PRAISE FOR
TRICIA LEVENSELLER

"Exciting, romantic, and filled with magic, *Blade of Secrets* is a fast-paced journey through a fractured kingdom. Ziva is an amazing main character, with a gentle heart and a fierce need to do what's right, even in the face of incredible odds. This is a book you'll want to read right away—and then reach for that sequel."

—JODI MEADOWS, *New York Times*–bestselling coauthor of *My Lady Jane* and the Fallen Isles trilogy, on *Blade of Secrets*

"*Blade of Secrets* is an impactful, eye-opening journey of social anxiety that is flawlessly blended with Levenseller's signature flair for adventure and romance. It's the best kind of story, inciting understanding and compassion while allowing the reader to escape reality."

—Bookstagram sensation **BRIDGET HOWARD**, @darkfaerietales_, on *Blade of Secrets*

"This fast-paced novel caters to popular romance and fantasy tropes while still feeling fresh, but it really shines in its portrayal of Ziva, who has an anxiety disorder . . . Readers will be craving not just the sequel but also more fantasy fiction that handles disabilities with this level of care."

—*THE BULLETIN OF THE CENTER FOR CHILDREN'S BOOKS* on *Blade of Secrets*

✦

"My favorite kind of fantasy: dark, mesmerizing, and completely addictive. With a gripping mystery and layered characters, it's a glittering tale of love and the pursuit of power. Put simply: it's the Slytherin romance we've all been waiting for."

—KERRI MANISCALCO, #1 *New York Times*– and *USA Today*–bestselling author of *Stalking Jack the Ripper*, on *The Shadows Between Us*

"A decadent and wickedly addictive fantasy."

—KENDARE BLAKE, #1 *New York Times*–bestselling author of
the Three Dark Crowns series, on *The Shadows Between Us*

"A wickedly fun romp with corsets and jeweled daggers . . .
The Shadows Between Us will heat up the page—and your heart."

—EMILY R. KING, author of the Hundredth Queen series,
on *The Shadows Between Us*

"The action! The world-building! The voice!
This book kicks so much ass."

—CALE DIETRICH, author of *The Love Interest*, on *Warrior of the Wild*

"This adventure sings."

—BOOKLIST on *Warrior of the Wild*

"This high-octane novel is filled with mythical creatures and showcases
a heroine who wants to be a warrior, a woman, and a leader."

—SCHOOL LIBRARY JOURNAL on *Warrior of the Wild*

"[Levenseller's] words will pull you in, and there's no escaping them."

—CHARLIE N. HOLMBERG, author of the Paper Magician series,
on *Daughter of the Siren Queen*

"With a cunning plot, robust writing, and complicated characters, any
reader will enjoy being manipulated in Levenseller's capable hands."

—ANNA BANKS, author of the *New York Times*–bestseller *Of Triton*,
on *Daughter of the Pirate King*

★ "Levenseller makes an impressive debut with this funny, fast-paced,
and romance-dashed nautical fantasy . . . This one's not to be missed."

—PUBLISHERS WEEKLY on *Daughter of the Pirate King*, starred review

MASTER *of* IRON

BY TRICIA LEVENSELLER

MASTER
of IRON

TRICIA LEVENSELLER

FEIWEL & FRIENDS

NEW YORK

A Feiwel and Friends Book
An imprint of Macmillan Publishing Group, LLC
120 Broadway, New York, NY 10271 • fiercereads.com

Our books may be purchased in bulk for promotional, educational, or business use. Please contact your local bookseller or the Macmillan Corporate and Premium Sales Department at (800) 221-7945 ext. 5442 or by email at MacmillanSpecialMarkets@macmillan.com.

Library of Congress Cataloging-in-Publication Data

Names: Levenseller, Tricia, author.
Title: Master of iron / Tricia Levenseller.
Description: First edition. | New York : Feiwel & Friends, 2022. | Series: Bladesmith ; book 2 | Audience: Ages 13–18. | Audience: Grades 10–12. | Summary: Eighteen-year-old Ziva, a magically gifted blacksmith with social anxiety, must race against the clock to save her beloved sister and stop a devastating war.
Identifiers: LCCN 2021047555 | ISBN 9781250756824 (hardcover)
Subjects: CYAC: Magic—Fiction. | Blacksmiths—Fiction. | Weapons—Fiction. | Social phobia—Fiction. | Orphans—Fiction. | Fantasy. | LCGFT: Fantasy fiction. | Romance fiction.
Classification: LCC PZ7.1.L4858 Mas 2022 | DDC [Fic]—dc23
LC record available at https://lccn.loc.gov/2021047555

First edition, 2022
Book design by Liz Dresner
Feiwel and Friends logo designed by Filomena Tuosto
Printed in the United States of America

10 9 8 7 6 5 4 3 2 1

For my fellow warriors who battle with social anxiety every day,
You matter. I see you. Keep fighting. There is so much good to come.

"I HAVE FOUND IT IS THE SMALL THINGS, EVERYDAY DEEDS OF
ORDINARY FOLK, THAT KEEPS THE DARKNESS AT BAY.
SIMPLE ACTS OF KINDNESS AND LOVE."
—Gandalf,
The Hobbit: An Unexpected Journey

GHADRA

PRINCE VERAK'S
Territory

Thersa

PRINCESS
MAROSSA'S
Territory

PRINCESS ORENA'S
Territory

Southern Mountains

CHAPTER

ONE

We don't have time for this.

There's a fallen tree in the road, blocking our access to the bridge ahead.

I glance down to my sleeping sister, noting the red dotting her lips as another wheezing breath turns into a cough. I turn Temra onto her side to prevent her from choking on her own blood. We're keeping her unconscious with a tincture so she doesn't jostle her wounds and make them worse. The stitches at her arm no longer seep blood, but the slice to her side nicked a lung. Blood continues to ooze in, which is the reason for her labored breathing.

She's fading away before my eyes, and we're still days away from reaching the magically gifted healer residing in Skiro.

My murderous gaze lands on Kymora, the warlord tied up only a few feet away from me in the cart. She is the reason for Temra's current condition, and if my sister dies, no force in the world can stop me from what I will do to her.

Kellyn stands from the driver's bench, removes the scabbard

from his back, and unsheathes the longsword I magicked for him.

"What is that for?" Petrik asks. "You can't hack your way through."

"Quiet. Slip into the back with Ziva. Keep your heads down."

The scholar does as told, and I scan the surrounding trees, finally registering the danger we're in.

Our party is small, and only three of us are trained fighters: my unconscious sister; Kymora, who is wounded, bound, and going to stay that way; and Kellyn, a mercenary for hire, who is somehow still tagging along after our group despite the fact he's no longer being paid.

The latter is impossibly still, his eyes peeled for danger.

A company of men rushes up from the slope to the river, staffs and clubs held loosely in their grips. Petrik's breath hitches, and I hover protectively over my sister.

The newcomers stop a mere ten feet away.

"Hi, friends," one of the men calls out. He's a big fellow, though not as big as Kellyn. He's got a rounded sort of muscle about his gut and hands big enough to palm a horse. His club drags along the ground as he walks ever closer toward our cart. His eyebrows have grown into one straight line of hair.

"We want no trouble," Kellyn says. "One of our party is sick. We seek help in the capital."

The eight men behind the leader grunt, loose grins upon their faces.

"That's good. We want no trouble ourselves. We're here to offer our services, see. Fifty ockles and we'll help you move this here trunk off the road."

Since one of the men is not so subtly gripping an ax over one shoulder, it's not hard to guess their game.

"That's a problem, because we haven't any money," Kellyn replies.

The club-toting leader uses his pinkie finger to clean out one of his ears. "I must have heard you wrong, friend. Sounded to me like you said you didn't have any money. Now, who travels to see a healer and doesn't carry any money with them? The price just went up to seventy-five ockles for our generous assistance."

It feels as though I've got a family of worms wriggling within my gut. I hate confrontations, but my anger and fierce need to protect my sister supersede all else.

I stand. "My sister doesn't have long. Let us pass. We've truly no money. The healer is a friend of ours. We're not paying for her services."

A different man comes forward, his staff clopping the ground in front of his feet. He peers into the back of the cart, and Petrik shifts with his movements, keeping himself between Temra and the danger. "Your sister might as well be dead. You needn't be in a hurry."

I try to force the bandit's fatal diagnosis to roll right off me, but I feel as though I've been punched in the gut.

He doesn't know about the magical healer. She's not beyond saving, I remind myself. There's still hope.

"Devran," the bandit continues, "they've got a woman tied up back here!"

The leader, Devran, tsks. "That's not very nice." He curves around the cart to get a better look at Kymora. "She got a bounty on her head? If so, we'd be happy to take her off your hands."

They absolutely cannot take Kymora. She's our bargaining chip. We need to turn her in to clear the bounty on our own heads. We're hoping her capture will endear Prince Skiro to us and convince him to let us use his healer.

And we need to be *moving*. Right now!

"Move back," Kellyn says, "and let us pass. I won't say it again."

Devran sucks his bottom lip into his mouth, looks around at our small party. "You'll pardon us if we don't take your word regarding that money. Lads, give 'em a thorough search. And if they don't have anything on 'em, we'll just be taking the horses and that sword." He points to Kellyn's longsword, Lady Killer. "It's real pretty."

Nine versus Kellyn, Petrik, and me.

We've certainly faced worse odds.

"It's going to be okay," I whisper to Temra, even though she probably can't hear me.

I jump over the side of the cart and right myself. The man nearest me takes a step back.

"Whoa," he says as he looks up at me.

Yes, *up*. I've always been taller than most men, reaching just over six feet. Normally, I hate my height. It makes me the object of constant staring and commentary. But right now, I like the way the brigand is looking at me. Like he's intimidated.

His eyebrows lift when I pull my twin hammers out from my belt.

I may not be a trained fighter, but I am a trained smithy, and there's nothing I know how to do better than swing a hammer.

Kellyn leaps down beside me, in front of my sister's side of the cart. I watch as Kymora holds her hands out to Petrik, a silent plea to release her. *I can help*, her face says.

But Petrik wordlessly grabs a long metal pole from inside the cart and joins us. It was once used as a cart axle, but now it's a magicked staff.

"Friends," Devran says, "you're outnumbered, and my men

will be far more gentle if you put down your weapons. There's no need for anyone to lose their heads today."

"I can take them," Kellyn says to me, "if you'd rather wait in the cart."

"If I'd wanted to wait in the cart, I'd be in the cart."

"Okay." His response is quiet, but I don't feel bad for snapping at him. Everything Kellyn says these days seems to set me off.

Devran listens to the exchange with amusement. "Maybe you got the wrong idea about us because we're being so polite. But you realize we're brigands and we're going to use force to rob you if need be?"

"We're aware," I respond. "It's you who has the wrong idea by believing we're easy pickings."

And I charge forward with my left hammer extended.

It's magicked, of course, like everything I've ever made. This one works as a shield, an invisible barrier between me and any oncoming enemies. And should anyone approach me with force? The weapon rebounds on them.

The first brigand plants his legs and raises his club to ward me off, but I plow him down and step right over the top of him before charging onto the next fellow. He retreats several feet after seeing me trample his friend, before finding his nerve.

He sidesteps me, swings toward me with his staff. I fling my left hammer outward, catch the blow on the invisible shield, and the man falls on his rump from the strength of the magical rebound.

With the swing of my right hammer, which doesn't have a lick of magic within it, I cave in his skull.

That's two down. Seven remain, staring at me like they've seen some mystical creature fall from the sky.

"Let us pass," I insist once more.

Flecks of red paint my fingertips. Blood and brain matter and Goddesses know what else. My stomach rolls over.

I've no taste for violence, but I'll do it to protect those I love. Even when it horrifies me.

Devran hefts his club in two hands. "Charge!"

I let Petrik and Kellyn handle the rest, preferring to stay near Temra in case I'm needed.

Lady Killer, Kellyn's beloved longsword, was magicked especially for the purpose of taking on multiple foes at once. Though Devran's men surround Kellyn, the mercenary grins as they approach him.

He dodges a swinging club from the left, strikes out toward the right, thrusting the tip of his sword into another man's gut.

Lady Killer encourages him to spin, nudging him in the right direction, and Kellyn just misses the tip of a staff jabbing where he once stood.

Three weapons swing toward him at once, and Kellyn bends backward in half, swinging Lady Killer in a wide arc to deflect every strike.

Petrik stands close to the wagon still, but that's only because his weapon works better from afar. He casts the metal staff, which twirls end over end until it makes contact with one of the brigands. He wears no armor, and I hear ribs crack before the staff flies back toward Petrik, the magic causing it to return to the caster, always.

Five left.

Kellyn and Petrik wheedle down their numbers until only Devran and one of his men remain.

The extra man flees while Devran stares at us in wonder. "Who are you people?"

Kellyn Derinor, the mercenary.

Petrik Avedin, the scholar.

Ziva Tellion, the bladesmith.

Our relationships with each other are more complicated than ever. But we're willing to fight, each and every one of us, to protect the other. Our adventures together have bonded us through blood.

Another cough comes from the wagon, and I've no choice but to wipe my hands on my own pants before climbing in to see to Temra.

"We're travelers in a hurry," Petrik answers, "and you've kept us long enough." He throws the staff, catches Devran at the temple, and the leader goes down in a heap of limbs. Petrik runs after the bandit who fled.

I pull my sister's hair away from her lips, trying to keep it from the blood gathering at her mouth. I look over my shoulder, about to throw another hateful glare at Kymora.

But there's no one else in the cart.

I blink several times, as though that will conjure the warlord.

"Kellyn!" I shout.

When Temra's fit subsides, I lower her gently to the floor once more and leap over the other side of the cart, where the cut ropes dangle.

Once my feet hit the ground, they're pulled out from under me. My hands catch most of my weight as I hit the ground.

I flip over to find the warlord under the wagon. She rolls out, clambers atop me, and jabs the flat of her arm against my throat. I claw at her face, try to roll the woman off. My lungs search for air that won't come.

And then Kellyn is there, hauling her away.

Kymora elbows him in the gut, and Kellyn bends in half as the air leaves him. I roll up onto my legs as she begins to flee. For a woman with a shattered knee, she limps along at an impressive pace, as though she doesn't feel pain.

I race after her, grabbing for my hammers once more. On anyone else, it might be excessive, but Kymora is the most fearsome warrior in the whole of Ghadra. She intends to overthrow all the royals, to subject all to her rule. In our last fight, it took Kellyn, Petrik, and me working together with our magicked weapons just to bring her down.

This woman who brought my sister to death's doorstep. Who made me an orphan. Who thought to use me to make magical weapons for her private army so she could take Ghadra without any resistance.

There is no one more dangerous.

She *cannot* be allowed to escape.

I dare not throw a hammer at her, for fear of giving her a weapon. The woman could make a twig threatening. Instead, I slam into her from behind with my shield hammer, sending her careening to the ground. She crawls along the grass, not missing a beat, reaching for a large stick—

"Touch it, and I will break your other knee," I say, my voice dropping to a tone I don't recognize.

She ignores me, her hand catching hold of the branch. She uses it and a nearby tree to hoist herself to her feet.

By then, Kellyn arrives, his sword at the ready.

"Get behind her," I order, but he's already moving that way.

"There's nowhere for you to go," I say. "Surrender."

Kymora flicks loose, greasy strands of hair out of her eyes. Her usual no-nonsense bun has come free, and she's slipped off the gag that was hiding the smooth scar on her cheek. Somehow, her disheveled appearance only makes her look more intimidating.

"How much time will you waste chasing me when your sister

needs to reach the capital?" the warlord asks. "I would have thought every second counted by this point."

Her words do their job, infuriating me, renewing my sense of urgency, probably making me reckless.

I grind my teeth as I leap forward, and Kellyn does the same from behind the woman. She can't properly deflect us both with only one good leg to stand on, but that doesn't keep her from trying. Her stick catches my hammer, and she spins into me to avoid Kellyn's strike. My instinct is to step backward, away from the hateful woman.

I ignore it and kick out at her shattered knee.

Kymora screams as she falls, dropping the stick.

I grab one of the warlord's arms, attempt to pin it to her back. Kymora swings outward with her other arm, tries to catch me in the head.

I pull her pinned arm up higher, straining the muscle and bone. The older woman grunts as I shove her forward, forcing her to the ground. I fumble with her other wrist, try to also get it pinned to her back. Meanwhile, I've got my full weight pressing into the woman.

"Yield!" I shriek at her.

"Never!" She tries to throw her head back, the movement making her look like a beached fish.

"If it's a choice between letting you get away and killing you, I *will* kill you," I say. "You've taken everything from me, and you deserve to die!"

Kellyn adds his weight to mine, practically sitting on her legs so she can't kick them outward. He produces a length of rope, and I use it to secure her wrists once more, tighter than is necessary.

We each grab an arm, haul her upward, and carry her back to the cart, Kymora fighting the whole way.

Petrik comes running out of the trees and bends over to rest his hands on the tops of his thighs. "The last man got away."

"Never mind him," I say. "Help Kellyn."

Despite his fatigue, Petrik helps haul his mother into the cart. When she's secured once more, he inspects the severed ropes. "How did she get free? She couldn't have stolen a weapon during the skirmish. These men had clubs and staffs, and the ax is still on the ground."

"Maybe somebody gave her something sharp," Kellyn says.

"I would *never*."

Ignoring the two men, I search under the wagon, looking for a dagger or something else to explain the warlord's attempted escape.

"Blood runs thick," Kellyn says.

"I hardly know this woman. She may have borne me, but there is no love between us. You know that. Why would I free the woman who hurt Temra?"

"Shut up, the both of you," I say as I right myself. I hold out the sharpened metal. "Hair clasp. It was holding her bun in place. She took it out days ago. Must have been waiting for the right time to use it."

Kellyn won't meet Petrik's eyes. "Sorry," he grumbles.

"When are you going to trust me?" Petrik asks. "I've done nothing but help. I may have kept my parentage to myself, but I have never betrayed the Tellions or you."

"We have bigger problems than your squabbling." I eye the bridge. "We're still blocked, and anyone who could have helped us move the trunk is unconscious, dead, or run off. Is there another way around?"

"Yes," Petrik says, "but it will add a half day's journey."

I want to sob. The timing is too close as it is. The healer back in Amanor said we had only a week before Temra would die from her wounds.

The exact time it takes to reach the capital.

Rage as I have never known floods my limbs as I haul myself back into the cart. I pull my unmagicked hammer from my waist and swing it toward Kymora's good leg.

The crack is sharp. Kymora's shriek is muted behind her replaced gag. Petrik's intake of breath and Kellyn's look of horror fill me with guilt, but—"A promise is a promise," I utter.

She won't be escaping again.

CHAPTER TWO

We travel all night to make up for lost time.

The road is awful, full of ruts and holes, but we don't feel the worst of it. Before we left Kellyn's hometown, I magicked the metal beneath the cart to provide Temra as smooth of a journey as possible.

Still, I don't sleep, not with Temra's constant coughing, Kymora's moaning, the crack of Kellyn's neck every time he looks over his shoulder to check on me.

I want to scream at him, to rage at everyone. They should all hurt the way I hurt right now. My body is in some weird state of exhaustion and extra alertness. I take to counting my sister's breaths to pass the time.

When a body moves, I raise a fist, worried that Kymora has somehow broken free again, but it is only Petrik, climbing into the cart bed next to me.

"You should rest," he says. "Let me watch over her."

"Thank you, but I'm okay."

"If there's another fight, you'll be more useful after some sleep."

I think the exhaustion is what compels my honesty. "I'm afraid she'll die if I close my eyes."

"She's tougher than that," Petrik says, all confidence.

It's so nice to hear, even if he has no way of knowing for sure what Temra's body is equipped to handle. He's a well-learned man but not in medicine. Petrik is a scholar from the Great Library in Skiro's Capital, and he's spent his life studying ancient magics. I met him initially because he was writing a book on known magics throughout the world. He wanted to learn everything there was to know about me and my blacksmithing abilities.

Along that first journey we took together, he fell in love with my sister. He's never said as much, but I can tell. How can anyone not fall for my brave and feisty sister? She's strong and stubborn in all the right ways.

When we learned that Petrik hid the truth about Kymora being his mother, Temra was furious. Personally, I don't much care so long as he gets us the help we need. His words from before were true. He's never betrayed us or done anything to suggest we can't trust him. He just kept one secret.

Who wouldn't want to hide the fact they're related to this monster?

But monster or no, she's still his mother.

I whisper, "I'm sorry I hurt her like that in front of you."

Petrik swallows. "It had to be done. We can't risk being slowed down again."

"I wasn't being spiteful; I told her I would do it if she—"

"It's okay, Ziva. Really."

His dark eyes sweep over Temra's face, her mahogany hair, her bow-shaped lips, her unblemished face—all barely visible in the moonlight. "She hasn't gotten a chance to yell at me for the secret I kept. She needs to do that. To tell me she doesn't want to hear my excuses. She'll want to throw things at me."

I let out a weak laugh to keep from crying. "She will. All of that will happen. Have you been working on the explanation you'll give her?"

He shakes his head. "I have no explanation. Only the truth. I was scared you would not let me come if you knew who I was. There are some who would not believe I don't have any warm feelings toward her." At that, he flicks his gaze in Kellyn's direction.

"I know why you did what you did," I say. "I don't hold it against you."

"You are a good friend, Ziva, and an even better sister."

"I failed her."

"You haven't. You're still fighting. We will reach the capital. Temra will be healed. Our names will be cleared, and Kymora will get the fate she deserves for her treachery."

I want to believe him so badly, but horrible scenarios flash through my mind in a loop and carry into my dreams.

It's the stillness that wakes me.

The cart has stopped. I immediately check on Temra, even as I call out, "Why aren't we moving?"

"The horses need a break," Kellyn says. "If we push them anymore, they'll give out before we can reach the capital."

He's pulled us off the road, and Kellyn already is in the process of unhitching the horses. Petrik leaves with his pack, likely off to prepare food.

That leaves me with Kymora and Temra.

I swear the warlord never sleeps. Every time I look over at her, she's perfectly alert. Her eyes rove over the scenery, our camp, searching for any opportunities to escape.

"Here," Petrik says sometime later. He hands over a bowl of broth. "I can feed her, if you'd like?"

"No, I've got it."

"I'll still help." He kneels behind Temra and raises her to a sitting position, while I bring a spoonful to her mouth on trembling fingers.

I force open her lips, pour in the broth, tilt back her head. I breathe out a sigh of relief when I watch her throat working to swallow.

"We're going to make it," Petrik says.

"This healer you spoke of—is she good?"

"She can work the body the way you work iron. She's good, Ziva."

The next spoonful of broth ends up being coughed out with yet more blood.

"She can mend the hole in Temra's lung?" I ask.

"I've seen her reattach limbs."

The hope burning in my breast is dangerous, but if I lose Temra, I'll lose the last of my family. I'll lose my heart.

Kymora really will have taken everything from me then.

When Temra's eaten enough, Petrik's gaze lands on his mother. "I guess I'd better go feed her."

He leaves me, scoops out another bowlful of broth, and pads over to his mother. He removes the gag gently, offers her some water first. Kymora drinks and drinks and drinks. She paces herself, as if not to show weakness, but by the amount she swallows, I can tell she's suffering from the journey. Her limbs must be aching from the way she's constantly bound. Her wrists and ankles are red and swollen from the tightness of the ropes, not that they would be forefront of her mind with her more severe injuries.

I'm glad she's suffering, and I feel no shame for that.

Temra's face has turned whiter over the last four days. Her lips are cracking. Her lungs are weakening. She has sores from lying in the same position for so long. But I dare not move her too much, lest I make her injuries worse.

These might be the last days I spend with my sister, and I don't even get to talk to her.

I try to will my thoughts elsewhere.

Petrik and Kymora converse in whispers when she's drunk her fill. I can't hear the specifics of the conversation, but Petrik winces at something she says. He spoons her up some broth and feeds it to her. Says something in response. Her face gives nothing of the conversation away, and I begin to wonder if I should move closer.

Then Temra begins coughing.

I gently turn her on her side and rub her back. Her shoulders heave, and her body tenses. Blood spills from her lips.

"I'm not leaving you," I say. "I'm here, Temra. Nothing is going to happen to you."

Movement out of the corner of my eye has me turning. Kellyn bends at the knees to scoop out some soup for himself. His towering six-and-a-half-foot frame has a long way to go to reach the cooking pot. With golden-red hair and soft facial features, he's a beauty in every sense of the word, even covered in grit from traveling.

He once meant so much to me. We were . . . together for a time. But instead of running to help my sister against her fight with Kymora, he came after me and the men who tried to steal me away.

He saved me instead of her.

And if she dies, I will never be able to forgive him.

Even if she survives, I don't think I can forgive him. He knows my sister is my whole world. He knew I wasn't in any real danger. Kymora wanted me alive. But she wanted my sister dead to teach me a lesson.

Still, he came after me.

He chose wrong, so how can I choose to be with him?

When he has his food, he pads over to my side of the cart. A jolt of awareness shoots through me to have him so close. I don't know how he can still affect me when we've spent so much time together. Yet it's always the same with him. Excitement and anxiety rolled together in a confusing mess.

"I'm sorry I doubted Petrik," he says.

"Again," I remind him.

"Again."

"It pains him to see his mother bound like she is, but every time she says something, trying to manipulate him into helping her, he looks at Temra. Reminding himself why his mother is a prisoner and must be kept that way."

"I know. I just worry. I can't help it."

"He shouldn't have kept his parentage a secret from us. But he's nothing like his mother. He's here with us now. Leading us to help."

I'd been staring at Kellyn's chest while we talked, but feeling his eyes on me now, I raise my own.

His brown meet my blue, and a hurricane of emotions battle for dominance in my chest. Fear. Want. Hate. Resignation.

I was once terrified of speaking to him. Couldn't even get a word out without my anxieties taking over. That changed slowly. During the journey where Temra and I hired him for safe passage to Thersa. From there we had to flee across two more territories, eventually landing in his hometown of Amanor, where I met his family. Where I felt like I truly knew this man and wanted him to know me.

I maybe even started to lo—

The thought hurts, so I don't finish it.

Because liking him, trusting him, wanting him—it all feels like a betrayal to the one person who has always been there for me.

Temra doesn't have my anxieties. She's protected me from awkward encounters my whole life.

And when I should have protected her, when I called on Kellyn for help, she was mortally wounded.

It's my fault. It's Kellyn's fault. It's Kymora's fault.

I can't be with him without hating myself.

He looks at me now, want and hurt in his own eyes. I watch his lips start and stop, looking for the right words to say.

But he and I both know there aren't any.

Kellyn gets in a quick nap before we're moving again. He and Petrik take turns with the horses, while I stay in the back, stuck between the person I love the most and the person I like the least.

A week has never felt longer.

Seconds sluggishly crawl by, while the day inches toward night again. Time has no meaning for me, except for the toll it takes on Temra. She grows paler, thinner, weaker.

We're running out of time.

Kellyn asks, "What's the plan when we reach Skiro?" Since the words are quiet, I assume they're not meant for me.

Petrik sits up straighter. "We'll immediately ask for an audience with Skiro. He'll get us everything we need."

"You sound confident," Kellyn says. "Why would the prince bother to speak with us? We're fugitives, for all he knows. We're not in a place to ask for anything."

Petrik looks off to the side of the road, his gaze falling into the passing trees. "I thought you would have pieced it together by now."

"Pieced what together by now?"

"Kymora is my mother. You haven't guessed who my father is yet?"

Kymora was King Arund's general. The late queen died not long after giving birth to Prince Skiro. He was alone and grieving, and then there's fierce Kymora, who gives birth to a child and sends him away to be tutored far from the palace . . .

By the Twins. He's the king's bastard son. Sent away so as not to be in the way. But when the realm was split, Skiro took leadership of the territory housing the Great Library. Petrik would have grown up close to this brother.

I should have put two and two together much sooner.

When Kellyn doesn't get it, I help him out. "He's the king's son."

"What?" Kellyn's voice raises an octave.

Petrik says, "I'm very close with my brother. We grew up together. He'd do just about anything I asked, including helping the woman I— Temra. Including helping Temra."

When Kellyn finds his voice again, he says, "Seriously? Is there anything else you'd like to share with the group? Any other secrets you'd like to just casually drop?"

"That wasn't a secret!" Petrik says. "Everyone who knows my brother Skiro knows who I am to him."

"Kellyn," I say. "It doesn't matter who his father is. It wasn't ever relevant to our plight."

"Really? It seems to me like knowing he has such a good relationship with his *prince* of a brother would have come in handy while we had Kymora chasing our asses!"

"If we had gone to Skiro for help, Kymora would have declared war on him and the innocents of that territory!" Petrik counters. "Would you put that on them? We can only go to my brother now because Kymora is no longer a threat! And besides, Ziva would never have allowed us to seek refuge from someone in a position of power like that while Secret Eater was still a problem."

He's certainly right about that, and Kellyn knows it, too, for the mercenary has nothing to say in response.

"So that's the plan," Petrik says, circling back to the matter at hand. "We ask my brother for help. He will give it to us. There's nothing more to worry about."

Except for Temra dying before we can reach the prince.

CHAPTER

THREE

I've never before felt relieved to step foot in a big city.

Ordinarily, I find them horrifying. Too many stimulants: the people, the animals, the smells, the sounds.

But as the horses carry us up the steep incline, through the city gates, into the fuss of city life, I feel like I can breathe for the first time. Kellyn urges the horses faster, and the people of the capital leap away from the wagon, shouting curses at our backs.

We've arrived later in the day, so the streets aren't as packed as they could be, but folk are still closing up their shops or rushing to find the last of their groceries.

The capital lies in the mountains, and the rumor is that Prince Skiro wanted to set up his rule as far from his elder brother Ravis as possible. The people are bundled in loose furs and thick boots. Fall hit the city early, it seems.

Petrik directs Kellyn toward the palace, taking us up winding roads with inclines that grow ever steeper. I can see hints of our destination peeking over the tops of the homes and businesses. The castle towers are the tallest structures in the city.

When we finally reach them, I see they're connected to a vast wall surrounding the palace grounds. The gate is left lowered, admitting us within its boundaries.

Two massive figures line either side of the palace doors. One carved in whitest marble, the other deepest granite. Ebanarra and Tasminya, the Sister Goddesses.

When the wagon rolls to a stop, a patrolling guard steps up to us. "Petrik, you've returned!"

"I'm sorry, Leona, but I don't have time for pleasantries. Please tell the prince at once that I'm here. I have a high-profile prisoner for him, and I beg the use of Serutha for our wounded companion."

I don't know if Petrik knows all the guards or if one just happened to be stationed who knows him, but I'm glad things are being set in motion. Leona shouts a few words to servants stationed by the doors, who disappear inside.

In just a few minutes, a pallet is carried out toward the wagon, and it's followed by a small garrison of guards bearing chains and manacles. I help the caretakers place Temra on the pallet. The guards wrest a wriggling Kymora off the wagon and bind her properly. She puts up quite the fight, earning her a few more scratches and bruises.

"Please," Petrik says. "Be as gentle as you can within reason."

More guards spill from the front entrance, all decked in deep blue tunics bearing a yellow sun on their breasts.

There's a faint murmuring from inside the palace, steadily growing louder. Then, "Just let me through!" a voice insists, pushing past all the others.

And he can be no other than Prince Skiro. He wears a deep golden tunic with the same sun as the guards beneath an open sapphire robe. Prince Skiro's brown skin is darker than Petrik's, his head shaved, and his features are so smooth that Temra would probably describe them as pretty. He's taller than Petrik but not so tall as me, though he comes close. He bears no special ornamentation to mark his standing, but he wears a jeweled dagger sheathed at his waist. He is the youngest of the royals, and I would place him at not a day older than twenty.

The prince eyes the wagon, my sister on the pallet, Kymora in chains, before his eyes land on Petrik. His face alights in a bright smile. "Petrik!" he exclaims as he embraces his brother. "Is it just me or have your muscles finally come in? And what are you wearing? I can't recall the last time I saw you in anything other than your scholar attire."

"Forgive me, Skiro," Petrik says, "but we're in a hurry. We need immediate help. One of my friends is severely wounded. She doesn't have much time. We need Serutha. Can you please call for her?"

Skiro's eyes land on Temra and her white face. "Come inside, all of you. Any friends of my brother's are friends of mine."

Every second that ticks by feels like a lash against my skin.

I watch as caretakers use warm rags to clean the travel away from my sister. They are so gentle with her, but I'm impatient for this Serutha to arrive and work her magic. One of the caretakers unbinds the bandages on her arm, and a rotting smell fills the space. It's infected, and a healer begins cutting the stitches away and reopening the wound so she can lance the injury.

But where is the magical healer?

When the door opens, I spin in relief, prepared to greet and beg and do whatever it takes to get my sister the immediate attention of the finally arrived healer.

But it's only an attendant of some sort.

"Petrik sent me to collect you. I'm to show you to your rooms so you can clean and rest. The prince would like for you all to be his special guests at dinner."

I blink at him.

Dinner and clean and rest?

My sister is dying. *Dying*. And they expect me to—

"Excuse me," someone says from behind me. I turn, already tense and wanting to rush over to my sister's side.

It's one of the caretakers. "We have her. She'll receive the best care we can give her. You should go."

"I'm not leaving her," I say.

"I don't know how to put this delicately, but you're contaminating our sterile environment."

At that, I look down at myself. There's dirt under each of my fingernails. My clothes are torn from wrestling Kymora, stained from travel. I can't tell freckles from grit on my skin. And I can only imagine the smell.

Embarrassment seeps in, but it doesn't override my need to see Temra whole. "Are you saying it's safer for her if I leave?"

The caretaker nods politely.

"I can return as soon as I'm clean? And you've sent for this"—I don't know if the magical healer's abilities are widely known—"Serutha?"

"You may return, and the prince has *all* of his resources at your disposal."

I take her meaning.

"Very well," I say, exhaling a breath. The attendant looks relieved when I turn back to him.

The room I'm shown to is clean and lets in lots of natural light. There are many fine carpets and draperies throughout, beautiful designs that look like they would have taken years to complete. A bath has already been drawn, and I hurry to it, knowing the sooner I'm clean, the sooner I can see Temra again and watch the magical healer work on her.

The water feels nice against my skin, and I allow myself to enjoy it while I scrape a week's worth of grime from my body. I towel off when done, brush through my hair quickly, and leave it down—it's far too short to do much with anyway. When dressed, I see myself back out through the door and nearly run into Petrik. He's also taken advantage of a bath and new clothes.

"Do you have news?" I ask. "How is she?"

"Unchanged."

What? "Why? Why hasn't she been healed? Where is this healer you promised? Why is everything happening so slowly? Do I have to go banging on doors in the castle?"

Petrik stops me before I can ramble further. "I don't know the answers to those questions yet, but Prince Skiro wishes to speak with us all."

Good, then I can demand answers from him myself.

I let Petrik lead me down a hall covered in the richest of tapestries. Music drifts to us from some faraway room, and I cannot guess the instrument. Something with strings. Petrik doesn't stop moving until we arrive in a room also decorated in woven tapestries and fine rugs on the floor. Between the tapestries are bookcases lined with shelves of tomes. The music is louder in this room, though the players are not within. Perhaps they are in the next room over.

A modest table is heaped with food. Rich sauces over juicy meats and no less than five different casks of wine. The prince's personal guard line the walls, Skiro himself seated at the head of the small table, Kellyn beside him, taking large bites of buttered bread.

I shouldn't be angry at them both for eating while Temra is dying, but I am *furious*.

"Ah." Skiro looks up. "Please be seated. Fill your bellies. You must have quite the stories to tell after such a journey."

Neither Petrik nor I move, and I couldn't be more grateful to have him at my side, united in my cause.

Skiro sighs and drops the leg of chicken he'd been bringing to his lips. "I am beyond grateful to you all for bringing me the traitor Kymora, though I am surprised, brother, that you would turn on her."

"I learned of her plans to kill you and the others and take the entire kingdom for herself. I couldn't allow that to happen. It was Ziva who learned of it and stopped her." He gestures to me. "Her sister is the one dying, and we beg the use of Serutha."

Skiro's eyes land on me. They light up, and a far-too-bright smile stretches over his lips. He shakes himself, as though just remembering something before turning back to his brother. "You should not have told them about her—I don't care how good of friends you are."

"I consider them family now," Petrik answers.

"Is it a life debt that binds you to them? Is that what caused you to betray the trust of our friend Serutha?"

"It's Temra."

"The dying girl."

"I love her, Skiro. And I need you to save her."

I shift uncomfortably at the words. I had guessed, of course, but hearing Petrik admit something so personal aloud has my secondhand embarrassment kicking in. But if it gets Skiro to finally *act*, then—

"Oh, I see." Skiro's expression deflates. "I'm so sorry, Petrik, but she's not here."

"Who?" Petrik asks.

"Serutha."

"Well then, send for her! Where is she?"

"A few weeks ago, our dear brother Ravis sent spies into the palace. They learned of Serutha's abilities and snuck away with her in the dead of night. She's in Ravis's Territory by now."

A desperate cry looses from my lips as I sink to my knees on the floor. No no no no no nonononononono . . .

We made it. We brought Kymora. Temra survived the journey.

But the healer isn't here.

My sister is going to die.

I feel my breathing pick up, but I force words through my lips. "Pack the wagon, then. We're going to Ravis."

"You can't move the girl," Skiro says. "Another journey would surely kill her, and she doesn't have the time left that it would take to get there."

Kellyn has all but forgotten the food in front of him. "You must have sent men after your healer? Surely they're returning with her now?"

Yes, that would make sense. I cling to Kellyn's reasoning.

"I did send men," Skiro says. "They were supposed to report back days ago. They've likely been found out and killed."

My last shred of hope slips through my fingers, and my cries fill the new silence as I crumple all the way to the floor. Petrik leaves my side, steps over to his brother. Meanwhile, Kellyn crouches next to me, even dares to wrap his arms around me.

My despair is too great to even care.

I don't lean into him, don't return the embrace. I just feel and hurt and—this must be what dying feels like.

All at once I stand. If Temra only has moments left to live, I'm going to spend them with her. She can't be alone.

"Wait, Ziva."

I turn, can barely see Petrik through my tears. I clear the moisture from my face, attempt to focus.

"Skiro," Petrik says, a harsh plea at the end of whatever conversation they'd just been having.

"It's far too dangerous," Skiro says. "If my trained men didn't make it back through, your friends can hardly be expected to return with Serutha. Besides, I'm not going to risk the doors like that."

"For me, brother."

"They're going to die."

"No, Temra is going to die!"

"You know I love you, but the answer is still no."

Petrik growls, rounds on me. "Ziva, I ask permission to tell my brother who you are and why we're perfectly equipped to undertake this rescue mission."

"No," Kellyn answers for me.

Rescue mission? We've already established that we couldn't get the healer back to the capital in time and Temra wouldn't survive another journey.

Anyone powerful knowing my identity has not gone over well in the past; why would Petrik ask me to reveal myself now?

At my hesitation, Petrik adds, "It could mean saving Temra's life."

I don't understand, but I nod, because what else can I do? And Kellyn is not permitted to speak for me. Ever.

"This is Ziva Tellion. Magically gifted bladesmith. We all carry weapons she's forged. We took on what must have been forty men back in Amanor. The three of us brought down the warlord together. We can get Serutha back. And isn't retrieving your healer worth the potential cost of the doors?"

Skiro's eyes land on me. I look to the ground, uncomfortable with the scrutiny, but my thoughts are still on my sister.

"Really?" the prince asks. "How does your ability work? What weapons have you made? How do you—"

"Skiro!" Petrik interrupts.

"Sorry." He thinks a moment. "I still don't like it. Those doors are the only advantage I have, Petrik."

"What would it take to convince you?" he asks desperately.

"How about a solid plan?"

At that, Kellyn perks up. The prince is speaking his language, but I'm still thoroughly confused by the whole conversation.

Petrik says, "How did you get your last spies into the palace?"

"They traveled on foot. Wore disguises to blend in with the people from Ravis."

"Do you still have clothing from the territory?"

". . . Yes."

"Then we will dress the part. We'll take the door, stash our weapons somewhere, do reconnaissance. We'll infiltrate the palace staff. Do you know where Serutha is being held?"

"She wasn't in the dungeons. My spies did a sweep of the castle, covering every floor save the one housing Ravis's rooms. He's keeping her close. That was the last I heard before they were found out. They must have gotten too close."

"That leaves us only one floor of the castle to search. We'll find her and bring her back straightaway."

"She'll be guarded," Skiro says. "You won't be able to just take her."

"We have magical weapons," Petrik reminds him. "We'll cause a distraction if need be to lure them away. Lessen their numbers."

Skiro still wants to say no. I can tell.

"Ziva will be indebted to you if you save her sister's life," Petrik finishes.

At that, Skiro looks to me before looking down at the hammers around my waist. He sighs. "Fine, the mercenary bloke can go. Ziva and you will stay here."

"I'm going," Petrik and I snap at the same time.

"You're far too important to risk," Skiro says to me.

"You just barely learned of my abilities! You don't even know me. That's *my* sister dying. I'll be damned if I stay behind when I can do something to save her."

Skiro cracks a small smile. "I like you," he says.

For some reason, that statement makes Kellyn shift awkwardly next to me.

"I'm going, too," Petrik says again.

"You'll be recognized."

"I'm the only one who knows the layout of the palace. It has to be me."

"You haven't been there in years."

"I've a good memory."

"I don't want to lose you, brother."

"If she dies, you'll lose me anyway."

Skiro reads that loud and clear. If he doesn't concede, Petrik will never forgive him.

"You'd better cover your face, then," Skiro says.

"I will."

Skiro reaches for a cord necklace he had hidden underneath his tunic. With a sigh, he hands it over to Petrik. The prince calls for an attendant, mutters something to him, and then returns to the table. "Are you sure you wouldn't like anything to eat first?" he asks me.

I don't answer. I'm still not certain what is happening, and I'm such a mess that I don't know what would come out of me if I did speak. I settle for a shake of my head.

When the attendant returns, it's with three sets of clothing. Petrik gathers them, walks over to me, grabs my upper arm, and hauls me after him. He's practically running through the fine halls, and I nearly trip in my haste to keep up with him. Kellyn plods along behind us.

"I knew he couldn't say no to Ziva once he learned who she is," Petrik says. "My brother is a lover of all art. Music. Books. Paintings. Tapestries. He's especially interested in the art of magic. He collects magic users, you might say. Inviting them to his court, paying them generous wages. Offering them safety and his silence."

We turn down another hallway, Petrik's boots squeaking along the stone floor.

"Did you have to tell him Ziva would be indebted to him?" Kellyn asks. "What if he asks for something she doesn't want to give? And what are these *doors* you kept mentioning?"

"We're almost there. You'll understand soon."

A few more turns. A set of stairs.

Petrik turns the necklace over in his hands. I spy a bronze key between his fingers.

We reach a door that has at least a dozen guards surrounding it. The man at their head nods to Petrik as the scholar promptly unlocks it before ushering us inside. When we're through, Petrik immediately locks us in.

I walk to the middle of the room and spin in place, taking in the gorgeous portraits on the walls. There are five in total, spaced at even intervals. Each is shaped in a long oval, each taller than my person. The first one is of a woman. She looks older than I am but not by too much. Her skin is a deep brown, with rosy cheeks, and hair separated into tiny braids that rain down over her shoulders. She smiles, showing off a row of perfect white teeth. She looks mischievous, as though hiding a secret from whoever looks upon her.

The second is of a man, perhaps the same age or slightly older than the woman. Also dark-skinned, hands in his pockets, eyes looking at something over my head. He wears his hair to several inches in length, and it stands up on end in a glorious halo around his face. He wears an earring in one ear, rings on his fingers.

After the man, there are two girls, and then a final man on the end. All with brown skin, different expressions, though similar features.

"Are these . . . ?" I ask.

"The rest of my half siblings," Petrik says. He turns to the portrait on the left of the door we just entered through. "Meet Ravis, because we definitely don't want to run into him in the flesh."

The oldest of King Arund's children appears to also be the shortest. He wears his hair shorn close to his scalp—the same way Petrik likes to wear his. But unlike Petrik, Ravis's eyes are more hooded, his nose smaller, his lips fuller. He looks dead-on at who-ever's watching, as though daring them to challenge him. He must be near thirty years of age.

"The detail is extraordinary. You'd almost think they were in the room with us," I say.

"That's because these were done by a magically gifted painter."

Kellyn and I both shift in Petrik's direction.

"I won't disclose his name or identity because I've also been sworn to secrecy on his behalf. It's no matter. We only need his paintings, which are magicked into portals."

"Portals," I repeat stupidly.

"Yes, if he paints the exact same image—detail for detail—in two different areas, they work as a bridge between the two places."

I take in the paintings again, stopping at Ravis's. "You mean—"

"With these, you can get to any capital in the span of a heart-beat just by stepping through them."

I reach a hand out toward Ravis's face, but Kellyn snatches it back.

"This is awfully convenient," he says. "Why didn't we use them to get here in the first place, then?"

"Like I said, the portals connect the *capitals*. You must be in one to get here. We were in Amanor."

"What about when we were in Lisady's Capital fleeing from the warlord? We could have traveled here and been safe!"

Petrik grunts. "I don't know where the portals are within each capital. I haven't gone through them before! I just know they exist. I'd have to be able to take us to the portal directly. But once we walk through this one, we'll keep track of where we go so we can bring Serutha back through it."

The breath expels from my lungs. "You're saying we can still save Temra."

"We can save her."

"Tell me what to do," I say at once.

"First, we need to get dressed." Petrik passes out the clothing, shakes out the wrinkles from his own garment, and begins to disrobe.

There's nowhere for me to turn for privacy, so I do the same, trying my best not to think about the male bodies behind me.

I get the garment on and then reach under the skirt because I'm sure the material must be caught on something.

Nope.

What must be a knee-length dress on a shorter girl, is mid-thigh on me. It must be warm in Ravis's Territory, because the dress also hangs off only one shoulder. I shrug my boots back on, but there's still too much skin between the top of the boots and the bottom of my dress for me to be comfortable.

This is for Temra, I remind myself.

When I turn back around, Kellyn and Petrik are both staring at my legs.

My cheeks heat to burning.

"Stop it!" I whisper-shout to both of them.

Petrik shakes himself upright. "Sorry. It's just, I don't think that disguise is going to work in your favor."

Kellyn raises his eyes slowly until they burn into my own. "You— I— You have really long legs." He swallows audibly before turning away.

"Yours are longer!" I say defensively. How dare he make fun of me right now. Of *all* the times.

Petrik coughs. "I promise he meant that as a compliment. You have very nice legs, Ziva."

"Stop talking about my legs!"

"Right." Petrik coughs unnecessarily again.

Kellyn wears knee-length shorts with a loose shirt above, while Petrik has some sort of skirt on beneath a similar shirt. The scholar has also wrapped a headscarf about him to hide the features of his face.

Without any further prompting, I thrust my hand against the portrait of Ravis. Instead of meeting the resistance of the wall, my fingers disappear down to the knuckles.

I take a breath and step through, slamming my eyes closed.

CHAPTER

FOUR

I walk through the portrait just like I would an open doorway, but my head bashes against something on the other side.

"Ow."

I can't see a thing. The air is stale and hot, and there's a solid wall in front of me. Am I in a box?

Oof.

Something slams into my back.

Or someone.

A large, warm body—far too big to be Petrik's.

I'm pinned against the hard surface in front of me, and Kellyn's body smothers me from behind. His arms brace the wall on either side of me, trying to keep the bulk of his weight off me, but I can feel him *everywhere*. His hips just above my hips. His chest against my back. His knees against my lower thighs. His nose in my hair.

And it shouldn't feel nice. I should hate it.

I do.

I . . . do.

"Ziva? Are you all right? Where are we?"

"I don't know. I can't move."

"Maybe if I try . . ." He tries scooting over, but that only causes our bodies to rub, his upper thigh sliding against the back of my ass.

His breaths come out faster. "Ziva, I don't like this."

I'm momentarily pulled out of my fascination over the way his body feels against mine. He doesn't like this? But I thought— Oh, wait.

"Small spaces," I whisper.

"I hate them." He starts shifting, his arms tapping against our enclosure. He's trying not to panic, but I can tell his movements are becoming more frantic.

And then the space becomes even smaller as a third body joins us.

Petrik's stepped through the portal. I want to tell him to go back, but Kellyn's arm is shoved between my shoulder blades.

A light burst of air. Falling forward. And then the weight of two bodies crashing atop of me.

I feel as though my lungs are forced from my body. I cannot breathe, even after the weight is removed.

"Ziva!"

I start to panic because I still can't breathe and I'm in a strange place in the dark.

And then the air finally comes back. I take the two hands offered to me, and the boys haul me up.

"A damned wardrobe," Kellyn says.

"Of course, a wardrobe," Petrik says. "These portraits have to be hidden. Otherwise, anyone could stumble upon them."

When my eyes adjust, I take in the new space, illuminated by silver light from the single window. We appear to be in some sort of storage space. I can spot vanities and mirrors and chairs.

Rolled-up rugs, wardrobes like the one we just came through, bed frames.

I cough, try to muffle the sound against my elbow.

Everything is covered in a thick layer of dust.

"Now what?" Kellyn asks.

"Let's find our way out of the room. I need to orient myself," Petrik says.

We fiddle along blindly against the walls. Someone knocks over a lamp, candles breaking and rolling across the floor. Kellyn hits his head on something. I nearly trip over a frame that's flat against the floor. Then my foot comes down on the glass, shattering it when I try to catch myself.

I pray that we're far enough away from those living in the palace not to be heard.

"A door!" Kellyn calls. I weave through the maze of furniture until I'm at his side.

He tries the latch. "Locked."

Of course.

Kellyn steps back from the door a few feet and then throws his weight against it.

I slap his back. "What are you doing? Someone is going to hear that!"

"Do you have a better idea?"

"*Yes.*"

Petrik reaches us as I start picking at the hinges on the door, pulling the pins out.

"Right," Kellyn says. "Having a smithy around sure is handy."

"Because we know how *doors* work?"

The bottom hinge gives me some trouble, so Kellyn pulls out his sword to work out the final pin.

"I feel attacked by that comment," he says.

"You were meant to," Petrik says for me.

The door pops inward as we pull, the latch snapping from the tension.

"We're just lucky we're stuck on the inside, where the hinges are," I say. "Otherwise, we'd have to watch Kellyn beat it down."

"What a shame to miss that display," Petrik says.

The hallway is empty, also dark. No torches lit for us to see the path.

"I had a look out the window," Petrik says. "We're in the attic. Ravis's rooms should be only a floor or two down. Look for a heavily guarded door."

We leave our weapons in the attic, stashing them behind a portrait propped against the wall. Kellyn tries his best to place the broken door back over the opening when we leave. It might pass as a closed door if no one looks too closely.

It'll have to do.

We keep close to the walls as we stumble in the dark. The floor is uncarpeted, the walls barren. I'd wager no one lives on these levels or bothers to visit them.

"Should we split up?" I force myself to ask.

It's the last thing I want to do, but if it means we could get Serutha out of here faster and back to Temra, I'll do it.

"No," both boys answer at the same time.

"We'd search the palace faster," I say.

"Yes," Petrik says, "but if we do find Serutha, we're far more likely to get her out of here if we stick together."

"I agree," Kellyn says.

I'm outvoted, and I'm glad for it. I do not want to be alone in this place. And if any one of the palace's occupants were to find me, I couldn't lie my way out. I'm terrible with people.

The corridor seems to go on forever. The lack of light doesn't help things, either. Only occasional windows let enough moon-light through to brighten the shadows. I'm convinced every single one is a person lying in wait to pounce.

We finally reach a staircase. My steps are louder than my breathing, but only just.

Temra. You're doing this for Temra. It doesn't matter if you're caught. The most important thing is giving your all to keep her safe.

Voices drift up to us, and we stop right where we are. Petrik has one foot up in the air, preparing to descend on the next step down. He holds the position.

I can't make out individual words; everything is too muffled, but they talk for what feels like hours before moving on.

Our eyesight improves as we continue our descent. Candlelight—faint but present—exposes the last steps of the staircase before showing us to yet another corridor. Windows on the left. Doors on the right. I register more voices but only briefly before they disappear behind the gentle closing of a door.

Sweat beads on my brow. I feel overheated, overextended, overwrought.

I'm scared, and I'm so desperate.

Kellyn reaches out and takes my hand. It's only when he does so that I realize I'm shaking, but I don't pull away. It's wrong to accept his comfort, yet I'm too greedy for it. I need something tangible to focus on so my thoughts don't spiral out of control.

A door just a few feet ahead begins to open, and the three of us dart behind the drapery around the windows to our left. Because our hands are still joined, Kellyn and I land behind the same drape, while Petrik is one down from us.

It's a poor hiding place. If anyone looks too closely, they'll see our feet peeking out beneath the fabric, the outline of our bodies behind the material.

I'm gripping Kellyn's hand tight enough to hurt. He returns the pressure, his thumb running over the back of my knuckles.

The footsteps fade, ending in the closing of yet another door.

I don't know how much more of this I can take.

"Servants' wing," Petrik whispers when we step away from the windows. "The high-ranking servants are kept close to the nobles' rooms in case they're needed. We should go down another level."

We continue our slow trek.

"What are you doing?" a voice asks from behind us, and I go still as stone. Only Kellyn's hand in mine is what allows me to turn.

It's an older woman with russet-brown skin, her hair held up in a messy bun atop her head, wisps hanging about her cheeks. Her clothes are very plain, like ours. A tan knee-length dress with a white apron, the stitching coming undone at one of the sleeve's hems. Her eyes are mostly in shadow due to the scant light.

I cannot determine her expression.

"We're lost," Petrik ventures.

The woman gives us the side-eye. "I'll say. You think you can sneak off to the attic for a tryst in the dust? Where are you supposed to be?"

My mouth opens and closes like a fish. Feelings flash through me in rapid succession. Embarrassment. Fear. Urgency.

Kellyn and Petrik both turn their faces to the ground, as though ashamed.

Oh, oh!

I quickly do the same, realizing I need to play along.

"Kitchens," Petrik mumbles.

"Then get there!" the woman says. She shoos us with her hands.

The boys shuffle off, and I'm jerked along because my hand still rests in Kellyn's. At that realization, I take it back, having collected myself after the confrontation.

Petrik brushes dust off his skirt while Kellyn runs his fingers through his hair, trying to put the strands back in place. I scratch at my exposed shoulder.

"Apparently we didn't think about how our run-in with the wardrobe would make us look," I say, my cheeks heating. No one's ever thought I was having a tryst before.

"Gave us a good cover story, though," Petrik says.

At that, Kellyn purses his lips. "She thought the *three* of us—"

"Who cares?" I ask to hide my own embarrassment. "Just be glad we didn't get caught. Where to now, Petrik?"

"I see the stairs ahead. We'll be on the higher nobles' wing once we descend. Everyone look docile."

Docile? I don't know how to *look* anything. Temra is the talented actress.

And for some reason, I want to take Kellyn's hand again.

I shake that urge and follow Petrik down the stairs.

The halls are lit up brightly enough to make me miss the darkness. There, I didn't feel put on display, like people are staring at me. And I know that nobility don't pay close attention to their servants. I *know* no one really is looking at me, but my body goes hot all over.

We only pass by the occasional courtier, nobles turning in for the night. They're dressed finely. Men in short-sleeved tunics that reach their ankles. The women wear sleeveless dresses made from light fabrics. No one in sight wears pants or cloaks. It's so much more skin than I'm used to seeing, but if I lived here, I'm sure I would follow suit. I loathe being too warm.

As I am now.

I watch Petrik take careful note of each door we pass. At one point, he mumbles, "Ravis's rooms," and pulls his headscarf tighter about his face. Four guards stand outside at attention. They eye us as we pass, and my nerves ratchet up, coiling tight like a spring about to pop free.

I breathe easier when they're out of sight, but only a little.

But then we come to a shorter hallway that deviates from the corridor we're walking down now. At the end, a group of soldiers stand, also at attention, spearpoints gripped in their fists, feet spread apart, eyes dead ahead, watching us.

Only, as far as I can tell, they're not guarding anything. There aren't any doorways down there. Nothing of value lines the walls. The palace is actually quite bare, as though the occupants hadn't moved in yet—or they're packing to leave . . .

My muscles tense as we pass by the group of guards, fully expecting someone to call us out or chase after us, but nothing happens.

Hold on, Temra. Hold on.

We reach the end of the corridor, a lone guard standing there in case he's needed. Though we know Serutha is being held on this level, we have no choice but to go down the stairs or to look suspicious.

"Now what?" I ask when we reach the bottom.

"We must have missed something," Kellyn says. "Or the prince's intel was wrong. Maybe the healer has been moved."

Petrik says, "I don't think so. If Skiro's spies were found, that would only make Ravis extra cautious. He would keep Serutha close. He would add more guards."

"Do you think she's being held in his rooms, then?"

Petrik shakes his head. "Ravis wouldn't dare let someone beneath his station into his rooms. I would have thought the short hallway with the guards, but—"

"There was nothing there," I finish.

"Exactly."

"Wouldn't there be a queen's suite next door? Could she be there?"

"She could, but the door doesn't have its own set of guards, and I doubt Ravis would risk having an interior door between himself and his prisoner."

"We're missing something," I say. A beat of silence passes, before I decide, "We turn around and look again. We must have missed something."

Kellyn looks wary, but he says nothing. Petrik turns and begins marching back up the stairs.

When we reach the guard stationed there, his eyes narrow. "What's your business on this floor?"

"We're looking for a set of rooms," Petrik says. "Having trouble finding them."

"Whose rooms?"

Petrik rattles off a name, and I don't know if he made it up or if he actually knows someone here.

The guard's gaze tightens. "You look familiar," he says to Petrik.

A deep sense of dread claws through me. We're about to be found out. Ravis is going to kill us, and then Temra—

Before the guard can even see it coming, Kellyn swings a fist and knocks the man out. Kellyn catches him before he can fall and props him up against the wall, adjusts his head and arms.

Trying to make it look like he's sleeping on the job.

"We need to move," Petrik says.

I'm rooted to the spot, so Kellyn takes my hand once more, pulling me along.

"Relax," he says. "Try not to look so frightened or we'll be found out for sure. Do it for Temra."

I swallow, close my eyes, and breathe, before turning my gaze to the floor.

"That works, too," Kellyn says.

Petrik halts suddenly, and since I'm looking at my feet, it's Kellyn who pulls us to a stop behind him.

"Up ahead is that hallway full of guards," Petrik whispers. "We can't cross without drawing the same suspicion. There's too many of them to handle quietly. We'll be spotted for sure."

"Any ideas?" Kellyn asks.

"Why are they even there?" Petrik asks to himself, ignoring Kellyn's question.

"Doesn't matter," Kellyn says. "We just need to figure out how to get around them. Is there another way to access the other side of this floor?"

The boys talk quietly, but my mind is picturing that little hallway, remembering it as we passed by. It just ends. No doors. No windows. No nothing. If the six guards are simply waiting for an emergency, then why do they look like they're on duty?

Why do they look like they're guarding something, when there's nothing around them to guard?

Unless there *is* something there.

And we can't see it.

"The door's hidden," I breathe. Neither boy hears me. So I repeat myself a little louder.

They halt whatever conversation (though let's be honest, it was probably an argument) they'd been having.

"What do you mean?" Kellyn asks.

"We arrived by way of a magic portal. We're in search of a magic healer. Isn't it possible there's a door down there concealed by magic?"

Petrik blinks slowly. "Of course! I should have guessed that. There's no other reason for them to be there."

"It'll be a risk," Kellyn says. "If you're wrong and we engage them, we won't get a second chance."

"Temra is fading," I say. "She doesn't have time for a second chance. We need to try this."

"If we attack them, things will get very loud," Kellyn says. "And we're unarmed, with no way to go back for our weapons now." He thinks a moment. "We need a distraction. You two hide. I'll lead the guards away."

"What?" I ask. "That's a terrible idea!"

"It's the only chance we'll have of getting Serutha out of here unseen."

"No."

"Temra is fading," Kellyn reminds me, throwing my own words in my face. "I can do this. Don't wait for me. Run for the portal as quickly as you can. Get the healer through. Save your sister."

"Kellyn—"

Petrik puts his hand on my shoulder, turns me. "He's right. Let him help. This is the best way."

I don't know what else to say. Petrik takes my silence as compliance. He darts behind one of those drapes again.

There's a tug on my arm as I start to join him, and then I'm being turned around.

Warm lips press against my own; the pressure is fierce, searing against my skin. I feel my stomach drop beneath the ground. When Kellyn pulls back, I want to look anywhere else, but he demands my attention. "Don't wait for me," he repeats. "I'm sorry Temra ever got hurt." Then he gently nudges me toward where Petrik is already hiding.

His back is to me before I can say anything in response. I lose sight of the mercenary as he ducks into the small hallway.

"Guards," he says in a cocksure voice. "I'm looking for that fancy healer. Is she down here?"

His question is met with silence.

"You shouldn't be here," someone says.

"I'm injured. Broken heart. Hoping she can work some magic."

"Identify yourself," another guard demands.

Kellyn sighs dramatically. "I was hoping you would hand her over. Fine. I'll just be going, then."

Hands clamp over my upper arms and haul me behind the drapes. The fabric settles into place just as I hear running footsteps fly by, followed by so many more. Where the end of the drapes meets the wall, there's the smallest gap, and I watch Kellyn barrel down the hallway, five men in pursuit.

"Come on," Petrik says, gripping my arm.

They left one guard behind with a spear, and she raises it at Petrik and me.

Our weapons are still up in the attic.

She rushes me, and I just barely dodge out of the way. On instinct, my hands wrap around the spear shaft, trying to wrest the weapon from her.

Petrik comes over to help me, but the guard kicks out at him, and the wind goes out from his lungs.

I have her beat in strength, but I'm untrained. I don't know what to do, and I'm scared to make too much noise. I yank at the weapon, pull the guard across the hallway, smash her back into the opposite wall. Then I shove the shaft toward her neck, cutting off her air supply.

It's horrible, standing there, hurting someone. At least with my weapons, it's over quickly, and I can move on before I have too much time to think about it. But here, I watch the guard's eyes roll back into her head, feel her body go limp in front of me, watch her slide to the floor.

A whimper escapes me, and no amount of blinking will make the scene in front of me change.

"Ziva!" Petrik's breath rushes into him all at once. "Search the walls. Look for any grooves or anything at all!"

I remember the task at hand, even though my hands shake, and my mind is a complete mess. Smoothing my hands flat against the wall, I pray for something to materialize beneath my fingers. Nothing happens when I move my hands side to side, but when I start to reach toward the ceiling—

"Petrik!"

Fabric comes up with my fingers, and then I'm yanking, pulling, until a long cloth detaches from the wall. When I catch it in my fingers, it still bears the same pattern as the stone wall surrounding it, obscuring the door hidden beneath.

I wonder for just a moment if Ravis has gotten his hands on another magical cloth weaver, before I toss the fabric to the ground and pull the pins from the door as I did in the attic. This one locks on the outside, clearly trying to keep someone from escaping.

My heart is in my throat when I finally get the last pin and pull. There's a noise, but I hope Kellyn's distraction is enough to keep anyone from noticing.

A woman, who I assume had been lying on a divan, is now bolted upright. She's in a nightdress, her hair loose around her face. It looks as though it's been recently brushed. The curls are somewhat flattened, but the volume is intense as it falls nearly down to her waist. Her eyes are a warm brown, her skin just a bit lighter. More amber-colored than Petrik's deep brown.

"Serutha!" Petrik says.

"Petrik?" She blinks, as though not trusting her eyes.

"We're here to rescue you."

The woman holds her arms around herself. "You shouldn't be here. The last people who tried to save me were beheaded. I know because Ravis left their heads in here for a week. I couldn't breathe for the smell."

All I need is confirmation that she's who we're looking for. The rest can wait until later. I get behind the healer and push her in the right direction.

"You can tell us all about your stay later," I say. "Right now, there is someone who needs your help."

Serutha doesn't resist. She pads barefoot beside me, my hand on her arm to steer her in the right direction.

"How did you find my room?" she asks. "It was hidden. Magicked."

"We guessed," Petrik answers.

"Where are the guards?"

"One of our companions is dealing with them."

"You sacrificed him for me? Skiro must be truly desperate."

"We sacrificed no one," I say. "He's very capable. Now hurry. We have to get you through the wardrobe."

The healer's doubt suddenly turns to hope. "You're really going to get me out of here."

"Yes," I assure her.

"All right."

Our pace picks up. We race past confused servants who don't recognize us, and we only make it halfway down the hall when an alarm sounds—large bells tolling from far overhead.

They know she's gone.

We sprint for the next staircase, skipping steps, racing for the top. Back down a level, I hear an uproar go through the servants. Someone shouts, "That way!"

We're being followed.

My legs burn. Serutha is slower without shoes on the hard floor. But I don't have time to think of her comfort. Temra doesn't have time. Kellyn doesn't have time.

When we finally reach the attic, I'm ready to collapse, but I shuffle along the floor, trying to find the broken door.

"Here!" Petrik exclaims, shoving it aside, not bothering to place it back over. Speed is our number one concern now.

We grab our weapons before weaving through the dark, trying to find the damned wardrobe.

Serutha winces as she steps on broken glass from the frame I stepped on earlier. I pick her up in one motion, try to retrace my steps.

"Ow," she says as she bumps into something. Or rather, I bump her into something.

I don't apologize.

"It's here, Ziva," Petrik says. He throws open the wardrobe. Steps sound back out in the hall, growing closer.

Serutha eyes the painting, but she must already know what it is. She says, "Thank you."

"Just save my sister, please."

Serutha stands on the toes of one foot to account for the glass and steps into the wardrobe and through the portrait.

I turn around, eyeing the way we came.

"What are you doing?" Petrik asks. "We have to go."

"Where is Kellyn?"

"You don't know?" His voice softens, but the question is still infuriating.

"How would I know, Petrik? He disappeared from both our sights ten minutes ago!"

"Ziva, he's not coming back."

"What?"

"He was the distraction so we could save Temra. They'll have caught him by now."

"No! He's a master swordsman. He said he'd meet us here."

No, that's not true. He said not to wait for him. And then he kissed me . . . as if to say goodbye.

"Oh Twins," I whisper.

"They're coming, Ziva. We have to go. Temra needs you."

Petrik steps through the wardrobe.

But I pause. Yes, Temra needs me. She's hurt and dying . . . But Serutha is the only one who can save her now. I can't do anything more for her as far as her health is concerned.

And Kellyn—

Why would he do this? Stupid man! Stupid me for not realizing—

Guards pool into the room. One spots me, yells to the others.

It's now or never, Ziva.

I pull my hammer free. Prepare to step into the wardrobe.

No.

I'm not leaving him.

Instead, I step to the back of the wardrobe. Just on the other side of this wood, a picture of the feared Prince Ravis is painted.

I raise my hammer.

And I shatter the portrait.

CHAPTER

FIVE

I fell seven guards before I realize there's no way I'm going to
fight my way out. They fall so quickly beneath my shield and
hammer. Unlike Kymora's men, these aren't prepared for my
magical weapon. Skin splits beneath my right hammer, and blood
flies into my eyes.

I'm a creator, not a killer. I've spent my life forging steel
for others, yet here I am, fighting with weapons that have seen
enough battle that they deserve names.

I don't want to kill these men and women. They're only following orders. Only trying to fulfill a job. It's not their fault Ravis
ended up ruling their territory, and I don't fault them for making
a living by serving him.

But I will do what it takes to find Kellyn and get the hells out
of this place.

I need to see for myself if we got Serutha to Temra in time.

But first I need to find that oaf of a mercenary. That self-
sacrificing pig. That imbecilic—

I only experience a few seconds of disorientation when I gain consciousness in an unfamiliar place, the back of my head throbbing like a beating drum.

I'm in a cell in Ravis's castle.

We got Serutha through the portal.

And Kellyn—

"This is the second time you've gotten me locked up," a voice says.

And Kellyn is somewhere in the dungeon with me.

I groan as I rise to a sitting position. "Yeah, well, this is the second time I've woken up in a prison after being knocked out."

"What happened? Where are Petrik and the healer?"

"They made it through the wardrobe." I test all my limbs slowly, seeing if they'll move when I tell them to. My arms really ache. Blood is dried between my fingers.

"Why didn't *you* make it through?" His voice has an edge of frustration to it.

"The guards spotted us. They found the wardrobe. I stayed behind to destroy their way back to Skiro and Serutha." And Temra, most importantly.

Kellyn shifts position. I finally catch sight of him against the opposite wall. We're in the same cell. A wooden door with a barred window blocks the only exit from the room.

"You could have destroyed the portrait from the other side. Once you'd gone through it."

His words send a jolt of fear through me. "Didn't think of that," I say lamely.

"You are such a bad liar. Why did you stay behind?"

I don't answer him. I fiddle with my fingers, trying to get the dried blood off them. I try to force my mind away from the discomfort in my stomach. The awkward ball of worms wriggling.

I hear him stand, and that only makes the nervous fear more pronounced. I'm terrified of this conversation. Of this confrontation. Of him finding out the truth.

When Kellyn crouches down in front of me, he grabs my hands, even though they're filthy, stilling my nervous habit.

"Ziva," he says. "Why?"

I pull my hands out of his grip. A hot flash of anger rips through me. "You were supposed to join us at the wardrobe! You weren't supposed to get caught!"

"I knew I would get caught. I never said I wouldn't."

"No one told you to sacrifice yourself, you idiot."

"No? Isn't that what you wanted? You hold me responsible for your sister's injuries. Isn't it only right that I be the sacrifice to get her healed?"

I finally look into his face. Open my mouth. Close it. "No" finally comes out.

"To which part?"

"You shouldn't be sacrificed to get her healed. I should! I didn't realize what you were doing. Why didn't you tell me? I would have distracted them so you and Petrik could get away with the healer."

A faint smile touches his lips. "I was the only one who could hold them off long enough. We were all unarmed. It had to be me, or you wouldn't have had the time to get Serutha out of there.

"And," he continues, "if you think for one second that I would ever allow you to throw your life away like that, you don't know me very well."

"Oh, so you're allowed to throw away yours, but I'm not allowed to?"

"You're special. You can change the world with what you can do. Ghadra needs you."

"I—" *But you're special, too*, I want to argue. He's so talented and kind and funny—

And I hate him right now.

"Your family depends on you," I shriek back at him. "You've spent your whole life putting them first, and you would just cast that aside to fix a mistake?"

Kellyn shrugs. "You would take care of them if anything happened to me."

Of course I would. But that's awfully presumptuous, and why would he stick me with that responsibility?

I love his family. They're wonderful and kind, and they don't deserve to have this stupid oaf of a man as a son and brother. I'm still so furious with him. My skin is getting hot, despite the dropping temperature of the cell.

There are so many things I want to say, but finding the right words has always been so difficult.

Perhaps that's why I blurt, "You kissed me!"

If Kellyn is surprised by the new direction I've taken the argument, he doesn't show it. "And?"

"Why did you do that?" He knows I broke things off. I didn't say it outright, but he *knows* that I can never be with him because of my sister. The guilt of still wanting him is already more than I can bear.

"Lots of reasons," he answers.

"Name them."

"I wanted to. I didn't think I'd see you again. I thought I might be imprisoned or killed once Ravis's men caught me. I wanted something good to hold on to if they tried to torture me for information. I wanted the last moment I shared with you to be something sweet instead of an argument or a stiff silence."

A stiff silence fills the space when he finishes talking.

He sits beside me on the filthy floor. "Why don't you just tell me why you're upset? Is it because I kissed you? I'm not sorry. Only sorry that you had to stick around to talk to me about it afterward. Are you still angry about what happened to Temra? I tried to fix it. I'm sure Serutha got to her in time. Or is there another reason, Ziva? Just tell me. Tell me what I need to apologize for this time."

"You're an idiot," I say at last, not answering his question at all, because I can't put what I'm feeling into words anymore.

"You want me to apologize for being an idiot?"

"I want you to stop talking. I'm furious right now, and I need to think!"

"You mean to break us out of jail? There are no torches within reach. I checked. And even if there were, that door is mostly made of wood. The walls consist of stone. If we get out of this room, it won't be by your magic."

I want to cry. I wipe at my eyes before I remember my hands are still covered in blood. Now it's on my face, and I just want to be clean, and I don't want to hurt people anymore.

Why can't everyone just leave me in peace? Temra and I mind our own business. We didn't ask for any of this. I wanted to make the world a safer place with my weapons. Temra wants to keep people safe as a soldier. If she's dead—

I can't think like that.

When the night grows colder and I start shivering, I don't let Kellyn share his warmth. I don't want it. I want to be miserable. It somehow makes me feel better inside.

I can't fall asleep because I'm so cold. But Kellyn's snores eventually fill the room.

My teeth begin to chatter. Still I don't move. If I'm going to die in here, I'll do it without losing my dignity.

I think I might have started to nod off when the door opens. A guard enters holding a ring of keys, and Kellyn bolts to his feet. They don't need to use any force to get us from the cell or through a series of locked doors until we finally come up out of the dungeons, where there is still warmth in the world. Too much of it, in fact.

The palace is quiet. I don't hear courtiers laughing or music playing. All is still, and that somehow makes everything worse.

We're led into a large throne room, which is the only place in the castle I've seen so far with any sort of decoration. Ravis, the eldest of Petrik's siblings, sits atop the mighty chair. A spearpoint juts out on either side of the back of the chair, the shafts leading down to the rear feet of the opulent piece. The armrests shape out into giant cat claws, along with the front feet.

The prince wears a loose scarlet surcoat. The sleeves reach past his wrists, and the hem brushes his ankles. His feet are in jewel-studded sandals, and each of his fingers is gripped by a sparkling ring. The crown on his head is massive, each spire coming to a deadly point. At the base of the six spires are six jewels: red, blue, green, yellow, orange, and purple in color.

He looks bored.

"Who are you, and what have you done with my healer?" the prince asks. He hasn't even looked at us yet. He's staring at the long dagger gripped in his right hand instead.

Neither Kellyn nor I answer.

"Skiro has taken her back, hasn't he?" Ravis asks, undeterred by our silence. "Who would have thought he had the guts? Or the manpower. No matter." Ravis flicks his wrist, spinning the long blade in a wide arc repeatedly. "I beheaded the last fools who attempted to steal Serutha from me. What should I do to the fools who succeeded?"

My voice is so far from me, I don't think I could find it if I tried. I can barely breathe for the fear pounding through me with each beat of my heart.

"Send us to get her back for you," Kellyn says.

A flare of panic washes over me at the words. Just what is Kellyn playing at?

Ravis begins laughing. He sits up straighter in his chair, finally looks down at us. "Why would I do that?"

"We're mercenaries," Kellyn says. "Your brother paid us to retrieve the healer. Offer us a bigger sum, and we'll get her back for you."

Ravis huffs before focusing on twirling his overly long dagger once more. "Tell me about how you came to be here and how Serutha disappeared so quickly. What new magic has my brother discovered?"

"I'm not sure," Kellyn says. "All I know is we stepped through a portrait of you and we were suddenly here."

"Hmm. A painter, is it? Well, I shall have to locate them when I storm the gates to retrieve Serutha."

Kellyn thinks quickly. "Why do yourself what you could have us do?"

"Because I'm traveling to Skiro's pathetic territory anyway, and I have no patience for liars. Strax, test my dagger's sharpness for me, will you? The girl first, I think."

A guard standing several feet behind the prince steps forward.

"We have not lied, Prince. Let us do your bidding. Spare our lives, and we will get her back for you," Kellyn says.

"Liars claiming not to be liars. Must be a Tuesday." Ravis sighs. "Tell me, why would a mercenary destroy the very portrait which could have taken her home? What mercenary doesn't save her own skin?"

Ravis points his dagger right at me.

I look away. I still can't find my words. All I wanted was to get Kellyn out of here, but there is nothing I can do. There is nothing either of us can do. We're surrounded by guards. Our weapons are nowhere to be seen. There's an entire castle's worth of men and women between us and the exit. Never mind a whole territory to traverse before we can get back to Skiro.

"One with a good heart," Kellyn whispers too quietly for Ravis to hear.

"Strax," Ravis drones, and he thrusts his dagger into the hands of his guard.

Who then approaches me.

A strange calmness settles over me, and I feel suddenly as though I'm not actually in the room but watching this scene from afar. Is that what happens when you know your death is coming?

"No, please, Prince. You don't need to do this. I'm the mastermind behind everything. Let her go." Kellyn's words don't do anything to sway Ravis. He turns sideways in his chair, throws his legs atop one of the cat-claw armrests. Then his eyes turn on me, waiting to watch his man end me.

It's not a terrible way to go, I suppose. I did everything I could to save Temra. I can meet my parents in the next life guilt-free. Or mostly guilt-free. There were probably lots of things I could have done better. But at least I did everything I could to save my sister's life.

I've lived a good life myself. I've left my mark, leaving behind weapons for the world to use. I've seen much of the world over the past few months. I had my first kiss. I knew what it was to be with someone for a time. I raised my sister to adulthood, and if she survives, she'll be okay. Petrik will take care of her.

My only regret is taking Kellyn down with me. He didn't deserve this. The stupid man shouldn't have gotten himself caught.

I look at him now, without an ounce of discomfort toward him. I suppose there's a sense of clarity that comes with dying. How can I be anxious when I know I won't be around to regret anything? I take in his golden-brown eyes. So beautiful when they're searching my own. I trace a lock of hair with my eyes, marveling at the red color, remembering the texture under my fingers. His lips are perfect. The color of light roses and softer than anything else in the world. I'm glad he kissed me today. I close my eyes to savor that memory one last time, just as the dagger angles toward my neck . . .

"This is Ziva Tellion! The magically gifted bladesmith!"

My eyes fly open at the words coming out of Kellyn's mouth. *He didn't.*

"You don't want to kill her when you could use her to storm Skiro's gates."

How, *how*, can he be suggesting such a thing? My consciousness slams back into my body in full force, and I return to being a nervous wreck.

Ravis raises a hand, which signals his man to hold. "Prove it."

"Our weapons," Kellyn says. "They're magicked. She made them. Have your men retrieve them, and you will see. My sword is stashed up in the attic behind a framed portrait."

Skiro's feet slam loudly back onto the floor in front of him. "If you're lying to me this time, I will cut out your tongue and feed it to you. Strax."

The tall guard disappears from sight, and I glare at Kellyn.

"What are you doing?" I whisper.

"Saving you."

"By betraying our friends?" By betraying *me*?

"Silence your mutterings," Ravis says. "I'm still of half a mind to have you killed, magic or no."

I want to slap Kellyn and slap this haughty prince while I'm at it. I want to see my sister, to know if Serutha made it to her in time. And for the millionth time, I want to be alone in my forge.

When Strax returns, he holds my hammers in one hand, Kellyn's longsword in the other.

Ravis takes Lady Killer in one hand and swings her about like he did his dagger a moment ago. "What does it do?"

"Have your men charge you all at once," Kellyn instructs.

"Strax."

The head of Ravis's guard signals to some of the men and women on standby. They rush at their prince, though tentatively. I watch as they flip their spears around, trading the pointed ends for the shafts, before attempting to strike at their prince.

Ravis is a skilled swordsman, that much is clear. But Lady Killer makes him untouchable. He spins and ducks and jumps all the spears jutting for him. He doesn't throw any of his own strikes—he doesn't wish to harm his own men. But he puts on quite the act of dexterity as he dodges slash after slash.

When satisfied, Ravis leans the longsword against his throne. "The hammers?" he asks Kellyn.

Kellyn explains what the left hammer does in detail, and Ravis practices with it, using his men again. He marvels as he deflects blow after blow on the shield hammer.

Satisfied, Ravis sets my hammers next to the longsword before turning to me. "You will make me and my men weapons before our attack on Skiro's Territory." He nods, as though satisfied by his own conclusion, and turns.

"No."

I haven't said a word during the entire ordeal, but now one comes flying out of my throat like a battering ram against a door.

Ravis doesn't turn around, but he halts in his tracks. He doesn't speak. Doesn't move for a whole minute.

Then he turns.

"Strax, my dagger."

The guard tosses the weapon to his prince. Ravis catches it deftly.

"You can kill me," I say as he steps toward me. "I won't do it." I will not craft anything that could hurt my friends or sister. Not again. I've learned my lesson with Secret Eater.

But instead of taking the remaining steps to reach me, Ravis veers in Kellyn's direction.

"No!" I shout, just as he brings the blade against the side of Kellyn's head.

A wet noise. A grunt of pain. Kellyn shrinking in on himself. The dagger comes away bloody, and Kellyn's hand goes to cup the side of his face.

Ravis is holding part of his ear.

I feel my stomach turn, my lips quiver.

I never knew that one little word could do so much damage. *No.*

I can't so much as move, I'm so shocked.

Ravis presents the ear to me as though it is a gift, then drops it at my feet. "You care about this man, else you wouldn't have stayed behind for him. Make me my weapons, or I will gift him to you, one piece at a time."

He doesn't wait for my answer. Ravis turns to go once more.

CHAPTER

SIX

I stare at Kellyn, who still bleeds on the floor.

He doesn't make a sound, and I wonder if he's in shock. I know I am, but the knowledge doesn't seem to help. I can't make my limbs work. I can't feel . . . anything. The heat of this place is now lost on me.

But I do register the hands that eventually grip me.

"This way, smithy," Strax says. "You'll need a full night's rest before starting work tomorrow."

"Kellyn," I say, trying to get his attention, even as I'm dragged backward.

The mercenary doesn't move. If I could just get him to look at me so I can see his face. I need to know he's okay. In pain, of course, but okay.

But he doesn't turn before they take me from the throne room entirely.

"Someone needs to see to him," I say, finally daring to speak to the men holding me.

Their grip only tightens, and I try to pull from it.

"Won't you send someone to help him?" I beg.

"That will depend entirely on how well you cooperate," Strax answers.

At that, I stop fighting. I place my feet on the ground and walk willingly toward whatever our destination may be.

I recognize it after too long.

They put me in Serutha's old rooms. Her prison is now my prison.

And Kellyn put me here. He's bleeding somewhere. I don't want him to die and I want to kill him myself and *could he stop being so damn confusing*!

The door to the rooms closes, and Strax locks me inside.

It's been so long since I've been alone.

But this is not the kind of aloneness that heals and refreshes the mind. I'm in danger, in a strange place. My sister might be dead. Kellyn might be bleeding out.

And I'm alone.

Terrified.

Hungry.

Exhausted.

I collapse to the floor and weep. It's not long before my breaths come too quickly and the panic takes over entirely.

Helplessness pervades everything. I bang against the walls of my own mind, trying to find an escape. The air is sucked from my lungs, my whole body is on fire, and I'm certain I'm going to die. Eons pass as the walls close in, and everything grows blacker and bleaker.

And then exhaustion takes over.

I don't sleep long. Of that, I'm certain.

A bag of bricks weighs my shoulders down, and my brain has been replaced with cotton. My eyes are crusty, and every muscle I have is sore and bruised. None of this is consequential, however.

Ravis has Kellyn, and he's going to use him to force me to work.

Unless he let him die in the throne room overnight.

My thoughts try to spiral out of control again when someone enters my room. A maidservant, dressed plainly in a lightweight dress that shows off her calves and arms. She doesn't speak. Doesn't say a word to me. She holds a rather large pot in two hands and takes it right to the washing room, dumping the steaming contents into the tub. It takes her several minutes to bring in each bucketful of water.

I try to catch her eye, even try speaking to her. But she won't say a word.

By the sixth time she enters the room, she brings up a set of clothes. And food. She sets the tray on the divan by my feet. The clothing she lays carefully on the bed so as not to wrinkle the outfit.

"I will return for you in one hour." She leaves before I can respond.

I'm apparently not too proud to refuse the food or the bath or the fresh clothes.

If I'm to escape, I need a full stomach, I reason. A bath will clear my head, rinse the blood from my fingers. I need to be as ready as I can for what's ahead.

I don't recognize my breakfast, though I eat it to quell my hunger. There's some sort of pink fruit that I have to peel first, a citrus with a bitter aftertaste. I like it, by the fourth or fifth bite. The bread is soft and fresh, peppered with spices I'm unused to, but covered with a deliciously salty butter. I wash it all down with a cup of water.

I have to wait another ten minutes before the water is cool enough not to scald. Even then, my skin is blushing pink when I emerge and don the clothes left for me: lightweight trousers, a sleeveless shirt, and thick sandals.

When the servant collects me, no less than twenty guards follow us down through the castle, outdoors, and then to the forges.

Yes, multiple.

A quarter mile from the palace, Ravis has a massive outdoor area with more kilns than I can count. Men and women hammer away at various weapons, others man the bellows, while even more take steel to the grinding stones.

It doesn't take a genius to realize Ravis has been preparing for war for quite some time.

"Isn't it marvelous?" a voice to my left says.

The prince has joined us, his own guard trailing behind him.

I lack any tact at the moment. The truth comes out. "Your forges are impressive."

"I meant the weapons. As someone who makes them for a living, surely you must appreciate the sheer volume we've managed to produce in just half a year."

I swallow. "What are you planning?"

"Don't be naive."

"This isn't right."

"I didn't take you for a hypocrite."

I round on him. "I make weapons for people who want to defend themselves from bandits. I keep people safe while they're traveling on Ghadra's dangerous roads. You want to hurt them."

Ravis is undaunted by my tone. "I do want to keep people safe, smithy. Safe from my father's mistake. My siblings are running their territories into the ground. They should never have been entrusted with such responsibility.

"I'm the eldest," he continues. "I was the only one trained to rule. Ghadra is my birthright. I'm taking it back. The world will thank me one day."

This is worse than I feared. I thought Ravis wanted to invade Skiro to retrieve the healer, that perhaps he craved magic in a dangerous way. But he wants what Kymora wanted.

The world.

The irony of the situation is not lost on me. After King Arund sentenced his brother to death for a failed assassination attempt, he wanted to avoid future familial disputes over the land, so he split the realm into six territories, bequeathing one to each of his children.

But Ravis clearly feels cheated.

I gentle my voice into what I hope is a reasoning tone. I'm not gifted with words, but I try anyway. "I've been to several of the other territories. They are starting to find their feet after the split. Don't hurt the people by changing everything again so soon." Don't hurt my friends and loved ones by bringing war to them.

Ravis pulls his long dagger out from the sheath at his waist, twirls the point lightly against the pointer finger of his left hand. "You do not command me, smithy. You know nothing of politics. You know steel. Why don't we focus on what we're good at, hmm?"

Ravis eyes one of the nearest workers. "You there. Bring that weapon over."

A burly man takes his foot off the pedal working the grind-stone and brings over the sword in his hand. It's a bastard sword, though bulkier than the weapons the warlord's men used.

The metalworker kneels on the ground dramatically and holds up the sword to his prince with a bowed head.

Ravis takes it and thrusts the weapon in my direction, hilt first.

I accept the sword, thoroughly confused. The guards around me straighten ever so slightly. Ready to pounce should I try anything.

"Magic it," the prince orders.

"I can't."

"No? Do I need to send you another piece of that brutish mercenary locked up in my dungeons?"

Fear licks down my spine, but at least he confirmed Kellyn is alive. "I can only magic metal when it is hot. I must be part of the forging process. I cannot magic an already-finished weapon."

A partial lie, but I force it out. Everything is happening so quickly, and I need all the time I can get.

"Then bring the smithy a hot weapon!"

"You misunderstand me. *I* have to make the weapon, Prince." Another lie. I'm not really good at them, but hopefully Ravis doesn't notice.

He rolls his eyes. "And just how long does it take you to make a weapon?"

"A couple months usually," I answer truthfully.

"Then what bloody good are you? What am I supposed to do with a single weapon every other month? Wait a few years so there are enough for my generals?" Ravis starts swinging his dagger about again, twirling it in wide arcs at his side. Clearly a habit of his.

The smithy who knelt on the ground rises and steps toward his prince, whispering something to him.

"Ah, good point, yes. How long, lady smithy, will it take you to make a weapon if you have help? I have an entire legion of metalworkers who are here to assist. They can make dozens of weapons a week."

"My name is Ziva."

"I'll call you whatever I like. Now answer the question."

"I couldn't say. I've . . . never had help before."

Except Temra.

"Well, there's a first for everything. Elany!"

A girl my age saunters over from the back of Ravis's personal guards. I hadn't spotted her before now. Her skin is the palest I've ever seen, hair a bright yellow, long enough to reach her waist. Her features are friendly, open, but if she works for Ravis, I'm not about to let that fool me.

"Ziva, meet Elany. Consider her your right-hand woman. You need something to assist you with making my weapons, you tell her. She is to be involved in every step of the smithing process. You don't go anywhere in the forge without her. Understood?"

"Yes."

"Good. Now get to work."

"But, Prince, you haven't told me what you want!"

"What I want? I want weapons, girl! By the Twins, have you no brains?"

I chafe at the words but press on. "What *kind* of weapons? What do you want them to do? What do you want them to look like? What embellishments?"

Ravis tilts his head to one side, then the other, observing me like he's never seen me before.

"I'm a specialty bladesmith," I explain, uncomfortable at the scrutiny. "People come to me for one-of-a-kind weapons. No two are the same. They usually have specific requests. I don't want to displease you." Or, really, to cost Kellyn the other half of his ear. "I just need to know what you want."

"This is war, lady smithy. I'm not looking for uniqueness. I'm looking for volume. I don't care if all the weapons do the same thing! Just make me swords." Ravis points to the head of his guard, Strax. I notice for the first time that the man has Kellyn's longsword strapped to his back.

"Make my men unbeatable. I need weapons fit to conquer Ghadra. I don't care how you do it. Just get it done. Any further questions can go to Elany. I might just decide you're not worth the trouble if I hear another one. We're done here."

Ravis leaves me, his guard trailing behind him. The soldiers assigned to me remain, fanning out along the sides of the forges.

I turn to stare at everything behind me. Noise and people and roaring fires and *people*. I want to run.

The girl called Elany steps up to my side before I can do something foolish.

"They won't bite," she says kindly.

"I'm not used to working in front of others."

"For the sake of your friend, I hope you get over that quickly."

That makes two of us.

"Shall I show you around?" she asks.

"Do I really have a say?"

Elany doesn't answer; she takes me in a wide arc around the area so we can better observe the space and how everything works together. My assigned guard is never less than twenty feet away.

I count at least four dozen men and women before I give up. They're all massive, well-built individuals. Elany explains that there are sixteen kilns, twenty-five anvils, a dozen grinding stones. She introduces me to some of Ravis's most talented smithies, but I don't remember a single name. I'm too busy battling the anxiety that tries to creep in and take over. I don't look anyone in the eye if I can help it. I couldn't attach faces to names if I tried.

Children sweep the forges free of soot, oil down weapons, stack them neatly against tall racks. The forges are busy and noisy and full of chatter. I feel as though I can't quite ground myself, as though every new sound quakes in my bones, setting me off balance.

"Here's where you'll be working," Elany says, showing me to a forge in the heart of the sprawling smithies. Where I can be observed by everyone. Where escape is impossible.

Beyond the forges, I can spot a single road leading away from the castle, but there's no cover on either side of it. Tall, prickly plants unlike any I've ever seen dot the area. Sparse bushes and shrubs grow intermittently. In the distance, past the sweep of the city, I can see the start of a tree line. The sun is to the left of the woods, so I know they sprawl to the south. Toward Skiro.

But I'd never reach them with how heavily I'm guarded.

And then an approaching contingent of guards has me feeling even more trapped than before—until I notice who they're escorting.

Kellyn walks in the middle of the throng. The relief at seeing his face is a tangible thing. There's something about taking in his features that makes me feel a little more hopeful. A little stronger. Like we can get through this together.

It battles against the part of me that wants to rage at him for getting me in this mess, for putting the idea into Ravis's head to use me to build weapons to hurt others. But at the sight of the gauze that wraps around his head and covers his left ear, the nicer Ziva wins.

"Are you all right?" I ask him.

"No talking!" a guard yells back.

"Oh, shove off," Elany says to him. "There's no harm in her asking after him. Go ahead, Ziva."

"Kellyn?" I ask.

His eyes meet mine. "I'm just fine. They cleaned me up. My sleeping arrangements leave something to be desired, but they're not hurting me."

"Yet," the guard who spoke before says. "But anymore daw-dling, and that will change. Get to work."

So they've brought Kellyn to keep me on track. To encourage me to get my job done with all haste. I'm to outfit an entire army with magical weapons.

This is what I feared most just months ago when we were running for our lives from Kymora.

Now it's my reality.

The bite of despair is powerful, but I can't let that poison set in. If there's a way to get us both out of this, I'm going to find it. I've bought myself some time to think. I've convinced Ravis I can't just magic the weapons he's already made—which was, of course, a total lie. I could heat them up one by one and magic them on the spot.

But now I'm permitted to start the process from scratch. It'll be weeks, surely, before I finish a single weapon for the prince. I'll stall wherever and whenever I can. But I must always appear to be doing my best.

For Kellyn's sake.

"I need an apron and gloves," I say to Elany. "Show me your iron stores."

Aside from the guards lining the whole area, about seven men and women wait at the edges of my new forge. I realize soon enough that they're my team. And they're awaiting instructions.

"Um . . ."

Temra is the only person I've ever had in the forge with me, and I'm struck with unimaginable grief at the reminder. It's been too long since I've heard her voice or seen her laugh. What if I don't get to see her again? Not knowing what's become of her might kill me before Ravis's guards ever do.

I try to sort through the mess of my thoughts. I shove all

musings of my sister to the back of my mind. Worrying over her will only distract me from my current task.

Which is to talk to people. To tell them how to best help me in the forge. I look to Kellyn as a reminder of why I have to do this. Why I have to push aside the panic and discomfort. My fingers tangle together, and my gaze drops to the floor as I mumble out instructions.

If the smithies think me odd, they say nothing. Ravis clearly has them well motivated to work. They haul iron ore into the forge for me. Light the kiln. Man the bellows. Begin the process of creating steel.

And I see right away how I'm in trouble. This is going to be over much too quickly.

"No, let me hold that," I say to the woman filling the crucible with charcoal. I take it, finish the mixture myself, and then put it in the kiln, which is already raging from the man working the bellows.

Another group has already finished filling another crucible, and they hand it to me for inspection. When done, it's added to the kiln. Then a third and fourth. Five total fit in the kiln at a time. Then Elany leads me to another forge, where I have a hand in carburizing more iron. Over and over again.

With every new crucible added to the kiln, a stone weight drops into my stomach.

The forge used to be my safe space. It was where I was most happy and comfortable.

Now it's my prison.

Now it's where I will craft the very weapons used to threaten everything I've ever known.

CHAPTER SEVEN

Every night I fall into bed sore from my efforts. It's been too long since I've hammered at anything for a significant length of time. I love the burning in my arms. It means I'm growing stronger. But it also exhausts me, and my team of helpers insists on doing the hammering themselves once I can no longer do it myself.

On top of that, there's the stress of constantly being surrounded by people. It's an exhaustion of its own. It makes me want to stay up late at night just so I can be awake and alone for a time. Otherwise, I don't have time to think. To regain my mental fortitude, such as it is.

They bring Kellyn to the forges every day, but they don't hurt him. I don't give them the chance. I'm hammering, shaping, heating, reheating the metal of the swords we're furnishing. If Ravis is also fond of the bastard sword, then that's what I'll make for him.

We do not stop for meals. Workers from the kitchens bring

food at even intervals to the metalworkers, and we take turns eating. The forges are never quiet. Someone is always doing something. There's barely time to breathe.

By day six, my sore muscles are mostly a dull throb. I've learned the names of all the men and women in my crew, and I even occasionally forget they're there. At times, when I'm lost in the sound of my hammer pounding on metal or gazing at the white-hot steel of a blistering sword tip, I can almost pretend I'm back home doing the work I love.

And then someone will ask me a question or a guard will bite out a threat toward Kellyn just for the fun of it.

Then I remember where I am and fear sets in.

When the pressure becomes too much, I look up, stare at the freshly replaced gauze at Kellyn's head each day, and remind myself the cost of failing. It's a terror that battles with my anger day after day. I don't want anything bad to befall Kellyn, yet I want to beat on him myself for making me a slave to Ravis's will.

Elany is never far behind me, observing everything I do, and she regularly attempts to strike up conversation with me.

"How long have you been magicking metal?"

"Do you magic with your will or your voice?"

"Does using your ability weaken you?"

I don't know if she's genuinely curious or if Ravis has put her up to the interrogation. Either way, I answer so the guards near Kellyn don't get any ideas.

"Since I was nine."

"Both."

"Not really."

Sometimes she brings a bit of mending to work on. Cloaks or shirts or dresses that she stitches up—but for the most part, she watches me, as though she could learn something. But my gift isn't something that can be taught. Magic is there or it isn't.

"Who are you?" I ask her one day. "Why does Ravis have you watching me?"

She shrugs. "He hopes I'll learn a thing or two. And there aren't enough guards to go around."

At that, my gaze whips to her. "You're a prisoner, too?"

"Not really. Ravis is my employer, but he doesn't trust me entirely."

"But he trusts you with me?"

"Guess so."

"And what does he employ you to do?"

She rolls her lips under her teeth but doesn't answer, and I've no choice but to let the subject drop.

While the newest batch of blades is cooling, we set to forming hilts for the swords. The steel process is started again, but this time we hammer the heated metal into a cross guard. That done, I set to shaping metal, chiseling at it while it's still hot.

"What are you doing?" Elany asks.

"Shaping."

"It's already shaped like a hilt."

"Embellishing, then," I say, and I realize my mistake. When I look up, Elany is smiling at me gently.

"You're an artist, Ziva, but Prince Ravis doesn't want art. He wants practicality. As long as there's a place for a soldier to grip the sword, no extra embellishments are required."

I'd been preparing to add the designs of some of the local fruit I've tasted, adding what I think the blossoms of such trees might look like.

But my skills are not what Ravis wants.

Only my magic.

I sigh, trading the chisel for a hammer so I can pound the hilt back into a smooth shape. As I do so, horse hooves clop into view, pulling a heavy cart laden with iron ore.

"Another shipment?" I ask.

"Every Tuesday and Saturday," Elany responds. "The prince doesn't ever want his stores to run dry.

Since the capital of Ravis's Territory is the farthest from the Southern Mountains, I can't imagine where he's getting the ore from. I ask Elany about it.

She says, "Prince Ravis has friends in the southern territories. There are many who recognize the need for a unified Ghadra."

I take that to simply mean the prince has deep pockets, and he's buying the ore from men who have no idea where it's being taken or what it's being made into. There could be miners in my own city of Lirasu aiding the prince without knowing. The thought makes me sick.

I search for Kellyn through the countless guards stationed to watch me. He's where they always keep him, far enough from any of the smithing tools that he can't get any ideas. Instead of watching me, as he usually does, Kellyn only has eyes for the newly arrived cart of iron ore.

Every Tuesday and Saturday.

As Elany's words echo in my mind, Kellyn looks up. He looks back at the cart, then at me. I nod slowly, taking his meaning.

A team of horses arrives on the premises twice a week like clockwork.

They're exactly what we need to escape.

But that doesn't solve how I'll get Kellyn away from all those guards before they can hurt him, or how we'll get out of here without Ravis's men right on our heels.

When just a few days later all the hilts are shaped and welded to their blades, everyone turns to me expectantly.

It's time for me to magic Ravis's swords.

Ten days. That's how long it took for my team to craft over five dozen swords. So many, even with my efforts to slow down the process by having a hand in making each one. They're simple blades with no finery or ornamentation, but they'll kill a man just as well.

And now I have to make them even deadlier.

"You need them put back in the kiln, yes?" Elany asks. "You mentioned they needed to be hot in order for your magic to work?"

I nod.

My team does the task for me, which is good, because my hands have started to sweat. As if I weren't already under enough pressure with Kellyn healing from a head wound and countless guards watching my every move.

I don't like magicking in front of others. Sometimes I even make Temra leave the forge when it's time for that part of the process. It's something that comes from inside me, and outside distractions will often lock that part of me away.

Or cause whatever I'm magicking to have unanticipated abilities.

That's how I made Secret Eater, the sword Warlord Kymora was so eager to possess that she chased me all over Ghadra for it. I'd been distracted by Kellyn while trying to make the weapon. It was the first time I'd ever seen him, and I ended up creating the most dangerous sword the world has ever known. Thankfully, Secret Eater is tucked away in the small town of Amanor, buried in a rock of iron, where only someone worthy may pull it free.

When the steel has had enough time to reheat, Elany treads over to the kiln, pulls out one of the swords with a pair of tongs, and thrusts it at me.

I take it, and for the first time in my life, the tools that I hold so very dear feel wrong in my hands. Today I'm not using my abilities for protection. These blades have one purpose, that of destruction.

The knowledge makes my heart ache, but I cannot bear to see Kellyn chopped into small bits.

I have no choice but to try and do the least amount of damage.

Back when I had a shop in Lirasu, I would make smaller items in bulk: daggers, buckles, arrows, nails, and the like. They were imbued with simple magic. They'd never dull or rust or break. Arrows would always hit their mark. Everyday items that more ordinary folk could afford.

Maybe I could do that. Imbue Ravis's swords with simple magic. He didn't ask for specifics. He asked for volume.

Fine.

That I can do.

As I inspect the weapon, the forges go quiet. Everyone around me ceases working. The constant hammering and scraping and bellowing all cease. Breaths are held, and heads lean in.

To watch me.

I close my eyes and pretend no one is around. That it's just me in the forge. Me in my safe space.

And I think of Temra.

We're bound by blood and years of sisterhood. Our love for each other is warm and accepting and unbreakable. I hold that feeling close as I think fondly through my memories of her.

Watching her take the lead in city plays. Seeing her face light up when she dances. Seeing her bent over her schoolwork or listening to her babble about boys. They're little things, but I would give anything to have more of those moments with her.

I feel the light pulse of magic from the weapon before me. Satisfied, I quench the blade and hand it off to a nearby worker, before starting the process over again on another sword.

Elany interrupts me after I finish magicking the second one.

"What did you do to them?"

"Extended their life spans—and that of Ravis's soldiers."

When she says nothing more, I look up. She and everyone else around me have expectant faces.

A demonstration, then.

I find the biggest man in the forges. "Come over here. Bring a hammer."

He listens at once, and I slap the sword onto the nearest anvil, holding it by the hilt and letting several inches of the tip hang off the end.

"Try to break it," I instruct.

The man looks to Elany, as if for permission. She nods.

After a shrug, he hoists his hammer and slams it down on the end of the sword. There's a noise like a clap of thunder, and the man's arm flies backward when it meets the resistance of the blade.

Which is still intact and perfectly unmarred.

"Take it," I say, holding it out to him.

He examines the sword carefully. "Not a scratch on it. I should have shattered it with that swing. Wait a moment." He reaches out a hand, brushes it along the tip. He draws in a sharp gasp before putting his finger in his mouth. "It's sharp. We haven't taken these to the grindstone yet."

"Nor will you need to," I say. Ravis ought to be happy about the saved time.

Elany takes the sword from him and examines it herself. "It's impressive, but I don't think it's what the prince had in mind . . ."

"If the prince wanted something different, then he should have asked for it."

And with that, I continue.

By the end of the day, all five dozen swords are magicked, and the team has already started up a fresh iron-and-charcoal mixture, preparing to make more steel. I dread the work ahead and the end result of it. I think of how each swing of my hammer will weigh down my soul.

And then the prince shows up with his personal guards, Strax at the head still bearing Kellyn's longsword.

Ravis doesn't say a word as he grabs one of the finished weapons. He twirls it about as he's fond to do with his dagger. Strax picks up another one of the weapons, puts himself through a series of drills, striking at an invisible foe.

When done, Strax holds the sword out in front of him, balances the blade on two of his fingers. "This is better work than anything your smithies have made yet. The balance is perfect. The blades are light yet powerful."

The prince listens to Strax's judgment before he turns to me. "What do they do?"

My gaze drops to the floor, unable to bear the scrutiny. "They'll last forever, Prince." I try to think of something else to say. Something to convince him of the worthiness of these blades, but my mind goes totally blank.

Elany clears her throat. "As soon as Ziva magics the blades, they're instantly sharp. We don't have to take them to the grindstone. These swords will never dull, never rust, never break. Your warriors' blades will never fail."

My fingers interlace in front of me, and distantly I hear my joints popping. I think I might hold my breath as I wait for the prince's judgment.

"I know you can do better, lady smithy. Strax's new weapon is proof of that. I expect the next batch to be more powerful, else your mercenary friend will suffer the consequences."

My gaze snaps up. "Prince, I can't control my more powerful magic. Sometimes it works, sometimes it doesn't. Bigger things are more unpredictable. And if you expect volume, as you've requested, simpler magic is the way to go."

I'm mumbling. I'm not really even aware of what I'm saying. Truths or falsehoods? I just know I can't make him dozens of unbeatable weapons or else the world is doomed.

"Do better," Ravis says. "You have been warned."

I can't sleep that night. My brain turns over every possible thing that could go wrong. Visions of Petrik and Skiro falling before my magical weapons. Kellyn's family fleeing for their lives. My home city burning. It haunts me into the early hours of the morning.

With drooping eyes, I begin hammering at the next round of weapons.

"Ziva," Kellyn says from the corner of the forge. "Don't do this for my sake."

"Quiet," a guard snaps at him.

"I'm not worth it," he says. "I can't bear to see you like this."

"Not another word!"

Oh, *he* can't bear it? *What about me?* I want to snap. What about when I was ready to die in Ravis's throne room, and Kellyn sold me out? Once again, he was only thinking about how he would feel if I died, not about how I would feel, forced to—

"Ziva, please—"

I look up just as one of the guards slaps at the injured side of Kellyn's head. His face contorts in pain, and I leap forward.

"You stay right there, smithy," the guard who struck him says, "or I'll give him another good wallop."

Tears prick my eyes, but I turn my head back to my work. I will not let Kellyn suffer because of me. I will not let the world suffer because of me. I *will* find us a way out of this.

The pain of sleep deprivation pounds like a drum at my temples, and each slam of my hammer only intensifies the throbbing. I cannot think like this. Not when I'm worrying about what the next batch of swords will do or if Temra is alive or if Kellyn is smart enough to keep his stupid mouth shut.

Elany puts away today's mending and stands next to me. "What's your plan for the next batch?"

"I don't have one yet."

"And your plan for escape?"

I shoot her a glare. I can't find it within myself to look innocent or surprised or anything else. "If I had one, I'm not about to tell Ravis's lackey about it, now, am I?"

Elany twirls a lock of her golden hair around one finger. "That's fair." She pauses. "I know it doesn't help, but I want you to know that I don't approve of the way you're being treated. We need a united Ghadra, but this isn't the way to go about it. You can't force loyalty. It's something that can only be earned."

I wipe the sweat from my brow with the back of my arm. "A united Ghadra doesn't do anything except create more problems at this point. And if my current situation is any indication of how Ravis intends to lead a united Ghadra, then I have no hope for the future. Just look at Kellyn."

Elany doesn't say anything for a moment, and I focus on my swings, turning the metal just so.

"I cared about someone once," she says at last. "The way you care about your mercenary."

I don't stop my hammering or correct her assumption about Kellyn and me. Maybe once we were close like that. Now I don't have a name for what Kellyn and I are.

"Raiders from the west sailed across the sea and ransacked my village in Orena's Territory. They butchered my Verryn right in front of me."

"I'm sorry," I say quietly.

"No one has done anything about it. Princess Orena isn't about to stage a war against the western isles, nor demand justice from the individuals who attacked. She doesn't have the manpower or the inclination. She's too busy trying to figure out how to rule.

"Don't you see?" she continues. "We have to be united. None of the other royals were meant to rule. We must have a united army. A force who can stand up for the people and make sure that all are looked after."

At that, I pause in my hammering. "Who's looking out for me right now, Elany? Who's looking out for Kellyn?"

"I am, dammit!" she says. "I'm helping you however I can. But you need to do this for Ravis. For all the people who are being neglected."

We stare at each other. Neither willing to back down.

"It isn't right what happened to your village," I say. "Your princess should do better, but this"—I gesture to all the work going on in the forges—"it isn't right, either."

"This is all I have left," she says.

"And you're trying to help destroy all that I have left."

Elany turns away, puts distance between the two of us.

And I continue hammering.

CHAPTER

EIGHT

The next batch of weapons takes a little longer.

Along with the swords, Ravis demands spears and war hammers for some of the higher-ranking members of his army who have requested specific weapons suited to their tastes. Though it shouldn't, the variety brightens my mood.

When it comes time to magic the weapons, I still don't have a plan for escape. I do, however, have thoughts on the magic. Ravis said to do better, and I've decided the best strategy here is defensive magic. I can't bear to create anything that will make killing easier for the army bent on world domination.

But if I made Ravis's men a little harder to kill?

That's better, isn't it? In a way, I'm protecting.

Even if I'm protecting the wrong people.

I take the swords one by one and think about what I want them to do. Once again, my thoughts turn to my sister. She's not like me at all. She's strong and smart, and if anything bad happens to her, she bounces right back from it.

I remember when the governor's son made her a social outcast at their school. How he bullied her and got her friends to turn on her. She was upset at first, of course, but afterward, she became as determined as ever to live her life as she saw fit.

When the glow of the memory fades, I feel the magic heating my fingers from where I touch the metal. I turn to Elany and gesture for her to take the weapon, extending it to her by the blade. She grips the hilt and waits for instructions.

I don't give her any. Instead, I grab an unmagicked sword and swing at her, knocking the weapon from her fingers. Elany jumps backward, as though afraid I'll run her through now that she's weaponless and I'm not. The guards at the sides of the forge jump forward.

But the moment her sword hits the ground, the hilt flies back into her hand, even though she'd stepped away from where she'd dropped it. The guards freeze, and Elany stares at the sword as though confused by where it came from.

I smack the weapon from her fingers a second time, and the blade does the same thing. Hits the ground, bounces back into her waiting fingers.

I don't wait for a response from anyone before I proceed to magic the next sword. And the next. And the next. Elany mumbles to some guard behind me, but I try to put everything from my mind. I can't work if I'm stressing about all the people around. It's just me and the sword, me and the next sword.

Kellyn shifts somewhere out of the corner of my vision, and I'm astounded that I can still be so aware of him when my focus is somewhere else.

To mix things up, I reach for one of the war hammers, hold its mighty weight in my hands, and think on what I want the heated steel to do.

"Show me," a voice demands.

In my concentration, I hadn't heard the prince approach, and he startles me so badly that I jump and gasp in a breath of air, my concentration completely shattered.

Ravis rolls his eyes. "Don't be so jumpy, smithy. You'll injure yourself." He turns his attention back to Elany, who shows him how the new swords work. She gives him a blade, tells him to hold on to it lightly, then has Strax knock it from his fingers. Ravis grins as the weapon jumps back into his hand.

But the prince only has half of my attention as I look in horror at the war hammer I'm holding.

It's magicked.

But the prince had interrupted me when I was trying to imbue it with power.

"And what of the hammer?" I hear Ravis ask, as though from a great distance away. "Does it move on its own as well?"

I blink once, raise my eyes to the prince's.

"Well?" he asks.

"I don't know," I mumble.

"You don't know?" he asks, his tone taking on a hint of irritation.

"You startled me while I was working, and now it's magicked."

Ravis sighs. "Lady smithy, trying my patience is a game you don't want to play. Izan, grab the hammer and see what it can do."

One of the biggest men I have ever seen steps away from the prince's personal guard and stomps over to me. A meaty hand reaches for the hammer, and I drop rather than place the weapon within. Izan turns it over, inspecting the work. He trods some twenty yards away from the forges before taking an experimental swing through the empty air.

When nothing happens, he shrugs at the prince before

approaching one of those tall, prickly treelike plants. Izan rotates his arms, sending the hammer head flying forward. When it connects, the plant splinters into a million pieces before raining to the ground in a powdery dust.

My insides crawl, and my mind goes completely blank at the sight.

The forges go utterly silent, until Ravis commands, "Again."

His man finds another plant, smashes the hammer into it, and the result is the same. The plant breaks into pieces so tiny they can only be described as powder before falling to the ground.

The prince's face splits into a wide grin. "I think the cacti have had enough. We have some traitors in the dungeons. Let's see if the results are the same."

The prince and his retinue leave without giving me another glance. My gaze fixes onto the heaps of what look like green ashes from here. A breeze blows by, stirring up the remains, carrying the top layer away in a cloud.

My knees connect with the hard ground as I stare and stare and stare, willing the ashes to form back together into what they once were. Waiting for this new nightmare that has become my life to end.

"Wake up, wake up, wake up," I whisper to myself.

But this is very, very real.

I just made something that will turn people to *powder* with a single swing. The faces of the people I love rotate through my mind, bursting into pieces before falling like ash to the ground.

I'm a menace.

My eyes lower to my hands, freshly calloused.

These hands were forced to kill. Forced to make weapons meant to kill.

Was I always made for death? I only ever wanted to help

people. To enjoy the process of creating. To feel closer to my mother by practicing the ability that we share.

But all I ever seem to do is cause trouble.

I ruined our lives in Lirasu, then put the world in danger by making Secret Eater. And now I'm mass-producing weapons intended for world domination.

I lose it, laughing hysterically one second and then sobbing the next. I wrap my arms around my torso, as though I can make myself smaller, compress myself until I'm nothing at all.

Why do I exist? What is the point of creating when it's only going to be used to destroy?

Distantly, I hear someone shouting, "Let me go," and the sounds of a scuffle.

"Release him," someone else says. Elany. "Just this once."

Warm arms enfold me, and I let them, thinking maybe they'll do a better job of hiding me from the world than I'm doing now.

Lips at my ear. "Ziva, it's okay. It's not your fault. None of this is your fault—do you hear me?" Kellyn's voice is like a balm on my nerves, and I wish it wasn't, because I'm not supposed to want to be comforted by him. I'm supposed to be letting go of him for a million reasons. Because he chose me over Temra. He thought to sacrifice himself. He betrayed my trust by giving my abilities away to Ravis. He made me care about him enough to put the rest of the world in danger with the weapons I'm making for this army.

Kellyn might be all I have right now, but that doesn't mean I have to lean on him like this. We're not together anymore. I need to be strong on my own.

I shove Kellyn away from me, dust off my clothes, and walk into the center of the forge. I grab the next heated weapon from the kiln and go back to imbuing swords with defensive magic.

I'm present. I'm focused. I control my magic.

The words don't feel true, but I have to cling to them for now.

✝

A few days later, our working hours are cut short. Elany ushers me from the forges, the guards following behind us.

"What's going on?" I ask.

"You get a break tonight."

"Really?" I ask, relishing the thought of more time spent alone.

"Yes, we're going to a party! Isn't that exciting?"

I feel my whole face fall. "Why does the prince want me to attend a party?" And more important, how can I get out of it?

"You're to meet some of the influential nobles of this territory. They're fabulous. Just you wait."

I feel sick. As if making weapons for Ravis weren't bad enough. Now he expects me to socialize.

The last time I was at a party, I insulted the host's son, and the whole affair was cut short. I was publicly shamed and humiliated, and everything only got worse in my life from there.

"This isn't a good idea," I say.

"Nonsense," Elany responds.

In my room, an army of ladies awaits me with tortures I'd never dreamed of. They wash me, dress me, primp me with makeup, take a hot iron to my hair. They pluck hairs from my brow and pinch my cheeks and hoist up my breasts into some monstrosity of a dress. It's tight. Too tight to move, though there's a slit in the skirt, which shows off way too much of my right leg. The top is sleeveless, strapless, to show off my arms, I think, and I cannot glean what sorcery is keeping the foul thing from falling off my breasts and showing even more of me to everyone. It glitters, a silvery color that hurts my eyes if I stare at it too long. My attendants paint swirling designs on my bare shoulders and beside my eyes. I sneeze from the loose bits of sparkling grains they drizzle onto my skin.

I want to be in the forge or the dungeons or really anywhere else.

When Elany comes to collect me, she smiles brightly. "You're so beautiful!"

She's dressed in red, with short sleeves and a skirt that really isn't long enough to be called such. I don't like how exposed everyone is in this territory. There's too much skin showing. I know the climate calls for it, but I hate the fashion choices. Just another thing that puts me ill at ease in this place.

Guards escort us to the throne room, which is bedecked in new finery that wasn't there before. Glittering rocks cover every flat surface. They're unlike anything I've ever seen. Most of them are rounded with crude gray or brown exteriors, but they've been broken through the middle, exposing beautiful twinkling lights within.

"They're called geodes," Elany explains. "Our territory is rich with them, and all the finest specimens are to be found in this room."

An array of purples and whites and creams wink at me from the exposed centers of the rocks. Others are smooth reds and blacks, almost like glass.

"Obsidian," Elany says, as though that's supposed to mean anything to me.

The people are almost more elegant than the rocks. Nobility

spatter the floor in their finest fabrics and ornamentation. Many of the girls are done up in a style similar to the one I wear. It must be the height of fashion, then.

I try not to meet anyone's eyes as I attempt to make myself familiar with my surroundings.

Musicians play in a corner, the music soft and slow, and the floor is filled with courtiers swaying to the sound of it. Ravis sits on a raised platform, his bejeweled crown on his head, his dagger sheathed at his side. He's in a different version of the outfit I saw him in the first time we met. Another surcoat, which I'm beginning to suspect was what the late king used to wear—this one made of fine silk with epaulets covered in winking gems. Nobles parade in front of him, one by one before joining the throngs of people already dancing.

The guards march me up the dais steps, where two wooden chairs have been added beside the prince's throne. Elany sits at his right hand, which leaves me to take the left.

Everything feels wrong up here. I don't like being higher up than the rest of the room. Put on display. It *invites* people to stare, and how am I supposed to pretend I'm in an empty room if people are *actually* looking at me?

Before I can lose myself entirely to panic, Prince Ravis leans toward me. "South doors."

I haven't a clue which direction anything in this palace is, but I look at the different doors before spotting what Ravis must be drawing my attention to.

Kellyn.

It takes me a moment to recognize him because of the large seaman's hat on his head, which must be there to hide the bandages. It's a rich black leather that comes to three distinct points. He's done up in finery like everyone else. Red silk tunic. Shimmering lightweight pants. Silver-buckled boots. And over the whole thing, a captain's coat, with matching silver buttons down the sides. Ravis must be passing him off as some foreign dignitary.

Kellyn must be roasting under all those layers.

He's escorted by two ladies, one on either arm, each wearing just a little less clothing than I am.

All the sights and smells have been making my stomach turn, but a new emotion takes hold at the sight of Kellyn and those women.

Something hot and angry.

Kellyn's eyes meet mine, as though sensing my gaze. It's impossible to tell for sure at this distance, but I think he takes in my dress and my proximity to Ravis.

I stare at him. He stares at me.

"Leave a good impression for me, and he won't come to any harm," Ravis says.

And I realize then that those women aren't courtiers. Obviously not. They're guards. I see their swords sheathed at their hips. I notice the upright way they hold themselves, the way their heads turn to take in the room, searching for any trouble.

And more guards line the walls nearby, ready to pounce should anything happen.

Kellyn is here as an incentive for me to behave.

When the next group of nobles reaches the dais, Ravis greets them warmly. "Lork and Vanya! My friends, welcome to my party."

"Prince Ravis." The man, Lork, nods.

"My prince," his wife echoes.

Insects crawl down my spine at the proximity of more people, and I wish this chair would swallow me whole.

"Do enjoy yourselves tonight!" Ravis says. "As two of my most loyal supporters, I hope you'll consider tonight's revelries as being held in your honor."

Lork shifts his weight onto his other leg. "About that, Prince, I'm afraid we can spare no more financial aid in your efforts. I'm sure you'll understand, given that we've donated more than anyone else and have yet to reap any rewards."

Vanya takes her husband's arm, offering him her silent support. They both eye the prince, unafraid of his response.

Ravis has gone still. So still that I can't tell if he's breathing for a moment.

"This is most distressing news," the prince says after a moment. "When we are so close to achieving the whole of Ghadra."

"A pile of swords does not equate to more land in my name, Prince," Lork says. "Nor slaves to work said land. I've had a talk with the other upper nobility. They are also inclined to withdraw their gold. We will not be able to support our own staff and households much longer at the rate you wring us dry."

"And," Vanya adds, "when you throw such opulent parties that do not bring us closer to our goal."

"The party, Duchess, was financed by the crown," Ravis says through clenched teeth. "The gold from my supporters goes to the army. Men need to eat. Swords need to be sharpened. You understand."

"I'm afraid all I've seen is a lot of talk and no action."

"No action? Well, let me introduce you to my newest hire. Ziva, tell the duke and duchess what you do."

My mouth goes dry. An invisible hand squeezes my heart within my chest. I can barely focus on what the prince has said, the panic is so strong.

The two nobles turn to me, and the sensation only grows worse.

"Ziva," Ravis prompts, the threat clear in his voice.

"I—I make weapons." My voice is no more than a squeak.

"You've hired another smithy," Vanya says, unimpressed. "Really, now, Prince. The promise of action has been too long coming. This does not help things."

Ravis glares at me, and only then do I realize the vital piece of information I left out.

"Magic!" I blurt a little too loudly. *Pull yourself together, Ziva.* "I make magic weapons."

The duke and duchess say nothing for a moment. Then Lork's eyes glance at Elany before returning to me.

"Magic weapons?" he repeats.

"Yes."

"What do they do?"

The spaces beneath my arms start to sweat. Everything is too hot, yet I still wish for more fabric to cover myself.

"Um, all sorts of things," I say. "For the prince, I've been making swords that can't be broken and never need to be sharpened. I also made blades that return to the wielder's hand immediately if they're disarmed." I rack my brain for any other safe details. Ravis knows about my hammers and Kellyn's sword, so I mention those as well.

The nobles eye me with suspicion, as though they think I'm some sort of trickery drummed up by Ravis to fool these idiots into giving him more money.

I can feel Ravis's glare burrowing into the side of my head, and I just know he's going to hurt Kellyn some more if I don't think of something quickly.

I shout the only thing I can think of. "Strax!"

From behind the dais, the head of the prince's guard steps forward.

"Show them what your sword can do."

Strax looks to the prince. When Ravis nods his assent, Strax calls a halt to the music, waves everyone off the floor, and brings out an assortment of guards for a display.

While he's fighting about seven men at once, I explain to the nobles, "Watch the way the weapon shifts subtly in the direction Strax is meant to go. It's leading him out of danger."

I used to feel such pride when I would see Kellyn use his sword. But to see it in the hands of our enemy, I feel nothing but regret.

I can't do this again.

When the demonstration is done, Ravis says proudly, "You can see why the schedule has been delayed somewhat. I intend to make our men unbeatable in battle before we start storming the territories one by one. We have scores of magical blades now with many more on the way. With victory assured, you can hardly pull your support now."

"Hmm," the duke says.

"When do we march?" Vanya asks.

"Three months' time," Ravis says.

"You have our apologies for ever doubting you," Lork says. "This development is most exciting."

"And perhaps I'll have the smithy make a weapon for your household."

"That would be most generous."

"Do the kingdom proud," Vanya says to me before the two depart.

And then another set of courtiers approaches, and Ravis makes me repeat the whole ordeal.

I suppose it gets a little easier to say the words after about the fifth time, but I feel my energy draining, each set of nobles carrying away a little bit of it as I speak.

I'm literally winning over Ravis's nobility for him. I'm guaranteeing him more funding, rallying support. On top of that, I am making the weapons that will help take over all of Ghadra.

I'm doing all the bloody work for him.

I'm dooming all of Ghadra by myself.

I never knew I had such power.

A stupid sailor's hat bobs in the corner of my vision. Kellyn's got a glass of something in his hand, and he appears to be doing his best to charm the guards on either side of him. They laugh at what he says but don't loosen their holds on his arms. He just effortlessly manages to win people over. He's probably looking for openings to get us out of this. How does he do it? I can barely think as I try to block out all the stimuli around me.

When a new song strikes up, Ravis leaves, inviting one of the ladies of his court to join him on the dance floor. Someone asks Elany to dance, and she also leaves. I start to panic when courtiers try to approach me, but my guards fend them off before they can reach me. It would seem no one is allowed to speak to me without Ravis present.

Thank the Sisters.

I shut my eyes and massage my temples. It's been weeks and weeks of bladesmithing and magicking. I feel my soul wearing down little by little each day, and I just want it all to stop.

But I don't see how we can escape. The only way to get out of this is by stealth. We need to sneak away without being spotted. We can't be followed. Ravis has too many men at his disposal, and if we're caught, we'll surely be overrun.

Maybe I could craft a weapon that would make us unseen?

But how would I do that when I'm constantly under guard, and any weapon I make with new abilities goes straight to Ravis? And if I started swinging a weapon around upon finishing it in an attempt to escape, the guards would slit Kellyn's throat before I could get to him.

I need to make something that doesn't kill. Something that won't hurt Kellyn if he gets caught in the cross fire.

The wheels start turning in my head.

Ravis wanted me to make an impression on his nobles. I wonder what would happen if they were to know I was suddenly gone . . .

CHAPTER
NINE

If Elany notices that I'm fidgeting more than usual, she doesn't say anything.

Two separate needs clash within me. On the one hand, there's survival. If I'm caught trying to escape, I don't know what Ravis will do to me or Kellyn. I'm absolutely petrified that something will go wrong. There are a thousand ways it could.

But on the other hand is the desperate desire for freedom. The need to see what's become of my sister. Kellyn and I must warn our friends that war is coming.

I'm going to execute my plan today.

My hands shake as I pull weapons from the kiln and begin magicking them one by one. Every time Elany opens her mouth, I startle, convinced she's going to call me out on what I'm planning—as I try to work up the nerve to magic another too-powerful weapon.

"What are you thinking about when you use your magic?" she wants to know this time.

I steady my breathing before answering, "The people I care

about usually. It helps to focus me. I have to coax the metal gently. Usually, I have to . . . give of myself, in a way. But it's different every time."

Did any of that even make sense?

"Give of yourself? What do you mean by that?"

"Sometimes it's physical. The metal needs the wind of my breath or the touch of my skin." My blood and sweat have landed on weapons before. "Sometimes I just share my thoughts and feelings with the weapon, whether I verbalize them or not."

And the more I give, the more powerful the weapon—I hadn't noticed until Petrik made the observation while questioning me for his book.

Another pang of longing fills my breast. I miss my friend. His sharp wit and open way of looking at the world. He would have come up with a much more clever plan for escape and executed it more quickly, too.

As self-doubt sets in, I lose my resolve and magic the weapon I'm currently holding to do the same as the others that have come before. Return to the wielder's hand when disarmed. I hand it off to a waiting smithy, who stacks it with the others before retrieving another bastard sword from the kiln.

Kellyn looks much improved after several weeks spent healing from his sliced ear. The color has returned to his face, and he doesn't scratch about the bandages the way he used to. He's also growing more restless, and I can't tell if that's a good or bad thing. As a mercenary, Kellyn is used to movement. Traveling from place to place, swinging his sword. He likes to be active, so he can't be happy standing around the forge day in and day out. Being captured has been worse for him than it has for me.

Good, the selfish part of me thinks. If he didn't want to suffer, maybe he should have kept his big mouth shut.

It was that or die, the nice Ziva argues, surfacing now, perhaps, because the hope of escape is before her. *He saved you by revealing your abilities.*

At what cost? He saved himself. And, yes, me. But in exchange for the lives of an entire kingdom if Ravis gets his war.

As if my thoughts have drawn his notice, Kellyn meets my gaze, and his eyes narrow, as if he knows I have a plan and if he can just stare at me long enough, perhaps he can figure out what it is.

I desperately wish I could talk to my sister, ask her thoughts. About Kellyn and me. About what I'm about to do. Would she think me irredeemable if I intentionally make another powerful sword? Will my mother look down on me in shame from one of the Sisters' heavens?

"You're remarkable, Ziva," Elany says. "Whatever our differences, I hope you know that."

I don't believe her. "I need to focus," I say gently.

"Of course," she says, disappointed by my answer. I wonder for a moment if she hoped the two of us would be friends, but the notion is so ridiculous that I discard it immediately.

All right, this is it. This is the weapon that I will magic differently.

Ripe, tangible fear courses through me, as though infused in my veins. I can feel my heart pumping it out to every limb. My body feels hotter than the fire I approach to grab yet another sword.

I need to ground myself, or I'll never be able to pull this off. Be present. Focus on what's real and right in front of me. The bastard sword, also known as a hand-and-a-half sword, glows white. It's an arm span in length, the blade the width of my four fingers pressed together. The hilt is long enough to be held in one or two hands, which is where its name comes from.

I feel the smooth metal under my fingers, loosen and

tighten my grip on the hilt to focus on the friction. I smell the heated steel, a tangy yet earthy scent that is usually so comforting to me.

It's time, Ziva. No more stalling. You have to do this. No one can save you but yourself.

The sword and I size each other up. I often talk to my weapons while working. They're far more forgiving than people are in conversation.

I run a finger over the cross guard, let it hover over the heated blade as close as I can stand without getting burned.

I'm so, so tired. Too many nights with not enough sleep. On top of that, living with fear is exhausting. The two try to battle for dominance within my body.

Kellyn gives me an encouraging smile. His golden-brown eyes are too trusting. I'm likely going to butcher this for the both of us.

"We're tired, aren't we?" I whisper to the blade. "You've been beat about, and I've been overworked. Perhaps we could use that on our enemies, hmm?"

I resist the urge to look about me and see if anyone suspects anything. Sometimes a weapon takes longer to magic. It's nothing unusual for me to take more time with a stubborn blade.

Keep going.

"I want you to take my fatigue and build it into something. Can you do that for me?"

I try to be as specific as possible. Going through the motions of what I want it to do, begging the blade with my will and words to be my salvation.

When I feel the magic take root in the weapon, I feel shockingly refreshed. I feel strong. Like the weapon has taken the weariness right out of me, infused it into the blade.

A small smile creeps onto my face.

"I hear another batch is ready to be magicked today," a voice says.

My whole body grows cold as I turn to find the prince entering the forges with his retinue of guards, all of whom now have magic weapons.

"Ziva's already begun," Elany says in response.

"Any surprises today?"

"No extraordinary weapons so far."

"Pity. Maybe someone should try to scare the smithy. The results seem to be better when she's under duress."

The men behind him laugh, and I feel myself shrink away from it.

"Don't mock her," Elany says. "She's helping you win a kingdom. Show some respect."

Ravis stops laughing and rounds on my overseer. "You remember your place. You do not command a king."

"You're not a king yet, and if it weren't for me and Ziva, you'd never become one. I came to *you*, Prince, don't forget that. We're on the same side."

Ravis scoffs. "Not that you've been much help."

I hadn't realized I'd been backing away slowly until Ravis's dark eyes land on me, freezing me in place.

"What do you have there, smithy?" he asks.

My hands tighten on the hilt. "A sword I'm working on."

"Bring it to me."

My stomach sinks. *I cannot hand this one over.*

This very scenario right here is why I shouldn't be allowed to have this gift.

I dart a look in Kellyn's direction. The men around him have relaxed somewhat in their hold on him. He hasn't tried to escape once, and he's injured.

"Actually," I say, "I was just going to duck out for a bit. Get some food. I haven't had lunch yet."

"I didn't ask for chatter. I ordered you to bring the weapon to me."

Another look at Kellyn from me. "Really, I'm just going to *duck* out for a moment. I'll be right back."

Kellyn cocks his head.

"I'm *ducking* out *right now*," I snap.

And like the smart man he is, Kellyn's eyes shoot up in realization at the same time he bends at the waist.

Right as I swing the sword in his direction.

I aim at the shoulders of the men surrounding Kellyn, swiping at them from a dozen feet away. They fall in heaps to the ground, chain mail clinking, weapons rolling out of sight.

A light snore comes up from the vicinity of the fallen men.

The forge goes perfectly still as everyone *not* in the direction I swung looks up from their work. Kellyn rises from his crouched position, finally free of guards.

"Run," I tell him as I turn, my new sword held at the ready.

Ravis has his dagger drawn, and he points it at me with fire in his eyes. "You think very carefully about what you're about to do, smithy. This might turn into a decision you can never come back from."

"I choose freedom," I say as I swing the sword.

Ravis catches it on his dagger before I can complete the full swing, preventing the magic from unleashing. I step away and slash at him, but he catches that, too.

The prince was trained to be a ruler. With that training would have come swordplay. He's no amateur. The men behind him step forward, drawing their own weapons. The smithies throughout the forge fidget, and I can just imagine them grabbing whatever weapons are around, preparing to jump in.

This wasn't supposed to happen this way. I had a plan. I waited until a Tuesday, so the iron shipment would be here, giving us a getaway cart. It's after lunch. Food is sprawled around the forge, enough for us to pack and get a few days under us before it spoils.

Everyone in the forge is supposed to be sleeping. The prince wasn't supposed to be here yet. Kellyn is running on foot behind me somewhere, Ravis has a weapon pointed at me, and nigh fifty individuals are preparing to pounce upon me.

They're going to catch him. They're going to kill us both, and then Ghadra will be doomed.

The prince doesn't wait for me to strike at him again. He launches himself at me, and I just barely manage to block the blow.

But that's what Ravis wanted. In a quick and powerful move, he catches the guard of my sword with the length of his blade, flicks his wrist, and sends the weapon sailing off to my right.

We both leap for it, the two of us tangling into a heap on the ground. I wince as I feel the prince's dagger slice across the back of my arm, and Ravis drops the knife, likely in fear of killing his smithy. He gets both hands on the hilt of the new sword, and I grasp his forearms from behind him, doing my best to still his motions.

"Stay back," Ravis orders his men, halting their advance. He must *really* not want me injured in the scuffle.

"After the mercenary!" I hear Strax shout, and men race past us in blurs. The head guard doesn't go with them, staying nearby in case the prince asks him to intervene.

Ravis is shorter and weaker than I, but he holds on to the weapon with a death grip. He manages to spin onto his stomach, so I reach around him, grip his arms, haul his body upright at the knees, and force him to swing the weapon.

Strax and the men who remained with him go down, collapsing to the floor in sleep.

"Ziva, stop this!" Elany shouts. I force Ravis's arms toward the many forges and swing again. She and the smithies slump toward the earth.

Bells ring from somewhere in the palace, alerting everyone that there's trouble. I hear running feet in the distance. More guards are coming.

"Get off me!" the prince shrieks as he manages to rise to his feet, bringing me with him. He backs up, stepping on my foot, trying to shove me away.

I leap onto his back, wrap my legs around him, hooking my ankles together in the front, keeping my hands gripped over the top of his on the sword.

He turns his head to the side and bites my upper arm.

On instinct, I release my right arm and shake out the pain, let my legs drop. I try a new tactic, throwing him forward with all my strength.

Ravis hits the ground again, flat on his stomach. I wait for him to roll over before leaping upon him—not allowing him to get in a swing.

I'm straddling the prince as I shove his arms above his head.

"That's it," Ravis says, clearly embarrassed by the indignity of the situation. "Grab her!" he screams to the fast-approaching guards.

They'll tackle me in seconds if I don't get the sword from him!

To me, he adds, "I'm going to hang you for this! I should have killed you when I had the chance."

"Let go of the sword!" I demand.

"No!"

And then a new sound fills the space. Something louder. Pounding hooves and wheels crushing over rock and plant alike.

I take my eyes off Ravis for just a second and see Kellyn speed by atop one of the carts used to transport iron ore. He sends guards and other staff leaping away.

But some aren't quick enough.

Bones crunch under hooves, and the wheels take the bumps so quickly that Kellyn nearly loses his seat a couple of times. He slows the team of horses, turns the cart around, and barrels back this way to take out a fresh wave of new arrivals.

Meanwhile, my struggle with Ravis continues. He's using his training to uproot me while I push into him with all my strength. I think my stamina will outlast him, but how long will that take?

Ravis releases an arm and throws a punch. I dodge, but the distraction is all he needs to roll us. He comes up on top this time, presses into my lungs, jabs at me with his elbows while trying to release my hold on him.

At the corner of my eye, I see jewels wink in the sun, and I reach out a hand to grab Ravis's dropped dagger.

Then I've got the blade pressed against his neck with one hand, the other clasping his against the sword.

"Drop it or I will slit your throat with your own weapon," I say.

The sword clatters to the ground.

"Now get off me," I command.

He stands, leaving me lying in the dirt. His eyes land on something behind me. He lets out a laugh. "You've lost, and now—"

The prince collapses to the ground, his chest rising and falling in deep and even breaths. I finally stand, coming up with the newly magicked sword I just flicked in Ravis's direction.

I'm breathing heavily as I turn, sweat and blood dripping down my arm, snores sounding all around me.

"Not a step closer," a guard says. She and half a dozen others have swords pointed at Kellyn's chest. What feels like hundreds more are pouring out of the palace, heeding the call. But those already present have seen what the sword can do and clearly have no desire to get any closer to it, instead thinking to help their sovereign by threatening me with my weakness yet again.

That mercenary!

"I did my best," Kellyn says. "But you're free. Go. No one will dare stop you while you carry that thing." He flicks his chin toward my new sword.

"Here's what's going to happen," the guard closest to Kellyn says. She must be the next in charge after Strax. "You're going to drop the sword or I'm going to gut him like a fish."

I'm still so many leagues beyond scared. Adrenaline pumps through my veins. Yet the magic of the sword keeps me feeling refreshed and alive.

There's only one choice to make.

"Sorry, Kellyn," I say.

I swing faster than the guards can react.

Kellyn goes down with all the men surrounding him, their weapons falling uselessly to the ground. Soldiers out of the sword's reach charge forward, but I swing before they can get too close, until Ravis's palace lawns are covered in sleeping bodies.

I wait a few minutes to see if anyone else will come, but with the leaders of Ravis's ranks all sound asleep, there's no one to give orders. Seeing the scene around me, any servants or guards left standing aren't daring to approach me. The warning bells have long since stopped ringing.

I'm surrounded by enemies at their most vulnerable. Anyone could come up and slit their throats. If Ravis had gotten his hands on this sword, he would have used it on the front lines, taking out enemies in droves before his soldiers silenced them forever without any resistance.

My gaze snaps downward. As I stare at the prince, I'm almost overcome with anger. He tried to make me his slave. He might have cost me Temra by stealing Serutha. He's the reason I'm parted from the rest of my friends.

And he threatened Kellyn.

Maybe it's foolish, but I take the sheath from around the prince's waist and slide the dagger within. Ravis took weeks of my life for himself, so I'm taking something of his.

I steal a sheath for the bastard sword off one of the guards. Once I'm outfitted, I search through the sleeping bodies for Kellyn.

He's snoring louder than anyone else. I fight a smile at the sight of him.

It takes some maneuvering, but I manage to get the horse-drawn cart as close to Kellyn as possible without crushing anyone, then haul the sleeping mercenary over to it. I hoist him onto my back and ease him into the bed of the cart. Then, remembering Lady Killer, I find Strax among the bodies and retrieve Kellyn's longsword. I've no idea where my hammers have ended up (or the war hammer I've magicked), and I don't have any time to waste searching for them. I'll have to leave with what I have.

I gather as much food as I can, searching for anything that'll keep for a while. Bread, dried meat. I take some fruit and vegetables as well. We can eat those for the first few days.

I roll a barrel of water into the cart. Then I don a stolen cloak, make sure my face is concealed, leap atop the cart, and give the reins a good flick.

We're off.

CHAPTER TEN

I have no clue where I'm going.

The castle is an imposing shadow at my back. My only concern was to get *away* from Prince Ravis's home, but now I need to figure out how to get to Skiro. I've got a cart full of sleeping mercenary. Finding the right road is crucial.

I suppose as long as Kellyn sleeps, I know that Ravis and his guards are also sleeping.

But that means I can't rely on the mercenary for anything.

It takes me a minute to search through the city square for the least intimidating figure, a young girl my age. I ask her for directions to the quickest road to take me south.

"Only road that will take you that way is the one to Briska. From there you can head south."

I hide my grimace. Things did not go so well last time we were in Briska. We were beaten and imprisoned.

"It's a long journey," she warns. "Beg your pardon, but you don't look like you have enough to get you there. Most of that food will spoil."

I waste a few moments bartering fresh food for more hardy food. I sell Ravis's dagger and purchase saddles, saddlebags, waterskins, bedrolls, and other supplies.

We're not going to make it far if we don't have everything we need to travel. The last time we tried, we were only making a week's journey to Kellyn's family's farm, and he knew the land well enough for us to forage for food.

We have no such advantages now.

With a much fuller cart, I find the road and set off again, pushing the horses as quickly as possible.

I've got Kellyn's longsword across my back and the sleeping sword at my side. Still, I'm not confident in my abilities should we run into trouble.

I start to relax when we leave the city. The homes give way to cottages, which disappear entirely after a while. The cacti and sparse shrubbery turn into trees. Some pine and fir. Some kind of deciduous trees with yellow leaves and white bark. Dried leaves crackle under the wheels of the cart; the light breeze sends more drifting off the branches.

A few people pass me by on the road, but they say nothing. No horns sound. No barking dogs. No signs of pursuit. And Kellyn is still fast asleep.

I check on him a few times, just to ensure he's breathing. I even try rousing him. I shake his shoulder. Shout his name.

But he doesn't stir.

Magic is indeed a powerful thing.

Afternoon gives way to evening. Still, I don't stop the horses. I slow their trotting into walking. It's the only reprieve I can give them. We need distance between us and Ravis, especially when I've no choice but to use the road. I can't very well get a cart off the beaten path.

I remember the last time I traveled with an unconscious Kellyn. Temra and I barely managed to strap him to a horse. We sort of abducted him. He agreed to be our protection on the road to Thersa, but then he passed out drunk after a day spent celebrating his twentieth birthday. He's two years older than I am.

I remember the argument Temra and I had that day. She insisted that we needed Kellyn for protection, whether he was sober or not at the moment. I didn't want a stranger with us on the road, especially one I felt attracted to.

I would give anything to be able to argue with my sister some more.

I don't know what I will do if I arrive in Skiro only to learn she's dead. That I wasn't quick enough. That Serutha couldn't do anything for her.

Tears gather at my eyes, just at the thought of losing my sister.

"Stop it," I scold myself, forcing my thoughts elsewhere.

But the only other thing for me to think on is the dark woods. During the day, the deciduous leaves were a stunning array of golden yellows, bronze oranges, and fiery reds. Now everything is grays and blacks. Shadows and whispers.

I haven't passed another traveler in at least an hour. Most have probably camped for the night.

But I don't have that luxury.

Every sound causes me to turn my head. The horses grow a bit on edge, startling at the sounds of cracking twigs, a fierce rustling of leaves.

I wish I had eyes in the back of my head. I begin to imagine dark figures creeping behind me, waiting to pounce. My skin is chilled, but I can't bring myself to grab a blanket. It seems safer not to move.

I don't know how long it's been now. The exhaustion that the sword removed from me has long since returned, and I feel ready to snap at the slightest provocation.

"What's going on?"

I jump straight into the air before Kellyn's voice registers.

I think I must have shrieked because he tacks on, "Sorry."

When my heart doesn't feel as though it will beat its way out of my chest, I say, "We're running for our lives."

"Nothing new, then."

He climbs up next to me, and I feel my whole self relax to have another body beside me. The dark has never scared me before, but add the fear of being recaptured, and it takes on a whole new terror.

Kellyn's body is incredibly warm, and I hope he doesn't notice as I sidle closer. I'm beyond relieved that he's okay, and I take so much comfort from having him here with me. In this outrageous situation.

But I shouldn't want to be physically close to him. I should shove him out of this cart for telling Ravis my identity and for what came after. All those magical weapons are now in the hands of Ravis's men.

Later. I'll rage at him later. For now, I'm just trying to grasp the fact that we're both somehow okay.

"I don't remember . . ." Kellyn trails off. "Wait, you'd just beaten Ravis and taken the sword back. His men had me."

"I had no choice but to start swinging. You succumbed to the sword's power with the rest of them."

"I have no complaints." Kellyn wraps both arms around me, squeezing me tightly to him. I feel his lips briefly against the side of my head.

It feels so nice, except for the sting of guilt that accompanies it.

"I knew you would free us both," he says. "I had zero doubts."

That makes one of us.

"If you're awake, then so is everyone at the castle," I say. "We need to saddle the horses and disappear off the road. It'll take us to Briska, but if we go directly south, we'll reach Skiro's Capital much quicker than Ravis's men."

Kellyn releases me. "You're dead on your feet. Let me take the horses for a bit. You rest for an hour or so in the cart. Then we'll saddle the horses."

"We don't have the time. We need to go now. They'll travel faster without a cart to slow them down."

"One hour," he insists.

"I won't risk being caught again!" I snap. I hope the *because of you* is heard even though I don't say it.

"How about we share a horse and you can sleep against me?" He seems undaunted by my outburst. Kellyn draws the horses to a halt before I can respond. We make quick work of it. Saddling the two horses, loading up the supplies.

"How did you get all this?"

"I sold Ravis's dagger."

He smiles at that.

We do our best to hide the wagon, pulling it as far off the road as we can manage and covering it with branches and whatnot. Afterward, he mounts his horse and holds a hand down to me.

"I can ride," I say.

"I know you can, but you don't have to. Come on, Ziva. Let me keep watch for a while. Thanks to you, I'm fully rested."

Only because I'm now dead on my feet do I take his hand. I ignore the shock of warmth that travels up my arm. My skin prickles when my back is pressed against his front, this strange mixture of terror and elation and frustration. There was a time when I managed to relax around him. But things are different now. Ravis threatened his life, and I toiled day after day to keep him alive. I obviously still care about him, but that doesn't change the fact that he's hurt me and betrayed my trust. I don't know where we stand with each other now. I don't know how to even begin to sort through it all in my head.

I must be even more tired than I realize, because the next thing I know I'm suddenly rousing from sleep.

Kellyn has one arm loosely around my middle, keeping me from falling. The other directs the horse. My gelding is attached to the saddle horn with a lead, and he follows behind.

I'm so warm and comfortable, though I shouldn't be, having slept upright. But I felt safe, and that's something I haven't felt in a long time. And it's such a pleasant feeling to have Kellyn behind me, cradling my entire body. I want to stretch, to lean my head back against his shoulder. Turn into his neck and breathe him in.

"I'm awake," I announce instead.

"Go back to sleep. It's only midday. You need more rest."

"Don't tell me what to do." I grab the reins from him and draw the horse to a halt. Once on the ground, I untie my gelding, a midnight-black horse, and mount.

Then I can think more clearly. Because Kellyn is not touching me.

He doesn't say a word as we continue forward, and the silence is so awkward it infuriates me. I resist speaking for as long as I can.

"Do you know where we're going?" I ask.

"Sun rose from over there. We're headed south. Don't worry. I travel for a living, remember?"

More silence ensues, and it feels so wrong. We were trapped together for weeks at the forges, unable to speak to each other, but now that we can, he doesn't have anything to say to me?

Surely, he can tell I'm upset. Why isn't he asking me about it?

"What are you doing?" I ask.

"Leading us to Skiro."

"You're being quiet. You're not usually quiet."

"If you want to talk, you're welcome to talk. I gathered that anything I said would only make you angrier. Am I wrong?"

Him being right makes me angrier.

"Kellyn," I say to his back, halting my own horse.

He turns his russet mare around to face me, raises a brow.

"Don't you *ever* tell someone about my abilities without my permission again." I manage to look him in the eye as I say it, put as much seriousness into my voice as possible.

"He was going to kill you," he volleys back.

"I would rather die than be the cause of making weapons that will destroy Ghadra."

"Then you should have refused him."

"He wasn't threatening my life; he was threatening *yours*!"

He turns his horse around, urges her forward once more. "Then I don't see the problem."

I encourage my own mount into a trot and use him to block Kellyn's path. "The problem is that I don't want to be the cause of anyone dying. And you forced me into that position!"

"You should have gone through the wardrobe. You forced my hand."

"And you shouldn't have left me!"

His eyes widen, but he doesn't say a thing.

My abdomen feels tight, like there's not enough room for all my organs. My eyelids are heavy, and tears slide down my cheeks.

"My sister was dying. She might already be dead now, and then you thought you could just sacrifice yourself and force me to lose you, too."

I turn my head to the ground, wipe the tears away, and make other pathetic attempts to collect myself. Then I urge my horse back in the direction we'd been traveling a moment ago.

When Kellyn next speaks, his voice is deeper than usual. "I thought you didn't want me anymore. I thought you didn't care what happened to me as long as your sister was okay. I was only trying to give you what you wanted. What you deserve."

I think the fact that I'm turned away is the only reason I'm able to get the next words out. "Just because I can't be with you doesn't mean I don't still care. It doesn't mean that I'd *ever* be okay with you being killed or imprisoned or anything less than living a happy life."

"How was I supposed to know that? After what happened in the fight against Kymora, you gave me the cold shoulder. We didn't even talk about what happened. Temra was injured, and she needed your full focus; I get that. But there's nothing that needs your immediate attention now, so I'm going to defend myself. It was during the heat of battle, Ziva. I didn't process what you were saying when you told me to save Temra. I saw you being dragged away, and I acted. Blame me for that all you want, but Kymora hurt your sister, not me. All my actions since then have only been to help Temra."

"Really? How does revealing my abilities and suggesting to Ravis that I make weapons to destroy the world help Temra? Or Petrik? Or all the people who are going to get butchered in the war Ravis is bringing to them?"

"First of all," he snaps back, "I didn't exactly have time to ask for your permission to tell Ravis who you are. Someone was coming at you with a knife! I was thinking quickly and under pressure. It was the only thing I could come up with to save your life. Second, I knew you would get us out of there before any damage was done."

"You couldn't have known that! And you didn't, because Ravis now has scores of magicked weapons to aid him."

"Most of them aren't that powerful, and you got Lady Killer back for me."

"Someone has my shield hammer, and then there was that war hammer . . ."

"Ziva, it's okay."

"It's not okay! We're the only warning Prince Skiro has that war is coming. If we don't get there in time, it'll be a mass slaughter. People I care about will be killed with weapons *I made*! And do you think Ravis will stop when he's done with Skiro's Territory? He won't. He wants his so-called birthright back. He's going to claim all six territories for himself and unite Ghadra. I didn't just doom my family and friends. I've doomed the entire kingdom. How am I supposed to handle that? It hurts, Kellyn. Right here, in my chest. I can barely breathe." In fact, my breathing picks up dangerously just at the thought.

"Hey, now," Kellyn says. He grabs the reins of my horse, drawing us both to a stop, and then he takes my hand in his. There isn't much else he can do from atop his own horse. He squeezes gently. "Do you remember what I told you when you were panicking about Kymora and Secret Eater?"

"I panic a lot. You're going to have to be more specific."

He fights a smile. "You're not that important."

"Excuse me?"

"That's what I told you. You're not that important. You don't get to put the whole world on your shoulders. That's not fair, and it's not your fault. Kymora was at fault. Ravis is at fault. Those who give him their loyalty? They're at fault. While you're still fighting for what's right, you don't get to blame yourself."

I sniffle. "It doesn't matter what my intentions are if I still cause innocents to die."

"We've no way of knowing what will happen, but we'll do our best to fix it when the time comes. For now, maybe try to focus on what you've saved. You saved the world from Secret Eater. You saved Temra. You saved Petrik. You saved *me*. But most important, you saved yourself. You've done *good* things."

"I can't even see those things. They're buried too far beneath all the bad I've done." The stuff he drove me to do.

He squeezes my hand one more time before giving it back to me. We start moving again.

"I don't always know the right thing to say," Kellyn says. "But you just remember that I'm here. You're not alone."

"Thank you."

"Thank you for saving me," he says. "Even though you probably didn't want to in the end."

How can he think that? "I would never leave you behind. I wouldn't have been able to stand it if I'd gone through the wardrobe. I couldn't be in Skiro's Territory safe and sound while I had no idea what happened to you. I'm going mad as it is wondering what's happened to Temra."

"I didn't know."

"You think me so fickle as to just stop caring about what happens to you because you did some things I didn't like?"

"The only constant in my life has ever been my family," he says. "I travel so much. I can make friends with the people I work for, but when I get them to their destination, that's it. I never see them again. I have to move on constantly. Otherwise, it's just too damn depressing. I shouldn't have assumed that you would be the same way."

Does that mean that he's moved on? Because he's used to doing so constantly? That would be . . . good, right? We've fought too much and hurt each other too much to get past everything, haven't we? I'm unsure. I've never broken up with someone before.

And yet, my heart feels hollow at the idea of him having moved on already.

After a moment, Kellyn lets out a single puff of a laugh. My neck cracks in his direction, certain he's somehow heard my thoughts and laughing at me for some reason.

"Sorry," he says, "I was just thinking about how last night was the second time I've woken up to you carting me off somewhere."

"You should be grateful."

"Oh, I am." He laughs again.

"If you're going to poke fun at me while I'm hurting, you can strike out on your own." I really don't want him to leave, but I have my pride. I tack on, "But all the food and supplies are mine. I bought them."

"With the prince's stolen dagger."

"My argument still stands. And don't forget it's your fault that you're in this mess."

"As is everything."

"Naturally."

His smile is bright as he looks ahead at the road again. "I'll take my chances with you, vicious though you are."

The silence becomes companionable after that.

CHAPTER ELEVEN

Before it gets too dark, I pull my gelding to a stop in front of some sort of maple tree with red leaves and branches close to the ground. Then I begin my climb.

Kellyn doesn't ask what I'm doing. He wordlessly follows.

I used to climb trees all the time when I was little. It was an easy escape from everything. A hundred feet in the air, no one can find you or talk to you. What with our home in Lirasu on the edge of the city, access to the forest was quick.

My hands are covered in sap, my knees are scratched up, and I couldn't feel better. The trees smell delicious. Different from the forest back home, but still fresh and green and free. The wind causes the tree to sway as I get closer to the top, and I giggle at the sensation.

And then I break the canopy.

It's a sea of green with the occasional golds, oranges, and reds reflecting fall. It's beautiful. Peaceful. Why can't Ravis be satisfied with what he has? His land is gorgeous.

I point when Kellyn joins me up top. "There."

He's a bit out of breath, but his eyes land on the smoke. Just a few miles behind us.

"They're closer than I thought," he says.

"But they look camped for the night. Let's push the horses a little farther before we do the same."

"I think they're still on the main road. They didn't spot the wagon. They think we're going southeast to Briska. We should make camp now. We've pushed the horses long enough. The poor things need a break."

We don't risk a fire, lest our enemies be able to see us as easily as we spotted them. But Kellyn stakes up the tent, while I retrieve the bedrolls and dinner.

It isn't until I'm walking back over to the mercenary that I'm struck with the most violent bout of nerves.

Sometimes it happens like that. It'll come out of nowhere, and I can't even immediately place why I'm feeling it. Sometimes there's no reason at all. But most of the time, it has to do with the people around me.

And I've just realized that there's only one person around me.

It's just me and Kellyn and one tent.

The mercenary and I have traveled across Ghadra before, but we were joined by my sister and Petrik. It's never been the two of us alone like this and we have a history and there was kissing and touching and feelings and then Temra was wounded and things were bad and—

"Ziva."

I look up into those golden-brown eyes, and the anxiety only gets worse.

"Hey, just breathe. It's okay. What can I do?"

"Could you just, um, go away for a moment?"

A beat of silence. Then, "Yes. I can do that."

I feel like a monster for asking, but I don't take the words back. I wait as he walks away in the direction of our pursuers, putting himself between them and me. I watch him go until he disappears entirely.

And then I can breathe again.

I focus on the task of unrolling our bedrolls, plumping the flat pillows, adding extra blankets. I unsaddle the horses. Give them long leads so they can rest and roam. And then I return to the tent and sit on my side of it.

With nothing left to do, I'm forced to deal with my thoughts.

Kellyn's not going to hurt you. Nothing scary is going to happen. He won't say anything to embarrass or humiliate you. He's not like that.

Well, he's usually not like that. Sometimes he can't help his teasing.

And you like his teasing. You like teasing him. It's a give-and-take.

I focus on my breathing, try to rub the uncomfortable tingles out of my arms. I feel a little better being alone, but now I'm stressing out over the moment Kellyn returns. What if I say something humiliating? What if I do something embarrassing? I'm stuck with him for Goddesses know how long until we make it back to Skiro.

I rock in place, trying to soothe myself, trying to calm my out-of-control thoughts.

Kellyn finds me like that, huddled in the tent. I'm sure he was gone at least an hour, and yet I'm still a mess.

"I hate that I'm this way, and I hate that you have to see me this way," I mumble. I pull my blanket around my arms and let the edge rest over the top of my head, giving me a small barrier between myself and Kellyn. He takes a seat atop his bedroll. I keep my face straight ahead so he can't see it.

"We were talking just fine while we traveled. What changed? Did I do something?" he asks.

"It was, um, the realization that we're alone and sleeping in the same tent."

"You know I would never—"

"I know," I interrupt. "It's not that. It's not about you. It doesn't work like that. It doesn't make sense. I just feel this way sometimes. And it's painful and it makes it hard to think."

He folds his hands into his lap. I see the movement out of the corner of my eye. "Do you want to talk about it? Talk through it? Would that help?"

"I don't know."

"Okay."

I talk it through with Temra all the time. She's forgiving. She accepts me. She loves me unconditionally because she's my sister.

Kellyn isn't forced to accept me. He could reject me at any moment, and that makes this so much harder. He's only doing this to be polite. I don't want to be pitied.

But we must work together if we're to get through this, and if there's anything I can do to lessen my anxiety, I have to try.

Kellyn waits, and I search for words in my clouded head. Every nerve in my body screams at me to leave. To be alone. To go somewhere safe.

But there are enemies on our trail, and I'm safest here.

"Think of the most embarrassing moment of your life," I say.

After a few seconds, he says, "All right. I've got it."

"Think about how that made you feel. Now multiply the sensation by a hundred and imagine feeling that way every time another person is around you. Or just feeling it for no reason at all. And how all it does is force you to reflect on every stupid thing you've ever done in front of another person. Each moment adds to it as you remember them, and soon you're spiraling out of control."

Kellyn draws in a breath. "*That's* how you feel every day?"

"Yes. And sometimes I feel so tired, even though I haven't done anything. It's like my head and heart have run a marathon on their own, and only solitude will help them regain their strength."

I feel Kellyn rise, notice the dip in my bedroll as he places himself next to me. Then there's warmth as he wraps me in his arms.

"Does this help or make it worse?" he asks.

"Both."

"And if I squeeze tighter?"

"It might tip on the side of helping more."

He leans his head against mine, and there's just something about having someone try to understand that makes me feel a little better.

"I need you to know that I'm really glad I'm not alone," I say. "I'm glad you're with me. I am. It makes me feel safer. But there are just times when I need to be alone for my own sanity. Does that make sense?"

"I think so. Thank you for telling me. For helping me understand. I will never know exactly what you go through, but I hope you know you can always trust me with how you're feeling or with what you need."

"Thank you."

After a time, he asks, "Do you want to hear my most embarrassing moment?"

"Of course."

As he holds me, he tells me about one of his first jobs as a mercenary. "He came out of nowhere. Stole the purse right off my charge's saddle. I chased him down through the middle of the crowded road. I didn't see where the water had gathered into a puddle from the rain the night before. I hit it at a full run, slipped, and fell flat on my back in the filthy muck. He got away."

"That doesn't sound too bad," I say.

"Well, at the time, I thought my employer was attractive. I slipped, had the wind knocked out of me, and lost the money in front of a beautiful girl. If that weren't bad enough, that night, they were telling stories about me in the tavern I visited to find a new job. Someone pointed me out, and I got to relive the humiliation all over again. I had to travel to the next town over for work."

Now I'm giggling, the tension and discomfort finally abating.

But my thoughts go wild. I try to picture the beautiful girl he met. Did they have something while they traveled together? Did they kiss? Did they do more than kiss? Does he still think about her?

I shut my eyes as tightly as I can, as if that will make the thoughts go away.

And then one of Kellyn's hands rubs up and down my arm, giving me something else to focus on. That pleasant warmth and friction. I count the strokes as my breaths deepen and my mind finally goes quiet.

A few days later, I climb through the treetops to try and spot our pursuers again. What I find is worse than I ever could have predicted.

I half crawl, half slide down the tree, scraping the skin at my palms in the process.

"We have to go," I say, packing away what remains of our lunch.

"What is it?"

"Dust. The sky is filled with it. I didn't make sense of it at first, but—"

"Ravis's army has begun their march," Kellyn says.

"They shouldn't have been ready yet! What is Ravis thinking?"

We leap atop our horses, urge them into a trot.

"He wants the element of surprise," Kellyn muses aloud. "He's marching, ready or not. If they don't have enough food for their soldiers, they'll likely loot Briska first. There's only a meager city guard there. They don't stand a chance."

"We have to get to Skiro immediately. He can warn the other royalty with his portals. It's the only way we can help now."

It's impossible to gallop with all the foliage. We push our horses as fast as we dare without causing them to trip or stumble. A broken leg on a horse is a death sentence.

We have the advantage, I reason. We're on horseback while Ravis's men are on foot. We're taking a direct route to Skiro, while they're limited to the roads.

We'll get there first. Skiro will be warned.

I'll find Temra laughing with Petrik, waiting for my arrival.

It'll all be okay.

Pushing the horses faster only means they need to rest more. I ache to be *doing* something. Traveling doesn't feel helpful. It feels wasteful somehow.

And even though every step brings me closer to my sister, I grow more and more on edge.

"You're confusing your horse," Kellyn says one day, about a week into the journey.

I stop my fingers from tangling together, and the horse's strides grow smoother beneath me. Poor thing wasn't sure whether I wanted him to go or stop with the way I kept jiggling him about.

Over the next ten minutes, I realize I'm veering to the left.

"Your leg," Kellyn points out.

It's dancing in the stirrup, bouncing slightly up and down. My horse is moving away from the contact, thinking I mean for him to turn left.

"You shouldn't be so worried. The prince's army is barely noticeable in the distance. Our lead is growing."

"Sometimes I don't want to reach Skiro." In fact, all I seem to be able to think about today is how badly I never want to reach Skiro.

"Why?"

"Because if Temra's dead, then I'll know. Not knowing is safer than knowing she's dead. And not knowing is killing me. But if she is gone, I want to stay not knowing a little while longer."

Kellyn's voice grows quieter. "It's better to know. Better for you to be allowed to grieve or celebrate. Not knowing will only tear you apart."

"I don't want to grieve again. I've already been through that. If Temra dies, I'll have lost the rest of my family."

"No," Kellyn says firmly. "You'll have me and Petrik. We'll be your family. After what we've been through together, we're already family."

How can he say that after all that's happened? I dragged him into the whole mess with Kymora. I called things off between us. He's moved on. How can he say that he'll be my family?

I feel heavy inside, like all the blood and bone has been replaced with brick. Just thinking about the possibility of Temra being dead has me silently crying again. Because I know her odds weren't great. She was barely holding on as it was, and it took us hours to get Serutha out . . .

"I don't think I will be able to survive if she didn't make it," I say.

"You will."

"I can't live without her."

"You can."

I close my eyes tightly. "I know you're trying to be helpful, but it's only infuriating when you talk like that. You don't get it. Not only is Temra my whole world. My whole heart. She is my rock. She keeps me safe from all the things that terrify me. I mean it when I say I won't survive without her."

Kellyn is silent for all of five seconds before he says, "Forgive me, Ziva, but that's a load of shit."

My breath catches at the words. Kellyn doesn't swear that often, and when he does, it always packs a punch.

"I don't know how you got it into your head that you're some helpless thing," he says. "You provided for yourself and your sister when your parents died. You outran a warlord. You saved the world from an all-powerful sword."

I open my mouth to speak.

"And before you can say Temra was with you through all of that, let me add that you destroyed a magical portal so your sister's savior could escape. You outsmarted a prince and his entire court and army. You smuggled me out of the city. You did that all without your sister. You can be strong without her."

"That was different."

"That wasn't different. That was you! Under pressure. Scared out of your mind. Alone. And you did it anyway."

"I wasn't alone. You were there."

"I didn't do anything. I didn't come up with a plan for escape. I didn't make a magic sword to get us out of there. I didn't fight Ravis one-on-one and win."

"You kept his men off me, with the horses and the cart."

Kellyn throws his hands up in the air. "Why do you do that?"

"Do what?"

"Look for ways to downplay yourself. Why can't you accept that *you've* done amazing things on your own? That you're strong and persevering and compassionate? You're a protector, Ziva. You've done so many good things."

"Because that's not how I *feel*. Inside, I'm not any of those things. I'm weak. Scared. Self-conscious. All the time. It's all I can think about. My failures and shortcomings. They scream louder than any accomplishment ever could."

Kellyn sighs. "I wish you could you see yourself the way others do. The way Temra does. Or Petrik. The way *I* see you."

I know he's not trying to send my anxiety off to run a mile through my body, but he manages to anyway with that last line. I don't want to talk about the way he sees me. How did the conversation even get here?

I get us back on track. "Even if I could be strong from time to time alone, I don't *want* to live without my sister."

"No one does. The world is a better place for her being in it. But, Ziva, you have lots to give the world, too. You're an adult. Your sister is basically an adult. Have you ever thought that maybe it's time to start living for you?"

He rides ahead of me, signaling he doesn't actually want to hear an answer. I don't know that I could have given him one if I tried.

His words ring through my mind as we make camp.

Living for you.

My black gelding makes pleased noises as I brush him down.

Living for you.

The dried elk is tasteless in my mouth at dinner.

Living for you.

The rain starts to come down, and Kellyn and I huddle in the tent. We give up our extra blankets to the horses so they can stay dry better. The trees block most of the rain but not all.

"Kellyn," I say all the sudden. "You're an oldest child."

"Eleven times over."

"How did you justify leaving your family to become a mercenary?"

Kellyn pulls off his boots before sitting atop his own bedroll. "I gave the first years of my life to my family. I still send them money all the time to help out. But I wanted to see the world. There was no reason why I couldn't have a family and do that. There was no need to justify it. I'm a person, and I deserve to be happy."

"Being with your family doesn't make you happy?"

"It does. But I get restless after a time. Seeing my family is made even more special when I've been away for a while. Does that make sense?"

"Sort of. Temra has always been in my plans for my future. I want to make weapons in a secluded place where no one can find me. Somewhere safe, just me and Temra."

Kellyn flicks a couple droplets out of his hair. "I've spent a lot of time with your sister, and I can promise you those aren't her plans for the future."

"But of course they are! She can be a soldier in a small, secluded town somewhere—"

"No, Temra wants to be seen. She wants to be around other people. She wants to laugh and make more friends and more memories. She likes attention and camaraderie. She loves you and being around you. But she also loves more."

His words ring true, hollowing out my chest. Because of course

Temra wants more than just me. She's always been enough for me, but just me is not enough for her.

And I think that maybe, even if Temra isn't dead, I've lost her in a different sense. She's had a taste of adventure; she's never coming back from that. She has Petrik to make a life with, if she'll stop being stubborn and realize she loves him, too.

And she loves me, obviously. But she will live for herself. Because she's always done that. She's never had to live for me the way I've lived for her. Maybe it would have been different if she'd been born first. If she'd had to sacrifice and work harder to protect me. But she's only ever had to look out for herself and her own interests. I mean, she's always stepped in when she's noticed I needed her, but she's never had to sacrifice anything on my behalf. I don't love her any less for it. It's just the way life was for her.

I want Temra to be happy. Isn't that more important than having her close to me always? Of course it is. I can let her go and do what will make her happiest, even if it takes her away from me.

The self-pity is stronger than ever as I try to imagine a life without my sister living with me, but I'd rather have her alive and happy than dead. No matter what happens, I'm losing my sister one way or another. And if I can survive the first alternative, then why can't I survive the second, as Kellyn suggested earlier?

And if he's right about that, can he be right about everything else he said, too? That I'm strong and persevering and compassionate? Even if those aren't how I see myself?

How can I see myself more clearly? I certainly don't *want* to be scared and unsure all the time.

"What are you thinking?" Kellyn asks.

"I'm trying to decide if you're right or not."

He smiles. "About what?"

"All of it."

"You let me know if you decide I am. I do like hearing that."

I throw my pillow at him. He catches it before it can hit him. Then tosses it harmlessly back at the top of my bedroll.

"Good night, Ziva."

CHAPTER

TWELVE

The next day, while we're traveling, I try something I've never done before. Kellyn says I always downplay myself, and he suggested earlier that I focus on what I've saved. So, every time I think something negative about myself, I force myself to think something nice about myself. Or, if I start to fixate on something negative, I try to replace it with something more positive.

My first thought upon waking (after registering Kellyn's loud snoring) was about how I should have done more for Temra to protect her from Kymora.

And then I stopped myself and thought the following:

You gave Temra a real home and got her out of that orphanage. You raised her to be the amazing person that she is and worked so she could focus on her schooling.

And though my anxiety doesn't go away, I feel a little better as I start my day.

As we travel, and I start to fixate on the fact that I miss the way

Kellyn and I used to be together, the fact that he's moved on, that I let him go—I force my brain to think the following:

The time we had together was precious to me, and I wouldn't trade it for anything. Sometimes relationships don't work out, and it's very unrealistic to think that my first one would be the one that sticks.

My eyes drift over to Kellyn, the way he concentrates on the road in front of him, deep in thought. Then my eyes lower to his lips. And I forget what I'd been thinking about altogether.

I feel foolish, after a time, forcing myself to think more positively, but I make a promise to myself to do it again tomorrow.

After another week of riding, we stumble upon a road in the woods. It's clearly not well traveled, with plants finding purchase in the spaces between where the wheels have worn down the ground. I find another tree to climb and take a look ahead.

I'm surprised by what I find: rooftops and chimneys in the breaks between trees.

"There's a village up ahead," I tell Kellyn when my feet touch the ground again.

"I didn't know there was anything out here. I've never traveled so far from the main road in this territory, and I've never seen anything on a map this way. Should we skirt around it?"

"It'll add time to the trip. It's a pretty big village." The left-over money from selling Ravis's dagger is attached to my saddle-bags. I don't like the idea of interacting with anyone, but if Kellyn is willing to do the talking . . . "Maybe we could get lodging for tonight? Sleep in real beds?"

"That sounds nice."

I keep my horse close to Kellyn's as we enter town. The temperature has cooled somewhat as we've traveled south, and the people here wear more layers than those back in the capital. No one stares at us, which leads me to believe they're used to visitors. Whatever this place is, it's much bigger than Amanor.

There's even an inn.

We keep our weapons and money with us after leaving the horses with a stable girl. Once inside the inn, I feel my nerves ratcheting up. As I look around, I try to turn the people into blurs. I don't want to register faces or anything else. It'll just make me more unsettled.

I follow Kellyn up to the bar, where he exchanges greetings with the owner.

"This here is Vinder. We're a community of hunters and farmers. We work with many merchants who sell pelts to the nearby territories. Some folks like to camp out this way before heading to find food for their families. We're so far from the capital that the prince can't catch us for poaching." The owner winks.

Kellyn pays the man for food and baths and a room with two beds.

At the mention of *two beds*, the owner looks between the two of us.

"My sister," Kellyn says.

The man nods in understanding before putting in our order to the kitchen.

Kellyn turns to me. "Would you mind terribly if we ate in here?"

"With all the people?" I ask.

"I just . . . want to do something normal for a change. Feel normal."

I'm reminded of just how different we are that being around people is normal for him. But I don't blame him. Being around people who don't want to hurt him must be a nice change. He doesn't wear bandages around his head anymore, and his hair covers his injury. But it's still there, and as I remember that I got him hurt, I find that I can't deny him this.

"Sure. Pick a table," I say.

Kellyn looks to me in surprise, as though he fully expected me to refuse and beg him to take me upstairs.

"Are you certain?" he asks.

"Yes."

We settle into a couple chairs at a small two-person table. I hide my hands in my lap immediately, and my fingers tangle together, twisting the joints before picking at my cuticles. Kellyn looks so relaxed, but I feel a prickling at my back. Half the room is behind me and can see me without my knowing. I hate that.

I can practically hear Temra's voice in my head.

No one is looking at you. No one has a thought to spare your way. They're doing their own things. Focus on having a good time. Think of the hot food coming soon.

I look up at the beams of the ceiling, two stories above my head. Stare down at the grains in the table, look at my lap. Anything to avoid noticing the people around me or the man opposite me.

Because he most definitely *is* staring at me.

"What?" I ask finally, turning to him. I look at his neck to avoid my mind blanking by looking into his eyes. It still happens sometimes, when I feel overwhelmed.

"I'm just trying to gauge how you're doing."

"I'm fine. I don't need you to look after me."

"I know you don't, but I still like to do it."

"Why?" I ask, but he's stopped from answering. Our food and drinks have arrived.

A bowl of creamy potato chowder with corn and some sort of meat is placed before us.

"Thank you," I mumble, but the server doesn't answer. In fact, she's not looking at me at all.

I look up from my food to find the girl smiling at Kellyn. She lowers two glasses of ale to the table. She's a pretty thing with creamy-smooth skin, short curls, and a beautiful figure.

For some reason, I hate her immediately.

"Could we get some water, as well? My sister doesn't like ale."

"Your sister? That's good to know."

"Is it?" he asks.

"Yes. That leaves me free to tell you my shift is over at ten."

Kellyn grins, showing all his teeth. When was the last time he gave me a smile like that? Does that mean he wants to see her after her shift is over? Will he leave me alone in our room tonight?

"I'm flattered, but I'm not available," he says.

"Sometime tomorrow, then?"

"Sorry, miss, I didn't mean my time wasn't available. I meant I'm already spoken for."

She looks heavenward. "The pretty ones are always taken. I'll be right back with that water." She glides toward the kitchens, as though the conversation hasn't hurt her ego one bit.

My mind has so many thoughts running through it, I can barely snatch them out to examine one at a time.

Why is he telling everyone I'm his sister?

Why did he tell the girl he wasn't available?

And how is he already taken? Did he meet some girl in Ravis's dungeon?

That's ridiculous and you know it, Ziva.

Did he find the time to romance someone in the brief moments we were apart in Skiro's castle?

Also super unlikely.

Then he must have lied.

But why bother? Does he not find her attractive? And if so, how did he ever find me attractive? Because I'm certainly not as stunning as she is.

There's obviously something wrong with him.

I shove food into my mouth as I continue to mull this over. When the server returns with my water, Kellyn doesn't even spare her a glance. He's enjoying his food, looking about the inn, the people.

"If this were a normal day for me, I'd be trying to find work," he says. "Looking for someone who needs protection on the road."

"You miss it," I say.

"A bit," he admits.

"I'm sorry."

"I wasn't looking for apologies. Just making conversation."

"Then why don't you make conversation tonight? At ten? With her?" I point with my eyes at the server who walks by and curse myself for ever opening my mouth.

Why don't I just tell him outright that I'm a jealous idiot who needs to get a handle on her feelings?

The innkeeper stops Kellyn from answering and spares me further mortification by saying, "The bath is ready."

I snatch the key from his lowered hand, ditch the rest of my dinner, and run upstairs as though my life depends on it.

The room is much smaller than I expected. The tub barely fits at the foot of the two beds, which might as well be one bed with the mere foot of space between them. I have to squeeze between the tub and the wall just to be able to shut the door.

I lock it, undress, and climb into the tub, trying my hardest to forget the stupid thing I just did.

I last about two seconds.

Why didn't Kellyn accept the pretty girl's invitation? Maybe he wants some alone time, but if that were the case, then why did he want to eat dinner surrounded by strangers? I dunk my head below the surface of the water and hold my breath.

Why did I have to ask him about it? Now he knows I'm thinking about him and his romantic exploits.

My lungs burn, so I come up for air. When I'm done, I scrub my clothes clean and hang them up to dry on the footboard of my bed. I slide into the nightgown, courtesy of the inn, left on my bed. As I run my fingers through my short hair, I wonder what the odds are that Kellyn will take his time with dinner.

A heavy fist hits the door in quick succession, causing me to jump.

But I don't make a sound, hoping whoever it is will go away.

"Ziva, you took the only key."

Oh, right.

I unlock the door before sitting back on the bed.

If I weren't still so panicky about my earlier comment, I'd probably find it funny watching Kellyn trying to squeeze into the room. It takes him a couple tries to get the door shut, and he nearly falls over while taking off his boots.

"Would you rather wait up here or downstairs while I bathe?" he asks. His voice has a strange edge to it. I cannot place his mood.

More important, though, I don't know the answer to his question. Downstairs there are people. Up here there is a naked Kellyn.

"I'm in a nightgown," I say, as though that's any answer or explanation.

"Then why don't you turn around?"

Still sitting upright, I shift my body to face the small window in the room.

Where I can see Kellyn's reflection.

I snap my eyes closed as I hear clothing start to drop. Water splashes. And I think I might stop breathing.

If I thought the earlier conversation was bad, this is much, much worse. I should have left. I should have gone downstairs no matter what I was wearing. Maybe my food is still on the table, not that I have any appetite anymore.

"What's the matter, Ziva?" he asks as I hear the soap scrape against his skin.

"Can we not talk right now?"

"Why?"

"Because you're naked."

"So? My mouth still works."

"Well, mine doesn't."

My eyes fall open for just a moment, and they connect with Kellyn's in the reflection of the window.

I think I might go up in flames as I snap my gaze shut once more.

"I wondered if you'd peek. You ought to be ashamed of yourself."

"I can't see anything important. You're—you're in a tub!"

He laughs, and I don't know why that only sets me more on edge.

But then he stands, and I can hear the water running down his skin, hear the towel scratch against his hair, hear his heavy tread. Feel the heat of his body as he grabs the nightgown off his own bed.

When the opposite bed creaks from the weight of him, I relax my eyelids finally.

"Now can we talk?" he asks.

I shake my head. "Definitely not."

"Ziva, it's me. You don't need to be afraid."

"You are the most terrifying thing."

"That's ridiculous."

Is it? Is it so ridiculous when his words can scare me, hurt me, reject me? And there's not even anything to reject, so why does he still have that much power over me?

"Why are you telling everyone I'm your sister?" I ask, thinking to claim control of the conversation.

"I thought it was an easier description than to call you my past romantic partner."

Why do those words sting? "You could have said we're friends!"

"Friends who share a room?"

"It's safer if we stick together!"

"I know that, but I wasn't about to give everyone the finer details."

I wrap my arms around my bent knees, my face still pointed at the window. "There's not another reason?"

"No. What secret motive could I possibly have?"

Distancing himself from me. Letting other women know he's a romantic prospect?

"Fine, don't answer," he says. "Tell me instead why you're so worked up over that serving woman."

No, I want to groan. "I'm not worked up. It doesn't matter to me how many women throw themselves at you."

"So you wouldn't care if I went down there and flirted with her?"

"Nope."

"How about if I spent the night with her?"

A pause. "Nope."

"What if I wanted to stay in the village and become a hunter so I can see my new true love every day?"

At those outrageous words, I finally spin in the bed and plant my feet on the floor. I'm prepared to give Kellyn a tongue-lashing, but I pause when I see the laughter he's just barely containing.

"What are you doing?" I ask him.

"Witnessing you not worked up."

I lean forward. "Stop playing games with me, Kellyn. I don't like these conversations. Tell me straight. Why did you reject her invitation?"

He leans his elbows onto his knees. "How do you still not know? How can you still doubt?"

"How about, instead of belittling me, you tell me what it is I don't know? Just make the point you want to make instead of dancing around it!"

"That's rich coming from you."

I stand, thinking to storm out, before I remember the tub is still in the way of the door. And there's nowhere for me to go.

I let out a growl before settling right back on my bed. My heart is racing, my breath is heaving, and I just want to be alone. Somewhere he can't see me or read me or try to poke fun at me.

Instead, Kellyn grabs my hands, stilling the fidgeting I hadn't even noticed I'd been doing. Our knees touch in the small distance between the beds. He looks down at that point of contact, looks to my hands, where his warm fingers wrap around my palms. His gaze settles on me.

He lurches forward, catches himself when he's only a breath away. "I'm going to kiss you," he says. "If you don't want that, pull away now."

I cannot even process the words before his lips are on mine. It's not his fault; he waited a good three seconds, and I could tell even that cost him. It was all me and my inability to think when he's so close.

Never mind what happens to my brain when he's touching

me. Kissing me. His lips are so desperate as they move against mine, trying to get a reaction. Meanwhile, my head is spinning, and my chest is constricting, and why can't I do something other than just sit there?

After a few seconds of no response, he pulls back, but not far. "Ziva, I still want you. I haven't stopped wanting you since I first met you in your smithy shop. You were so quiet and ridiculous." He laughs at the memory. "I don't want anyone else. I don't even see anyone else because I'm too busy obsessing over you. If I seem distant or uncaring, it's only because I'm trying my damndest to be okay with the fact that you broke things off. But I'm not okay. I'm constantly wondering what you're thinking. I'm trying to guess how you're feeling. Sometimes, I can read you as plainly as a book. Sometimes, you're a complete mystery, one that I love trying to solve.

"But I want you, Ziva. I don't want there to be any confusion on where I stand where we're concerned."

My eyes drop so I can think, but I feel the burn—or glow?—of my cheeks.

He says, "You don't have to say anything in response. I know it makes you uncomfortable. I just wanted you to know. Since you've clearly got it into your head somehow that I don't want you anymore."

My next breath hurts as it leaves my lungs.

CHAPTER
THIRTEEN

He wants me?

Doesn't he know he's the only person I've *ever* wanted?

But I can't have him.

Because . . .

Why can't I have him?

I forget the reasons as his breaths mingle with mine.

I'm so sick of thinking. Of worrying all the time. Sometimes I can't control my thoughts. Sometimes I'm just a ball of nerves spiraling out of control.

I want him.

That thought is as real and bright as a light beam breaking through the clouds. And if I could just have him, even for a little while, I think things would be better. But I'm terrified. Just touching him feels like I'm burning from the inside out. I lost him once. I don't want to lose him again. I'm not supposed to have him again, because . . . reasons.

But I miss him so much. I miss the way he made me feel. I miss being with him, and above all else, I miss kissing him.

Look up.

My hands tighten against his. We're in this room until morning either way. Why not just enjoy him while I have him? I'm not brave enough to put myself out there. To reason with him. But I can just look and trust that he'll do the rest.

My eyes raise to Kellyn's lips, and that's all the encouragement my mercenary needs.

This time when he kisses me, I'm ready. This time, I kiss him back.

His knees part, so one rests on either side of mine, and I clutch at his arms, holding on as he kisses me senselessly. My memory is a huge disappointment. It focuses on the bad, remembers every detail so I can be tormented by a single embarrassment years later. But the good things? It glosses over them. Lets them fade.

Kissing him now is like the first time. So new and exciting. So wonderful and life-changing.

My hands explore the planes of his face, loving the roughness of the beginnings of the beard that's growing with our travels. His strong neck. The curve of his jaw. His damp hair in my face.

I love all of it, and my mind is so blessedly quiet that I hope this moment never ends.

A deep noise comes out of the back of his throat when I suck on his lower lip before exploring the inside of his mouth with my tongue. I might be pressing against him too roughly, though, because he's tilting backward, falling against the bed with me on top of him.

We've never kissed while lying down.

Our legs tangle, and I worry that I'm crushing him. I try to raise my weight up on my arms.

"Don't," he whispers before pulling me right back down.

All right, then.

I stop thinking about my weight and instead focus on every point of contact between us, how it makes the kissing even better. After an indeterminable amount of time, Kellyn rolls us over. Rolls me beneath him.

And I see exactly what he means.

I love having his weight atop me. Love feeling his strength and the entire length of him spread across me from his head to his feet.

I've never been this close to anyone. Had no idea what I was missing out on.

"Don't ever stop kissing me," I say. My first words in what feels like hours.

"You choose when we stop, then."

I don't stop him until I can barely keep my eyes open. And we collapse into sleep together.

The next morning, Kellyn doesn't treat me any differently.

He brings up breakfast from the kitchen, hands me my food, and asks, "How did you sleep?"

"Deeper than usual."

"Same."

He doesn't look at me while we ready the horses. I know, because I'm staring at him every chance I get.

And when we start riding, leaving the town far behind, he hums to himself.

Is that a happy hum? Or a nonchalant hum? Or an I-need-something-to-pass-the-time hum?

Maybe I'm thinking too much about him and what he's doing. Why should he act differently just because we kissed? Though the humming is a little unusual for him. Whatever. The point is, he's fine, and I need to be fine, too.

Just act normal. And everything will feel normal.

Eventually.

Maybe.

When I am finally able to get Kellyn out of my head, it is only because my mind finds something else to worry about. I catch sight of the sleeping sword attached to my horse and remember how conflicted I was about making it in the first place. Especially when Ravis could have gotten his hands on it.

And now his men are following us, likely gaining with each day . . .

After a while, I say, "I've been thinking about the sword."

"Which one?"

"The bastard sword I made to aid us in our escape. I think we should get rid of it."

"Why?"

I give my horse a pat when he catches himself after stumbling on a rock. "It's too powerful. It shouldn't exist. If Ravis gets his hands on it while trying to conquer, he'd knock out legions of men and be free to murder them in their sleep.

"The sword served its purpose," I continue. "I think it's time to return it to the ground."

Kellyn doesn't say anything for a moment. "It makes sense to me. We want to help our friends, but we can't risk anything too powerful in the wrong hands. How do you propose we get rid of the sword? Do you want to forge another stone?"

"I don't think I need to. The sword shouldn't be indestructible the way Secret Eater is. I didn't put so much of myself into it. I created this one for a very specific purpose, with a very specific ability. The magic should disperse if the sword is broken."

Kellyn nods. "We could take care of it right now, then, if you want?"

"I think that's best. Before anything else can happen."

"All right."

We dismount, and Kellyn strides over to a fallen tree. "May I?" he asks.

I hand over the weapon.

He wedges it under the trunk as far as it will go, so the hilt sticks out of the ground at a forty-five-degree angle. Then he places a rock the size of his head beneath it. He climbs atop the fallen tree.

"Stand back," he cautions, and I lead the horses away.

Kellyn jumps, and the sword snaps, the sound ricocheting through the entire woods.

I feel the magic leave the weapon, as though a sun-warmed stone suddenly lost its heat. We leave the pieces there on the ground. Kellyn mounts his horse once more. The matter is done with so quickly.

"If only Secret Eater had been so easy to dispense with. Maybe Kymora would have left me alone," I say.

"I doubt it," Kellyn says.

He's likely right. "What do you suppose Skiro's done with her?"

"If he has any sense, he's removed her head from her shoulders. A person like that is too dangerous to let live." He shudders, and I think I know exactly what appeared in his mind. The fight outside the Amanor smithy. Him fighting her, sword to sword—the mercenary far outmatched.

He'd have died if Petrik and I weren't there to step in with our magicked weapons.

Kymora is the greatest swordswoman to ever live.

"What do you think Petrik is doing?" I ask. "If—" If Temra

didn't make it. Is he waiting around for us? Is he counseling his brother? Staying close to his mother if she's still alive?

"If he thinks we're alive, he's waiting for us, trying to convince his brother to send men after us. If he thinks we're dead, he might have returned to the library."

I sit with that a moment, and then I ask the question that I shouldn't give voice to. Hope can make truth all the more crushing.

"And Temra, what do you think she's doing?" I ask, my voice faint.

"I bet a whole team of doctors is forcing her to rest and finish healing as she tries to fight them off and come after you instead."

That brings a soft grin to my lips. The thought of Temra wanting to come save me warms my heart, but I wouldn't want her to actually *try* it. The whole point of going to Ravis was to save her. If she were healed only to put herself in more danger . . .

Kellyn doesn't say anything more as we travel. He doesn't initiate conversation, not if he can help it. If I want to talk, I have to start and direct the topic. I can't tell if he's silent because he thinks it will make me more comfortable or if he has other motives entirely. Either way, I like that he isn't forcing me to talk about what happened between us. How he's keeping things from becoming awkward despite it. And though he's being more quiet than usual, I don't call him out on it.

But *I* need to talk about normal things if I'm to stop thinking about what happened and the million questions that come with it. Have I forgiven him for everything? Does he forgive me for everything? Do we just go back to normal now—whatever that is for us? He said he wants me, but maybe he didn't mean right away, since he hasn't initiated anything since the kiss.

I blurt, "I miss my hammers."

"I really liked watching you with those," he says. "I'm sure we'll find a way to get them back. Ravis will probably bring them when he invades. Or you could make new ones before he reaches us? I'm sure Skiro will give you the use of anything you want. He seems as fascinated by magic as Petrik is. Must run in the family."

"Thank goodness none of them possess a lick of it. Can you imagine people in power like that with magic?"

"It would be horrible," he agrees. He turns to me, as if about to add something.

By the time I register the sound of an arrow flying through the air, it's already too late.

Kellyn growls in pain, and his horse startles from the noise and the sudden, involuntary pull of the reins. His mare goes up on her back legs, sending Kellyn tumbling to the ground. The mercenary doesn't move again.

"No!"

I push off my horse without bringing him to a stop, then go to my knees in front of him.

"Kellyn, say something!"

The arrow is protruding from the back of his arm. Blood stains the area, and my hands hover over the spot for just a moment.

A shot to the upper arm, but why isn't he—

Blood drips down the side of his face.

He hit his head on a rock after the fall. He's out cold but still breathing.

I register all of this in a second. Then I stand. Lady Killer's hilt peeks over the top of Kellyn's back, and I draw the longsword, holding it in both hands before turning around.

I count five of them, dressed in Ravis's colors.

The party he sent after us didn't take the road, then. They were smart and picked up our trail.

And they caught up to us.

"Bladesmith," one of them says, a man with a full beard and thick brow. "King Ravis wishes to speak with you. Put the sword down and come with us."

As if it weren't bad enough already that I have to fight while vastly outnumbered. They want to *talk* first.

"Ravis isn't a king, and he has no authority to command me." There, that sounded impressive, didn't it? Maybe, if my voice had managed any sort of bite. It was rather weak sounding.

"He has an army greater than any other in all of Ghadra, and he has the birthright. Firstborn of the late King Arund. He has all the authority he needs."

I want to say something dangerous. *If you want me, come and get me.* But the words will only taunt the soldiers forward, and I want them to stay far away from me.

"He will not sweep across Ghadra unchallenged," I say.

The guard laughs. "Who's going to stop him? You?"

If need be. That would be the intimidating thing to say. But I have no intention of doing any such thing. I just want to reunite with my sister and move north. Away from Ghadra and all the trouble it's caused me.

"Turn around and don't stop walking," I say.

"If we return empty-handed, the king will have our heads."

"If you step forward, I will have them. I suggest you make a run for it." I try to look imposing. I stand up to my full height, flex my arms while they grip the sword hilt. The weapon doesn't feel natural in my hands at all. I've never had to wield a sword before.

Please don't make me kill you, I want to beg. I've had enough of killing.

The soldiers advance, fanning out around me.

"Has Ravis not told you what I can do? Do you not know what abilities this sword possesses?" I ask.

They don't falter, but my hands shake along the sword. I only have three of the guards in my line of sight. The other two must be behind me.

And then the sword moves to the left, dragging my hands after it. I spin on my toes in that direction, bring the sword up just in time to stop the pommel that was flying toward my head.

But the only way to stop it was to slice at the arms of the man holding it.

He shrieks, dropping his weapon and backing away.

I relax a little, reminding myself that they've no wish to kill me. Ravis wants me back unharmed, likely so he can kill me himself. These soldiers are going to try to disarm me, knock me out, bind me, take me away.

And then Kellyn might bleed out on the rocks alone.

I can't let that happen.

The longsword nudges me back around in time to see a sword point coming for me. I dodge, jumping to the side, but the movement is so awkward.

The sword is heavy and just so *long*. It's nothing at all like holding a hammer, and I ache for my beloved weapons once more.

I kick out at the man in front of me. Bring Lady Killer around to block the strike from the female guard. When our weapons connect, the force of it almost sends the sword flying out of my hands. I tighten my grip, and the woman makes some sort of flicking motion, shuffling the weapon away while she moves in for the kill.

If she were intent on my death, I'd be dead. Instead, the blade rests an inch from my nose.

"Surrender," she says.

I jump backward, throw my weight behind my next swing, feeling like a failure.

This sword is magicked, and I still might lose this fight.

It can yank me about all it likes, but I lack the instincts to protect myself. I wonder if I could magic a self-fighting sword in the future? Clearly I have need of one.

Lady Killer jerks upward, and I thrust my arms up with the motion, catching the bastard sword. A hidden knife sails toward me, but the sword doesn't move. It keeps the more dangerous hit away from my face. I need to stop being on the defensive. I have a longsword. They have bastard swords. Mine is the longer reach.

The knife makes contact with my arm, drawing blood before trying to go to my neck. Trying to force another surrender from me.

But they won't kill you, I remind myself.

I leap back once again, swinging the sword around and around my head. Four opponents, all of them in front of me. I can do this.

I slash and lunge, but the trained guards deflect my blows. Two weapons sail at my head at the same time, and Lady Killer drags my body down. From below, I stab one of them through their boot. The second jumps into the air to avoid my strike.

Two down.

Three left.

While on the ground, I grab a fistful of dirt and rise, throwing it into the eyes of the female guard. Her eyes slam closed, trying to free the grit from them, and I slice her across the ribs in the midst of the distraction.

Two more.

Blood drips down my elbow. Sweat stings the wound as I exert myself. Though it might be a result of my nerves than any actual physicality on my part yet.

The sword lunges toward the ground, and I follow after it. The man I stabbed in the boot made a grab for me, and Lady Killer goes through the flat of his hand, sticking him to the earth.

Oh, gross.

The air is full of shrieks. Blood runs down Lady Killer as I pull her free and size up the remaining two guards.

There's no going back from this. I need to finish it.

I bring the longsword down, and when it catches on the nearest soldier's sword, I release my left hand from the hilt and send a closed fist toward his head.

They're not expecting me to fight with any skill. I'm catching them by surprise. That, my magical weapon, and the fact that they're trying not to hurt me are the only reasons I'm able to do anything well.

When he takes a step back from the blow, I slash down, and the weapon wedges into his side. He screams, but not as loud as when I pull the sword back out.

The man whose arms I cut comes up behind me, having dropped his weapon and thinking to grab me. I deal with him easily, slicing across his gut.

One left. The one in charge.

I face him, raise my sword in preparation.

And then a figure appears behind him. I hear a *crunch*, and then the soldier falls to the ground, revealing Kellyn behind him, rock in hand.

"Well done," he says right before he collapses.

CHAPTER

FOURTEEN

I try to catch him on the way down, but I'm still holding Lady Killer, and I don't drop the sword in time.

Kellyn groans with every breath he lets out. One hand on his head, the other at his arm.

"It's okay," I tell him. "You're going to be okay. Just wait here a moment."

As if he could go anywhere.

I try to track down the horses. These weren't trained warhorses, and they spooked at the first sign of trouble. Kellyn's mount is nowhere in sight, but I find my gelding grazing in a rich patch of grass about a hundred yards away.

When I bring him back to the blood-soaked clearing, I retrieve one of my waterskins and return to Kellyn. I clean the blood from his head and wrap it with an unsoiled shirt from one of the dead soldiers.

Kellyn snores lightly, and I flick his nose. "What!" he shrieks. Then he's back to groaning.

"Stay awake."

"Why?"

"You hit your head."

"So?"

"So, when you hit your head, you're supposed to stay awake."

"Why?"

"I don't know! That's just what they say."

"I have to sleep eventually."

"Will you stop being difficult? I need to figure out what to do about this arrow."

The wound is deep, but it doesn't quite poke out the other side of his arm. Do I push it the rest of the way through? I can't pull it back out. The wound itself isn't bleeding terribly, but *there's an arrow in there and that's not good.*

"Wake up!" I snap.

Kellyn jolts back to consciousness. "Ziva, I'm tired."

"No. Stay awake. Help me figure out what to do with this arrow."

"Leave it," he hisses. "We don't have anything to help get it out or to patch it up or . . ."

"Kellyn!"

"I'm awake!"

"Can you climb onto the horse?"

"I don't know if I can sit up."

He starts drifting off again, and I know that the arrow shaft is going to be a problem. It's so long; it'll bump up against things, causing him all kinds of pain.

If the blow to his head doesn't kill him first.

Don't think like that!

I place both hands on the arrow shaft, grip it as close to Kellyn's skin as I can.

Then I snap it.

"TWIN HELLS! GAH!" Kellyn's suddenly upright, shoving me away. I know he's not in his right mind, on top of being in unimaginable pain, so I don't take it personally.

I discard the broken piece of arrow, cover the wound as best I can above and below the shaft, then pull Kellyn to his feet. "Come on. On the horse. Then you can rest."

I have to find a large rock for Kellyn to climb in order get him into the saddle. I come up behind him, and he sags against me. He's a lot heavier when he's all deadweight.

"Kellyn, talk to me."

"You said I could rest," he slurs.

"You can. You're not moving. You still have to talk to me."

"I don't want to talk to you. I want you to talk to me."

The horse leaps over a smaller tree trunk, and Kellyn groans again.

"What is that supposed to mean?" I ask.

"I'm always the one instigating everything. When we talk. When we kiss. The flirting. All of it. At first, I did it because you're shy, because I thought that's maybe what you needed . . ." His words trail off.

"Kellyn!"

"But it's not fair!" he shouts when he jerks awake again. "I want someone who wants me. I want someone who puts in an effort to be with me. A relationship takes two people, and they have to be equal partners. And no matter how badly I want you, I can't make you want me. So I'm backing off, and if you want me, you have to try harder . . ."

He slumps into sleep again, and I'm so stunned by his words that I let him be for a moment.

Twins, that's what he's been doing. Acting normal. Not making a big deal out of the kiss. Not being extra flirty. He wants me to make an effort. He wants an equal partner in a relationship, and I don't know if I can be that for him. I spend so much time alone, preferring it to anything else, even. I don't know how to be what he needs. What he wants.

He's not asking you to change who you are. He's asking you to make an effort.

But what if that makes me uncomfortable? What if I say or do something awful to push him away for good? Doesn't he realize I'm doing him a favor by letting him start things? I don't want to start anything that he doesn't want.

I tell myself that I don't have to make any decisions now. Right now, I have to get Kellyn to the capital so Serutha can put him to rights. How far away are we now? Three weeks? A month?

How long can that arrow stay in there before more serious things happen?

"Kellyn," I say.

"Hmm?" he asks sleepily.

"Just checking on you." Though to be honest, I have no idea what I'm checking for. But as long as he's coherent every time I wake him, he should be fine, right?

And Twins, but I hope he forgets everything he said to me today.

We ride through the night. Though most of those guards were unconscious, I don't know how many of them were dead. I just hope their injuries are severe enough to seek help and not pursue us.

Kellyn returns to himself over the next couple of days, and he tries to hide the pain in his arm.

"Here," I say, handing over a makeshift sling.

"Thank you."

If he remembers anything of what he said while concussed, he doesn't say anything about it.

With the other horse long gone, we have to continue to share. We spend more time walking than riding, however, because the poor gelding can't carry two for as long.

"I can hold the reins," he says one morning after we've had a good night's rest. He climbs atop the horse behind the saddle, clearly intending me to take the spot in front of him.

"You're injured. I'll continue to take the reins."

His eyes shadow beneath his brow.

"If something were to start chasing us, it's better that I be in control. Me taking the reins isn't going to make you less manly."

"That's not—"

"Isn't it?"

When he doesn't answer, I say, "Scoot forward."

He does.

Every day, we replace the bandages on Kellyn's arm. I boil water from the stream to clean the bloodied strips, then replace them. He needs to keep the open wound covered, lest infection set in.

But after another week on the road, I feel the extra heat from his right arm. That night, when I remove the bandages, a smell comes from the wound, and white liquid drains from it.

I draw in a breath through my teeth. "We need to clean this out."

He's silent a moment. "All right." He reaches on the ground with his good arm, finds a broken stick, and bites down on it.

"Do it," he says, the words barely intelligible around the wood.

I'm terrified I'm only going to injure him more than he already is. I've never done anything like this before, but I've seen it done. I've cut myself on metal plenty of times and had to visit the Lirasu healer.

I angle his arm up gently so the wound is parallel with the ground. "I need you to hold your arm like this."

He brings up his knee so he can rest his elbow there.

"Do you want to look away?" I ask.

"No."

"All right." I place my fingers on either side of the wound and press down and slightly in. Something like a whimper, only much louder comes out of Kellyn's mouth.

"I'm so sorry," I say as I watch the white liquid ooze to the ground.

I rinse off the top of the wound with more water, then go again, pinching the spot around the arrow shaft.

Kellyn's scream is barely muffled by the stick, and his free hand reflexively goes to me. He grips my shoulder, his fingers digging in.

"That's it. Just one more time."

"I—I don't think I can," he says, letting the stick fall from his mouth.

"You can. We have to get as much out as possible."

"I think I'd rather die."

"Don't say that!"

His breathing is ragged, and I know he needs a distraction from the wound.

The obvious solution hits me like a hammer.

Kiss him.

Go on. Initiate it. Right now.

No, no. I can't. I'm not ready.

You'll never be ready. This is something you just need to do. It's an important step for you. Time won't make it easier. You'll just overthink it more.

But what if I do it wrong? Or if he doesn't want it? Or—

"I can promise I will never refuse a kiss from you."

Didn't he say that to me once? But what if he's changed his mind? So much is different now, and—

For Twins' sake, Ziva, he's in unimaginable pain, and you sit there arguing with yourself like an idiot.

He took an arrow. The least you can do is distract the man.

The unbelievably beautiful and kind and wonderful man you never stop thinking about.

Fine!

Before I can talk myself out of it, I grab Kellyn's face with both of my hands to angle him toward me and lean in.

My nose stubs against his cheek before my lips touch his, and I think maybe I've done something very wrong when his whole body tenses beneath me.

Oh Goddesses, back up. Back up. But I've lost my balance, and I'm already here. And I can't just shrug this off. However will I explain it away? I should at least do what I set out to do, shouldn't I?

I move my lips across his in the way they've done dozens of times before. It's hard to tell if I'm doing it right, when he's just sitting there like a stone. Am I pressing too hard? Too soft? Should I say something?

Maybe I should stand and walk away. Pretend it never happened. Maybe I'll trip over a rock and fall into a ditch and die from embarrassment so I won't have to face him again after this.

I tighten the hands pressed against his jawline, preparing to push off, when he suddenly moves.

At first, I think maybe he's going to shove me away, but the hand on my shoulder is pulling me closer, and his lips start moving with mine. It takes me far too long to realize *he's kissing me back*.

There's some sort of victory in having a kiss returned. Knowing that it was wanted. That it was accepted. That *I'm* accepted.

Unless of course he's just humoring me. Oh, I really hope he's not doing that.

But he's the one who deepens the kiss, not me.

He pushes his tongue between my lips and pulls me flush against him. I bite at his lips, taste as much of him as I can, thread my fingers in his hair so I can weld our mouths together.

I used to think that once I'd been kissed for the first time, I would just be part of some select group of people who *know*. Some experience that once you have, you just know what to expect every time. Like cutting your hair.

But there are different kinds of kisses. Some are achingly soft. Some are deep and searching. And some are so powerful they almost knock me onto my knees.

Kellyn traces my upper lip with his tongue before sucking the lower into his mouth. His lips trail down my throat, each kiss harder than the last. When he finds that spot I like, he lingers, drawing an ache out of me that I feel low in my belly.

Soon I'm the one with ragged breathing, and that thought reminds me of my purpose. I slowly remove my hands from his hair. I angle my head so I can see the arrow shaft, and then I dig in my fingers.

He pulls back with a violent gasp, biting my neck inadvertently, but I don't let up on the pressure until the white liquid turns to blood.

"There!" I say triumphantly.

Kellyn slumps to the side, losing consciousness, and I wrap the wound while he's out, comforting myself with the knowledge that at least he can't feel any more pain.

We kissed so many times while we were staying with his parents, back before Temra got hurt. So many kisses that I couldn't recall the details of every single one anymore. But I'm going to remember that one forever.

The days progress, and Kellyn doesn't improve. His arm only gets more infected the longer we travel, and soon, lancing the wound does nothing to help. He grows feverish, and by the time our southern trek through the woods finally meets the main road, he's grown too weak to be of any use. He rides the horse whenever we travel at my insistence, but soon he becomes too sick to sit atop it by himself.

It's like with Temra all over again, taking the same road to help. Only this time I at least know Serutha will be able to help. Unless Skiro sent her somewhere for some task.

He wouldn't do that. He just got her back.

He can't have done that.

Kellyn groans and mumbles incoherently while we travel, and I find myself missing my sister immeasurably. She would know what to say to help me calm my thoughts. To help me focus on the positive and not let my thoughts spiral out of control. She would point out all the good things. I do my best without her.

That evening, I use cold water from the stream to wet a

rag and dab at Kellyn's forehead. I've never seen him like this before.

Helpless. Rendered useless by a measly arrow.

"You're not going to die," I tell him. "Not on my watch. We need to think about positive things. Like, we're not dead. Petrik made it out. We know he's at least safe. And Serutha is free."

But Temra could still be dead.

Positive, Ziva!

"Because we escaped, we can warn Skiro about the invading army. We got your sword back. I'm mostly uninjured, so I can get us safely to the capital. We're just days away now."

If only the woods had spat us out before the trail to Amanor. I could have taken him to the healer there. It would have been closer. And then I could leave him with his family.

But Serutha will do a better job fixing him up. He only has to make it.

What if he can't last a few more days?

Again, positive, Ziva!

"We have plenty of food to eat and water to drink. We have a horse. Can you imagine if I had to drag you all this way with my own strength?"

I'm strong, but I'm not *that* strong.

"We're going to make it," I say again. But Kellyn doesn't acknowledge a thing I say.

When we approach the bridge over the river, I recognize where we are instantly.

Especially with the hacked-down tree covering the whole thing.

A crew of bandits runs up from the slope to the river.

"Good evening, friends," the bandit leader—what was his

name?—says. He must have found new men to replace the ones we killed, because he's toting a full gang.

"Devran," I say as the name comes to me, and an edge of warning enters my voice.

"How do you—" he starts, and then his eyes go wide. "You!" he shrieks, taking a few steps away from me. "Didn't you just come through here? What are you doing back?"

"I really haven't got time for this." Not that I had any time when we first met, either. "Move this tree out of my way, or I will kill all your men a second time!" Then I realize how that sounds. "Not the same men, obviously. I'll kill the new men. I'll kill lots of different men like I did before!"

Sometimes I think I'm getting braver at speaking out, but then I go and make a fool of myself.

"Of course!" Devran says, and he makes a motion with his hand. "Move the tree, lads!"

"But we haven't been paid yet," one of the smaller ruffians says.

"This one already paid the other time she came through."

"You only make 'em pay once?" another asks. "That don't seem too profitable, boss."

"Just shut up and do your jobs."

"I don't think she looks very scary," says a third.

"Any man who doesn't put his back into moving this here tree will be cut loose from the gang, you hear?" Devran snaps.

And slowly but surely, the men crawl atop the bridge and get to work. I sigh in relief. I don't think my horse could make the jump carrying me and Kellyn.

When they're done, I wait for the brigands to step away before making my way across. I halt before I reach the end.

"Devran?"

"Yes, miss?"

"Don't let me catch you on this bridge a third time."

"No, miss. I mean yes, miss. You won't."

"Good."

"But don't you mean a fourth time?" he calls at my back while I ride away.

He really needs a new job, but I don't see how he'll find anything good if he can't count properly.

CHAPTER

FIFTEEN

The castle couldn't have come into view any sooner. Kellyn keeps losing balance and listing out of the saddle. I have to constantly wrestle him against me at the same time I hold the reins, yell at people in the street to move, and egg on the horse.

He almost falls to the ground when we pull up to the front entrance, but I catch him, muscles straining. I shout to the men on duty. "He needs the healer Serutha. Now! And I need to see Petrik."

Only after the words are out of my mouth do I realize I have no authority. They probably don't even know who I am. I was barely here before.

"At once, Mistress Ziva," one of the guards says.

Then again, I've been wrong before. Maybe these are the men who were here last time and they have really good memories?

Or, more likely, Petrik has told them to keep an eye out for me.

A handful of attendants appear at the door with a pallet.

They help Kellyn off the horse, before placing him atop the pallet and carrying him inside. I begin to follow, hating how familiar all of this feels.

"Ziva?" comes a voice from behind me.

"Petrik!" I shriek, throwing myself into him.

He startles backward, before his arms slowly come around me. He gives me two soft pats. "What's the matter?" he asks. And then he catches sight of Kellyn. "What happened?"

"We were attacked on the journey back. He took an arrow through the arm. I had no way to get it out, and now it's infected. The wound, I mean. Not the arrow, obviously."

He takes in my filthy travel state with one sweep of his eyes. "The journey back from where?"

The attendants disappear with Kellyn around the corner, and I grab Petrik's arm so we can follow as we talk.

"The journey back from *where*?" I repeat incredulously. "Honestly, Petrik, did you not notice we were gone?"

"Well, you didn't tell me you were going anywhere, now, did you? Who shot Kellyn?"

"Ravis's men."

"Ravis's men are here?"

"Not yet, but his army is marching. I need to talk to Skiro! But first, what about Temra? I need to know. Tell me!"

My arms come to Petrik's shoulders, forcing him to give me his full attention.

Petrik's face falls, and a pained expression crosses his features.

I feel all the air leave me.

My feet lose their traction, and I fall to the ground right there in a heap. "No."

I bury my face in my hands and weep.

I hear some shuffling about, and I think Petrik might be

scuffing his shoes on the floor. I want to be angry with him for not showing more emotion, but I suppose he's had well over a month to process Temra's death. I'm just now hearing about it.

My cries only get louder as time goes on. For once, I don't care who sees me or who hears me. I don't have any space in my head to worry over what someone else will think about my display. I can't think past the pain where my heart used to be.

"Ziva?"

I sniffle as I bolt upright, recognizing that voice.

It's my sister. It's Temra. Unless I've grown so hysterical that I'm now seeing things.

She looks different. Her face is so careful. Almost hesitant, like she doesn't want to break me.

I throw myself at her, hug her to me as though I could crush her body into mine. Fuse us together so she can never be separated from me again. Temra's arms come up, enfolding me with just as much force.

"I missed you," she says.

I don't have the words to explain how I felt while we were separated, so I stay silent.

Until I remember what happened before I saw her.

"The hells, Petrik!" I yell.

I spin around and plant my fist right in his face.

"Ah!" we say at the same time. His hands go to his nose, while I shake out my throbbing fingers. I haven't gotten any better at striking people. It still hurts every time.

"What was that for?" he asks around his fingers. A few drops of blood run onto his upper lip.

"You let me think she was dead!"

"What are you talking about?"

"Why did you hit him?" Temra asks.

"Your face!" I say to Petrik. "You looked about to give me bad news."

Petrik looks me up and down, taking in my disheveled state. He appears utterly confused.

"Shit," he says suddenly, and he steps forward, grabs Temra by her arm, and yanks her away from me.

"What the hell?" I ask.

Petrik uses his body as a shield between me and my sister, and I want to punch him again.

"Let go of me!" Temra says to him, trying to shake him off.

"Stop it!" Petrik says. "Ziva, what was the first magicked weapon you ever made on your own?"

"What is going on?" I ask.

Temra tries to sidestep Petrik, but he moves with her. She looks on him with such malice, as though disgusted just by being in his proximity.

"Answer the question, Ziva," he says.

"Why?" I ask.

"Because I saw you yesterday evening when you arrived at the palace, so clearly there are two of you walking around, and I need to know which is the fake."

At that, Temra rounds on him. "Ziva came back yesterday and you didn't tell me?"

"How was I supposed to know she didn't come to see you?" Petrik asks.

Their bickering is taking off to speeds I can't keep up with, but my stomach drops to my toes. Someone with my face is walking around.

"Midnight!" I shout, breaking up the pair. "My first weapon was Temra's shortsword. Honestly, the other me didn't want to see Temra immediately and that didn't clue you in that it wasn't me?"

"You were different, but I thought it was because of whatever Ravis put you through. How was I supposed to guess magic was involved straightaway?"

"Ravis?" Temra asks. "What does Ravis have to do with anything?"

"The cotton spinner is clearly working for him," Petrik says. "First the linen hiding Serutha's door, and now this. He must have gotten ahold of her after Kymora was captured."

"Did you see Kellyn yesterday, too?" I ask.

Petrik nods.

"Why are we talking about Ravis and Serutha and hidden doors?" Temra asks. "What am I missing?"

At that, the guiltiest look I've ever seen crosses Petrik's features. He looks embarrassed before he turns to me. "We need to talk in private after we root out the imposter."

"When was the last time you saw . . . me?" I ask him.

"Last night. We talked about"—his eyes flit to Temra—"things, and then you went to bed. But not before Skiro asked you to have lunch with him . . . the next day. I thought it odd that you accepted so readily."

"What time is it?" I ask.

"Midday," Temra replies.

"And where is the prince now?"

"Oh no," Petrik says.

Temra and I race side by side, just behind Petrik.

"Just so you know," she says, "you really smell."

"I've been traveling!"

Petrik's sapphire scholar's robes disappear around the next corner, and Temra and I slide after him.

"Yes, but from Ravis's Territory?" she asks. "Why would you be there?"

"Stop talking and focus on running!" Petrik yells over his shoulder. "Guards!" he calls to men as we pass them by, and they fall into step with us.

We reach some doorway, burst through, and then find Skiro seated at a private table tucked away in a cozy room. He'd been laughing when we entered, but it cuts off when he sees us.

"Petrik, what is going on?" he asks.

I feel my eyebrows raise at what we find in the room. Skiro has his hand on the arm of the girl sitting next to him, and he's leaning forward.

Toward a girl with my face.

She jumps to her feet, comes behind Skiro's chair, and raises a butterknife to his neck. Not the deadliest of weapons, but effective if she jabs it into just the right spot.

"That's not Ziva Tellion," Petrik says. "We've imposters in the palace."

"Yes, I think I've gathered that now." Skiro groans. "And we were having such a lovely time, too."

I feel my face heat at the close proximity we found them in, but that's hardly my fault. I wasn't the one seducing the prince. I couldn't seduce anyone if my life depended on it.

"Put down your weapons," the girl with my face says.

"She doesn't even sound like me!" I say.

"I thought you were coming down with something," Petrik says defensively.

"Weapons," the imposter says again. "Down. Now."

Skiro grunts. "Do as she says."

I hear a clattering as the guards behind us drop their spears. Temra lowers her sword, Midnight, which I now note is black as night, warning us that someone who means us harm is nearby.

The girl backs away with the prince until she's cornered at the wall; then she slides along it until she's at the door. "Follow us and he dies."

"Could you loosen up just a bit?" Skiro asks. "Ow!"

She must have gripped him harder. We watch, our feet rooted to the floor as they walk back down the corridor. It's a slow trek down, down, down. Just before they disappear out of sight, the imposter gives Skiro a shove in our direction and runs.

"After her!" Petrik yells, now that Skiro is free.

The guards are already moving; a few break free to surround the prince while the rest race after the girl.

Temra, Petrik, and I reach Skiro.

"Are you hurt?" Petrik asks.

"Only my pride," Skiro says in return.

"She wasn't here to assassinate you," Temra observes. "She had plenty of time to kill you otherwise."

"What did you talk about?" Petrik asks.

Skiro finishes righting his robes and waves off the guards, who give him some space but keep their eyes peeled for other intruders.

"I was wooing her," Skiro groans. "I've always had a thing for tall women. You know that."

I feel my face heat up and turn my gaze to the ground.

"But what did you say? Did she ask you anything?" Petrik wants to know.

Skiro lets out a groan. "I thought she was the smithy. She wanted to know how many men to make weapons for, wanted to know what fortifications we already had in place so she could expand on them with her magic. Whoever sent her wanted to learn about our defenses."

"It was Ravis," I say, looking up. "Kellyn and I saw his army on the road behind us. He must have sent spies ahead."

That gets Skiro's attention. "Ravis is marching an army here? How far behind you was he?"

"I couldn't say. We didn't take the road, but not more than three to four weeks, surely."

"Less than a month." Skiro swallows audibly. He steps away until his back hits the wall for support. "We don't have an army here. There are city guards. Castle guards. A handful of men and women."

We all fall silent, and Skiro's personal guard fidgets at the news.

I see the moment Skiro realizes he probably shouldn't have said those thoughts aloud. The last thing he needs is rumors to spread before he can take the time to process the situation. He stands up straight. "But that's for us to work out tomorrow. One problem at a time. Let's deal with these imposters first."

After a few minutes, a guard comes jogging down the hallway. He bows to his prince before brandishing something. "There's no sign of her, sire, but we found this."

I recognize it instantly. It's the same kind of mask Kellyn pulled off the guard in Lisady's Capital, the one who wore his face. A variety of blues stitched in a scale from light to dark. The mask of my own face. I know that whoever puts it on will instantly look like me.

"There was another," Petrik says. "Find the mercenary and arrest him. The real Kellyn is in the hospital."

As before, I'm forced to wash up before they'll allow me in the infirmary to check up on Kellyn. Temra offers to take me up to her room, where we can have a bath brought in, but Petrik steps in front of me.

"Ziva, a word in private, please?" he asks.

"Not a chance," Temra says in return, one hand coming to rest on her hip. "You're not having any private conversations. You're keeping something from me."

"Ziva, please—" he tries again.

Temra cuts him off. "I need to know what happened. Why were you in Ravis's Territory, and how is it that Kellyn got shot?"

I try to remember the conversation earlier. I was panicked about Kellyn's injuries and the realization that there were imposters around us. I can't remember much else.

And what is Petrik's game? Why did he lie to my sister?

"When we arrived in Skiro's Capital," I say, "Serutha wasn't here. She'd been kidnapped by Ravis."

Petrik groans at my words and hides his head in his hands. I feel a little guilty, but my first loyalty is to my sister, not my friend.

I continue, "The three of us used a portal to travel to Ravis's Territory to find her. We did, and she and Petrik made it back through the portal. Kellyn and I were captured. It was awful," I rush to add. "I didn't know if you were safe. If you survived. I was trapped a territory away, trying to escape to get to you. I'm sorry it took so long."

For the second time today, Petrik gets socked in the face.

But Temra doesn't stop there. She throws herself at him, fists and feet flying. Petrik holds his arms up to try and stop any more blows.

I grab her and haul her off him, her limbs flying every which way as she tries to leap back at him.

"She was in danger! She was captured!" Temra shouts at the scholar. "Oh, just when I started to consider forgiving you for keeping secrets about Kymora! Then I find out that you went and *lied* to me about where my *sister* was. How could you? Put me down, Ziva!"

"Not until you calm down," I say.

"I'll calm down when I get some answers!" she shrieks.

Petrik works his jaw; I think her fist clipped it hard. A popping sound comes out of his head.

"I was trying to spare you," Petrik says feebly.

"What?" Temra says. I don't think she heard him over the sounds of her fidgeting and grunting. But her body finally goes still, so I set her down but prepare myself to intervene if need be.

"You were so injured," he explains. "You almost didn't make it. I didn't know if you could handle learning Ziva was in danger."

"Oh, so now I'm some delicate thing!" Temra snaps.

"No, no one would ever say that!" Petrik says. "Ziva had just sacrificed herself to save you. I wasn't about to let that sacrifice be wasted by you plunging yourself into danger to go after her. Ziva wouldn't have wanted it."

"You mean *you* wouldn't have wanted it," she spits back at him. "What about what I wanted? I deserved the truth!"

"I know you. You wouldn't have been able to help yourself. You would have marched across the country and stormed Ravis's gates. You can't take on an army alone. You can't—"

She hits him again before I can react.

"I hate you," she says before stomping off.

Petrik's nose is bleeding again. He hunches rather than stands upright.

"Petrik," I say. "Thank you. Truly. You saved her more than once." And then I follow after Temra.

I hadn't seen much of Skiro's palace the first time I was here. My mind was set on saving Temra and little else.

But now, as I run after my sister, I'm taken through unfamiliar passages. Unlike Ravis's empty halls, Skiro's are fit to bursting. Tapestries and carpets insulate the rock. Portraits line the walls, and I wonder eerily if any of them are magic portals to other places in the world. The artist's signature is the same, a looping mess of letters that I can't actually read. Any empty space of stone has been painted directly. Animals, sceneries, anything living and flourishing.

Skiro is a lover of all kinds of art, and it shows in every bit of his palace. He has a fondness for creation, not destruction. There's no way he'll be prepared for the fight Ravis is bringing to him.

Temra lets herself into a set of rooms, leaving the door open so I can follow.

When we fled Lirasu, we took nothing with us save essentials. No personal trinkets or mementos, so Temra doesn't have anything from our old lives to decorate her rooms at the palace. But her walls are filled with books—gifts from Petrik, I'd wager—and a weapons rack has been recently mounted to one wall.

She's too angry to talk right away about what happened, so I bathe in silence while she paces back and forth in her room, mumbling her fury to herself.

As soon as I'm clean and in borrowed clothes, I tell Temra I'm leaving to check on Kellyn. As much as I'd love to stay, I already know she's safe.

I need to know how Kellyn is doing.

He's unconscious but clean when I find him, and the arrow is gone, which has to be a good sign. Serutha stands over him with her fingers held out over the wound.

I don't say a word, lest I break her concentration.

Instead, I move to Kellyn's other side and take the hand attached to his uninjured arm.

"He'll be fine," the healer says, her eyes closed. "I've cleared the infection. All that's left now is to mend the muscle and skin."

"Thank you," I say.

"No, thank *you*," she says. "You saved me. This is the least I could do."

"You also mended my sister. I think I am still in your debt."

She shakes her head, and her dark eyes flutter open. "This is what I do. It's what I love. Surely, you can relate? I've heard quite a lot about you since I've been back. You work with metal the way I work with flesh. I hope you don't mind Petrik telling me. Once he got to talking—apologizing, really—for revealing who I was to you, I think he felt the need to even the score."

I shrug. "I don't care that you know." I watch as Kellyn's flesh stitches back together under Serutha's careful ministrations. "Your ability is far more impressive than mine."

"It's not a contest."

"No, but you save life, whereas I seem to be good only for threatening it."

Serutha massages her left hand with her right when she's done. "I would wager there are hundreds out there who would testify otherwise. I'm sure your weapons have saved them in ways you will never hear about. The only difference between you and me is that I get to see the results of my work firsthand."

The words are kind, and I accept them. For now. "How does it work? Your ability?" I ask. "You're the only other person with magic I've ever met."

She smiles, takes a seat opposite me. And though she can't be much older than I am, she feels older, like she's seen more of life than I have somehow. I suppose she's witnessed many die while honing her craft and learning. It would age anyone.

"I doubt that's true. Didn't you meet Elany while you were trapped with Ravis?"

"Elany. Yes, she followed me practically everywhere I went under Ravis's orders. She's gifted with magic?"

"Yes. The carefully crafted camouflage over my prison door? That was her doing."

It takes me far too long to put it together.

"Elany is the cotton spinner!" I ought to be shocked. Instead, I'm enraged. "How could she betray her own kind!"

"She has her loyalties, just like we have ours."

"But Ravis is awful."

"You don't need to tell me. Elany is the one who needs to figure that out. I hope she does it sooner rather than later."

A moment of silence passes as I process the new information. The invisible assassins on the road, the soldier wearing Kellyn's face, the prison camouflage—that was all Elany. She's caused me unimaginable grief, and I had no idea she was right in front of me for weeks.

What would you have done if you'd known?

Nothing, I realize. I could do nothing while Ravis's prisoner. I suppose things would have still played out as they did.

I sigh as I try to force the tension from my body.

"Do you still wish to know how my ability works?" Serutha says, perhaps thinking to distract me from the pain of the past.

Either way, I'm glad for it. "Yes."

"I can sense all the parts of the body, and I can feel what's broken or dying. And then I guide it. I encourage bones to move back into place, tell muscle to knit itself back together. I ask the infection to leave. I talk to the body, though not aloud, and it listens."

"I talk to metal in much the same way," I say. "But sometimes aloud."

"It's fascinating how gifts so different can still be so alike."

"Do you think we're gifted? That these abilities are blessings from the Sister Goddesses?" Or are we cursed? Forced to be pawns in the hands of those in positions of power?

"The Goddesses created the first woman in their image, who then gave birth to the human race. I believe that they've gifted a select few of us even more than their images. We have the ability to create as they do. Not on a cosmic scale, but a smaller one."

"For what purpose?" I ask.

"To see what we would do with that kind of power. I've heard some speculate that we are Ebanarra's creations, but I think we were made by Tasminya."

"The chaotic Goddess. Why?"

"Doesn't it just feel right? Like she wanted to spice up the world with more flavors? With magic? Just to see what would happen."

My whole life, I've only ever wanted to have control over everything. What I say and do. How people react to what I say and do. I always thought I must take after Ebanarra. But Serutha's words make far more sense.

Maybe there is no other purpose than to just live our best with the time and gifts given to us.

"Is there anyone else like us living here?" I ask. I want to meet more. I want to know what else the magic users of this world can do.

"Yes, but I will let them reveal themselves to you when and if they are ready. Just as I will keep your identity secret and hope that you will do the same with mine."

"Of course."

"Good. I will leave you alone with your man now. I've done my part. I don't know when he will wake. Healing is exhausting, and the body needs time to recuperate. Don't force him awake before he's ready."

"I understand. Thank you again."

She nods before disappearing.

The rest of the hospital is mostly empty. I spot one woman sleeping on a cot in a corner, but she looks to be another caretaker, sneaking in a much needed nap, rather than a patient. It would seem that Serutha makes quick work of anyone who comes through the infirmary.

I don't want to risk waking Kellyn since Serutha warned against it, so I don't say anything. I hold his hand, stroke his fingers, let my fingers brush back his hair.

I really am fond of this brute.

CHAPTER SIXTEEN

When the hour grows late, I return to my sister's room. Temra is not ready for bed but, rather, she stands in the middle of the chamber with a short-sword that isn't Midnight held in her left hand. I carefully dart around her and settle myself on the bed while I watch her go through fighting stances.

"It's weighted," she says before I can ask. "I'm learning to train with my less dominant hand, as well as up my endurance levels."

"Clever," I say.

She spins and thrusts, practicing drills that someone taught her in secret. She knew I would never approve of her training to be a soldier, so she did it without my knowledge or permission. I've come to terms with it, mostly.

A light sweat breaks across her brow after a few minutes, and I watch in silence. She's so determined. So fierce. Though I'm sure she practices like this daily, I can tell tonight's exercise is because of a certain boy and his lies.

When she's tired herself out a bit, I say, "You should forgive him."

"I will not."

"Temra, he saved you when I could not."

"He prevented me from saving you when I *could have*."

"It's all right. I got out. I saved myself."

I saved myself.

The words rise so effortlessly, yet I'm startled by them. Kellyn was right, damn him.

I saved myself. I am not helpless. I can do things without my sister.

A pleasant warmth floods my whole being, as I realize a core truth about myself.

"But you shouldn't have had to do it without me," Temra says. "I should have been there."

"You needed to heal."

Her panting makes her words almost unintelligible. "It's not okay, Ziva. You always get to do all the saving! You saved us from Kymora. You saved me from a cult in Thersa. You saved Ghadra from Secret Eater. You saved me from death. You get to do all the saving, while I'm the one helpless. *I want to do the saving.* It's what I've trained for. It's what I've always wanted. And yet I'm the one unconscious while you get to go on another adventure!"

The sword slips from her hand on the next move, and she grunts as she goes to retrieve it.

"You think I've enjoyed any of this?" I ask. "You think I liked running for my life and having to protect you from danger? You think I liked wondering if you were dead, knowing it would be my fault?"

"*I* enjoyed it," she says while she resumes her workout. "I loved it. Being on the run. Fighting for my life. I've never felt more alive."

"And when you were dying? When you took a sword to the arm and lung? How did that feel?" The words come out snappish, but I don't apologize.

"That part obviously wasn't great, but the rest of it!"

I will never be able to forget just how different we are.

"So you're mad at Petrik because he denied you an adventure?" I ask.

She rounds on me, lets the sword point stab straight up into the air. "I'm *furious* because he *lied to me*. I'm inconsolable because you were in danger, and I didn't know about it. We're sisters. That means we look out for each other. Not *you* always looking out for *me*. When am I ever going to give back when you're doing everything all the time?"

"Temra, you don't owe me anything."

"But I do. I owe you everything. My life. Everything that I own back home. Everything I am is because of you. And Petrik is a no-good liar. If he weren't the brother of the prince—another fact he kept from us, I might add—I'd gut him right now."

She returns the sword to the rack before sitting on the floor to stretch. She reaches out with her hands and touches her feet, keeping her legs straight.

"You don't mean that," I say.

"I do. If he values his life, he should stay out of my sight. Who knows what I might do if provoked?"

"He traveled with us all over Ghadra. He sided with us against his own mother. He fought and killed for you. He came with me to save Serutha." *He loves you* is what I don't say but want to. "You didn't see him after you were wounded. He was just as inconsolable as I was. He broke a promise to Serutha by revealing her identity and leading us to the one person who could save you."

"He let you get left behind. How can I forgive that? He chose me over you."

I open my mouth, then shut it, realizing just how much of a hypocrite I would be if I said anything. Kellyn let Temra get hurt, and I held that against him, convinced I could never forgive him of it.

Though I've already forgiven him for it, hearing Temra's own thoughts helps me realize just how unfair I'd been to him.

I want to tell Temra that she had it easy. She didn't know where I was or what I was doing. She had no clue that I was in danger. She didn't find out until I was already back safe and sound. So really, what does she have to be angry about?

"Will you tell me the story?" she asks. "How did you get caught, and how did you escape?"

"That was actually Kellyn's fault." I tell her all about how the idiot sacrificed himself for her in order for the rest of us to escape, and then how I stayed behind to help him.

"You stayed. On purpose?"

"He would have died without me."

She looks inward, and I can't even guess where her thoughts are spinning to, so I continue. Telling her how Kellyn told Ravis what I could do. And then how I got us out. How we were followed on the road. How he was injured.

"Sounds like I owe a lot to the mercenary," Temra says at the end of it. Then she wraps me in a hug.

"Can you believe him?" I ask, relishing the feeling of her arms around me. "Such an idiot."

"He has a knack for getting under your skin."

"No, he doesn't."

"Oh, yes, he does. And he can't win. He lets something bad happen to me, and you hate him. He saves me, and you hate him."

"I don't hate him."

"I know you don't. I just hope he knows that."

"It's good for him to stew a bit," I joke.

She laughs, and I can feel her head shake against my shoulder. "I think he's perfect for you. If you two could just get over yourselves, I think you would both be happy."

"You could say the same thing about you and Petrik."

Her muscles go taut. "No. He's a boring imbecile who cares more about books than he does people."

"Boring?" I ask.

"Yes."

"You find his stories fascinating. The two of you would talk for hours while we were on the road together."

"Fine, he's not boring, but he still doesn't care enough about people. Certainly not enough to prevent himself from lying to them."

I let out a sigh. "I might argue that he cares enough *to lie*. He cares so much that he's willing to risk you hating him to keep you safe. It proves that he cares about you more than himself."

"I—" She cuts off. She tries to pull away, but I hug her to me more tightly.

I change the subject to make her feel better. "You're sweaty."

"Then maybe you should let go of me."

"Never." I grin.

I want to stay up all night talking to Temra, but I'm so weary from all the travel and worrying over Temra and Kellyn and everything else. Everyone is finally okay, and I'm free to just pass out in Temra's warm, comfy bed.

My eyes are crusty when I resurface. My limbs ache, and I really need to relieve myself.

But the true tell that I've been asleep for a long time is Kellyn sitting in the chair in the corner of the room. He has a book in front of him, and he turns a page idly. He crosses his legs at the ankles in front of him.

"You *can* read," I say. My throat sounds croaky from disuse.

Kellyn looks up at me, gives me a smile that warms every part of me, and then sets the book aside. "It's Petrik's. The story he wrote about our journey escaping from Kymora."

"Is it any good?"

"It's exceptional. He has a real talent for words. Makes us sound much more heroic than we actually are."

"I don't think that's possible, where you're concerned."

The mercenary rises to his six and a half feet, treads over to the bed, and sits on the edge of it. "How are you feeling?" he asks.

"I'm fine. I'm not the one who was shot. How's your arm?"

He rolls up his sleeve to reveal a thin white scar. "It's almost like it was never there. It's a little stiff, but Serutha says the feeling should go away after a while."

"I'm so glad. And your ear?"

Kellyn blanches, before hesitantly lifting his hair off the left side of his face.

"It looks good!" I say.

"It looks hideous," he says, lowering his red locks almost immediately.

"Don't be ridiculous."

"I'm not. I'm missing half an ear. It doesn't look right. And I don't hear quite as well on that side."

"But the skin is perfectly healed around the cut. You're going to be okay."

Kellyn doesn't say anything, staring at the wall behind me.

"Are you . . . upset because I'm the reason he hurt you?" I ask hesitantly.

"Twins, no! Ziva, I don't blame you at all. How could you have known that's what he would do? You saved me! You got me out of there. You brought me here."

"Then what is it?"

He sighs. "I'm worried others might look at me differently. That they'll find me . . . less."

"That's stupid. Nobody would think that. If anything, it's proof that you're *more*. That you survived something horrible and are stronger for it. You're allowed to feel upset for what happened, but don't be so hard on yourself. And if anyone treats you any differently, you tell me. I'll give them a piece of my mind."

Kellyn's grin is just a ghost of a smile as he looks down at me. "And what about you?"

"What about me?"

"What if you treat me differently?"

He's not—he doesn't seriously think I wouldn't want him anymore because of it?

"Kellyn," I ask, "just how vain do you think I am? Just how vain are *you*?"

"I'm being ridiculous."

"Yes!"

He nods to himself once, as though satisfied, then gives me a true smile.

And then I *really* can't ignore my body any longer.

"Excuse me for a moment." I rise and go to the washroom, shutting myself in to take care of my basic needs. When done, I spot a hairbrush on the vanity and take the time to run it through my hair. Then I glance in the mirror above the washbasin.

It may be silly, but I haven't had much time to look at myself over the last few months. It's not like we had any mirrors on the road or while we were in prison. Kellyn's mother owned one, but it was mounted on the wall in her bedroom, and it felt impolite to invade her personal space.

My face has bloomed with freckles, more than I've ever seen on me. All the travel, which has exposed me to the sun, has caused them to multiply. They're darker across my cheeks, lighter across my lips. My short hair has lengthened. It's always grown in quickly. When we fled from Kymora, Temra cut my straight brown hair down to my chin. Now it brushes my shoulders, the ends flipping outward slightly. I used to wear my hair up in a ponytail, but it's been too short for that for so long. And now I don't own a band. Maybe I could locate one eventually—Temra doesn't have any in here.

I'm stalling, I know it. I look into my own blue eyes. *It's all right. There's nothing to be scared of. It's just Kellyn.*

But he wouldn't be here if he didn't want to talk. And talking is scary.

As if there's anything further I could do to embarrass myself in front of this man. We've been through hell together.

I take a deep breath before leaving.

Kellyn's not in the room.

Yet, instead of relief, I feel irritation.

I rush for the door and find Kellyn striding away, about fifty feet down the hall.

"Hey!" I shout after him. He stops and turns.

I don't want to yell this conversation down the hall, so I jog over to him, hating the way he watches me the whole time.

"Why did you leave?" I ask.

"You left first. I assumed you were politely giving me the brush-off."

"No! I really did have to use the washroom."

"You took a while."

"Well, I needed to prepare myself to talk to you first, and then I came out to find you gone." I realize how stupid that must sound, but it's too late to take back the words.

"You needed to prepare yourself?"

"Yes. Sometimes I have to calm myself down before a conversation."

"Were we about to have a serious one?"

I can't look him in the face, so I settle for just below it, at his strong neck. "I don't know, but you know how I am. I get all worked up and have to talk myself off a ledge."

"Then shouldn't you have been relieved that I left? No scary talking?"

My eyes flit to the ground. "I should have. But I wasn't."

"No?"

I force my gaze to meet his. "No."

"Tell me, why is it so different talking to me now than it was when we were traveling on the road together?"

"Because before it was a necessity to be together. Silences weren't awkward"—not always anyway—"because you can't possibly talk all day every day. But now, if there's silence, it's because I'm failing at the conversation." I groan. "Does that make any sense at all?"

"Yes." His fingers twitch, as though he wishes to reach out and touch me, but he holds himself back.

Does he . . . want to touch me?

I remember his words back in the woods, when he was likely

concussed. He wants an equal partner. He doesn't want to be the one to do everything. Instigate everything.

And I do want to hold his hand.

So even though it terrifies me, I reach out and brush his fingers before clasping his hand in mine. Kellyn's brows jump up on his forehead, but he schools his features in the next moment.

"You really scared me," I say. "You were delirious with fever on the road. I wasn't sure if you were going to make it."

I step up beside him, and we both walk wherever it was that Kellyn was headed before. My heart beats quicker than usual at our close proximity. I try to make myself relax.

"With you taking such good care of me?" he asks. "How could I not?" He gives my hand a gentle squeeze before threading our fingers together. Somehow it feels even more intense than simply having our palms pressed together.

I really do like touching him.

Kellyn seems to know exactly where he's going, so I let him lead.

"How long was I asleep?" I ask.

"About twenty-six hours. I only just woke up in the middle of last night. Temra asked if I'd keep watch over you while she went to the training grounds. She's practicing even harder than before with the news of Ravis on the way."

She can practice all she likes, but I have no intention of letting her get anywhere near Ravis or his army.

"Where are we going?" I ask.

"To find you some breakfast," he says.

"Oh."

"You sound surprised."

"I'm not used to someone else taking care of me or thinking about what I might need." I clamp my eyes shut and immediately backtrack. "Not that Temra doesn't think about me. I meant someone else, other than my sister."

"Don't get used to it," he says. "I owe you one for saving me from Ravis, but after this we're even."

I laugh, feeling some of the tension in me leave. "Finding me breakfast isn't quite the same as me getting you out of a highly defended castle."

"All right. You get two breakfasts; now stop being greedy."

Kellyn pushes through wide double doors, and I smell fresh bread and melting butter. My mouth begins to water.

"I sniffed out the kitchen the second I awoke," Kellyn says. "The cook loves us, so we can have free rein of this place whenever we want."

A thin woman with her hair in braids on top of her head pulls a pan from the oven. She's young, maybe mid-twenties, and she's quite pretty.

Kellyn walks us right up to her. "Paulia, hello again!"

"Kellyn!" she says. Ignoring me, she throws her arms around him, and Kellyn lets go of my hand to return the gesture.

I feel myself frowning, my appetite leaving.

She asks after Kellyn's arm, and he shows it to her. Though if Kellyn woke last night, how long ago could it have been since she last saw him? And why are they so chummy already?

Kellyn asks how her morning was, and they chat among themselves as though there's no one else in the room. Normally, I adore being left out of conversations, because coming up with something to say is always a chore. But not now. Right now, I feel like blurting out anything just to keep this Paulia from looking at him. From touching him.

"I have someone I know you're wanting to meet," Kellyn says at last. He seems startled for a moment when he sees my expression, but he presses on. "This is Ziva."

Paulia's whole face lights up. She lets go of Kellyn's shoulder and rushes at me. Her head only comes up to my chest, so the hug is a bit awkward, but she pulls away as though it was some gift. "I can't thank you enough. You have given me my whole world back. You come by here anytime you want, and I will make you whatever you wish. What will you have this morning?"

I'm overcome by her generosity and sincerity, yet still battling the jealousy that's trying to take over.

I look to Kellyn for help.

"Paulia is with Serutha," he explains. "They're engaged."

"Oh . . . oh!" I say, turning back to the warm woman before me. I saved Serutha from Ravis. That's why she's grateful. It takes my mind far too long to process all of this. "It was nothing. I'm happy she's back and grateful she healed my sister and my—and Kellyn."

Kellyn looks like he might be fighting a grin at my stumble.

"I still owe you everything all the same, so what will you have this morning?" Paulia asks.

"Is that bread I smell?" I ask.

She presents the pan that just came out of the oven. "Rolls. Will you have some?" She sets before me a plate and silverware, a slab of butter, and a pot of honey.

Now I like her even more.

Paulia fills the kitchen with a steady stream of chatter, and I love only having to nod or answer questions occasionally. She has a natural way of putting people at ease. Kellyn helps himself to a roll, butters it, and drizzles honey on top. I watch as he takes a bite, swipes at a stray drop of honey on his lip with his tongue. My mouth starts to water again.

When he catches me staring, I look at the floor, mortified.

My body grows uncomfortably hot, and I can't seem to take part in the conversation any longer. I think Kellyn might excuse us because suddenly he's ushering me away, our hands clasped together once more.

His strides are so long, I almost have to jog to keep up. While most of my height is located in my torso, Kellyn's is all in the legs. He shoves open some door, pokes his head in, and then pulls me after him.

I only catch a quick glimpse of the room—an unused bed-chamber. White sheets cover everything. The air is somewhat stale, and a thin layer of dust coats everything.

"Are you all right?" Kellyn asks. "Was that too much? I know she's a talker, but—"

I launch myself at him as soon as I realize that we're alone. We're alone and safe, and for once there isn't any immediate danger.

His back slams against the nearest wall right before my lips cover his, swallowing his gasp. He tastes like butter and honey, and if that weren't sweet enough, it is nothing compared to when he brushes my hair back with gentle fingers, cups my cheeks with his hands, angles me just where he wants me so he can taste me in return.

My hands slide down his chest, loving the hardness of him through his clothes. When I reach the end, I'm startled by a soft warmth.

His shirt has ridden up, and my fingers find bare skin.

Either he hasn't noticed or doesn't care that I'm touching his skin, because nothing changes in the movements of his lips. So, tentatively, I press the flat of my palm against his bare stomach.

He gasps, and I pull away as though I've been burned.

"I'm sorry!" Oh no, I ruined it. That was too much. I should have—

Kellyn yanks me right back. His lips find mine again, and with one of his hands, he returns my palm to his skin.

But I'm unsure based on his previous reaction. What if I do another thing he doesn't like? Is he only humoring me? I find myself too scared to move, so I try to ignore the feeling of his skin, focusing on his lips instead.

Kellyn kisses along my jaw, bites my earlobe before blowing cool breath along my skin. "You only surprised me," he whispers, his voice deliciously husky. "I love it when you touch me."

I think about the way his arms move up and down my back. The way I feel when his fingers brush my cheeks. When he touches me, I feel alive. Is that what he feels, too?

I let my second hand join the first, and then my fingers rove to his bare back, where I apply pressure, fusing us together.

Kellyn makes a humming noise, and I love the sound of it. I think I could spend years kissing this man, learning the noises he makes, the places he likes to be touched the most.

One of his hands slides down my side until he reaches my thigh. He grips it, raises it up, so the inside of my leg brushes against his strong muscles.

And then he tries the same thing with the other leg. Only, then I won't be able to balance myself. Does he mean for me to . . . ?

I jump, and he catches me effortlessly. He spins us, rests my back against the wall, holds me up with his strong arms. His shirt is cinched up between us, and I rake my nails up and down his back, loving the way his muscles tense up underneath me.

I don't understand. Temra always becomes so bored with men, hopping from one to the next. She seems to need variety to keep herself entertained. But I don't feel that way. I want to learn all the different positions I can kiss this one man in. I think I could do this all day without tiring.

After what could be one hour or five, Kellyn lets me slide back to the floor. I almost don't catch myself in time, but he holds me in place, our foreheads resting together while we share the air between us.

"I thought *I* decided when we stopped kissing," I say.

He laughs, kisses the tip of my nose, and takes my hand. "If we don't go find your sister, she'll come looking for you."

"She'd never find us in here."

"You're probably right. But we have a meeting to get to."

"A meeting?"

"With Skiro and Petrik. About Ravis's approaching army?"

"Why didn't you say anything before?"

"You distracted me."

"So it's my fault?"

Kellyn leads us out into the hallway, takes us up a level of stairs. "Most definitely, but I loved every second of it."

With a smile, I say, "Me too. Attending a meeting sounds less fun."

"If you want, we can go back to kissing when the meeting is over."

"No!" I say.

"That's a strong response."

"I mean, we can't *plan* when we're going to kiss."

"Can't we?"

"No. Because if I know it's coming, then I'll overthink it. I'll be stressed and panicking until it happens. I won't be able to focus on anything else."

"Why?"

"I'll worry over all the ways I'll do it wrong."

"You can't do it wrong," he says confidently.

"But my mind will worry that I might. I can't control it. It just is."

"Fine, we won't kiss after the meeting. Is that better?"

"... No."

He laughs so hard, we have to stop in the middle of the hall-way. When he's done, he purses his lips, as though he wishes to say something. Then, thinking better of it, he simply tugs me after him.

CHAPTER
SEVENTEEN

The meeting room consists of a large oak table with elaborate carvings running up the legs and sides. The Southern Mountains are depicted in perfect clarity, the table legs showcasing streams and trees. The chairs have hand-stitched cushions, each with a native blossom in exquisite detail.

When we admit ourselves into the room, Petrik stands from where he'd been sitting. "About time! Kellyn, I told you to wake her if she wasn't up by four o'clock."

"She was up."

Petrik hisses between his teeth, "Then why are you both so late? I think we can agree the situation is grave enough to warrant some seriousness." Petrik cocks his head to one side. "Why are your arms covered in dust?"

Kellyn notices the gray streaks on himself and tries to brush them away with his fingers.

"And, Ziva, it's all over you, too. What have you been doing?"

I swallow, feel my cheeks heat.

But, like usual, Temra rescues me. She's suddenly there. "Why don't you stop embarrassing them and resume the meeting?"

"I thought you weren't speaking to me," he says. "And I'm not embarrassing them. I'm asking a perfectly valid question."

"They're both covered in dust, Petrik. What do you *suppose* they were doing in a secluded, abandoned area?"

Petrik's eyes widen, and he stammers a bit before retaking his seat.

"Idiot," Temra mumbles.

"What did we miss?" Kellyn asks.

"They caught the spy wearing your face," she says. "Unfortunately, he took his own life before we could question him. He had something on him. A poison of some sort."

"So we have nothing?" I ask.

"Just the warning you've brought us. Come sit. We're discussing a siege."

The table is full of empty seats, but I take one next to Temra, while Kellyn occupies the chair on my other side.

It isn't until I sit down that I find Skiro's eyes on me. He grins, winks, and I feel hot all over again. Did he just overhear the conversation between me and my friends? Or does this have to do with how attracted he was to the imposter wearing my face?

To you, Ziva. If he was attracted to someone wearing your face, then he's attracted to you.

"Ziva," the prince says, and I cringe at being singled out. "I haven't gotten a chance yet to thank you for bringing Serutha back to us. You have done me a great service, and I shall not forget it."

I nod, unable to do anything more.

"As I was saying," a woman I don't recognize says, "there are just over three thousand people in the city. We can fit that many within the palace walls, but it'll be tight."

"Bring them in," Skiro says. "If it can be done, then it must. It's the only way to ensure Ravis doesn't slaughter innocents on his way to the palace."

"And when he reaches the castle?" a man I don't know asks.

"We negotiate," Skiro says. "There has to be a peaceful solution. If Ravis wants something that will spare my people, then we need to give it to him."

Temra leans in next to me. "The man is Saydan, and he oversees all the guards in the palace and city. The woman is Bida. She's a sort of caretaker over the city and its people. She's been helping Skiro's Territory find its feet when the land was split. She knows numbers, food, trade—all of it."

"And the last woman in the room?" I ask.

"Isulay. She is the person who keeps the castle running. She knows who lives here at any given time, servants and all. She'll be working closely with Bida to prepare for the siege."

When I look back up, Kellyn is speaking. "Ravis doesn't want to negotiate, Prince Skiro. He has every intention of claiming all of Ghadra for himself. Ziva and I were there. We saw his forges and armories. We saw his army. I don't think he would bring so many if he intended to talk."

"That's possible," Skiro says, "but I know my brother. He's reasonable, even if he is ambitious. And if we can come to some sort of arrangement, then we have to try."

The man, Saydan, nods in agreement. "There are only some one hundred trained men in all of the city. We do not have the numbers to withstand a battle of any kind. Negotiation must be attempted."

"And if not," Skiro says, "we wait him out. We can withstand a siege indefinitely."

Thanks to the portals, I realize. They can make supply runs as needed.

Except, they have no hope of keeping these walls intact long enough.

I count to five before forcing myself to speak. "I don't think a siege is possible."

"And whyever not?" Saydan, the older man with graying hair and a face buried in wrinkles, demands.

I reach under the table for Kellyn's hand and slam my eyes shut. "One of Ravis's men has a war hammer that turns everything it touches into powder. He'll slam through the gate with a single swing."

"Really?" Skiro asks, his tone one of fascination, rather than horror. "How did you—"

Petrik coughs gently, which seems to do the trick and keep his brother on track.

Skiro says, "We have sharpshooters among my ranks. We'll keep them near you on the wall. Anyone who tries to approach with the hammer will fall."

He makes it sound so simple, as though I didn't do something terrible by empowering the enemy. Is truly no one angry about what I did?

"Is there anyone you can call on for aid?" Kellyn asks.

The prince says, "No one else has a standing army. There hasn't been time to recruit since Ghadra was split. I don't know how Ravis managed it.

"I am close with my sisters, but they do not have the numbers to help us make a significant difference, and we have no room to house them within the walls to aid with a siege."

Desperately, I ask, "Can you not leave?"

"And just hand over the territory to him?" Saydan asks.

"Land is land. It can be reclaimed. People are harder to replace," I respond, my heart hammering a million beats a minute.

"Ziva, I appreciate your input," Skiro says. "Truly. But I have to try to keep what is mine first. Besides, it is not only mine. It belongs to the people who live here. Ravis will not leave them be. He'll tax them. Force them to feed his troops before moving on. He'll take what he wants, leaving people to starve."

What he says lines up with everything I know about Ravis so far. I nod in understanding.

And then I'm struck by the absurdity of the whole situation. *Am I in a council meeting? Did I try to give advice?*

However has it come to this?

I don't envy Skiro or his people. They've got a brutal time ahead of them.

I sit silent for the rest of it, feeling ridiculous for speaking in the first place.

Afterward, Temra and I walk back to her rooms. Kellyn tried to meet my eyes as I exited, but I refused to look at him.

I know what he's thinking about. What we did in that abandoned room and how he wants to do it again.

And though part of me wants to also, another part wants to get away and have some more time with my sister. If we didn't need to leave this territory right away, I would likely insist on my own room and lock myself inside until I was ready to come out.

When we reach her rooms, I ask, "Has Skiro cleared our

names? With everything that's been happening, I never got the chance to ask. And it seemed insensitive during the meeting."

"Good instinct. And yes, Petrik explained everything to Skiro. The prince has cleared us of all charges, sent notices to all the major cities and rulers within those territories. We're no longer wanted, and with Kymora imprisoned, there's no one coming after us."

"So the warlord is still alive?"

"Skiro is keeping her in the dungeons. He's acquiring as much evidence against her as possible before holding the trial. I have no doubt she'll be executed when the time comes."

I sigh in relief. "Good. Then we can leave. Let's get you packed."

Temra blinks. "Leave?"

"We need to get as far away from Ravis as possible. We'll go to the northern continent like we always planned."

"We can't let Skiro fend for himself!"

My fingers open the nearest dresser and start pulling out clothing, setting it all on the bed in neat piles. "We have to, Temra. We don't have enough forces to withstand Ravis. His soldiers have too many of my weapons. It'll be a slaughter."

"The prince thinks he can negotiate, and I believe he knows his brother better than you do."

"Perhaps when they were little and living under the same roof. People change. Ravis is greedy and power-hungry. You know all too well what that can make a person do. We saw it with Kymora. We need to go, and we need to go now. Talk to Petrik; I'll talk to Kellyn. We can all leave together."

She narrows her gaze. "So your plan is to run like a coward and ask our friends to go with us?"

"It's not cowardice; it's sense! You weren't there, Temra. You weren't captured by Ravis, forced to do his will, just praying that you did things quickly enough and well enough so he wouldn't hurt the person you care about."

I wish I could make her understand just how dangerous Ravis is. That I could pull my pounding heart out of my chest and shove it into hers so she could get a taste of my own fear and understand the severity of the situation.

Temra's face gentles. "You're right. I cannot imagine what you went through, but, Ziva, we can't go now. We must try to reason with Ravis and withstand a siege if nothing else. What about those too poor or too weak to flee? What about Amanor?"

At that, I feel my stomach sink to the floor.

"What about Kellyn's ma and da?" she presses. "His siblings. The little ones? They're not leaving. They can't afford life on the northern continent. You would leave them to be butchered by Ravis?"

I feel tears prick my eyes just at the thought. "They live far off the main road. Ravis won't find their city on his march over here!"

"And what about after? When people start settling and expanding and exploring? They may be safe for now, but what about after everything has been taken?"

"Temra, we can't do anything." I think I might be begging now. "Come with me. Let's get our money out of the bank in Lirasu, and then we'll go. Anywhere safe."

"I can't. I've sworn my allegiance to the prince. He's accepted me into the ranks of his men. I'm a soldier, and I belong here now. Even if I wanted to go anywhere, I couldn't."

"You didn't!"

"I did."

Now the angry tears start to fall, my attempts at packing

forgotten. "What can you do! There's an army, Temra. How have you forgotten that?"

"We're not fighting them. We're negotiating, and if need be, holing up in the castle walls until Ravis runs out of food and money. Then he'll return home. That's how we save everyone. I can guard the walls. Keep watch at night to ensure no one sneaks through."

I don't even have words now. What she's saying is so preposterous. It's foolishness and stupidity, and my parents are rolling over in their graves right now knowing what a terrible job I've done protecting my sister.

"You can help, too," Temra adds. "Use your gift."

"No," I nearly shout. I'm almost as surprised by my negative outburst as Temra. "My gift is too dangerous. What if I make Skiro's men magical weapons and then Skiro gets greedy and decides *he* wants to conquer? Making weapons for powerful people has never gone over well for me. I can't do it. I almost destroyed the world once. I can't do it again. It's bad enough that several of Ravis's men carry my weapons."

"Don't make world-dominating weapons, then. Just make us blades that will give us an edge, like you did while trying to placate Ravis. If word spreads that the magical smithy is aiding Skiro, more people will flock to his territory. We can build the forces to take a stand against Ravis in the future. We can do some real good here."

"And if Ravis captures me again? If he takes you and hurts you to force me to build more weapons for him and make him truly unstoppable?"

"I'll kill myself before I ever allow him to use me like that."

"Temra!" I say in utter horror. "You can't mean that."

"I do, but that's the absolute worst-case scenario. It won't come to that, Ziva. We will get you out of the palace if things grow desperate."

"You want to save the world. You're addicted to thrills and adventure, and that's only going to get you killed."

"Then at least I die living. I'll die protecting something I believe in."

"You're so fanciful. Thinking about glory in death. How did you get this way?"

She levels me with an unwavering stare. "My sister raised me to be my own person. She taught me to love who I am and to fight for the things I want. I'm proud of how I turned out."

I leave the room without another word, because what can I possibly say to that?

A servant shows me to my own rooms at my request, and I promptly lock myself inside.

But for some reason, I don't feel any better.

I've been craving this. A space in which I can be totally alone. A place where I can feel like myself and not worry about anyone else.

Instead, I feel sick.

Selfish.

Lonely instead of alone.

Is my desire to keep myself away from Ravis selfish? Is my need to protect the world from what I can do just an excuse I'm giving to hide true cowardice, as Temra suggested?

I'm not brave like her. I run from trouble. I hide until it passes. I like feeling safe. I crave feeling safe.

What am I supposed to do when my little sister throws herself into harm's way on purpose? I can't control her. I can't make her see reason.

"But I won't abandon her," I say aloud. "I promise, Mother and Father. I won't ever leave her."

Even if she gets me recaptured.

At dinner, I find Petrik and Kellyn sitting together, talking like they used to on the road.

"You've become all-important now," Kellyn says. "Look at you, advising princes and setting up meetings."

"I can't exactly go back to the library with all that's happening," Petrik says. "Besides, look at *you*! Rushing into danger when there's no money to be earned. Be careful or everyone will think you've grown a heart."

I set down my tray of creamy tomato soup and sourdough bread and sit across from the two of them.

"What's wrong?" Kellyn asks.

"Temra."

"What about her?" Petrik asks.

"She's joined Skiro's personal guard, and she's determined to stay for Ravis's arrival. She's going to get herself killed!"

"She joined the guard?" Petrik says, becoming just as grumpy as I am. He looks over my shoulder, glaring at something behind me. I turn to see Temra take a seat among a bunch of men and women dressed as guards. Her new friends, likely. She was always so good at having people flock to her.

"How do I convince her to leave?" I ask.

"Wait, leave?" Kellyn asks. "Why would you leave?"

"So Ravis doesn't capture me again!" Does nobody remember what happened the last time? "Weapons I made are heading toward us right now!"

"Ravis didn't want to recapture you in the end," Kellyn says. "He wanted you dead. Not that that's better."

"He can change his mind! I'm too dangerous to stick around. Isn't it better if I go?"

"No!" both boys shout simultaneously.

"I don't believe you, but it doesn't matter," I say with a sigh. "I would never leave Temra behind."

Kellyn looks relieved. "Good. We can't abandon these people."

And yet I feel like I'm the one that's putting them in more danger. Both boys are staring at me, as though trying to read my thoughts.

Though too much time has passed since Kellyn's comment, I ask in jest, "Since when do you care about other people?" Anything to get the attention off me.

Kellyn doesn't miss a beat. "Why does everyone talk about me as though I'm some monster?"

"You're not a monster. You're just often self-serving," Petrik says.

"I am self-serving right now! If we don't stop Ravis here, he'll be unchecked as he ravages through Ghadra, which is where *I* happen to live."

"Ziva," Petrik says, as though an idea has just come to him, "do you think you could—"

Any traces of humor leave me as I cut him off. "If you ask me to make weapons, I will hit you again."

Petrik slams his mouth shut.

"I'm not going to be anyone's pawn ever again. I'm not making weapons for anyone ever again. I won't be trapped or forced against my will."

The table goes quiet, and any nearby folks wisely scoot away.

"No one is forcing you to make anything," Kellyn says. "I won't let them."

I spoon up some soup, feeling no better about the situation.

I hoped Petrik might have some words of wisdom or that Kellyn would see things my way.

No such luck.

The boys start up a new conversation, but I stay out of it. I'm too consumed with worry over what I will do if Ravis captures me again. He won't let me get away with using a magical weapon against him again. He won't make the mistake of keeping the person I care about near enough for me to free them again. I can picture him ordering Temra locked up in a tower, his men observing my work in the forges with a spyglass, ready to slit my sister's throat if I make one wrong move.

My thoughts only turn darker and darker from there, and I look up from my food, desperate for an escape.

I find Petrik staring longingly over my shoulder, and I reach for the distraction.

"Give her some time," I say to the scholar. "You know how stubborn she can be. She'll probably forgive you eventually."

"I messed up," he says. "I shouldn't have lied to her."

"Yes, you should have. You did everything right."

"I took away her choices. That wasn't fair."

"But you saved her."

"I kept her from what's most important to her. You," he adds at my confused look. "I don't think that's something she can forgive."

Shyly, I look up at Kellyn. "You'd be surprised."

The next morning, I wander the halls, unsure of what I'm searching for. Answers maybe? A solution to a problem that can't be fixed?

Eventually I find myself back at the kitchens, since it's one of the few places in the castle I know the location of. Paulia and Serutha are in there together. Serutha mixes a bowl filled with some sort of dough, while Paulia checks on something in the ovens.

"Hello," I say feebly.

Both girls immediately halt what they're doing and usher me forward. Paulia shoves food under my face, while Serutha leans forward on one arm, asking me how things are with Kellyn now that he's healed. I guess they're both romantics.

"He's great. We're great, but—don't you both know what's coming our way?"

"The army," Serutha says.

I sigh. "Am I the only one afraid? The only one who wants to run?"

"Not at all," Paulia says. "I'm terrified, but I'm going to do what I can. I'm making food for all those who will soon be within the palace gates. We should go through all the perishables before resorting to hardtack and dried meats. Serutha is helping me bake up a storm."

"But you're staying? You have no desire to flee? You're about to start a life together, and Ravis is threatening that. He's already stolen Serutha once. What will happen if he gets ahold of her again?"

That's why I'm really here. Because Serutha is the one person who understands my fear. Ravis had her captured for a time, too. She has to be thinking about that.

Serutha stands, drums her fingers on the table once, twice. "I can't live afraid of what might happen. All I can do is live."

"I'm afraid," I say. "What if he catches me again? Why would I stay when I could run?"

The healer stares at me with hardened eyes. "Ravis took

something from us. He forced us to use our abilities in ways that we hated. Now you doubt yourself in something that is precious to you. Now you see how your abilities can be used to harm rather than help. Don't let him have that power over you."

"But your abilities are for good!" I argue. "Even if you're healing bad people, you're never truly doing any wrong." It's not the same. Why can't everyone see how much more dangerous I am in the wrong hands?

Serutha stiffens, and Paulia runs a hand down her back. "Do you not think that if I can heal injuries, Ziva, I can also make them?"

My mouth pops open in a little O.

"Ravis did not just have me heal his scrapes and bruises. He also had me torture men and women he suspected of deceit. Do you think that doesn't weigh heavy on my soul?"

Quietly, I say, "I'm so sorry. I didn't know. Please forgive—"

"You are not the one who needs to seek my forgiveness. I've had time to practice healing from those wounds, by using my ability when I choose to. By associating good with it, instead of bad. I suggest you find a way to do the same."

"I don't know if I can."

"You can. There is a castle forge."

"No, I mean. I can't make weapons for Skiro." Not with the risks involved. Not after all the damage I've already done.

"Then do not make weapons for Skiro. Make weapons for yourself."

I want that so desperately. To forge for myself again. But any weapons I make would be wielded by someone in the upcoming war. I can't exactly hide them.

Unless—

I literally make a weapon for myself.

Didn't Kellyn suggest on the road that I make new hammers? Wouldn't I feel safer to have something to protect myself with?

An image forms in my head. Two beautiful hammers with smooth handles and heavy block-shaped heads. A combination in design between forging hammers and war hammers. I'm running through possibilities in designs for the detail work, something Ravis never permitted me to do.

"Serutha," I say. "Thank you. Please excuse me."

CHAPTER
EIGHTEEN

When I find Petrik, he's in conversation with Isulay, from the meeting room.

"The earl wants more space for his pregnant wife. He's taken to having his men bully the servants out of their rooms. I've already told him that if he persists, he and his family will no longer be welcome within the protection of the palace."

"Then what's the problem?" Petrik asks.

"If we lose him, we lose his men. That's twenty fighters who can aid during the siege."

"How far along is his wife?"

"Eight and a half months."

"You remind the earl that we have all the midwives within a fifteen-mile radius within the walls of this palace. If he wants the best care possible, he would do well to behave. Perhaps we could arrange for a bigger room if we have a midwife stay with them."

"I could arrange that."

"See if that helps."

Isulay walks on, and I approach as Petrik rubs at his temples.

"And I thought manual labor was tiring," I say.

"Every day there are dozens of these petty squabbles to solve. They're exhausting." His fingers move to pinch the bridge of his nose.

"You seem to be good at fixing them."

"I know. It's strange."

"Not at all strange. You're the most brilliant person, I know."

"If I were truly brilliant, I'd find a way to convince Temra to forgive me."

I feel bad for him, truly, but there's nothing more I can do for him. Except maybe—

"Have you tried cake?"

His dark eyes narrow. "Cake?"

"Chocolate cake is her favorite treat. I bet if you asked Paulia, she could show you how to make it. Tell her I sent you."

A small smile graces his lips. "Thank you, Ziva. I will try that straightaway." He turns to leave.

"Wait! I need your help first."

He pauses instantly. "What is it?"

"Can you take me to see your brother?"

"Yes, of course. May I ask why?"

"I need access to a forge."

"I honestly think he's been dying for you to ask that very thing. Follow me." Petrik yawns as we round a corner.

"Are you sleeping?" I ask.

"Not well. I'm reading up on sieges and battles in times past."

I've seen Petrik carrying armloads of books to and from the palace—likely borrowing volumes from the Great Library. It's within walking distance of the palace.

"Have you found anything to help us yet?" I ask.

"I don't know. I guess we'll see when the time comes."

Petrik leads me to what must be the prince's rooms, nodding to the guards on either side of the door. They knock for us.

"Your brother to see you, my prince," one calls out.

"Send him in."

We enter.

"Should I stay or . . . ?" Petrik asks.

"Would you?" I ask.

"Of course."

If I thought the rest of the palace was beautiful, it is nothing compared to the opulence of Skiro's rooms. Bright greens, blues, and reds call attention from every corner of the receiving room. Statues, paintings, taxidermies, and much more cover the space. Skiro adores beauty, and he's filled this room with all of it. I can only assume the rest of the master suite to be the same.

The prince looks up from a finely carved table, where he is finishing up his lunch. The same carrot and potato stew the rest of us had.

"Ziva," he says excitedly. "Won't you sit?"

"There's no need for that. I only wished to ask if I could have the use of your forge?"

"You are welcome to whatever you may need! Hail down a servant to show you the way."

"Thank you." I turn to leave, pause, then turn back around. "Why?"

"Hmm?" he asks as he takes a sip of his tea.

"Why do I get whatever I need?"

"Because you asked."

"Yes, but why do you want to give it to me?"

"Because I want you to stay, of course. Join your sister here at the palace. When this business with my brother is settled, you will have your own permanent rooms within the palace, should you wish them."

"Do you expect me to make weapons for you?"

His brow furrows. "No, did you want to?"

"No."

"All right, then."

I'm still so confused.

Skiro continues, "You make glorious works of art, Ziva, and if I can just look upon them from time to time, that will be more than enough payment. Besides, you've brought me the traitor Kymora, unearthed not one but two plots for world domination, and saved my brother's skin when he was foolish enough to tag along after you. As far as I'm concerned, you deserve whatever you want until the end of time."

I bite the inside of my cheek. "Would you release my sister?"

"Release her?"

"From her oath of loyalty. From the guard?"

Skiro brings a napkin to his lips. "She begged me to take her on, and she's welcome to leave at any time. Oaths of loyalty are simply a tradition of the past. I wouldn't want anyone to serve me and this territory who didn't want to. That doesn't sound pleasant for anyone. Why? Has she asked to leave? Maybe I didn't make myself clear during our last conversation."

I wish I could lie, but that will do neither of us any good. "She has no wish to leave."

"I'm glad to hear it. Please make yourself comfortable in the castle forge. Do let me know if there's anything else you require."

"Okay. Bye, then."

Why is saying goodbye always such an awkward affair? I exit as quickly as I entered, my cheeks heating.

Where Ravis had dozens of forges and hundreds of workers, Skiro's palace has one large smithy on the palace grounds. It's not quite as big as mine back home, but close. Just the sight of it fills me with fear and dread, and I curse my body's reaction.

You're walking in there of your own free will, and you can leave as soon as you'd like.

I flood my mind with good memories of the forge. Of halberds and throwing stars and swords and spears. Items I crafted on my own. Weapons I carefully designed and lovingly brought to life. I think of Temra sitting on one of the worktables chatting at me while I hammer. The time I saw Kellyn walk by my windows.

There is far more good than bad in my memories of forges. I just have to hold on to them, and make new memories, too.

So I put one foot in front of the other, determined to see this through.

Inside, I find a grizzled old woman, with hair out of control and arms too long for her torso.

"What do you want?" she asks when I enter.

Her tone isn't encouraging, but I push aside my nerves as I remember Serutha's words. I need to reclaim this for myself. I *will* make the forge a safe space for me once more.

"To help," I say. "What are you working on?"

"What *aren't* I working on? Broken shields. Bent armor. Snapped spears!"

"Do you have a spare work apron?" I ask.

"Do I bloody look like I have the time to teach you anything? Skiro expects me to work a miracle, and he thinks—"

I roll up my sleeves, exposing my biceps. I step up to the

nearest anvil, take note of what the smithy's working on, and grip the tongs she'd discarded when I entered.

"I hold, you hammer?" I ask.

When she says nothing, I look up. She's squinting so hard at me, I can barely see her pupils. My heartbeat quickens, anticipating the rejection that must be coming.

"Who are you?" she asks.

"My name is Ziva. What's yours?"

"Abelyn."

The ensuing silence only lasts for a few seconds. Abelyn steps forward, but I can tell I haven't won her over yet. While I hold the breastplate firmly in place, she begins to hammer. Before she can ask me to turn the metal, I'm already flipping it over.

After a few minutes of this, she pauses. "You can stay."

The staff may be shorthanded (it's only Abelyn), but the forge is well stocked. The capital is practically on top of the Southern Mountains, so there's no shortage of iron ore. I'm also delighted to find that Abelyn is proficient in making steel.

While she takes a break from hammering to sip from her waterskin, I peruse her worktables. Chisels, molds, drawplates, swages, fullers, punches, drifts, bits, and hammers. So many hammers in so many sizes. Every tool is finely made and well used.

"Don't touch anything," the old smithy says when she catches me staring.

"My last set of forging hammers was stolen by Prince Ravis," I say.

"And why should the prince care about your hammers?"

I only deliberate for a moment before answering. I can't very well magic anything in here without her noticing. Either I commit to this, or I leave now.

"Because they were magicked," I say. "I'm no fighter, but with those hammers, I felt unstoppable."

Abelyn narrows her eyes again; I'm coming to find that the suspicious look she gives me isn't a look at all but the natural set of her face.

"Magic? In weapons?" she asks. "Rubbish. I've never seen such a thing."

I smile. I can't help it. "Would you like me to show you?"

Her eyes narrow (again). "You're telling me you can do this?"

I tilt my head to the side. "You really haven't heard of me? Ziva, the magically gifted bladesmith."

Abelyn spits on the ground. "I don't care for gossip, and I hate small talk."

I really like her, despite everything about her that's off-putting. There's nothing pretend about Abelyn. What you see is what you get.

"And how do you feel about magic?" I ask.

"Never seen it."

"Would you permit me to use it?"

"If you didn't clearly know your way around the forge, I'd kick you out now for being a looney."

"Can I make my own hammers? I'll show you how the magic works firsthand."

I take her answering grunt as assent.

With the two of us working, we're able to get through Abelyn's to-do list much quicker. I help her with all the preparations to have our measly one hundred guards as properly outfitted as possible for the battle ahead.

And we also craft my hammers together.

It's a speedier process than most other weapons would take. Not so much pounding is required to turn a clump of white-hot steel into the shape of a hammer head.

Because of this, I take the time to add my own embellishments.

The sides bear the design of winding ivy—a beautiful plant that flourishes in Lirasu with all the rain. It's a weed in a lot of areas, thriving where it's not meant to.

I can relate. I never do feel like I belong, but even when things get tough, I somehow survive.

We make the shafts short—about the length of my forearm, with rounded pommels and a thick wrapping of leather on the grips.

The hammer meant for my left hand, I magic just as I did before, giving it the properties of an invisible shield with rebound power.

But I don't stop there.

Its right-hand twin will also receive the energy from each blow taken on the left hammer. Each swing will not only have my strength behind it, but the strength of my opponents in battle.

I name them Echo and Agony.

Echo for the shield. My enemies will get more than an echo when they try to smash their weapons upon it, but I like the gentleness of the word. Something needs to be gentle amid all the brutality of battle.

Agony for the right hammer. Not only will it cause pain to those who feel my strikes, but to me as well. I don't like fighting. I hate how it changes me and gives me memories that are impossible to forget.

But I will be prepared for the fight ahead. Just having these new hammers at my side brings a small sense of safety I didn't realize I'd been missing.

Working clears my head.

Maybe it's being in a familiar setting or having my friends and family close by once again. But I feel stronger and braver each day, like things aren't as hopeless as I once feared.

I forgot how hammering at steel helps me to relieve stress. Not having it has been awful. While captured, someone was always looking over my shoulder while I worked, but now everything is different. Serutha was right. I needed to take this back for myself.

And I realize during the passing weeks in Abelyn's forge that I've spent so much time worrying over others, to the point where I forgot to think about me. I worried about what my recapture would mean for everyone else. My own safety was always secondary.

But here, in this safe place, with only the grizzled smithy for company, I realize just what Serutha meant. I realize what Ravis did.

He took something I love and made me afraid of it. He caused me to lose my confidence in my abilities. He temporarily made me lose my love of forging. He threatened Kellyn.

He made this war personal.

If Ravis is allowed to spread throughout Ghadra unchecked, he will make life a misery for me and any other magic users in the realms.

I want to stay to make a stand for *my* right to live how I wish.

I'm not running. I want to see Ravis's supplies slowly dwindle and watch him flee with his tail tucked between his legs. I want to stay to build something. To help the world truly defeat tyranny. Maybe Temra is right and my presence will rally people to the cause. Maybe we can build an army large enough to stand up to him someday.

I won't give up my decision not to make weapons for powerful people again, but I can still help. I can still forge. I can still be me.

I will fight for *me*.

There is much to be done to prepare for the imminent threat. Even when I'm not in the forge, I'm kept busy. The people need help bringing themselves and their livelihoods within the palace walls. We carry children on our shoulders, herd wayward sheep through the palace gates, lift baskets full of food and clothing into the outer courtyard.

Skiro opens the palace to the people. They cram into the servant wings. Servants cram into the empty wings of the nobility. Temra, Petrik, Kellyn, and I shove our belongings into one room to make way for others.

But not everyone will fit inside the palace. I help erect tents out in the courtyard. Cows, goats, and other animals wander aimlessly without any fences to keep them contained. Chickens scatter from the boots of guards running around the space. Skiro's men carry weapons, shields, and anything else needed to the lookout points atop the wall.

Fear drips through the palace like rain, speeding and slowing at its own pace. The guards especially are ripe with it, but Skiro tries to assuage everyone's fears. He leaves the palace daily to go and speak to his people. He offers encouragement, safety, food to all.

He makes pretty speeches, but they don't calm my own worries. I try to cling to my newfound resolve instead as I watch day after day slip by.

I'm staying for me, becomes my new mantra.

Now that I'm seeing things Temra's way, there's only one thing for me to do.

Apologize.

"I'm sorry," I say, catching her alone in the room. She's staring at a tray of food like it's offended her.

"What?" she asks, looking up.

"I said I'm sorry. You were right. We need to stay and make a stand. I shouldn't have been mad at you. I'm sorry we fought."

Temra grins brightly, as if nothing was ever rocky between us. "It's a nice change when it's you who apologizes. I'm usually the one who messes up."

I let out a guffaw as I sit next to her on the bed. "I don't think that's true. I mess up *almost* as much as you do.

"Mm-hmm." She punches me lightly on the shoulder.

"Why are we glaring at your dinner?" I ask when I finish laughing.

"It's not the dinner. It's the cake."

"Cake?"

"Chocolate cake."

"And what has your favorite dessert done to offend you?"

She smacks her lips together. "I suspect it's from Petrik, since it's obviously not from you."

"Why isn't it from me?"

"You can't cook."

"Neither can you!" I say defensively.

"The point is, I can't accept the cake."

"Why's that?"

She gives me a look. "Because I hate Petrik."

"So? That doesn't mean you can't eat his cake."

She taps her thumb against her leg. "Paulia has her hands full in the kitchens cooking for everyone."

"I don't follow."

"She didn't make this *for* Petrik. He had to have made it himself."

"And?"

"That makes it so much worse."

"I still don't understand."

"He"—she searches for the right word—"labored. He made this while he was thinking of me, and I hate him, so I can't eat it. Otherwise, it would be like forgiving him. I can't accept it, because I don't accept him."

"You've put way too much thought into this."

"I have to, Ziva. It's *cake*."

"He's not going to know whether or not you eat it."

She turns her head to stare me down. "You won't tell him?"

"I would never."

She thinks for a moment. "Maybe just a bite. It's probably not even good. Maybe if I just sampled it . . . for more fuel for my anger . . ."

"That's very wise," I say, fighting a laugh.

She uses her fork to break off a section and brings it to her lips. "Ugh," she says.

"It's bad?"

"Worse. It's really good."

She pulls the tray close and eats the rest without a word.

My hammers stay hidden in the forge until I'm able to finish a new belt. It hangs low around my waist with perfectly measured holsters, one on each hip. The shafts slide into the holsters, so the hammers are positioned heads up. Their weight is evenly distributed, and I can now carry Echo and Agony with me effortlessly wherever I go.

I can't seem to stop smiling.

The new safety that comes with these hammers is partially the reason, of course, but I also know it's more than that. I've spent a couple weeks with Abelyn now, working on the guards' armor and equipment. It was the first time in as long as I can remember that I did my job as a smithy without imbuing metal with magic.

And it was fine.

It wasn't quite the same as what I used to do, but I still felt useful and at home in a way.

Maybe there is a place for me here in the long run. I could open up my own forge in the capital. There's plenty of space on the palace grounds. Or maybe I'd get my own place in town, visit Temra on the weekends.

After we deal with Ravis.

It will be different, but I don't have to hate my life. I don't have to spend it without Temra.

There's a new bounce in my step as I make for the great hall just in time for supper. It's more packed than ever with all the new city folk occupying the palace and its courtyard, but Kellyn stands out like a beacon. He's a full head taller than anyone else in the space, and his golden-red hair practically dances in the candlelight.

He's surrounded by men wearing the guard uniform. They're laughing loudly in between mouthfuls of rabbit stew.

He's made some friends. Good for him.

I don't think Abelyn counts as a new friend, since we don't really talk, just work. But I'll take it. Better than nothing.

Then I see it.

An open spot directly on Kellyn's right.

Could he be saving it for me?

Stupid. It's not like his every waking thought is about you.

But what if it is for me? It would be rude to pass it up.

And what if it's not for you? How awkward will it be when

he says he's saving it for someone else? Then all those men will laugh as you walk away.

No one is going to laugh. It's not funny.

Yes, but you're thinking through worst-case scenarios. And being made fun of is always the worst.

So which am I afraid of more, then? Offending Kellyn or making an idiot of myself?

I turn away. I can't possibly set myself up for such a spectacle.

But Kellyn wants an equal partner. And you want him.

I can be brave when I want to be.

To prove it to myself, I take my tray of food to the nearly full table. A few heads notice me approaching and look up, but I keep my gaze firmly fixed on the back of Kellyn's head.

Otherwise I just might bolt.

When I come to a full stop behind him, I realize he hasn't noticed me yet.

Obviously. His back is turned, idiot.

Do I clear my throat? Speak up? Tap Kellyn on the shoulder? Another person at the table is speaking, and it would be rude to cut him off. Yet, if I do nothing, I stand here like a dolt.

I'm panicking. I feel my legs shaking, and I want to run far, far away.

I take the seat without asking.

Every muscle in my body snaps taut. I'm stuck here, and I probably just stole someone's seat. What if they were just in the lavatory or something?

Oh Twins. What have I done? Why did I ever think I could—

And then a big arm wraps around me, and Kellyn puts his lips to my temple.

And everything is just fine.

Well, not really. I'm still surrounded by strangers, and I hate most everything about this situation. But Kellyn is touching me, and I really like that.

I did the hard part; now I just need not to overreact.

I try listening to the conversation.

"...and then the mercenary lands me flat on my back!" one of the younger men at the table says. The rest break out into more laughter.

Kellyn leans into me. "I helped with some of the training today. Made some new friends."

After one day?

I've never made this many friends in my entire life.

"They seem to like you," I respond.

"What's not to like?"

"I can think of some things."

He grins and nuzzles my hair right in front of everyone. As though he wants to make it perfectly and publicly clear just who I'm with. As though he's proud to be with me.

But such a public display of affection makes me a little uncomfortable, so I think I'll let him know that when we're alone. He won't mind, I'm sure.

"Who's this?" another one of the men asks, clearly meaning me. I try not to visibly shrink back.

Kellyn turns to me, giving me the option to answer.

"I'm Ziva."

"You didn't tell us you were married," one of the men says to Kellyn.

"I'm not," Kellyn answers. "Ziva and I have only been together for a few weeks."

It would have been longer, had I not broken things off while we journeyed. But Kellyn makes no indication to show his thoughts have turned where mine have.

A man across from me says, "Well, if things don't work out with this big oaf, you come talk to me." He winks.

Kellyn and I both tense. Things are so fragile right now, and the man across from us has no idea. He probably means it as a joke. Even so, I should say something.

But what? Giving my name is one thing. Offering something to the conversation? That's entirely different.

Unthinkable.

And how do I avoid being confrontational and rude?

"You're not my type," I say, perhaps too harshly.

The table erupts into laughter, and one of the men ruffles the hair of the one who spoke.

Kellyn gives me a gentle squeeze with the arm still around me.

"And what is your type?" another asks.

"Big oafs," I say before I can overthink it.

More laughter.

"Don't let that one go," someone says.

Kellyn looks to me. "I don't intend to."

My cheeks turn red for all to see.

After the meal, I tell Kellyn about my day in the smithy, and I ask if I can take his longsword to work with me the next day.

"Yes," he says, "but what for?"

"I have ideas."

"Sounds dangerous."

I grin but only briefly. "War is coming. I need to keep everyone safe. I'm already making adjustments to Midnight for Temra, making the blade lighter to help with dexterity and endurance."

"And what are you going to do to Lady Killer?"

"Because of her sheer size, you have to remove your scabbard before you can unsheathe her. You lose time, and if you were ever in a hurry, I thought it might be nice to have a quicker way to get her into your hand."

"So you're magicking again?" he asks carefully.

"Not really. I'm only doing this for people I know and trust." For those I can't bear to lose to this war.

Once done with Kellyn, I seek out Petrik.

He's in another meeting with the prince and his advisers. Patiently, I wait outside the door. I blush when one of the guards outside asks if I'd like to enter.

I shake my head vigorously. "Just waiting for Petrik." Then I turn my gaze to the floor and keep it there.

I can't hear much, but every so often, I think I hear Petrik shout something about "contingency plans," but his voice always peters off.

After only a few minutes, the doors burst open, and Prince Skiro comes striding out.

"Oh," he says, his face losing the look of frustration and replacing it with one of delight. "Hello, Ziva. What can I do for you?"

I know he doesn't mean to make me uncomfortable, but it's impossible for me not to be weird around him when I can still picture him leaning suggestively toward the imposter with my face.

"I'm here for Petrik."

"Oh," he says again, and his tone lowers. "Well, I'll see you around, then."

His blue robe sweeps behind him as he takes off, his advisers trailing behind him. Petrik exits last.

"Everything all right?" I ask.

Petrik doesn't hide his frustration from me, which I like. "No. All anyone wants to discuss is strategies for negotiating with Ravis. What we're willing to give him to go away. No matter how many times I try to bring up a discussion for what we should do should Ravis attack, my worries are discarded as though meaningless."

"Why would they do something so stupid?"

"It's like they can't even entertain the notion of a battle, because . . ."

"We'll all be slaughtered if it comes to that."

"Tactful, as ever, Ziva."

"At least I agree with you."

We start walking toward our bedroom together, and I bring up the reason for my visit.

"Why do you want my staff?" Petrik asks.

"I wanted to try magicking it so no one but the caster can catch it. See if I can get rid of the weaknesses in its magic."

"Wow."

"It's no big deal," I say, feeling my cheeks heat.

Petrik shakes his head. "Sure. I'll grab it for you." He doesn't exactly carry the large weapon with him wherever he goes.

But before he enters the room, he asks, "Did she eat it? Did she like it?"

"I am sworn to secrecy," I say.

"Fine."

CHAPTER
NINETEEN

Another week passes. The palace now looks gutted, most of the supplies having been taken to the people living outdoors. Bedding, storage chests, washroom supplies. Anything to help Skiro's subjects have an easier time of it.

I finish magicking the weapons belonging to Temra, Kellyn, and Petrik before returning them to their owners. Skiro's men are all properly outfitted with repaired weapons. Most walk the palace halls fully armored, just waiting for the warning bells that will signal Ravis's approach.

Yet the prince doesn't come when he ought to come, and everyone grows more edgy than ever.

Time crawls by, as it always does, and I start to worry that everyone will think Kellyn and I made the whole thing up.

Especially when he's late by a whole fortnight.

But we stay busy. Kellyn and Temra continue to train with the guards. Petrik remains an adviser to the prince. I keep working with Abelyn.

With all the official work done in the smithy, only the occasional cookware request or horseshoe replacement comes to us.

Abelyn grows grouchier than usual with nothing to do. "Ugh. Another dull day. Let's not bore ourselves with small talk. Go. Find something useful to occupy yourself."

Trying not to take that personally, I return to the castle.

I'd hoped for work today. Free time means thinking time, and there is much to fret over.

Like *where is Ravis?*

What does it mean that he's taking longer than he should? Did something bad happen? Has disease swept through his camp?

Or maybe something good happened for him? Maybe he's detoured to meet up with even more forces?

I'm about to enter my shared room in search of Temra but stop outside the door when I hear talking.

"You need to stop it." Temra's voice. "I don't want food or gifts from you. I don't want to catch you looking at me or thinking about me or anything else where I am concerned. You lost that right."

"The right to think about you?" Petrik asks sardonically.

"Yes."

"That's not— You can't—" He cuts himself off twice before saying, "I messed up."

"Twice," she cuts in.

"I messed up twice. I'm sorry. Please, can you ever forgive me?"

Her voice rises. "You can't ask for forgiveness. This kind of offense is unforgivable."

"I only wanted to keep you safe. Please understand—"

There's a crash, and I think Temra might have thrown something at him.

"No, you understand! You had a choice to make, and you made the one that results in us never being friends again."

"Friends?" Petrik's voice takes on a nasty edge I've never heard before. "We were never friends."

"What is that supposed to mean?"

"You used me. Always."

"What?"

"The playful flirtations. The compliments. The light touches. I was always something you kept around to amuse yourself. You only wanted attention from me."

"And you always kept yourself away at arm's length, so whose fault is that?"

Petrik scoffs. "Because the second I showed even a trace of interest in you, you would have become bored and moved on to someone exciting."

"Are you calling yourself boring? Or are you calling me a flake?"

"Girls like you don't go for boys like me."

"Pathological liars? I don't think that's anyone's type."

"I mean beautiful girls don't go for smart boys. They go for dangerous ones. Exciting ones. Boys with big arms who can swing swords and bash in heads."

"Then it's a good thing I'm pretty. How else could you stand to be around someone so stupid!" she growls at him.

"I never said you were stupid."

"It was implied. Because if all I am is some pretty girl, then clearly I have nothing else going for me. And if all you see in yourself is your ability to read a book, then you need to build your confidence. Being with a pretty girl won't fix that."

It goes quiet for a full ten seconds. No one moving. I can barely hear them breathing on the other side. Secondhand embarrassment floods my senses, and I want to flee almost as much as I want to stay and listen.

"I don't see you as just a pretty girl!" Petrik finally blurts. "You're protective and talented at everything you do! Almost in an obnoxious way, I might add. You have such empathy for those around you. You are beautiful inside and out!"

I don't know why he's still yelling at her, but his voice doesn't drop.

"And I know I'm more than my books. I am also loyal to my friends. I like to learn how things work. I will fight even when I know I can't possibly win. I'm kind, generous, and, on occasion, even funny. Material wealth doesn't matter to me. People matter to me. I have a confidence in what I do. The only thing I'm not confident about is you!"

More silence, then, "You upend me," Petrik says so quietly I almost can't hear him. "I can't think straight around you. I worry over everything I say, convinced that will be the thing that drives you away. Instead, it ended up being my actions. I'm sorry for keeping Ziva's true whereabouts from you. I'm sorry for lying. I did what I thought was best in the current situation. But I didn't put your thoughts and feelings first, as I should have. As I will do from now on, should you ever agree to be my friend again."

"I thought you said we were never friends," Temra says just as whisper soft.

"You are my friend, even though I never wanted friendship from you."

"No, you only wanted access to Ziva and her magic."

"You misunderstand me. I never wanted *friendship* from you, Temra. I always wanted something more."

And then I can't hear any more talking. There are different noises. Noises that I can't quite make out. And then I realize—

They're kissing.

I leap away from the door as though I've been burned.

I have a million questions. Who started it? And how did it come to that? Weren't they just arguing? Kellyn and I don't finish arguments with kissing.

Maybe we should.

Maybe everything should be followed by kissing.

Bells ring from high up on the palace towers. The sound seems to become trapped within the stone walls, echoing down the hallways.

It takes me far too long to realize why they're going off.

Ravis and his army are finally here.

I bolt for the outer doors, Temra and Petrik somewhere behind me. I don't know if they've realized that I was right outside the door, but now is not the time to worry about it.

We've got bigger problems.

I find Kellyn and Prince Skiro already on the wall above the gate, overlooking whatever is beyond. I have to fight through the crowds of people calling for loved ones, trying to usher children out of the way. I leap over a sheep before finally reaching the stairs and taking them two at a time.

From up top, I can't see anything at first. And then, a dust cloud in the distance. The tiniest pinpricks of what might be marching soldiers.

Regardless of how small and far away they seem, fear grips my heart, pumps terror into my veins with every beat. I can do nothing but stare for a moment.

Skiro says, "Saydan, send riders to set up a time and location for the meeting. We're resolving this quickly. We don't want the people afraid longer than they need to be."

I turn in time to see Skiro stride past a disheveled Petrik, who has eyes for nothing but my sister. My face warms at the reminder of what I overheard. It's really not something I should know about unless Temra wants me to know about it, but it's too late to take back my eavesdropping now.

The thick wooden gate creaks open beneath where we stand, and five riders gallop toward the approaching army. They carry nothing with them, only wear the golden sun sigil of Prince Skiro.

"There's nothing to do except wait until the riders return with news of the meetup," Petrik says.

"I don't like it," I say. "What if Ravis means to trick Skiro? Kill him during the negotiations?"

"He won't," Petrik says. "He's not my favorite person, but he's not a heathen. If he agrees to a meeting, he will honor the stipulations surrounding it."

"Would you bet Skiro's life on that?" Temra asks.

Petrik bites his lip. "No."

We stand atop the wall, watching. Waiting. Skiro returns shortly, followed by the head of his personal guard, Tazar, who sticks to the prince like butter on bread.

An hour goes by.

Two.

Three.

Night falls, and still the riders don't return. Just how far away is the army? We see lights in the distance, torches flickering faintly. The barest sounds of the march carry on the wind.

And then, finally, a lone horse approaches, whinnying when the rider pulls it to a stop.

"Open the gate," Saydan calls. "He's one of ours."

Skiro descends the wall, and the rest of us follow on his heels. The gate slams closed once the guard is safely inside. I hope it doesn't open again for a very long time.

A small man dismounts from his horse; he was clearly chosen for the sake of speed. When his feet touch the ground, he immediately removes his helmet and bows to the prince.

"I sent out five," Skiro says. "Why have only you returned?"

The guard's voice wavers slightly as he answers. "Prince Ravis said he needed only one to relay his message. He kept the others. I know not for what purpose, except perhaps to weaken your forces."

Skiro does a poor job hiding his response to the news. Through gritted teeth, he asks, "What is the message?"

"'If you surrender your lands to me willingly, little brother, no harm shall come to you or your people. Otherwise, you will surrender them after much bloodshed. Either way, I will have them.'"

When the guard ceases talking, Skiro's jaw drops. "That's it?"

"That's the entirety of the message, sire. He will not negotiate. He will not meet with you."

I watch the prince's hands clench into fists at his sides. "What more did you observe? Of his forces and his march?"

"They will be here by tomorrow morning, and it will be no siege, sire."

"What do you mean?"

"His men bring with them ladders and hooks. Battering rams and projectile weapons. He has some two thousand men with him. They will breach the walls in no time."

At that pronouncement, I have no chance to see the prince's reaction. I'm too busy trying to keep my own under control. I bite back a whimper, and I can't help the glance I shoot Temra's way. As though I have to assure myself she hasn't somehow floated away.

"We can't stay here," I hear Kellyn say. "It'll be a slaughter."

"It's too late to leave," Skiro says. "We'd never move this many people, children and elderly, at a fast enough pace. He'd catch up. *Two thousand men*." He whispers the last three words to himself. No one thought the prince capable of rallying such forces.

"What if we use the doors?"

Everyone turns their gaze on me.

"I'm not sure what doors you're referring to," Skiro says, "but I'm certain they're meant to be kept *secret* and not spoken about in just anyone's company."

"I made no promise to keep them secret," I say. "And they might be our only chance of saving everyone."

"I can't simply sneak thousands of people into a new territory! Into a new palace."

"Then don't be sneaky!" I shout, uncomfortable and irritated and full of fear. Remembering I'm talking to a prince, I lower my tone. "We could let them know we're coming. You said you're close with your sisters. Will none of them be sympathetic to our plight? Surely they will want the added numbers when Ravis comes their way?"

Skiro places his hands atop his hips as he looks up at me. The scrutiny is unbearable, but I want him to take me seriously, so I don't look away.

"Marossa," Petrik says. "She would take us in."

I blink at the princess's name. She's the ruler over my home city of Lirasu. I know very little of her other than that. The capital is a couple weeks' journey from the city, and I've never had to make it.

Skiro lets a long breath out between his teeth. "Even if she lets us in, and even if I give away the one advantage I have over all my siblings, we'd still never get this many people through the portal before the army reaches us. We'd need more time."

"We can stall the army," Temra says, drawing her sword.

No one says anything for a moment.

I blurt, "You can't stall a two-thousand-strong army with a handful of soldiers."

"We have the advantage of height," she retaliates.

"Until they breach the walls."

"Then we will fight with our last breath to allow as many people the chance to flee as possible."

"You want all the trained men and women to give their lives so a handful more city folk can flee?"

"We promise to protect when we take the oath. We're prepared to lay down our lives."

"You're not laying down your life for anyone!" I'm bursting with anger. If I have to tie her up and haul her through that portal myself, I will.

"There are strategies," Petrik says softly in the thick silence following our argument. "Ways to defend the wall longer. I've been reading. I could go get my books . . ."

"Books are not helpful right now, little brother," Skiro says. "What we need is someone who can command the troops through the siege." He eyes his man Tazar.

"I am only trained in defending you, sire. And Saydan has never led men into battle. He hasn't any experience with sieges."

Skiro looks off into the distance, staring at nothing. "Then we must ask the city guards to give us as much time as possible. I will go speak with my sister and warn her we're coming. I will be back shortly. Temra, will you oversee the people through the portal?"

Though the last question was directed to my sister, Skiro looks to me as he asks it.

Temra works her jaw wordlessly. I know her dilemma. She wishes to be on the wall, fighting. But she also doesn't want to refuse the prince. In the end, she says, "Of course."

Skiro takes a few steps away.

"Wait," Kellyn says, drawing everyone to a stop. "We have someone here who *has* led men into battle. Someone who has experience with sieges. Someone who could lead the troops and buy more time for everyone to escape."

I turn to Kellyn. Who could he possibly—

"No!" I shout.

"You mean the warlord Kymora," Skiro says, drawing closer to the group.

"She's our prisoner. We should use her," Kellyn says.

"She can't be trusted!" I shriek. "She's nearly killed us more times than I can count! She'll flee at the first chance she gets, help our enemies if she can!"

"We could offer her something she wants," Petrik says hesitantly.

I round on the scholar. "And just what are you prepared to offer her?"

"Her freedom," Skiro says with a firm determination. He turns to Saydan. "See to it. I have to speak with my sister. Temra, Petrik, with me."

I think I must have imagined the whole conversation. Surely the prince couldn't have been so stupid as to—

And then I hear her voice.

"This is all the men we have?"

"Yes," Saydan answers Kymora.

"Huh. Then we best make use of the townspeople. Send them out in groups to collect rocks from the surrounding mountains."

"Prince Skiro ordered the gates closed."

"And I'm telling you to open them."

I watch them walk through the courtyard. So close now.

"I want fires built in every tower. We need large pots from the kitchens. Set water to boiling."

Saydan nods to some of the men behind him, and they break away to carry out orders.

"Give every man on the wall a torch to hold. Do you have pitch?" Kymora asks.

"We have oil."

"It'll have to do. Bring all the soldiers I have to command to the wall so I may speak to them."

"I will gather them up now."

Saydan looks to Kellyn and me before relinquishing Kymora into our custody.

Though I have a new set of magicked hammers at my sides, they do little to comfort me with the warlord standing to my left.

Kellyn, the traitor, stands on her other side, his arms crossed over his chest. He looks carefree, relaxed almost. As if there weren't an army approaching. As if everything were perfectly fine.

Why does no one but me seem to realize that we're all about to die? How am I the only one afraid?

After a silence that might be the death of me, Kymora bursts into laughter. "It's funny how quickly things can change."

Her hands are manacled together, and she isn't permitted a weapon, but she's still far too capable without the use of either. She can run. She can jump. She can do whatever she damn well pleases.

My eyes land on her perfectly working knees. Knees I once shattered with my hammer. Kymora notices my stare.

"They blindfolded me. Brought in some magic user, and then I was all healed up. Guess Skiro figured I would need to be able to walk if I'm to lead you all into battle."

A noise comes up from my throat. One of distaste. Serutha's abilities are wasted on her.

"In the heat of battle, anything can happen," I mutter. "Maybe one of my hammers will slip from my grasp. Maybe your skull will split in two."

"I'd like to see how you'd fare against the approaching army then," she responds.

"Probably better! For all we know, you'll order the men to do things to impede our progress."

The warlord turns her uncaring gaze on me. "I'm a woman of my word. I said I would do my best against the approaching army in exchange for my freedom. I intend to do exactly that."

"And after? I suppose you'll just give up your plans for world domination? I suppose you'll cease trying to hunt me and other magic users down?"

Her smile is vapid, her eyes vicious. "I made no assurances about what I would do after."

"If you come after me or mine again, I *will* kill you this time. You will receive no mercy a second time."

"You wouldn't get the best of me a second time."

"We'll see about that."

"Enough," Kellyn says. "Do not taunt her, Kymora. Focus on the task at hand."

She eyes Kellyn with renewed interest. "Why are you still here? I thought you were a mercenary. What sum could Skiro have possibly offered you to entice you stay for this suicidal endeavor?"

"It's not suicidal," I interrupt. "You're going to make sure we win!"

"I never said we'd win. I said I would do my best. Even the likes of me cannot make soldiers out of untrained men. I'd wager over half of these men were given positions in the city because they looked impressive holding a sword, not because they have any real skill with it. Besides, our preparations would go a lot faster if you two were helping."

"We are making sure you don't do anything stupid," I say. "And nothing you say will entice me to leave your side."

"How's your sister doing?" Kymora asks.

My eyes narrow in on the warlord. *She thinks she's dead*, I remind myself. She's trying to goad me into running away in a huff or charging at her so she can take my weapons from me. She has no idea Temra is alive and well. How could she? Those wounds were fatal. But now she knows there's a magical healer. Perhaps she put two and two together . . .

I ignore her. As much as one can when still having to keep my eyes glued to her.

After a time, Skiro returns, Tazar and Petrik right beside him. The guard puts himself between Kymora and the prince. "It's all set into motion," Skiro says to Kellyn and me. "Nothing more to do except wait."

Petrik looks over his mother slowly, and I can't imagine what he must be feeling. What would I do if my mother were a traitor and tried to kill someone I loved? Had ordered her men to kill me?

"Petrik," Kymora says with a solemn nod, as though he were a new acquaintance.

"Kymora," he says.

And the fierce, fearless warlord flinches. It is the most subtle movement. I would have missed it entirely if I hadn't been watching her like a hawk.

This is the first time I've heard him address her by her name instead of *Mother*. As though he's officially cut himself off from her, and she knows it now, too.

The warlord turns away, and her mask of indifference is in place once more.

There are so many people piled into the courtyard, but we watch as guards encourage them to step into the palace in small groups, ushering people through the doorway.

I'd imagine some would resist. Hesitant to step through anything magical, when they don't know it's safe firsthand. Hopefully, Temra and Serutha will be able to convince everyone.

Whether there are difficulties or not, it will take quite some time for people to step through single file with all their possessions.

And the army will be here before then.

When Ravis's forces are within throwing distance, only half of the city folk have made it through the portal.

The enemy's numbers seem larger, what with all the heavy weapons and armor they tote around. They all wear the sigil of Ravis, a lion in mid-pounce. They carry spears in their hands and swords at their waists. A weapon to throw. A weapon for close combat. I wonder if the soldiers are strong enough to throw a spear over the wall.

Maybe.

Horses pull covered wagons. Only a handful of men ride their own steeds; the majority are on foot.

It is one thing to know an army is approaching. It's something else entirely to see it for myself.

"Steady," Kellyn says.

I realize a moment later he's talking to me.

"I'm fine."

"We should get you off the wall, sire," Tazar says to the prince.

"I will not hide. I will help where I can. My sword."

Tazar hesitates, before handing over the weapon sheathed at his side, a broadsword. The handle looks worn, but when the prince unsheathes it, I see the sword itself is sharp.

"Give the prince a shield, too," Kymora says. "He'll need one."

Kymora has had the men line the wall with arm-held shields. Tazar hands one to the prince. Saydan stays right at Kymora's back, his own weapons at the ready. I still don't like that she's freed with only a single chain binding her hands together. It's not enough.

The formation of Ravis's men is not perfect, I note when they get closer. Their lines are lopsided, the men themselves tired after a full night's march.

It's a small advantage, when considering their sheer numbers. I can't see them all without turning my head. But I take comfort in our walls. In the defensive position of the palace. Skiro's castle is built right up against the cliff of mountain at our backs, so at least the advancing men will be forced to attack from the front.

They march until they are only twenty yards away. Then they halt, adjust their formations, until the line is straighter and more uniform.

And then I spot Ravis, parting his men so he and his mount can reach the front. He wears a full suit of armor that gleams without a scratch or nick upon it.

I take a step backward before realizing I'm moving. Then I walk right up to the wall's edge and hold my ground. I will not be afraid. I will show Ravis that he can't affect me. I will not give him that power.

"Brother," Skiro says to the older prince below.

"Skiro," Ravis replies. "Your gate is closed."

"You haven't been invited."

"It's to come to a fight, then?"

"If that's what you choose."

Ravis scoffs in a distinctly un-princely way. "I offered you peace. I told you what was required. You are choosing this."

Skiro shakes his head. "I stayed in my borders. You are the one trespassing."

"You are unfit to rule, and I hear you are also unfit to fight. My spy has told me you've barely one hundred men within those walls. Are you really going to force them to die for you?"

"I force them to do nothing. If they choose to fight, it will be for their lands and their families. You've come to take that from them."

Skiro plays his part well, dragging out the conversation as long as possible to allow more civilians to make it through the portal.

But there are still so many filling the courtyard.

Kymora, I note, hangs back, out of sight of the enemy prince. When I look at her, she says, "Never show your hand."

She doesn't want Ravis to see her. I wonder if the prince would be less inclined to attack if he knew we had her. He would know and remember her from her time serving their father. She had a reputation long before the king divided the realm.

"Enough," Ravis says at last. "This is your final chance. Open the gate now or my soldiers will attack."

"No, this is your last chance. Leave. I have magicians and fortifications aplenty. We are not so helpless as you may think. You advance at your own peril."

Ravis doesn't blink, but his eyes turn to me. "Lady smithy, you're on the wrong side of the wall."

I shake my head, not giving him the satisfaction of answering.

"I will see you hanged for the stunt you pulled. You remember that I gave you a chance to serve willingly. I am not without mercy."

"Just basic human decency," I hiss under my breath.

"Soldiers of Ghadra!" Ravis shouts to his men. "Advance!"

Ravis disappears behind the sea of his men to safety, coward that he is.

And then it's happening.

We're under attack.

CHAPTER

TWENTY

I've learned in my few experiences with fighting that it's chaotic. Bloody. Loud. Foul-smelling.

There's really nothing to like about it.

But engaging in a battle among thousands?

It's so much worse.

A hammer to the senses.

Fear so thick, you feel like you're swimming through it.

I've had panic attacks aplenty throughout my life, but I've never experienced anything quite like this.

Arrows loose into the air from the enemy, flying over the wall without any trouble at all. I raise my new left hammer—Echo—to shield me, crouch to make myself as small as possible. One arrow hits the side of my shield and goes flying backward in the opposite direction from the rebound. My other hammer, Agony, absorbs the same amount of force.

And then another volley propels toward us.

In the courtyard, the people are running for the castle,

cramming into every possible space as they await their turn with the portal. There's too much happening behind me and in front of me, but I decide to keep my eyes ahead, where the danger awaits.

"Hold steady now," Kymora says.

There's nothing to do while the men are out of reach. Skiro has a handful of skilled archers among his men, and they fire over the tops of our heads into the masses below. While a few land, it does nothing to deter or slow down the sheer numbers of the advancing army.

Ravis's men uncover the wagons they've brought along, revealing ladders and hooks. They line up to heave the large equipment toward us.

A scream down the wall reveals a man with an arrow through the heart, too slow with his shield for the third volley. He plummets into the palace courtyard, the men around him stunned for a breath.

"Bring the water!" Kymora shouts.

With padded gloves, a handful of our soldiers remove the boiling pots of water from the fires, replacing them with new ones, ready to be heated.

The first of the ladders is extended, the top reaching just above the wall's edge. Kymora looks down her nose at it, watches a flurry of men begin to climb.

I feel my hands start to shake as I watch their progression, waiting for Kymora to do something.

It isn't until the first soldier is nearly to the top that she steps aside and nods to the man holding the first pot.

He empties the scalding water onto the waiting soldiers below. More screams fill the air, followed by the sound of falling bodies crunching on impact with the ground.

When the ladder is emptied, Kymora grabs it by the top and

casts it aside. The wood splinters once it falls, the whole thing now useless.

Skiro's men follow the warlord's lead, needing no prompting. When a ladder lands against the wall, they're ready with more pots of boiling water.

It doesn't take long for Ravis's soldiers to pause with the ladders, his men too afraid of being burned to keep pressing on. They stick to sending more volleys of arrows our way.

For a while.

Soon they're back, this time with the grappling hooks, likely hoping to overwhelm us with their sheer numbers. Twenty different ropes are thrown upward, the hooks catching on the wall's edge. The enemy climb nimbly, despite the armor they wear.

"Oil!" Kymora shouts.

While some of Skiro's soldiers saw at the ropes with knives, Kymora directs the others to pour oil down the line of ropes. With a torch, she walks past them one at a time, lighting them up.

More shouts rip through the air as the fire travels down, engulfing those who were unlucky enough to get coated in the oil. The ropes eventually snap from the tension at the spots where the flames eat away at the fibers.

More hooks and ladders replace the fallen equipment, twice as many as last time, and I wonder if the first two waves were just for Ravis to test out our defenses.

I take position at the top of one of the ladders nearby, leaving Kellyn to guard Kymora.

I bash in heads as they reach the top, sending men and women flailing back to the ground with caved in helmets. Some die upon impact; others find their feet and wander before collapsing.

I feel sick.

Sick to be killing.

Sick to know this is all because of Ravis's greed.

Sick to think no one at all has to die.

The city folk are all in the castle now, at least, if not through the portal yet. Guards bring regular updates to Skiro.

And then some of Ravis's men make it atop the wall.

At the farthest left end, where wall meets rock, a grappling hook caught on the wall, with no one to burn the rope or slice it off.

Five men rush this way, with more trying to climb the wall behind them.

"Kellyn!" I shout because he's closer.

He sees them, takes one look at Kymora, and makes his decision.

What I see next is only snatches out of the corner of my eye. Kellyn raising his hand, unclenching his fist. Lady Killer sliding from his back sheath of its own volition, whipping into his hand faster than the eye can follow. The mercenary leaping over our men bent over the wall, where they pour more vats of hot water over the enemy below.

A sword point thrusts for my face from below; I get Echo between me and it just in time. The magical rebound sends the soldier sailing down the ladder, knocking each man on the rungs below him off along the way.

With the ladder free of the extra weight, I shove it away from the wall and watch it crash to the ground below.

When I look back up, Kellyn has dispatched the men on the wall. He attempts to saw through the rope with his sword, but I see that a new man will soon reach the top. The enemy pauses to draw his sword and takes a swipe at Kellyn, narrowly missing his neck. I don't think before rushing forward to help.

With me bashing in heads and him sawing, the rope snaps in no time.

I spin back around as soon as I remember we left Kymora unguarded, but she's still shouting out orders from atop the wall. I watch as she dodges an arrow without skipping a word.

She really is extraordinary. I just wish she were *actually* on our side.

Petrik casts his staff at the men below, trying to interrupt the flow of soldiers as best he can. One tries to grab ahold of the staff, but it slips through her fingers as if coated in oil and returns to Petrik without delay.

I feel a rush of pride to see my weapons doing just as I bade them.

At a noise farther down the right side of the wall, we all look up. An enemy soldier made it to the top. A large woman in light armor charges toward us. Men try to stop her, but she thrusts out a hammer and—

That's my *hammer!*

Men go flying to the ground as she charges forward with the hammer Ravis stole from me. She tramples them underfoot as she comes bolting for the prince.

There is a small voice in my head, one that begs me to flee. To be safe and live. But in this one instance, the brave Ziva is over-powering. Because that is *my* hammer that *I* made, and she has it, and she's hurting people, and I have to make it right.

I bypass Prince Skiro, veer around Kymora and Petrik, until no one and nothing is between me and the approaching soldier. She eyes me, eyes my own hammers, and grins. It makes my stomach turn over, but I hold my ground, thrusting out Echo, while the woman charges forward holding out my old hammer.

The two invisible shields connect in a loud *twang*, and I'm thrown backward, losing my feet entirely as my back smacks into the solid brick flooring of the wall. The breath leaves me, and I can't sit up for some time. When I do, I find the other woman in a similar state opposite me. Shakily, we both find our feet before advancing again.

This time, instead of plummeting toward me with the shield hammer extended, the soldier holds it at her waist, preparing to swing with the magicless right hammer.

But what she doesn't know is that Agony absorbed the power of our collision, and she sings with the extra force. I dodge the soldier's blow before making contact with my right hammer.

The soldier goes *flying*. Well over the wall, over the heads of many of the enemy soldiers below, before finally falling.

I turn away so I don't have to see the impact. Then I pick up my old magicked hammer from where she dropped it and slide it through my belt.

I catch Kymora pursing her lips in thought when I turn around. I know for certain that I don't want to know what she's thinking. I can just see the wheels turning, feel her mind calculating all the ways she would use me at the first chance.

When the warlord returns her attention to the men below, she swears.

I follow her line of sight.

They're bringing out a battering ram.

"Rocks!" she shouts. "Concentrate all throwing power on those soldiers! Stop them now!"

I sheathe my hammers to palm large rocks and throw them onto the enemy below. Even with their helmets, the falling stones are enough to bend the steel, sending several men and women to their knees. The large log they carry topples momentarily, until more men fill the spaces of the fallen.

I worried Ravis would order his man to use his war hammer to bring down the gate, but he isn't even bothering. He doesn't need to risk a higher-ranking soldier trained with a powerful weapon when he has pawns and supplies that will get the job done.

"Again!" Kymora shouts. "Don't let them reach the gate!"

Petrik flings his staff over and over. With Kellyn and I assisting, Skiro's men send more rocks pelting downward. The prince himself bends down to gather stones and throw them. But we're running low on supplies.

And then the wall shakes as the first strike of the battering ram hits.

"Archers!" Kymora says. "Up here with me! You men there! Go below and brace the gate. Don't let them through!"

The warlord's orders are obeyed with haste. Men switch positions. The gate takes another hit, and we officially run out of rocks.

"Hot water! Bring it!"

The next batch of boiling water gets poured onto those manning the battering ram. Several run off screaming. Yet more take their places. Always more. Ravis doesn't care how many he sacrifices so long as he wins.

"Loose every arrow you have!" Kymora calls to the archers when they're in place. "Don't let any man touch the trunk!"

But with everyone concentrating on the gate, more of the enemy make it atop the wall.

Just how many damned ladders did Ravis bring with him?

Kellyn fends off the entire left side of the wall by himself, Lady Killer's abilities just enough to keep them back. But on the right side, Skiro's men start dropping like flies, falling beneath the superior numbers mounting the wall.

Kymora eyes the right. Then she holds out her hands to me. "Take these off."

"No," I respond immediately.

"Do you want to be overrun right now? Take them off and give me a weapon."

I shake my head vehemently. She cannot be trusted. I don't care if she's gotten us this far. She killed my parents. She nearly killed Temra. Kellyn. Her own son. A person who would do that is not stable in the least.

"For Twins' sake!" she screams. Then she bends down, picks up a fallen soldier's sword and approaches the right side of the wall with her hands still manacled together.

Unsure what else to do, I follow.

Kymora steps into the fray with a soldier's ease, fighting alongside Skiro's men. Even with her hands bound together, she wields the sword like a master, felling foe after foe.

More of Skiro's men fall. I step in with my hammers, fighting at Kymora's side.

Wrong. This feels so very wrong.

How has it come to this? Me fighting beside my parents' murderer.

Blood cakes my hands, sprays into my eyes. Some from my kills, but even more from Kymora's. Her sword slashes through the air, moving with a dancer's grace, letting blood fly in every which direction as she delivers death efficiently and most surely effectively.

I slip on a patch of blood, go down on one knee. Thinking me fallen, an enemy soldier tries to creep past me. But I raise my right hammer, catch him below his chin on the upward swing. His neck cracks. Or maybe his jaw? Either way, he soars backward and doesn't move again.

Do people really acquire a taste for this?

They don't talk about how messy it is. Killing. In the storybooks, it's all about glory and honor. They don't mention how blood can get in your mouth. How bladders loosen. How the smell of death is so cloying, you choke on it. How a face that was once animated can suddenly become lifeless.

How every time you kill, you feel like you lose just a little piece of yourself.

And yet, I keep killing. My sister is in the castle. My friends are on this wall. Ravis is advancing, hoping to overthrow peace. Intending to enslave magic users to his will.

Anyone who threatens me and my family will face my hammers.

I don't hesitate before I swing, but that doesn't mean I like it.

I like even less that I'm getting better at it.

"On your right," Kymora says, and I spin just in time to see a soldier charging at me. I catch him with Echo, send him sprawling to the ground on our side of the wall. His arms and legs land at angles that make them useless.

And then I hear a large crash. The splintering of wood and clanking of metal. The grunting of men and cries of others.

I realize with horror that they made it through the gate.

"Get the prince out of here!" Kymora shouts. "Hurry, before they overwhelm him."

I spin to find Tazar already hauling Skiro away, Petrik helping.

"It's not over. We have to—" Skiro starts.

"It's done," Petrik says. "We have to get you through the portal now!"

Kymora narrows her eyes at the word *portal*, but she says nothing about it. She's distracted by a fresh batch of men climbing over the wall.

I go to help her, but a hand on my arm stops me from moving. I spin with my shield and stop just in time as I register Kellyn.

"You can't just grab me when we're in the middle of battle!" I scream at him.

"Sorry, but we have to go."

"But Kymora."

"Has done her part. She bought us more time. The prince promised her freedom. It's time to let her go."

"No!"

Kellyn drags me down the steps of the wall, stopping at intervals to fend off an advancing soldier.

"Duck!" I shout, and he obeys as I bring up Echo and send a soldier flying backward.

"We can't just leave her behind!" I say, picking the argument back up, even as we begin running once more.

"What else would you have us do? Bring her? How in the world would we force her to do that? And you can't break Skiro's promise to her."

"*I* made no such promise."

"So you'd rather, what? Stay here, attempt to kill her, and then die when Ravis's men surround you?"

I hate this. Hate that he's right. Hate that there's so much happening, so much chaos. This is the literal opposite of being alone and safe.

"Surely you want to see Temra make it through the portal?" Kellyn asks at last.

He knows just what to say to get me to move faster.

We plunge into the palace, Skiro and Petrik so far ahead of us they're already out of sight. Kellyn and I dispatch more soldiers along the way, making for the stairs.

And then Kellyn looks over his shoulder. I see his eyes bulge before he pulls me into some darkened nook between a bookcase and the space under another set of stairs.

My heartbeat pounds in my ears, and sweat drips from every pore. Still, Kellyn covers my body with his, shoving us into the corner of the space, blocking anything running by from seeing me. There's nothing heated in the gesture. This is survival. I cover my mouth with my hands to dampen my labored breathing. I'm nearly overwhelmed with the dried blood taste on my skin.

Frenzied footsteps sound everywhere in the palace, but I immediately register the loudest sets, which come to a halt when they reach a loud crescendo that can only mean they're right next to our hiding place.

"You're telling me you bargained your freedom for killing dozens of my soldiers?"

My body tenses at Ravis's voice.

"You should have waited for me before attacking. I would have spared the loss of so many of your men." I'm even more shocked to realize it's Kymora responding.

"You caused the losses!"

"And had I been on the right side of the wall, the loss would have been entirely on Skiro's side."

"I didn't have the time to wait around for you. You were gone for weeks! I thought you were dead."

Kymora scoffs. "I'm not killed so easily."

"Just captured and dragged about Ghadra by a bunch of adolescents."

"I heard the same adolescents got the better of you. Wiped out you and your entire regiment of soldiers with a single sword."

"It's that damned smithy. When I get my hands on her—"

"You will do nothing. We need her."

"Like hells we do. We have the superior numbers. I'm done trying to get anything out of that lady smithy."

"She only needs to be handled carefully and given the right motivation. She won't get the best of us again."

"Because she'll be dead."

"Ravis, use sense. Even once you have the throne, you need the resources to hold on to it."

"That's what you're for. I reinstate you as general over my armies. I rule as king. That was the arrangement. Not my fault you butchered the plan by detouring and wasting time with that magical smithy. If you'd only joined your men up with mine sooner, the world would already be ours."

"Instead, you took Elany and my men for your own," Kymora says, her voice dropping dangerously.

"They needed money to feed their families. I offered them jobs," he says in defense of himself. "What's done is done, but I'll not let you bungle this up again. The smithy dies. Her friends die. And my brother will spend the rest of his days in prison."

"And what of your other brother?"

"My father's bastard?"

Petrik.

"My son," Kymora says, her tone making it perfectly clear what she thinks about the word Ravis used.

"You can kill him or throw him in with Skiro. They can rot together. I don't really care. I just want what should have been mine from the start."

I can feel Kellyn's heartbeat where our chests are pressed together. It stutters out a too-fast rhythm.

Kymora laughs, the sound unkind.

"Yours?" she repeats with contempt. "Ravis, half the reason your father split the realm was because you couldn't handle the full responsibility on your own."

"That's not true and you know it."

"Fine. He did it because of his own misguided notions of love, but that doesn't change the fact that you'd make a terrible king."

"You watch yourself, Warlord," Ravis says. His voice sounds strained, as though it comes between clenched teeth. "I will not put up with such disrespect. I am your king, and you will give me the deference worthy of that title."

"You're no king. And you're certainly no warrior king. That display back there proved as much. You think you've got an edge on the rest of the royal children, but what happens when the northern continent decides they want to inhabit our lands? What about when the western isles build a strong armada and want to see if we have anything of value?"

"Then you'll fight them off, as is your job."

A pause. Then from Kymora: "Yes, I will. What I'm struggling to figure out is why you need to be in the equation at all."

Another pause. "I—I have an army! I have the birthright! I'm—I'm—"

Kymora lets out a bored sigh. "Did you actually think I did all of this because I wanted to serve another king? Do you think I built myself up, gathered and trained loyal soldiers because I wanted to hand them over to you? Ravis, I always intended to betray you. I used you and your connections because you were the most power-hungry. I let you rouse the nobles of your territory to your cause so I could reap the benefits. And now that the army is gathered in one place, all the support and money it needs here right now, I'm struggling to see why I shouldn't just dispense with you now instead of later."

A weird, pained breathing comes from the prince before he says, "Strax! Arrest the warlord."

There's a scuffle, though brief. Strax and his men clearly don't think that Kymora will get the better of them, especially while she's manacled. Yet, I hear bodies fall, and I know none of them belong to the warlord. The fight ends with the wet sound of a blade sinking into flesh.

Kymora tsks. "That was the only loyal man you had in this entire castle. Now you've gone and got him killed."

"I have near t-two thousand still under my command." Ravis's voice has grown weak.

"And you pay them for their loyalty. Most are my soldiers, who will rally to me once they know I'm alive. We will take Ghadra without you, and if the rest of your men are smart, they'll ally with me. Goodbye, Ravis. Tell your father I said hello."

Another wet sound.

A muffled cry.

A body slumping to the floor.

And then Kymora's voice ringing clear. "I don't care about Skiro. I want that smithy. The soldier who brings her to me will get riches untold and a place of honor at my side as we take the kingdom back."

CHAPTER
TWENTY-ONE

It's been several minutes since Kymora moved on.

Yet Kellyn and I haven't moved an inch.

I'm too stunned for movement. Either Kellyn feels the same way, or he's simply holding me up. My brain is working far too fast, and yet not fast enough to put everything together.

Kymora has been working with Ravis from the start.

She just killed him.

Kymora is free and now possesses her own army.

She's coming for me.

She's coming for us all.

She means to take everything, and now she has the manpower to do it.

Should she capture me, then she'll have everything she needs to stay in power forever. Especially if she gets her hands on Kellyn or Temra.

Temra . . .

"We need to get to the portal," I say. "Now, before Kymora and her men find it. It might already be destroyed."

Kellyn nods. "I'm not sure if we're lucky or unlucky that she's not looking for it at the moment. Because she's looking for . . ."

"Me," I finish.

I try not to stare at Ravis's body as we leave our hiding spot. But I see it and Strax's, and I can't help but think again—no one had to die. Why couldn't he just be content with what he had?

Was that my problem as well? Not being content with what I had. Should I have just been happy with the money I earned, lived contentedly in my mother and father's house forever? Maybe I got greedy. Maybe I never should have taken on more and more commissions. Never should have let word of me and my abilities spread. I should have lived as a regular smithy. Never making anything magical for anyone. Temra and I would have lived simply, but we would have *lived*.

I miss the days when I was living.

Now I seem to only be *surviving*.

We take the halls with purpose, like we know what we're doing and know where we're going. Ravis's—no, Kymora's—men are everywhere. We pause to hide behind things where we're able, and fake that we belong when we're not.

No one stops us. Everyone is looking for a smithy, not a soldier. And I certainly look like the latter with the blood coating every part of me.

When we make it to the room of portals, we find it unlocked. Kellyn opens the door, ushers me inside ahead of him.

I lose any sense of sanity I had left when I see what remains. Destruction.

The portals have been destroyed, rendered useless before Kymora or any one of our enemies could use them.

But everyone seems to have made it through. Except Kellyn and me.

Again.

We'll never make it out of this castle.

I lose my balance. Lose my feet. Lose my connection to the here and now.

I'm spinning out of control. I can't breathe. My body feels itchy, hot, and I want nothing more than to claw out of my own skin.

I'm trapped. Forever. I will never be happy. Nothing will ever be okay.

"Ziva . . ."

Kellyn's voice sounds so far away, and I don't feel him even as he grips me. I'm going to lose him. I'm going to lose Temra. I've lost everything, and it's still all my fault.

And then the room spins.

No, just shifts, and Kellyn places me in front of one of the portraits.

Marossa's.

And my eyes finally focus enough to note one very important thing.

It's still intact.

Every portal is destroyed except one. The one I had to turn my neck to see.

I grab Kellyn's hand, and together we step through.

I brace myself for impact. Last time I did this, I struck against a wall. But this time? Nothing. The air is still stale and dust clouds in front of my nose, but I'll take it. Lights flicker around us, and I think we're in some sort of hallway.

"Thank the Twins!" a voice I know all too well says.

Temra uses the sharp edge of her sword to scratch along the portal behind us, scraping off the paint. Then, for good measure, she grabs a bucket and throws water onto the portrait. Paint runs down in rivulets, before pooling onto the floor in a brown mess.

Her task done, my sister embraces me. "I'm so relieved you made it! I was getting ready to go look for you if you didn't show in the next minute."

"Me too." Petrik appears farther down the barely lit corridor.

"Where are we?" I ask.

"Secret passage in Marossa's castle," Petrik answers.

Kellyn says, "Not so secret anymore."

Petrik winces. "Things are a bit touchy right now between my brother and sister. Don't poke the hornets' nest."

He and Temra lead us down the tunnel. It's filthy, the floor coated in mud and feathers and whatever else got dragged through here from all the people evacuating.

"Marossa didn't like that Skiro revealed the passage to so many people?" I ask.

"Actually, she didn't even know about it, nor the portal, so you can imagine how she's feeling right now," Petrik says.

"But she still welcomed us into her territory?"

"*Welcomed* is a strong word. *Tolerated* is more like it. In fact, I need to get back in there so they don't kill each other. Ziva, Kellyn, would you both come? You know the most about Ravis and his plans. I know my sister would love to hear everything from your mouths firsthand."

I open my mouth, stutter for a moment, and then sigh. "All right."

Kellyn says, "We just fought a battle in which we were heavily outmatched, but it's meeting someone new that might do her in." If it weren't for the fondness in his voice while he said it, I might be embarrassed.

When Petrik comes to a halt, his hand reaches forward, searching for something along the wall. There's a click, and a section swings outward, admitting us into a much brighter space. I squint, unsure if I'm trying to get grit from my eyes or protect them from the sudden light.

Men and women in black livery with an emerald tree stitched on their fronts line the interior of the room. They turn their gazes to us as we walk past but say nothing.

In the corridor, we find more guards. So many guards. I can barely see the walls they're crammed everywhere.

Princess Marossa may have allowed us into her castle, but she is certainly not trusting anyone. Or perhaps they were only here to help escort the people onward?

"This way," Petrik says, leading us beyond the serious guards. They stand so still, they don't look as though they're breathing.

And of all the thoughts to hit me right now, I think, *I've spent a lot of time in castles lately.*

Before a few months ago, I'd never set foot in one. And now? Now I've been to half the royal palaces in Ghadra.

And then, before I'm fully prepared, I'm meeting a third royal, the sovereign over my home territory.

Princess Marossa has black hair braided into fine plaits raining over her shoulders. Her skin is a deep brown, just like Skiro's and Ravis's. With flawless skin and large lips, she's simply stunning. She's small, lanky like her brothers, though much shorter. She might reach my shoulder if I was standing next to her. Instead of a dress, she wears formfitting leathers. She has a bow over her back, the string looped over one shoulder.

". . . filthy!" she's saying now to Skiro. "Just filthy. Have you seen my halls after three thousand people tracked through them? And they brought livestock with them. Livestock, Skiro! Feathers and wool cling to everything! Poor Algarow has been sneezing up and down the halls. I never wanted to rule anything, and now you've just doubled the size of my city in one day!"

Petrik coughs, drawing the argument to an abrupt halt.

I nearly freeze in place when Marossa turns her icy stare on me. "This is them?" she asks as she sizes up me and Kellyn.

"Yes," Skiro says. "This is Ziva and Kellyn, whom Ravis held captive. They gleaned extensive knowledge about his plans and brought me warning." I notice right away that Skiro doesn't reveal my abilities, for which I'm grateful.

"Skiro, I don't need another person to tell me war is coming. I believe you! You brought it to my bloody doorstep! What I need is someone with answers. How do we stop Ravis and his men? How do we protect the people?"

"Actually, Ravis is dead." The words are blunt, sharp. But I say them before I think about softening the blow.

"What?" both royals ask simultaneously. Their gazes turn back to me. I shift uncomfortably, and Kellyn takes over for me.

"We saw his body. Warlord Kymora killed him. They've been working together this whole time to take over Ghadra. But Kymora said she didn't need him anymore. She doesn't want to be reinstated as a general. She wants the crown for herself."

Petrik is the first to respond. "Tell us every word you overheard. What exactly happened?"

Kellyn shares the whole story, and I sway on my feet. I'm exhausted, and my hands itch from the crusting blood. When he's done, Marossa rolls her lips between her teeth, closing her eyes.

"Now the warlord is coming for us?" Skiro says carefully, as though if he speaks the words any louder, Kymora will appear then and there.

Kellyn nods. What he says is absolutely true, but what he didn't specifically mention is that she's coming for me.

Again.

"Algarow!" Marossa calls. "Bring me my bow. I want to shoot something."

"It's on your back, Highness."

"Arrows, then! And targets. No, take me to the stuffed rooms. I'll shoot some of the heads!"

The princess storms from the room, her attendants following behind her.

Prince Skiro closes his eyes, presses a finger to the bottom of his nose.

"I'm sorry," Petrik says slowly. "He may have attacked you, but he was still our brother. I never knew him well, but I'm sure you loved him. Despite him."

After a few beats of silence, Skiro says, "It has been a long day. I imagine we all would like to get cleaned and in bed. Please see to it." The last bit he says to the attendants along the walls.

I stay in the bath for hours, long after the water turns cold, just trying to feel clean.

Thoughts of blood and death and screams and crushed skulls play on repeat in my head. Everything that happened, everything I did—I can't seem to quiet it. To stop it. My fixating mind has new horrors to contemplate after today, and I feel out of control.

I leave the room immediately after dressing and pause outside my door. Temra's rooms are on the right, Kellyn's on the left.

I knock on the right door.

No one answers, so I peek inside. The bed is empty, still made. But I hear voices one door down, and it takes me far too long to realize she's in Petrik's room.

At first, I don't know how to feel about that. But I can hear their voices. They're just *talking*, Ziva. And even if they weren't . . .

Ick, I don't want to think about it.

So then I have another choice to make.

Go back to my room alone or . . .

I knock on the fourth door.

I wasn't nervous until now, when I'm waiting for him to answer.

What if he's sleeping and you just woke him up?

What if he's still in the bath and he answers in a robe?

What if—

The door opens partially, and his red hair comes into focus.

"Ziva," he says, his tone one of surprise. Like I was the last person he expected to see outside his door.

"Kellyn," I answer.

And then silence.

I came to him. I'm supposed to say something. What did I want? Why did I knock on his door?

"Do you—do you want to come in?" he asks. He stumbles over the words. I have never heard him stumble before.

"Yes," I answer.

He steps aside. I find a room identical to mine. Though at the sight of his tub, I wonder how he managed to fit in the thing. I barely fit into mine.

There's a chair and a desk and a bed. Nothing else. Marossa has not cultivated the same style of opulence that Skiro has.

For some reason I can't look at the bed directly.

More silence ensues as Kellyn watches me take in the room. He's dressed in a similar nightrobe to mine, though he has the strings at the neck loosely undone.

"Temra is in Petrik's room," I blurt as soon as my mind snags on something to say.

"Is she?" he asks.

"Yes."

Why do I do this to myself? I think I can be brave and do hard things, and then I throw myself into these mortifying situations that make me wish I were dead.

Please, please, can the ceiling collapse and the floor swallow me whole?

When I can't stand the new silence any longer, I say, "Please say something. I need you to take the lead right now. I know you want me to step it up and initiate things. And I've been trying so very hard. Please tell me you've noticed?" Before he can answer, as though my mouth has a tidal wave pressing against it and the words *must* come out, I continue. "I've been touching you. Initiating kisses. Striking up conversations. You said you wanted an equal partner, and I've been *trying*, Kellyn, but it's so hard. And I don't know if I can do it all the time anymore. Can we say I've learned my lesson? Can we please initiate things equally now? Can you please meet me halfway?"

I gulp down air after the words are out, as though I just ran a race instead of speaking so many words in one go.

"What!" Kellyn says, his voice incredulous.

"Please don't make me repeat all of that. I'm certain I've already forgotten half of it."

In fact, all I can focus on now is the tight bunching under my skin. The discomfort. Always discomfort. I try to focus on the good. On being near Kellyn. I just need to push through the agitation. It will fade eventually. It always does where he's concerned.

"I heard you," he clarifies. "But I don't understand. Whenever did I say you needed to initiate things?"

"After you hit your head in the woods. When you were shot.

You said you were sick of pursuing me. You said you were backing off because you wanted an equal partner, and you wanted me to make an effort for once."

"I really said that?"

I nod, daring to look at him. "Did you not mean it? Was that your concussion talking?"

"Yes, I mean no. I mean, I *was* feeling that at the time, but I had no idea I said it aloud. And I can't believe I said it so bluntly. I'm so sorry. It shouldn't have happened that way."

"I'm glad you said something! I thought you didn't want me anymore. You were pulling back. Not talking. Not touching me. I didn't know what to think!"

"But I told you! In the inn, I *told* you I still wanted you!"

"But then you pulled away. You didn't bring it up. You stopped acting like yourself. I thought you might have changed your mind."

"Changed my mind," he deadpans.

"Yes!"

"In just a matter of hours?"

"Yes! Why should I listen to your words when your actions speak something different? I'm glad, because you dared me to be braver. To go after what I want. And what I want is you."

The full force of his gaze hits me like a lightning strike. I continue, "But please don't make me take charge all the time. Can we please take turns now?"

His gaze softens into something endearing. "Yes, of course we can."

"You won't make me initiate every conversation?" I ask.

"I won't."

"And you'll start kissing me again?"

"I will."

"Good."

Kellyn's gaze turns inward. He's thinking very seriously about something, and I want to know what it is. But he's clearly not done, so I'm silent. He needs time to process everything I've said. I've been stewing over it for weeks. He's just now hearing about it.

When he refocuses on me, he says, "I have noticed your efforts. I loved it. But it was also mean of me. I was being spiteful. I wanted you to have a sense of what I was feeling while we were running from Kymora. It was unfair. And I'm so, so sorry. Let's just be ourselves."

"I'd like that."

And then I'm hit with another wave of exhaustion. The reminder of the bloody battle. Fleeing for our lives. Killing. I close my eyes against it.

I say, "I need you to take charge tonight," reminding him of my words from earlier.

He finally closes the distance between us and wraps me in his arms. "Sweetheart," he says, and the word is so loving and delicious it makes my toes curl. "I'm happy to, but I don't know what you need right now. You have to tell me. Do you want to talk about today? Do you want me to hold you? Do you want me to pull Petrik off your sister and lock him in my room tonight so he can't touch her? Say what you need and it's yours."

I laugh at the last option, and he squeezes me tighter.

"I don't hear that sound enough," he says.

Sometimes I forget that just because I never know what to say doesn't mean everyone else does all the time. Kellyn isn't a mind reader. If I need something, I need to ask for it.

"Today was rough," I say. "I would like to be held, please."

"Would you like to move somewhere more comfortable?" he

asks. "We can stand here for a while. We could sit on the couch. On the floor. Wherever you want."

"Could we lie down on the bed? Could we sleep side by side like we did in the tent?"

"Definitely," he says, his voice so deep, it's almost impossible to make out the word.

I'm very aware of many things. The fact that we're both wearing so little. The fact that we're alone in this room together. The fact that we have a *bed* to share.

But the gore and screams still battle for dominance in my thoughts, making me sick to my stomach.

Kellyn leans us against a mountain of pillows, pulls the covers over the top of us, and holds me against his chest. His hair is still damp from his bath, but I don't mind. The rest of his body keeps me warm.

"I can't stop thinking about the fight," I say after a bit. "It was horrible."

"It was," he agrees. "I've never experienced anything like it."

"I feel dirty," I say. "No, my soul feels dirty. I've killed so many people now that I've lost count. I feel evil. Bad. Like I will be sent to one of the Sisters' hells when I die."

Kellyn tries to say something, but I continue, "But then I think about you. You have also killed, but you're not bad. Your soul is not evil. Why do I hold myself to a higher set of values than I do you? What we did was necessary. I know it. But I still don't feel right inside.

"I felt this way after the battle with Kymora in Amanor, but then I couldn't give the thoughts much space in my head. I was too busy trying to save Temra's life. Then I was trying to save your life. And then we made it back to Skiro and war was approaching. And then it happened. And now I killed some more. It's fresh in my mind, and I don't think I can sleep. And how do you deal with it?"

Kellyn squeezes me tightly again. One hand rubs from my shoulder to my elbow. "I think my mind works differently than yours. I mean, obviously it does. But I am able to push things from my thoughts when I wish. But you can't, can you? Thoughts consume you. They take all the energy out of you."

"Yes."

"Sometimes it helps to focus on the *why* instead of the *what*. I don't think about the death I dealt. I think about who I'm protecting. I think about my home and my family. About you. I remind myself about all the good things so there's no space for the bad."

"I used to focus my thoughts by forging something in my head from start to finish. But now—the end result is a weapon. And then weapons lead to fighting. And I'm back to thinking about what I don't want to think about. I used to only worry about talking to people. Being judged by them. Now I have to worry about people trying to kill me. I think it's making my normal anxieties way worse."

"That's so unfair. I'm sorry."

"I think I've gotten over blaming myself, though. That helps. It's not my fault this is happening. What I do doesn't affect the world as much as I think it does." That and the fact that I've vowed not to make powerful weapons for anyone I don't know ever again. Or anyone in power.

"I'm glad to hear that."

It feels so good to unburden myself. To say aloud everything that's troubling me. I let the next problem fall from my lips.

"She's free, and she's hunting me again."

The arms around me tighten to an almost-painful pressure.

"She can't have you. I won't let her take you away. I'll die before that happens."

"Don't say that. Don't talk of dying, please. Just tell me that we'll beat her again. That everything will be okay."

"We *will* beat her again. Everything *will* be okay."

Though I know he can promise no such thing, it feels so good to hear it all the same.

I love the way Kellyn smells. Like the woods and leather and his own personal musk. I turn my nose into his shirt and breathe even more deeply. Now that we're talking, I don't feel so nervous around him. I feel myself relaxing into him.

"I've been going crazy with worry over my family," Kellyn says. "If we fail. If Kymora's army wins, that's it. There's nothing else to stop her. And what will that mean for everyone I love? I'm just one fighter. I can't stop her by myself. I couldn't even stop her fighting one-on-one. She's too good."

And now she has a whole army to back her up.

"We're not alone this time," I remind him. "The royals don't want to lose their lands or their heads. They will band together to fight her. They must. And if, for whatever reason, they lose, we will go to Amanor and defend your family to the last."

The words float in the air, determined, fierce. I would never take them back. I adore his family, and I would never leave them to face this alone.

"Ziva," Kellyn says so softly, "I love you."

I freeze, feel my body snap tight like a bowstring. He doesn't mean that. He's only trying to make me feel better because I'm so messed up after the war, and—

Stop it. You will not let your anxieties ruin this moment.

I want to tell him that I love him, too. How could I not? He's the only man I've ever wanted to love in this way. The only person I've ever felt so close to.

But I can't say those words back to him. It's too terrifying, and I'm still half convinced he doesn't mean them.

"You don't have to—" Kellyn starts.

I put a finger to his lips. "I want to be with you always," I say. Even if he changes his mind, I never will.

"Done," he says.

But doesn't he know that's something he can't promise me?

CHAPTER
TWENTY-TWO

Knocking wakes me.

At first, there's the extreme disorientation of waking up in an unfamiliar place. You'd think I'd be used to it by now.

And then there's the snoring coming from the body beneath me. Kellyn.

I get to admire him for all of a second before the knocking comes again, this time louder.

Kellyn rouses.

"What?" he asks.

The door opens, and Petrik strides in. Dressed and clean and looking for all the world like he could take on Kymora and her army single-handedly.

He looks between me and Kellyn for less than a heartbeat. "Good, Ziva's here, too. Saves me the trouble of hunting you down. You've both been requested to attend another meeting with my brother and sister. You have one hour before it starts. A servant outside can lead the way. Try not to be late this time."

And then Petrik whistles—*whistles*—on his way back out the door.

Kellyn's head falls against his pillow. One arm shields his eyes from the light. "You probably should have had me lock him in here last night."

"Why?" I ask.

Kellyn moves his arm, looks at me with amusement. "Why do you think he's in such a good mood?"

"Because he and Temra finally made up."

"They did more than that, Ziva."

I feel my mouth drop open. "No! He wouldn't— She wouldn't—"

Oh, Temra absolutely would. And Petrik would be helpless to deny her anything she wanted, let's be honest. Not that he would have any desire at all to deny her that. He'd be a willing and eager participant.

"Ick," I finally say.

"Try not to think about it," Kellyn says.

"I think Petrik and I need to have a talk."

"What will you say to him?"

"That I'll kill him if he does anything to hurt her."

Kellyn rubs his lips against the side of my head. "I don't think you need to worry about that, but Petrik could use a good scare every once in a while. I've never heard you sound so terrifying."

"And I'll need to have another talk with Temra."

"About?"

"Being careful."

"Careful?"

I eye him. "Against pregnancy."

"Oh. You mean— Sorry, I didn't know there was a way for women to control that."

He looks extremely uncomfortable, which I find vastly amusing.

"There are herbs," I inform him.

"I didn't know. My parents obviously don't bother with such things."

That has me laughing so very hard.

And then I catch my breath, because what he's saying means—

"So you didn't know?" I ask.

"I just told you I didn't."

"No, I mean—all the women you've been with. You didn't know whether or not you both were being careful?" He could have children that he doesn't even know about.

That thought makes my stomach turn sour.

Kellyn bolts upright in bed. He hauls me up after him, holding me at arm's length so he can look me in the face. "All the women I've *been* with? Just how many women do you think I've been with?"

Oh, I hate this conversation: being forced to think about how much more experienced Kellyn is than I am. My jealousy is almost a tangible thing with the way it consumes every space in my body.

"With your pretty face?" I say. "You're probably approaching a dozen." And then I worry over my answer. Will he think it too low? Have I offended him?

Who cares, Ziva?

This is not the time to—

"Ziva, I've never been with anyone."

My eyes fly up to meet his. "What?"

"Not a single person."

"Oh. But *why?*"

He laughs at the question. Then sobers. "Have you been with anyone?"

"Are you joking?"

"I didn't want to assume—"

"You were my first everything, Kellyn. Well, not *everything*. Yet."

And then I feel the blood rush to my face.

"Oh no," I say, burying my face in my hands. "I didn't mean that," I mumble between my fingers. "Please ignore—"

"*Yet?*" Kellyn snags on that word like it's some tasty treat. "Did you have plans? I need to hear all the details immediately."

I try to grab the covers to bury my face within them, but Kellyn wrenches them from me.

"I need to go . . . get dressed," I supply, making an attempt to roll out of his bed.

But he will have none of that. He moves his big body, pressing me into the mattress, caging me in. "Ziva, please look at me."

He's hovering above me, with his delicious weight warming my whole body. I sigh, find my courage, and move my hands.

Only to have his mouth capture mine.

The embarrassment disperses like a match being struck, and I kiss him back with everything I have.

All too soon, he pulls away, resting his forehead against mine. "I love you." He says those words again, and my whole body melts through the bed, pooling in a puddle somewhere beneath it. "Don't hide from me. No more hiding. We're past that, aren't we?"

"I suppose," I say.

"Even when you say such beautiful words. I never thought *yet* would become my favorite."

I laugh at him. He's so ridiculous.

"*Yet* is now your favorite word?" I ask.

"Absolutely."

Shaking my head, I wrap my arms around his neck to pull his lips back down to mine. I love how warm and soft they are. I love how they part underneath mine. I love the sounds he makes and the way he touches me.

I love him, and it hurts.

Because now he's become another thing I can lose.

We kiss for so long that I'm convinced I want to turn *yet* into *now*, but then he pulls away.

"Meeting," he says between breaths. "We have a meeting to get to."

The sound that comes out of me is somewhere between a groan and a pout.

His lips against my neck, he says, "I would suggest we make plans to continue after the meeting, but I already know what you'll say to that. So maybe I'll just spontaneously kiss you afterward."

"It's not spontaneous if you're planning it!" I say, lightly smacking his arm.

"Maybe I'll spontaneously think of it again . . . after the meeting."

"You're hopeless."

"You're irresistible," he counters.

Another knock sounds on the door, and Petrik's voice calls out, "Twenty minutes!"

I flip Kellyn over, raise up onto my knees, and then roll off the bed. "What are the odds I could get away with not showing up to this one?"

"Very slim. Unless we found a very good place to hide."

"With all the guards spanning the full length of the palace? I don't think we'd have a chance."

"We could barricade the door," he suggests.

I laugh as I see myself out.

Dressed, groomed, and with my mind fortified, I exit my room to find Kellyn standing next to a servant, both waiting for me. As the servant leads the way down the hall, Kellyn and I reach for each other's hand at the same time.

Whereas Skiro's palace was bedecked in all manner of art, Marossa's is filled with taxidermies. Mountain cat heads, antlers, even an entire bear can be found spread throughout the path we traverse. It's somewhat disturbing, but given the princess's love of the hunt, there's no question where all of this came from.

The meeting room has too many people. Kellyn and I try to hide in the back, but Petrik forces us to the front, right next to the royals, their guards, and their advisers.

Really, it's amazing how many people fit in the room. And everyone's standing, like maybe there isn't a table in the palace big enough for us all to fit.

I fidget in place, and Kellyn pulls my back against his front, before holding both of my hands in his. It's like he's shielding me on all sides from everyone in the room. It's nice.

And then I catch sight of Temra, standing next to Petrik, and I feel my eyes narrow. As if she can feel the weight of my stare, she looks up.

I give a meaningful nod between her and Petrik, then raise a single brow.

She smiles and looks away.

As though that's all we're going to say about it.

Not a chance.

But I let it go when Prince Skiro starts filling everyone in on the situation as it currently stands.

I try to pay attention; I really do. But I quickly become distracted by something else.

Thinking about *yet*.

Kellyn's fingers draw pictures on the back of my hands, and I imagine those fingers trailing to other places. I blush furiously, but it's not like anyone knows what I'm thinking. They'll probably think I'm overheated. There's a lot of people in the room. Anyone who knows me will think that's the cause.

And damn my mind, but since we talked about it, about *yet*, now I'm fixating. And of course it's all I can think about. Because that is how my brain works.

Naked bodies.

I, Ziva Tellion, am thinking about naked bodies and bedrooms and sweat and heavy breathing and—

"We are adjourned until Ashper returns with news. In the meantime, we need to prepare for war."

I startle as I realize the meeting has ended, and I zoned out for the whole thing. Bodies shuffle for the door, and I spot Temra trying to sneak out the back.

I turn to Kellyn. "I'll see you later. I need to have words with my sister."

"Try not to mortify her too much."

"I will mortify her as much as I see fit."

He grins, and I grin, and then I depart.

Petrik is only a few steps behind her in the hall, as though they're trying to leave the finished meeting separately and failing miserably at it.

Temra lets herself into her room, and Petrik reaches the door a few steps later.

"Wait," I call out.

Petrik's back goes rigid. When he turns to face me, he has the look of a man caught in the act of some heinous crime.

"Petrik, I value you as a friend," I say.

At that, his face relaxes somewhat. "I value our friendship as well."

"Good, then don't do anything stupid to ruin it."

"Ruin it?"

"If you hurt my sister, I will personally come after you and remove your favorite limb with the bluntest tool from my forge."

He swallows. "I understand, and I will *never* hurt her again. She's more precious to me than anything."

"Good. Now leave. I need to talk with her."

He purses his lips. Thinks a moment.

"I will tell her you stopped by."

"Okay," he says finally.

He looks back over his shoulder when he leaves, as though maybe he can see my sister through the door.

"It's only a few hours, stupid man," I say under my breath.

Then I let myself into her room.

Temra stands as though she'd been expecting me, her arms crossed, her face defiant.

"Ziva, I'm a grown woman. And if I'm old enough to be fighting in battles, then I'm old enough to—"

"Are you being safe?" I ask, interrupting her.

"Of course."

"Is it what you want? You don't feel pressured or anything?"

"It's what I want more than anything. I love him."

"You hated him just the other day," I point out.

She quirks a smile. "I loved him then, too. That's why I was so mad. But we had a talk last night, and we have an understanding."

"Which is?"

"If he lies or hides anything from me again, we're done. He needs to trust me to be smart and make good choices when I have all the information."

"That's good. You do deserve someone who trusts you to be

smart." I know that, even if I want to control her choices some-times. I brace myself for the next question I should ask her. "Was it—was it your first time?"

She catches my eyes, quirks her head. "Yes. Would it have mattered if it wasn't?"

"I would have been disappointed that you didn't tell me if it wasn't. Do you want to talk about it?"

She smiles. "Maybe later, once it's not so new."

"But you're okay? No regrets?"

"None."

My heart hurts because for some reason I'm thinking about my mother. I wonder what she would say to her, what she would do. I can't do anything at all to help her, and I have no advice to give, because I haven't had that first.

Yet.

Damn that word.

"What did you think of Marossa and Skiro's decision?" Temra asks in a poor attempt to change the subject.

I let it slide this time. "Which one?"

"Using Ashper to send someone to each of the territories to rally the other royals for support."

"Who's Ashper?"

She narrows her eyes at me. "Were you not listening?"

"I was distracted."

"Of course, by all the people," she says. I don't correct her. "Ashper is the magical painter. He's going to paint new portals here, and then we can travel to the other territories to talk in per-son with the other royals."

"Oh, that's smart."

Temra crosses her arms. "Petrik said he found you in Kellyn's bed this morning."

She's hardly in a place to judge. "I was overcome with thoughts of the battle. I needed someone to talk to. I went to your room first. You weren't there."

A look of guilt crosses her face. "You only talked?"

"Yes."

"All right." She fiddles for something under her mattress, then hoists it up. "Does that mean you don't want any of this?"

From a leather pouch, Temra produces *herbs*, brandishing them with a wicked smile.

My mouth drops open. "How did you even—"

"I bought them while we were in Skiro's Territory. And I had them on me when we went through the portal."

"You had them *on* you?"

"Of course. I knew it would happen once I decided I wanted it. I wanted to be prepared. In case it was a spontaneous thing. And I knew we were likely to leave at some point. Better safe than sorry."

I narrow my eyes. "You and I have very different priorities."

She offers me half of the bundle. "That will change once you've had that handsome mercenary of yours."

I stare at it, thinking to refuse.

Because I should set an example. Because we're busy preparing for war and I really shouldn't be thinking about this at all. Because . . . surely there are other reasons?

I snatch up what she offers.

Temra looks more surprised than I am. "I didn't actually think you would take me up on it."

"Kellyn and I are getting closer," I say sheepishly, "and I'm getting braver."

"I'm glad for you. But if he even suggests something you don't like, you let me know."

I laugh, because again, I am the older sister.

"I mean it," she says. "Just because you say yes to it, it doesn't mean you can't change your mind or say no to certain things happening in the moment. You always have a voice, and you should always let it be heard. Especially if you're nervous. If he loves you, he will always listen to your needs."

"He says he loves me."

"But you don't believe him?"

"Part of me does. But the irrational part wants to think otherwise."

"Don't let that part win."

I smile. "I'll do my best."

The contraceptives feel like they burn a hole in my pocket for the rest of the day, but I don't take them out. Every once in a while I reach for them, make sure they're still there. I feel guilty for having them, which is ridiculous.

I'm just finishing lunch and contemplating what to do with the rest of my day when I hear someone call my name. I find Serutha and Paulia walking hand in hand. Petrik is with them, which makes me happy simply because he's not *with* my sister.

That's going to take some getting used to.

"I've been looking for you," Serutha says. "There's someone who wants to meet you."

I feel cold dread settle in my stomach. A new person? Talking?

"Don't look so sick," Paulia adds, "It's only Ashper."

"Though many know his name," Serutha says, "no one knows what he looks like. He wants to meet you. I thought it might be fun for us all to spend the afternoon together. Magic users uniting and all, if you're comfortable with him knowing your identity."

That changes my entire outlook. "I'd like that," I say.

"Why don't you take her over, and I'll go acquaint myself with the kitchen staff?" Paulia asks.

"Sounds perfect." Serutha leans in for a kiss before taking off down the hall. She looks back once to make sure I'm following.

Petrik stays right by my side. "I thought I'd come, too, if it would make you more comfortable?"

I can't speak for a moment.

Because I'm just so, so touched that he would do this for me. Not that he isn't thrilled to spend more time with magic users for the sake of his book, but I don't think that's foremost on his mind right now.

"Thank you," I say. I really am lucky to have someone like him to call a friend.

When we join Serutha, she says, "Is it weird for you? Being in the capital with your home so close? You're from Lirasu, aren't you?"

"Yes and yes," I answer. It's only two weeks to Lirasu. To my home and forge. "It doesn't feel like it should be so close. Not when all I did was step through a painting and appear here."

"I know what you mean. When Petrik took me through the portal and I was safe from Ravis—it took my mind far too long to catch up."

"I'll bet. But it helps that I can *feel* where I am," I say. "I can smell the forest in the air. The cool weather. The overcast sky. It looks like home outside, even if I'm not quite there."

She leads us through a doorway, which opens up into a narrow room. So many guards line this path—dozens crammed together to fill the space. "Hello," Serutha says to them before taking us through another door and trailing up a spiral staircase.

I hear voices before we reach the top.

"I'm just saying, Skiro, that if you'd told me about the portals, we could have spent more time together! We could have collaborated. Figured this whole thing out. Why were you so determined to tackle it on your own?"

"It's not about you and me, Marossa. I value my friends, and I'm not going to reveal their identities or talents unless they wish it."

"You're being dramatic."

"No, I'm being kind."

The prince and princess come into focus a moment later. Skiro is in his blue robes and golden tunic. Marossa wears leathers again, her boots polished to a shine, her bow over one shoulder.

"You're impossible," she huffs. "I'm going for a ride. See that he finishes *soon*. We can't afford to waste any time!"

Marossa strides past us without a glance, leaving the way we came in.

Petrik is shaking his head at his siblings.

"Sorry about that," Skiro says, and at first I think he's talking to me and Serutha.

But then I notice the other man kneeling on the floor. I can only see his back, but he's thin and graceful—I can tell by the gentle brushstrokes across the wall. His hair is much longer than mine, worn up and away from his face, the golden locks falling down to his waist in gentle waves.

"It's fine," the man, who must be Ashper, responds.

"She really is grateful for your services. We'll be forever in your debt."

Ashper nods without taking his eyes off his work.

Work that, I now note, is the beginnings of the portraits that will be identical to the ones destroyed in a locked room in Skiro's palace.

"I'll leave you to it. Do let me know if you need anything." Skiro turns about, startles when he sees me. "Ziva!"

"Prince," I say, uncomfortable to have his eyes on me.

He waves a hand. "Please, call me Skiro."

I absolutely will not.

"Actually, I'm glad I ran into you," he says. He gently grabs my elbow and pulls me after him to the other corner of the space, out of earshot of the other two magic users and Petrik. "I was wondering if we might sup together."

"Sup," I repeat stupidly. Goose bumps rise on my flesh, and fear rolls through my chest.

"Yes. Dine. Eat. Food. You and me. Alone."

"Why?" I blurt, certain that whatever is happening I should be embarrassed because I'm bungling it up.

He laughs. "Because I like you, and I want to get to know you better. Things have finally settled for a moment. I have time to think and pursue what I want for a change."

"You like tall girls," I say, then mentally kick myself for saying the words out loud as I remember them.

He laughs again. "I just thought we might get on well."

"I'm with someone," I say.

"Ah. That mercenary fellow."

"Yes."

"Is it serious?"

The herbs once again pulse from their hiding place in my pocket. "Very," I manage to get out.

"Shame. Well, do let me know if that changes." And then he leaves.

What. Just. Happened?

"Good talk?" Serutha asks when the prince is long gone and I still haven't moved.

I shake myself out of it, but the space feels sweltering now.

"Fine, just fine," I answer, then lower myself onto pillows on the floor.

Ashper still has his gaze locked on the wall, one hand holding a paint palette. His fingers are smeared with dried colors, and an unused brush is lodged behind one ear.

"Ziva, Ashper. Ashper, Ziva."

The painter pauses long enough to look over and nod. "Good to meet you."

"And you. We're very lucky to have you."

He shrugs. "I like to paint." Then he sets down his tools, places the used paintbrush in a glass of water, and spins in place, giving us his full attention.

Well, me.

He's looking very intently at me.

Makes my cheeks heat.

"You have high cheekbones," Ashper remarks. "And your freckles! It would take me days to get every one just right. Oh, I should like to paint you sometime."

I can't find words.

"He means it as a compliment," Petrik explains. "You're not an oddity."

"No, of course not," Ashper says in agreement. "You're a rarity. You're so tall, I can't even imagine how much paint I would go through to get all your height and details onto a canvas."

"Thank you?" It comes out as a question.

"Ashper, you're making her uncomfortable," Serutha says.

"Sorry." He turns back around to focus on his work. "I've never been good with people. I prefer paint."

At that, I feel my discomfort lightening. "I know what you mean. Except, I prefer metal."

Ashper grunts in response. He dabs his paintbrush into a few different colors before continuing his brushstrokes. It appears he's starting the outline of each of the three remaining royals.

"Don't you need to travel to the other territories to paint the portraits there, too?" I ask, now curious about his own magic.

"No, the portraits in Skiro's castle were the only ones destroyed. The portraits in Verak, Lisady, and Orena are already there. I just have to duplicate them here, and the portals will work."

"And they have to be completely identical?" I ask.

"Completely."

"How do you remember all the details?"

"I have a mind that never forgets a single detail."

"It's really quite annoying," Serutha supplies.

An involuntary shudder goes through me. I can't imagine a mind that never forgets anything combined with the way I fixate.

"When I save our lives by getting us the help we need through these portals," Ashper says, "we'll see how annoying you find me then."

Serutha smiles. "Your portals have already saved me twice, friend. I have no doubt they will do so again."

Ashper grunts again.

"I have a feeling it will take all three of you to pull this off," Petrik says.

"Pull what off?" I ask, wondering if there was an alternative motive for bringing me here. Did Petrik orchestrate this whole thing for a reason?

"Winning the war, of course."

Ashper nods. "I can get us the aid we need with my portals."

"And I can heal our wounded soldiers," Serutha says.

They turn to me expectantly.

I look down, my fingers already twisting together. Though I've been doing my job as a perfectly normal smithy to aid the war efforts, I have a feeling that's not what they want from me now. "I can't give what you ask of me."

"You make magical weapons, Ziva," Serutha says. "Can't you make our soldiers unbeatable in battle?"

But at what cost? I want to ask. What happens when one of those soldiers decides he wants to rule the world himself? What happens if those weapons land in the hands of the wrong person? A too-powerful person?

I fancifully think through the idea of weapons that would self-destruct after the battle is over. But it would be impossible to time such a thing.

"People get hurt by the things I make. My abilities aren't like yours. Painting and healing don't lead to world domination," I try to explain.

I glare at Petrik. He knows this. Is he trying to bully me by making me a spectacle in front of other people? He wouldn't, would he?

"Ziva," Petrik says. "I'm not trying to pressure you, I promise! I'm only looking to find a way around your reservations. I've been thinking about this a lot and then talking with Ashper and Serutha. Ashper can paint anything to make a portal. Serutha can heal anything broken in the body. You can magic anything made out of iron. Why should that be limited to weapons?"

"Because—" I blink. Weapons are what I've always made. Except that's not strictly true. Before weapons, I was making farming equipment, when I apprenticed under Mister Deseroy, the man who adopted me and Temra from the Lirasu Orphanage.

But weapons have been my life's work. They're what I've always been drawn to.

I've never magicked anything else except out of necessity. But I could.

I lock eyes with Petrik as I realize what he's suggesting.

A tingling sensation takes root under my skin. Something full of anticipation and excitement. Not fear. Something hopeful and real and beautiful.

A way to help. A way to magic metal again and feel like myself.

"Excuse me," I say, taking off down the spiral staircase at a near run.

CHAPTER
TWENTY-THREE

It takes some time to find Abelyn, Prince Skiro's ill-tempered smithy. She's with the other refugees, spread out in the forest behind the palace. I weave around countless tents and lean-tos, asking if anyone's seen her.

When I spot her, it takes very little explanation for her to agree to set off with me to locate Princess Marossa's castle forge.

It's not any grander than Skiro's had been, but it's well stocked at least, the palace being only a short distance from the Southern Mountains. We find an aged man sprawled on the floor of the forge. He has a bottle of rum in one hand and clutches the corner of a small blanket in the other. I think he might be snoring with his eyes open.

"Huh," Abelyn says, taking note of the finished arrowheads lining the nearest worktable. Her eyes return to the man on the floor, giving him a swift kick with her boot. He doesn't budge. "How does anything get done around here? Marossa's smithy is a drunk!"

Footsteps round the corner. A young boy maybe thirteen or

fourteen years of age startles at the sight of us. His hair is so long and tangled, I can't imagine it's ever seen a brush.

"You make these?" Abelyn asks, picking up one of the arrowheads.

The boy panics, looking over at the sleeping smithy. "No, Clivor does all the work. I just help with the chores."

Abelyn snorts. "I don't have time for your lies. We need able bodies! If you're useless, then get out of here!"

I place a hand on her shoulder, putting myself between her and the boy. "What's your name?" I ask.

He swallows. "He calls me Insect . . . when he's lucid."

"And you're real name?" I ask.

"Zovid."

"Zovid, I'm sure you've heard war is coming. We need to prepare. Can you handle the tools in here?"

After a brief hesitation, he nods once.

"And you made all these arrowheads?" I ask.

Another slow nod. "The princess requests arrows mostly. I can do those well. Anything else and I have to wake him." Quieter, he adds, "He's not happy when he wakes."

Abelyn grunts. "He's going to be less happy when he meets me."

I ignore her remark. "We're going to do some work in here. Will you help?"

Zovid nods.

"Good. Now, I need you to run some errands for me. Do you think you could do that?"

Another nod.

"I need all the soldiers in the capital to bring me their armor. Collect it for me. Or plead with them to bring it themselves. I don't care. Just get it here."

I'm fairly bursting with joy come evening. Temra notices the glow in my cheeks at once.

"What is it?" she asks.

"I was in the forge today."

"And? Don't stop there. What did you do?"

I settle next to her on the bed, making myself comfortable in her room. "Well, you know how I've been feeling conflicted about making weapons?"

She nods.

"And I've also been miserable because I want to help with my magic, but I didn't see how I could. Not with how dangerous the things I make have been of late."

"I know."

She doesn't say anything more, for which I'm grateful, but I'm all too aware of what she thinks about my conflict. Though they haven't said so, I suspect she and Kellyn and Petrik think I'm being silly. What use is a magical bladesmith who won't magic blades?

"I started magicking armor today," I say proudly. "There's no time to make it from scratch, but I've heated the armor belonging to the guards and then imbued it with protective qualities. Arrows and other projectiles will bounce off. No sword can pierce it. I can keep our soldiers safe in battle."

Temra's grin now matches my own. "That's wonderful."

"I got through over fifty sets of armor today. I'll do it again tomorrow and the next day—until everyone is protected."

"There's really nothing you can't do."

I nudge her with my shoulder. "I can't sing to save my life."

She shakes her head. "That's not what I meant. I mean, if you set your mind to it, you can do anything. I'm so glad you've found a way to use your gift without losing yourself."

"Thank you for your support. I know you don't always agree with the way I see things."

"The most important thing is that you're here. You're here to fight for your home." Quieter, she adds, "To avenge our parents."

Those words send a flare of heat down my spine. "I wanted to kill Kymora the moment she revealed her hand in Mother's and Father's deaths. But then you were injured, and I had to focus on you. And then I worried that Skiro wouldn't let us use his healer unless we had her to trade."

"Now she's free and more dangerous than ever."

"We won't make the mistake of letting her live a second time."

Temra's hand finds mine. "No, we won't."

Our agreement hangs in the air, and the two of us sit in stillness, trapped in our own thoughts. I can't imagine what Temra must be thinking, but I'm imagining what I might be forced to do if I'm the one with the opportunity to end Kymora.

Flashes from the earlier battle invade my mind. The sound of flesh tearing, the sight of blood spraying, the smell of all that gore.

I force myself to concentrate on the heat of Temra next to me. Bring myself to the here and now.

"I miss home," I say.

"Me too," Temra agrees.

"What do you suppose we would be doing right now if we were still at our normal lives in Lirasu?"

Temra thinks a moment. "It's November. The tournament is coming up soon."

The tournament.

A pang of longing fills my chest.

How long ago was it that I was fulfilling commissions for mercenaries wishing to enter? I try to think back to a few months ago, to the day when Garik came into the forge because he cut himself on his own weapon and demanded a refund.

I snort at the memory. I was going to start on more weapons for the tournament before Kymora came in to commission Secret Eater.

That feels like a lifetime ago.

"You'd be finishing up your second-to-last year of schooling," I say.

"And you'd be making more weapons, trying to grow ever closer to your goal of retiring in the northern continent," she says.

I close my eyes tightly. "Did you ever intend to come with me? Or were you just humoring me?"

Her body stiffens slightly. "I was going to go. To try it at least."

She doesn't need to say the rest, that she'd leave the moment she was bored.

"And your plans to become a professional fighter? A guard? When did you think you would tell me about those?" I ask.

She laughs lightly. "I thought I might share that once you were settled in paradise. I thought your temper wouldn't be so dangerous."

"I still can't believe you kept so much from me back then."

"You're a worrier," Temra explains. "I didn't want to stress you."

"Oh, so it was all for my feelings?" I ask doubtfully.

"No, it was a bit of selfishness on my part, too."

I suppose I can't blame her for that.

"I want you to be happy," I tell her. "When this is all over, if joining Skiro's guard permanently is what you want, then that's what I want you to do."

The words break my heart, but I go through with them.

"And what will you do?" Temra asks.

"Don't worry about me."

"Ziva—"

"No, I mean it. I'll be fine. I'll figure something out."

"Just promise me we'll still see each other."

I let out a noise between a laugh and a sigh. "It's nice to hear you say that."

She scoffs, offended. "Just because we want different things, it doesn't mean I don't want to see you again! You're the biggest constant in my life. I want you to always be there."

"I always will. Even if we see less of each other, we will still see each other."

We just have to survive Kymora first.

My days grow more repetitive in the next week. During the daytime hours, I heat armor and magic it. Over and over again. Zovid mans the bellows. Abelyn holds the individual pieces of armor before me with tongs. And I coax it to be strong. To be light. To be an unbreakable shield for the body.

My evenings are spent in the company of Kellyn or my sister and Petrik. We talk and laugh and reminisce. Sometimes I even seek out Serutha and Ashper, just so we can talk magic. It's so nice to spend time with people like me.

I've never warmed to anyone so quickly before in my life. I can honestly say I never had friends before I left Lirasu.

But I'm mostly shocked by how much I like having other people around.

In measured doses, of course.

Temra and Kellyn spend their time with the army. Preparing.

Running through drills. Exercising. Training horses and men alike. Though Marossa has double the guard Skiro does, it's still pitiful when compared to Kymora's numbers. However, the princess has an impressive collection of horses. Together they'll make up quite the cavalry, which will give us a better edge than last time, to be sure.

Petrik has an inquisitive mind that leads itself naturally to politics. I watch him navigate the meeting room like a royal adviser who has been doing so for years. Though they run him ragged, Petrik seems to come more alive day after day, as though finding a purpose for himself. A use for all his knowledge as a scholar.

I'm sure being back in my sister's good graces is also part of the reason for his better mood.

I try not to think about that too much.

Several weeks go by—though it feels only like days.

Ashper finishes the portraits.

He and Serutha appear in the forge, Ashper covered in paint, Serutha smelling of healing herbs.

"It's done!" he proclaims, ignoring Abelyn and Zovid (and the snores of the sleeping smithy, who hasn't move from his spot in all the time I'm in the forge. I suspect he drinks himself into a stupor night after night, wasting himself away).

"Prince Skiro and Princess Marossa are through the first portal," Serutha explains. "There's nothing for us to do now but wait. We thought we'd see if we could help here."

"No talking!" Abelyn shouts when she notices the other magic users. "You're distracting us from our work!"

"They're here to help," I say.

Her mouth curls up as though to suggest she's in physical pain.

I roll my eyes, then give Serutha and Ashper their own pair of tongs to hold. It doesn't take much time at all to instruct them on selecting a piece of armor, putting it in the kiln for a few seconds, and then hoisting it out for me to magic.

After we finish one set of armor (Abelyn still grunting all the way), Ashper asks, "Why don't you magic all the heated armor at the same time?"

I cock my head to the side. "Because I can't. I have to focus on one thing at a time."

Ashper and Serutha share a look, before the latter asks, "Have you ever *tried* to magic more than one piece of metal at a time?"

". . . No," I say. "But it's hard enough to magic one thing! I couldn't possibly do more!"

"At the risk of sounding arrogant," Ashper says, "I do it all the time. When I finish painting the portals, I magic them all at once, since I want each painting to do the same thing."

"Me too," Serutha says. "I'd cost many of my patients their lives if I took the time to heal each wound individually instead of coaxing many large injuries to heal at once."

I cross my arms, stare at the floor. "I've said before that what you can both do is more impressive than what I can do."

"Hogwash," Abelyn says. "You just said you never tried. So, try!"

"And waste time—"

"You're the one wasting time if we could be getting through all of this faster! Think, if you can pull this off, girl, then we can move on to the horses' armor!"

I growl. "Fine!"

They all try to hide their smiles. Only Abelyn succeeds.

In the next few seconds, a vambrace, gauntlet, and helmet are all thrust in my direction, heat drifting up into the cool fall air.

My eyes flick back and forth. "I don't know where to look. If I focus on just one piece, then I'll only magic that one!"

"It's not about where you're looking," Serutha says. "It's about where your focus is. I like to use magic with my eyes closed."

"I can magic something behind my back," Ashper says, flicking his long ponytail over his shoulder.

They're both *so great* at making me feel better about this.

"Don't be stupid," Abelyn says to Ashper. "Say something helpful or don't say anything at all."

His fair skin twists in a comical way. "Feel the iron. Feel the magic. Put the two together."

As though it were so simple.

I close my eyes, feel the heat coming off the steel, even though it wasn't in the kiln that long. Zovid is keeping it raging over 2,500 degrees.

I pull my hands into fists as I'd been doing while magicking everything else up to this point, muscles tensing, my mind thinking the word *strong. Unbreakable. Impenetrable. Untouchable.* Every synonym I can imagine going through my head.

But instead of focusing the thoughts dead ahead, to one item, I expand, imagine my magic filling the room.

And the magic—it catches on every heated iron item in the forge.

I'm grinning so wide it hurts my cheeks.

"It worked!" I say.

"Good," Serutha says. "Now enough of this nonsense."

She and Ashper go to the piles of armor just outside the forge. They bring back inside armloads, chucking individual sheets into the opening in the kiln. Breastplates, greaves, helmets, gauntlets, faulds, pauldrons, and more.

Serutha points to the opening. "Now do it again."

CHAPTER
TWENTY-FOUR

It's only the addition of the word *emergency* to Petrik's call of a meeting that convinces me to join him.

I was enjoying an afternoon off. With my new ability to magic several things at once discovered, it really only took another day to get through all the armor presented to me.

I sigh at the thought of what I'm losing. An entire afternoon to myself.

But I follow the scholar down the halls.

The shouting starts before I even reach the room.

". . . stubborn idiot!" Skiro's voice fills the halls, so I really hope the conversation isn't meant to be private. "Imbecile. Useless wretch!"

"Verak always was Mother's favorite," Marossa says as I step through the door. "She babied him. Gave him a complex. He's never been able to see danger with any real clarity."

"He'll see it when it's on his doorstep."

Princess Marossa cleans dirt from under her fingernails with the sharp end of a knife. "By then we'll be dead, so you won't be able to say I told you so."

Skiro rounds on her. "Yes, *that's* what I'm worrying about! Me missing my opportunity to be obnoxious! Could you take this seriously! We don't have enough numbers."

"Orena and Lisady are both sending troops through the portals."

"Barely a hundred men each! What are we supposed to do with those?"

"I imagine we'll send them to fight."

"And when they die, our sisters will have no men left to guard their own lands. If only they would come. If only they would join us here to strategize and plan so we can present Kymora with some semblance of a united front! Instead, they're content to hide in their own realms."

Marossa turns over her hand to inspect her nails. "Don't forget Verak, who's just being a horse's ass to spite us."

"This is all Father's fault. If he wouldn't have divided the kingdoms. If he would have just given the whole damn thing to Ravis—"

Petrik steps forward. "You don't mean that."

"I certainly do! If Ravis ruled everything, I wouldn't have so many people to protect. I'd be spending my days in the Great Library, meeting artists from around the globe."

"No, you wouldn't."

Skiro straightens, then shrugs off his blue robes as though he's become overheated. "Explain."

"If Ravis ruled, the rest of you would be dead or in captivity. He wouldn't take any chances that any of you had ideas to usurp him. And before long, Kymora would likely have murdered him anyway. And then we wouldn't be in a position to stop her."

Marossa finally looks up from her nails, "I believe what Skiro is trying to say is that we're not in a position to stop her now. He's already convinced we'll lose."

"We're not entirely hopeless this time," Petrik says. "We will get to choose the battleground. We have more men this time if we are besieged again. Z—the smithy has magicked every soldier's armor so it is impenetrable. The men are training. They will be in good physical condition, able to withstand a long battle, and Kymora's men will be tired from their march."

"Don't forget my horses," Marossa says.

"And we have a cavalry," Petrik adds, "also protected by magicked armor."

"It's not enough," Skiro whispers. "Five hundred cannot take two thousand. Just because our odds are better than last time doesn't mean we will succeed. We need more. Don't get me wrong, the magicked armor will certainly help." Skiro tries to be stealthy when he glances at me, but I don't know that he succeeds. "But armor doesn't cover the entirety of the body. There are gaps. How long will it be before Kymora's men utilize that?"

"Then perhaps you should have this smithy magic more than just armor for us!" Marossa says, finally looking as though she cares about the conversation. "We need weapons that can even out the numbers. Make each one of our soldiers able to counter ten of theirs. That would give us a real edge."

Skiro frowns. "I already told you that wasn't possible."

"Isn't it? It sounds more like you need a better handle on your subjects."

"Technically, I'm your subject." Though my voice fills the room, it doesn't seem to come from me.

"Excuse me?" Marossa asks.

This is what happens when I think without speaking. I put

myself on display. Forget the anxiety that creeps up as soon as the attention is on me.

I feel sick, but I say, "I was born in your territory. I've spent my life living in Lirasu. I'm your subject."

"Fine," the princess says, as though she doesn't care one bit that my identity has finally been revealed to her. "Then *I* order you to make weapons for the war."

Skiro scoffs. "And what are you going to do if she refuses?"

"She can't refuse. It's an order."

"Orders are refused all the time!"

"Fine, then I'll punish her. Algarow, do we have a stocks?"

"No, Princess."

"No stocks? How about a work camp?"

"Afraid not."

"A *dungeon*?" she asks, as though on her last nerve.

"I think we could lock one of the rooms in the palace from the outside."

Marossa nods, pleased. "There. We'll—"

"Stop it," Skiro snaps at her. "We need to reward our people for their work. Not punish them."

"Stop being so bossy. I'm your elder, Skiro."

"By eleven months."

"And don't you forget it."

"You're embarrassing yourselves," Petrik hisses to the both of them.

The prince and princess look about the room as though just remembering there are others in it.

"Well, you're our advisers! Advise us!" Marossa snaps.

No one says a word. The silence goes on and on and on.

And then Temra speaks. "The tournament in Lirasu is approaching. Many people will gather there to watch. They will be in Kymora's path. We can't let her harm them. We need to take our soldiers there. It's where we should have the final stand."

My stomach sinks to think of my home ravaged by Kymora's men. Temra is right. The city is vast, but she'll make quick work of it.

There's a niggling in the back of my head. Something that started when Temra brought up the tournament again, but I can't quite grasp what my subconscious is telling me.

"The city has a similar set up to Skiro's Capital," Petrik adds, putting his chin in one hand while he thinks. "It's against the mountains. More easily defended than the capital here."

"The governor of Lirasu has a small guard," Temra continues. "It's not much, but every little bit helps. He is also in possession of a weapon Ziva made him that might help in the battle."

A weapon.

The tournament.

I look at Kellyn.

Mercenaries.

Skiro and Marossa are already discussing the merits of what Temra is suggesting, but I cut them off.

"The tournament!"

My outburst brings all the heads in the room in my direction.

"Around fifty mercenaries are gathering for that tournament," I say. "And they all carry weapons that *I* made."

Temra's eyes widen as she catches on my meaning.

"We need to hire them," I finish.

"Hire mercenaries?" Marossa says reproachfully. "No fools would fight against such devastating odds, no matter how much they're being paid. Which they wouldn't be, because there's no money." Marossa looks to her brother for confirmation.

"Don't look at me," Skiro says. "I left everything behind in my territory. All I have are the clothes on my back."

Now the advisers pitch in, discussing money and funds and what could possibly be done.

And an image comes into my mind. That of the Lirasu Bank housing all the coin I've made over the last seven years. All the money said mercenaries paid me for their weapons.

My retirement.

But does it mean anything if I'm dead?

"I have money," I whisper. When no hears me, I repeat myself, fairly shouting. "I have money!"

"Ziva, no," Temra says. "You can't."

"Money is nothing when faced with death."

Besides, this is the answer. I won't make too powerful of weapons for people who might misuse them. But mercenaries? Those who are loyal to coin and themselves? Those who have no ambition except their next payday? Those who already possess weapons I've made?

They're exactly what we need.

"Then it's settled," Skiro says. "We leave for Lirasu as soon as the preparations can be made. How much time before Kymora is likely to arrive?"

"Could be as soon as three weeks," Petrik offers.

"Then we'd better hurry."

Kellyn's hand burns in mine as we walk to our rooms for the night. Though touching him always brings a pleasant warmth, I'm feeling more than just that. Speaking in front of others, throwing away the earnings of my life's work—it has me burning inside.

I'm overheated, stressed, but at the same time, I know what I did was right.

Instead of giving me a kiss at my door, like Kellyn usually does, he steps inside with me. He takes his hand out of mine to rest both hands on my shoulders.

"Are you sure about this?"

"I'm sure of nothing as far as this war is concerned."

"But, Ziva, your life's earnings! Everything you've worked so hard for. Those royals don't deserve it."

"I'm not giving it to them. I'm giving it to a bunch of sellswords."

"On their behalf."

"On behalf of *Ghadra*. And it's not just my money. Marossa and Skiro are pitching in, too. Everything that they can spare in taxes. Everything the nobility can give."

He stands straight. "I don't like it."

"I don't, either, but I don't see another way."

"Maybe we can rally the mercenaries to fight without the incentive of money. This is their home, too. They will also suffer if Kymora takes over."

I cross my arms. "Put yourself in their shoes. Would you take on such a job without money?"

"If I knew the extent of the situation. If I was fighting for my family—"

"How many of those mercenaries are likely to have families like you do?"

Quietly, he says, "Not many."

I wrap my arms around him, pull his head down to my shoulder.

"You're comforting me," he says with a tinge of humor.

"You seem to need it."

"You should be the one to need it."

"And yet, I'm holding up just fine all things considered."

Kellyn sighs into my neck. "You're a rock. Steady and unbreakable."

"And I like to stay in one place."

He laughs, the sound tickling my skin. His hands are in my hair, his fingers running through the strands.

"Will you stay with me tonight?" I ask. The anxiety doesn't creep in until the words are out. I should no longer fear rejection of this nature from this man, but I do. Constantly.

"Of course. Let me get changed, and I'll be right back."

I use the opportunity to change myself. I place my hammers on the bedside table, within reach. I've never had to do this with weapons before leaving my home. But now I seem to need something sharp or blunt nearby at all times.

I empty my pockets, thinking to tuck the herbs into a drawer out of sight.

But as I stare at them and think about Kellyn coming in for the night, I carefully pop a dried leaf into my mouth.

The taste is bitter, meant to be diluted with tea. But I'm not about to brew something.

I swallow quickly.

And then my face feels inflamed.

Which is utterly ridiculous. It's not like anyone knows what I've just swallowed. It's not as if I have any reason at all to be embarrassed.

And yet, when Kellyn knocks on the door, the burning in my cheeks only intensifies.

"Are you all right?" he asks when he sees me. "Should I open a window?"

"I'll be fine."

"Leftover anxiety from the meeting?" he guesses.

"Sure."

"Sure?"

The most awkward and unwelcome of giggles drifts up my throat, and I feel like a lunatic.

Just because I took the thing, it doesn't mean we have to do anything. It was just a precaution.

Because you were hoping, my internal voice says.

Shh, I tell it.

"You make me like this," I say when I get the ridiculous laughing under control. "You make me crazy. You make me awkward. You make me laugh."

Kellyn's face softens. He closes the distance between us, lets one finger trace from the back of my hand, up my arm. The trail sends flickers of heat through my skin.

"You make me happy," Kellyn says. "You make me scared. Now that I have you, I'm so very afraid to lose you."

"I know what you mean," I whisper. The fingers of my right hand reach up to play lightly with the laces at his throat. It helps so very much to have something to do with my hands.

"You also make me believe that there's hope for the world," he says.

"The world?" I question.

"So many terrible things have happened to you, and yet you haven't lost yourself. You're still kind. Still strong. Still determined. The world is a better place for having you in it. My heart is better for having you in it."

The words are unbelievably dramatic, but I love them. My ears ring with them, happy and full and *right*.

Now is the time.

"I don't want you to ever go away," I whisper as I stand on my toes. It's not an admission of love, but the best I can manage at the moment.

"I won't," he says.

And he lowers his lips the rest of the way.

I will never cease to be amazed by how breathless and

wonderful kissing him feels. It doesn't matter how many times I do it, he's never any less potent.

The feel of his fingers in my hair.

The smell of his skin.

The taste of him.

He's all I never knew I wanted.

And, oh, how I want him right now.

Though the kiss starts slow, I deepen it almost immediately.

Kellyn doesn't protest.

He grips me more tightly, lets me lead the kiss, as I press against him again and again, playing with his lips, licking them, biting them, savoring them.

They're turned up all the while, as though he can't help but smile. He likes this. Loves it when we're physical.

I love it more than anything.

I pull at the laces at his neck. The gap only goes down to his mid-chest, but I follow the opening with my lips, tasting new parts of him.

In one sudden movement, Kellyn picks me up and lays me on the bed, sprawling himself over the top of me, which impedes my progress at his chest.

But I don't mind one bit when he starts undoing the laces on my own nightgown.

Again, the gap doesn't go nearly far enough, but I love feeling Kellyn's lips against my collarbone, his heated breaths sliding beneath the cotton.

I need his lips higher. I need his lips lower.

I settle for the easier of the two, drawing him back up to my mouth.

And then I flip our positions, so I'm the one on top. I straddle his legs as I go for where his shirt is tucked into his pants, pulling the fabric free. He helps me hoist it over his arms and head.

I take in the sight of his chest greedily, let my fingers trace the pattern my eyes make. He's so solid. So *big*. So beautiful.

And I remember my desire so long ago.

The one to touch him.

My imagination could never hold a candle to the reality of it.

Kellyn pulls my mouth to his for more biting kisses, and I try to free myself from the confines of my nightgown. I hadn't realized at the time, when I wanted to touch him, just how much I would want him to touch *me*.

Kellyn's hands go to my hips, and suddenly finding them bare, he freezes in place.

I've got my nightgown bunched up to my waist, but I stop my progress in undressing at his sudden immobility.

He sits up, keeping me close, his hands tightening on my hips.

"Ziva, what are you—"

I kiss him. I can't help it. "I want you," I tell him.

He groans against my lips. His arms crush me to him, making it impossible for me to do anything more than return another open-mouthed kiss.

And then he stops. He rests his forehead against mine. Loosens his arms but doesn't pull away.

"I want you, too," he says.

I relax—I'd been worried that maybe I'd done something horribly embarrassing that would prevent me from ever leaving my room again.

"But . . . ," he starts.

I stop breathing. Though my skin was overheated before, it somehow grows hotter, uncomfortable—no, *unbearable*.

I throw myself off him, thinking to flee. To hide. Because

this is horrible, and I misread everything. And how could I be so foolish?

"Whoa. Hold on!"

He catches me before I reach the door.

"Let me go," I ask feebly.

"Ziva, please, hear me out first. Then I'll go if that's what you want. These are your rooms, after all."

"Fine, but I'm not looking at you."

If it were possible to hear his lips turn up into a smile, I'm sure I would have.

"That's fair," he says, and—as if he can't help it—he pulls me against him, lest I get any other ideas about escaping.

"I want this, Ziva," he says. "I want this with *you*. But not yet."

He said he loved that word. Right now I hate it. His words are so baffling; I can't help but step back to look at him.

"Not yet?" I ask. "I don't understand. I took the precautions. We won't— I mean, there's little chance of preg—"

He puts a finger to my lips. "You were prepared for this."

"I . . . hoped for it," I admit.

His eyes are open, wondering. Loving. It's the only reason I'm still able to look at him.

He swallows. "I made a promise to my ma. The first and only girl I would ever take to bed would be my wife."

I feel my brows drawing together in confusion. "You promised to wait for marriage? Why?"

He laughs at my tone.

"It's what I want," he says. "I don't want this act to be meaningless. I don't ever want it to be a temporary thing. I want it to be with my forever."

"Oh."

The heat is replaced with ice. I grow unbearably cold, new

anxieties taking root. He sees me only as a temporary thing. He's not as invested in this as I am. I've been too hasty. Too ridiculous. I—

"Ziva," he interrupts. "I want my forever to be you. I don't *want* anyone else." He says the words quickly, as though he can read my thoughts. "But marriage is a big commitment. And with a war upcoming, how could we possibly discuss any huge life changes? And I didn't want to scare you away if I started talking about forever too soon. I worry all the time that I'll say the wrong thing or do the wrong thing to send you running. That you'll become too scared to be with me. That you'll prefer a life spent alone."

His words tumble out of him like a cascading waterfall. But I catch his meaning.

The ice inside me melts.

"You want me?" I clarify.

"Yes," he says.

"Just not yet?" I ask.

"Yes."

"Okay."

As though a weight has been lifted off his shoulders, his whole frame sags in relief. He draws me to him again.

"Thank you for understanding," he says.

"Of course," I say. "I would never pressure you for something you didn't want. I'm sorry I didn't just talk to you about it first."

"You would never have been able to broach this topic," he answers in understanding.

I laugh at myself. "No."

We stand there for a bit, holding each other.

"Just to be clear," Kellyn says. "I want to marry you, but I don't want you to do anything before you're ready. I'm a little older than you are. You might want to see other people first. Figure out what it is you're looking for in a partner. I know I was your first, but that doesn't mean I have to be your only."

Now I'm jerking backward again. "You want me to see other men?"

"No," he answers firmly, almost angrily. "I'm saying I wouldn't hold it against you if you wanted to make sure I was what you wanted first. My feelings wouldn't change. And *of course* I hate the idea of you even *trying* to be with anyone else. But I don't want you to feel trapped or as though you have to settle—"

I silence him with a finger at his lips.

"I know what I want. Didn't I tell you before? I've never even been interested in anyone else before. I don't need to see what else is out there when I've already found everything I want."

He smiles. "You're sure?"

"Absolutely."

He sighs in relief, pulling me so tightly against him I can barely breathe.

"Will you still stay tonight?" I ask.

"Are you going to try to take off your clothes again?" he asks.

I laugh. "No."

"Then yes. I'll always stay if that's what you want."

It's only when his snores fill my room that a new fear takes root within me.

I feel like such an idiot. I spent so much time worrying over Kellyn. Worrying about him and me together. Stressing over what to say to him and how to act around him. Making myself sick just being around him. Thinking about instigating things.

And I never once thought about what would happen *after*.

What if we survive and I'm free to return home? Temra will live in Skiro's Capital. She's going to be part of his guard. And I've already thought about setting up shop there. Skiro hasn't asked a single thing of me yet. I could live comfortably in his territory. But I want walls that are my own. I want a house that is all mine. A space that is safe from everything. A place I never have to leave.

And Kellyn wants to roam. He's a mercenary who only visits home every once in a while.

What would a future with him even look like?

I imagine myself all alone day after day. Waiting for Kellyn to visit. Taking on my commissions and living my life. But alone most of the time.

That's not a life. Not when I don't have Temra to be with me all the time. She'll be off doing her own things.

And my hypothetical future husband would be, too.

There's no future for us, I realize.

I've been foolish, hoping I could make things work. Practice being an equal partner and initiating things with him. Wanting to be more intimate.

Why didn't I think about *after*?

Because I was too scared about now.

But now is fine. It's the future that is uncertain. It's the future, when the fight is over, and Kellyn has no reason to stick around that I have to worry about.

My thoughts string together. Another one starting before the last one has finished, each growing more and more dark.

I would never ask him to stay with me. Just as I wouldn't ask it of Temra. They have to be free, not shackled to me. To do what makes them happy.

Why does what I want make no one else happy?

I cry then, doing my best not to make a sound, because I can't handle talking about this with Kellyn right now. I don't want things to end between us so soon. And that's surely what would happen once I point out to him how we want different things in our lives.

I will keep Kellyn close for now. Because if I die in the upcoming battle, I want to do so having spent what time I have with the ones I love.

But after that? It's over.

I roll out of his arms, push my face into my pillow, and cry in earnest, getting it out of my system before pretending everything is fine.

CHAPTER
TWENTY-FIVE

It will take some time for Marossa and her men to be ready to travel. They need to gather enough food and supplies, both for the soldiers and the horses. The princess asks all in the city to contribute what they can.

There's no reason to wait for them to be ready, especially when there is much preparation to be done in Lirasu. It's decided that the prince, his guards, Kellyn, Petrik, Temra, and I will start the journey ahead of Marossa and the rest of the army, who will follow as soon as they can.

I had become accustomed to sleeping in a bed again. The nights on the road are rougher than ever. Even though I know Kymora is far away, I can't shake the feeling that I'm going to see her pelting through the trees. Or worse, find her slitting my sister's throat in the dead of night.

Skiro, at least, has an uncanny ability to fill awkward silences with his chatter. "Tell me more about this tournament and the men we're going to talk to," he asks of me.

I find myself turning to Temra, but I stop myself. I don't need her to speak for me. I know the answers to these questions. This isn't a social conversation but a necessary one. I can do this.

"The local governor hosts the tournament every year," I answer. "At first, it was a simple competition that he held to find new members for his personal guard."

"And now?" the prince wants to know.

"Mercenaries who commissioned weapons from me started entering for the monetary reward, and the game changed. Obviously those with Zivan blades had an advantage, so it ceased to be a local tournament. Fighters from all over Ghadra compete for the notoriety and money now."

"It must be terribly exciting to watch," Skiro says.

"It is," Temra supplies. "Ziva's weapons are extraordinary. And to see so many in the hands of trained fighters? It's better than a choreographed dance."

"And these fighters who enter," Skiro says, "they're all mercenaries?"

"Most of them," I reply. "There's the occasional member of the nobility."

Temra answers his real question. "Mercenaries and nobility are the only ones who can afford Ziva's work. You won't find regular folk among their ranks."

Kellyn leans toward me. "It's one of the reasons I was initially in town, you know. I was going to enter the tournament if I could get a weapon from you in time. Things really turned out differently than I thought they would."

I wince. "Sorry about that."

"Don't be. Things could have turned out far worse if they didn't play out the way they did."

How true that is.

"So," Skiro says, "we're to convince these mercenaries not to hack each other apart for a large monetary prize—instead we're going to ask them to take a meager wage in exchange for a vastly outnumbered battle in which we'll all likely die. There's more work ahead of us than I thought."

Kellyn and Temra pair off in the evenings, practicing harder than ever with their weapons. The prince's guards run drills, if they're not assigned to keep watch for threats. It's a huge comfort to have them nearby at all times.

I like to find gaps in the trees or shrubs, places I can sequester myself to give my brain the illusion of privacy. Time to think and replenish myself.

Petrik hasn't changed at all. He still spends his free time scribbling away in yet another notebook.

"Working on another book?" I ask him.

"I'm trying to recall everything I've ever read about Lirasu."

"For what purpose?"

"If it's to be our battleground, we need a strategy. We'll need to know as much about the lay of the land as possible. The local governor—is he likely to aid us in our efforts?"

After some thought, I nod. "He's a kind and fair man. He will hear us out, though I've no idea what actions he'll be prepared to take."

"That's good." Petrik writes another line. "We have some advantages with the landscape. The city borders the mountains. We can take the high ground. Your forge and tools are all there, in case we need anything else made before Kymora reaches us. There's a local mine, right?"

"Yes," I answer. "It's where I get all my ore from. The entire mountain to the south is full of rich veins of it."

"The entire mountain?" Petrik asks.

"That's what I've heard. Why?"

"I'm not sure. It's just something to note. You use coal in your kiln when forging?"

"Yes."

"Where do you get it?"

"There's a vendor in the city. He always has tons of the stuff. I think he has it brought in from Orena. There are natural deposits of it in the north of the territory. It's not even terribly expensive."

"Hmm," Petrik says.

Though it's upside down for me, I read what he writes next.

Coal, cheap

Mountain filled with iron ore

Accelerant?

"What are you planning?" I ask.

"I'm just jotting down my thoughts. It's nothing yet."

Still, what does he need an accelerant for?

When Petrik and Temra aren't together, I steal moments alone with my sister. We'll walk ahead of the group out of hearing range or snuggle by the fire together in the evenings when we make camp. I feel stretched thin, wanting to spend time alone with her, alone with Kellyn—cramming in as many new memories as possible before the fight ahead. Before my whole world can come to an end.

"I've never spent much time thinking about the future," Temra says one evening, while we're off collecting firewood together. "I normally like making the most of the present, but I'm so excited for after the fight, when I get to return to Skiro's Capital and begin my training as a royal guard in earnest."

I wish I could say I'm just as enthusiastic about her future. "Does Petrik approve of your intended profession?" I ask.

"He doesn't love it, but he loves me, so he's willing to support me no matter what."

"I suppose that's good."

"Don't sound so gloomy. I'll be fine. Besides, you'll be too busy enjoying your life with Kellyn to worry about me as a guard."

I don't answer her right away, so she says, "You will be with Kellyn, won't you?"

"I don't think so."

"Whyever not?"

"We don't want the same things. He wants to travel. I want to stay put. I don't think it will work out."

"Did you talk to him about it?"

". . . No."

"Then how do you know it won't work out?"

"Because I know him, and I know myself."

"But you have to at least have the conversation!"

"Why bother?" I ask. "It'll only be painful for the both of us, and it'll end whatever good times we're having right now."

"You are *dreadful* at communication," Temra says, as though I don't already know this. "Ziva, talk to the man and see what happens. Have you told him how you feel? Have you asked him to stay with you?"

I duck around a tree, bend over to pick up another log, not answering.

"You haven't!" she accuses.

"I would never ask him to do something that would make him miserable." And I'm not about to share my feelings only to have them rejected. Kellyn may have said he loves me, but that doesn't mean he means to stay with me.

"You both deserve to know your options, though, and you can't know those if you don't *talk*."

I scoff. "And I suppose you and Petrik have it all figured out?" It's a desperate attempt to get the attention off me.

"Yes! We're going to live in Skiro. Petrik will resume his duties at the library, and I'll be a guard. We'll see each other all the time, while still having our own lives."

"It's easier for you two! You both want to be in the same geographical area." Quieter, I add, "I may love Kellyn. He may even love me, but how can we support each other when it means being away from each other all the time?" Him to wander as a mercenary. Me staying put alone in my forge.

"I don't know," my sister admits. "But I refuse to believe that a future for the two of you is impossible.

"We will talk," I assure her. "Kellyn and I. But not yet. There's no sense until after the threat is past."

Because if I die in battle, there will be no need for talking.

The journey, for once, is uneventful. We reach Lirasu without so much as a dangerous wild animal sighting.

Skiro and Petrik separate from us to go talk to the local governor.

That leaves me, Temra, and Kellyn to return to the forge.

Home.

As I stare at the yard and the front door, I find myself surprised to see it just as we left it.

There's the cedar tree trunk on the ground, where I severed it with Secret Eater. The yard is full of dead grasses, the broken chicken coop. A few scraps of cloth that once housed straw dummies.

The front door is unmarred, unbroken.

Though we've long lost the key to the house in our travels, it doesn't take Kellyn long to break down the door.

A thick layer of dust coats everything. Wordlessly, Temra goes to open the windows.

It's . . . just as I remember it.

Was I expecting to see it vandalized by Asel's friends? Find that someone had broken in and settled themselves in our home? Find the whole thing burnt to a crisp in Kymora's rage?

I'm not sure, but it's unchanged, which somehow doesn't seem right with how much my life has changed.

Still, a shock of relief sweeps through me. After all this time, I'm home.

I waste no time throwing open the doors of the forge, finding everything in here also as I left it. Ash in the kiln. My tools laid out along the worktables. For nostalgia's sake, I light the kiln and open the windows.

Kellyn stands in the doorway as he watches me man the bellows, staring into the flames.

"Are you making something?" he asks.

"No. Just going through the motions."

He doesn't ask why.

I'm not entirely sure myself.

Temra enters through the shop and stands beside Kellyn. "All the food has gone bad, obviously. Shall I make a run to the store?"

I shrug.

Temra leaves wordlessly.

"Are you all right?" Kellyn asks me.

I genuinely don't know how to answer. Because I'm here, but I can never truly return home. I will never again be who I once was—that smithy who only worried about the next time she'd have to leave her forge.

I've traveled half the kingdom, seen its horrors and its beauty.

There's a sadness in not being able to go back. But I'm also awed by how I've moved forward.

"I will be," I answer.

Petrik leads Skiro and his men back to our modest home after their visit with the governor.

"Solid man," Skiro says when Temra asks how the visit went. "I like him. He's a man of action. He's ready to help. He's already pledged his small guard to our aid, and he's calling all the contestants of the tournament together for a meeting tomorrow."

"The pieces are in place," Petrik says.

"All that's left is a grand speech on my part. Lots of money from you girls. Maybe a testimonial from Kellyn, since you're one of their kind."

"How can I help?" Petrik asks.

Skiro thinks. "I want you to meet with the governor's husband tomorrow. Tell him all you know about Kymora. Work together to strategize where our troops can camp until the battle, what to do with the townsfolk until then. Learn all you can about the city and how to use it to our advantage. The governor will be unable to join you because he'll be at the meeting with the rest of us."

Petrik nods. "I can do that."

"Then it's settled. We all have our parts to play. Let's hope we can sway a bunch of greedy mercenaries to our cause."

"We're not all greedy," Kellyn says. "Some of us are just trying to make an honest living."

"Right," Skiro says. "Sorry." His eyes dart to me briefly before looking away. "What are the sleeping arrangements for tonight?"

We all agreed that the prince and his guards staying in a local tavern would draw too much attention. We're safer if we stay together.

But that doesn't change the fact that the house only has two rooms and two beds.

"Find a spot on the floor, Prince," Kellyn says. "The girls are taking the beds."

Skiro scoffs. "I wouldn't dream of taking one of their beds."

"You could stay with the governor," Petrik suggests.

"No, no," Skiro says. "This is fine. I want us to stay together. We have an early start tomorrow. We best bunker down now."

The prince's guards grab their bedrolls and blankets from their horses. They take up every inch of space on the floor of the kitchen and living room. I worried for a moment that we might have to stash some of them in the shop.

There's never been more than one or two of Temra's friends in the house at a time.

Now my living room is overrun with soldiers.

I know it's necessary, but I can't help but feel unsettled.

When I bought back my parents' house, I claimed their old bedroom as my own. The closet is full of work clothes and aprons and the occasional nice outfit Temra purchased for me, hoping I would accompany her out in public now and then.

A portrait of my parents hangs on the wall, surrounded by metalwork. I shaped steel into swirling designs to give my room more character. None of it is magicked, just decorative. Things I thought would look nice.

On one wall is a full-length mirror Temra bought me one birthday. The bedside table is mostly empty. Two books that belonged to my mother sit atop it. Smithing books I've basically memorized. There's an old empty glass that used to hold water next to them—in case I became thirsty in the night.

There are a few pamphlets from old city plays Temra starred in.

A soft blue rug takes up most of the floor.

And a single-person bed.

Looking at my room now, I'm almost embarrassed to have Kellyn seeing it.

He looks at the metalwork on the walls, the painting of my parents.

"I keep most of my stuff in the forge," I say defensively, "because that's where I spend most of my time."

"I like it," Kellyn says. "It's simple. Easy to keep clean, I'd imagine."

"I don't really collect things—unless they're forging tools."

Kellyn runs his hands over the comforter I've already beaten free of dust. "This is a tiny bed."

I laugh. "We're used to sleeping in palaces now."

"We've been spoiled," he agrees. "But I like this." He removes his scabbard and boots before lifting back the covers and sliding in. There's less than a couple feet free to the side of him.

"Why's that?"

"Means you'll have to snuggle closer."

I grin before joining him under the covers.

CHAPTER
TWENTY-SIX

Dawn comes much too soon, drawing us one day closer to Kymora's arrival. It's nice, at least, to dress in my own clothes.

Breakfast is a quiet affair. Petrik cooks a simple oatmeal for us all, spiced with cinnamon and sugar.

And then we head for the stadium, where the tournament is housed.

Strangely, traveling the city streets doesn't hold the same kind of fear it once did. There's still the discomfort of being surrounded by people, but it feels somehow less intense than it usually does. Have I changed? Or do I just have bigger problems at the moment?

Probably the latter.

It certainly has nothing to do with the fact that Kellyn's arm is thrown over my shoulders.

The local tournament is the one event every year that I actually enjoy attending. It's exhilarating to see my weapons pitted against each other in friendly sport. It fills me with pride. I even enjoy interacting with old customers. Asking how the weapons are handling. Hearing their stories on the road.

We won't get that this year.

The stadium is empty when we arrive, naturally. The competition isn't for another week at least. It's odd to be here when everything is so dead.

But the fighting arena is full. The mercenaries are waiting for us. Some sit on the ground, bored and confused as to why they've been summoned. Others are picking friendly fights with each other. Testing out their weapons early.

I only count thirty-four in total, so some clearly haven't arrived in town yet.

While Skiro and Governor Erinar greet each other again, I make a perusal of the weapons visible to me.

Twin shortswords that ignite in flames when commanded.

A halberd that allows the bearer to vault unnaturally high into the air.

A morningstar mace with the ability to catch the light no matter where the sun may be facing, and blind oncoming enemies.

Throwing knives that can be directed with hand motions, coaxed to hit exactly where the castor demands.

A double-headed ax that can hold an enemy at bay, simply by pointing in their direction.

On and on I see them, smiling at each one as I remember the forging process for them. The hours of my life spent in pure bliss. Creating.

And then my eyes land on a figure that leaves a bad taste in my mouth. He carries a flanged mace. One with the ability to steal the breath from those standing nearby.

Temra's eyes catch sight of him, too. "What is he doing here?"

"It would appear he's an entrant in the tournament," I say through clenched teeth.

Temra bursts out into laughter. "Magic weapon or no, the mercenaries would have eaten him alive."

"I'll bet he runs screaming when he hears what's about to be asked of the contestants."

Kellyn turns to us. "Are we talking about the fellow with the mace? Who is he?"

"No one of consequence," I answer honestly. Though my face heats of its own volition.

"Do you have a history?" The question sounds innocent enough, but I think I hear just a hint of something more in Kellyn's tone.

"He's the governor's son, and he tried to kiss her once," Temra says unhelpfully. "When Ziva refused him, he made up some story about her attacking him. In the end, the governor didn't believe his lies, thankfully. But Asel took the slight personally. Even had some of his friends vandalize our place."

Kellyn cocks his head to the side, sizing up Asel.

It's laughable when I think about the two of them standing side by side.

Kellyn's tall, strong frame compared to Asel's shorter, lean one.

Kellyn's gorgeous gold-red hair compared to Asel's dark locks.

Kellyn's beautiful face compared to Asel's ugly features (at least they're ugly to me).

Kellyn takes a step in Asel's direction, and I pull at his arm the moment I realize he means to approach him.

"Stop that," I tell him.

"I was just going to say hello to the governor's son."

"Why would you do that?"

Kellyn doesn't answer as Asel suddenly looks in our

direction—as though he finally felt our stares. His eyes widen at the sight of Kellyn, and I realize he must think him a competitor in the tournament at first. Then his eyes slide to mine, and they narrow in some mixture of confusion and distaste.

Abruptly, I feel a yank on my arms. I look up just before Kellyn's lips press firmly against mine. My mouth opens in surprise, and Kellyn kisses me in a way that is entirely inappropriate in public.

I place my arms on his shoulders and push him back. "What are you doing? We talked about this."

He blinks. "No kissing in public. Hand-holding is okay," he says, remembering the conversation.

"So what was that?"

"I'm so sorry. I don't know what just came over me." Kellyn doesn't release me from his hold, though our lips are no longer touching.

It's thrilling to think of him becoming overwhelmed with the desire to kiss me, but still. I don't understand the context.

"Were you—staking a public claim to me? In front of Asel?" I ask.

He purses his lips. "I think I was."

"Because you feel threatened by that little slip of a boy?"

He has the good sense to look embarrassed. "He mistreated you," he says. "I think I wanted to show him you picked someone better."

I fight a grin. "Did I pick someone better?" I can't help but tease him.

Kellyn glares at me. "Isn't it just a little nice to show Asel that someone else finds you entirely desirable?"

"Yes. It is a little nice."

"If you object to me talking to him, fine. But let me know if you ever want to use me to get revenge. Whether that includes public displays of affection or something else."

I'm grinning like an idiot, worrying who might be watching, but unwilling to remove my eyes from this ridiculously handsome man.

"I'll let you know," I say.

Kellyn nods, steps back, then pulls me to his side so he can throw an arm around me again.

I slide what I hope is a sneaky peek at Asel.

He's glaring at Kellyn.

I like that a lot.

"Ziva!" a voice says. I find the governor mere feet away, appraising me carefully.

"Governor Erinar," I say. "How nice to see you again."

"You're back in the city! I feared my son's poor behavior had you fleeing Lirasu for good."

Asel was part of the reason we *were* going to leave the city for good. Something more pressing became the main reason, however. But I'm not about to explain all that.

I settle for "It was a warlord who chased me out of town, actually. The same warlord who is intent on attacking us now."

Erinar's features tighten. "Prince Skiro has explained the situation. We'll be ready for her. It's so good to have you back."

"Thank you."

The governor looks as though he wishes to say more, but I see him glance at Kellyn's arm slung across my shoulders. Instead he turns his attention to the contestants. "Welcome to Lirasu, warriors! I'm sure many of you are wondering why you've been called together for an early rendezvous when the tournament is still a ways away. With me today is Ghadra's very own Prince Skiro, of the territory to our east. A situation has arisen, and the prince has come to speak with you all."

Erinar steps back from the edge of the stadium platform to allow Skiro to take the center.

"Greetings," the prince says. "My sister, your sovereign, Princess Marossa, is on her way to us now with our fighting forces. She has entrusted me with making you all aware of the situation and requesting your aid in the upcoming battle."

At the word *battle*, murmurs go up through the crowd of gathered warriors. And the few who were staring aimlessly out at the fighting grounds now have their full attention on the prince.

"Many of you are familiar with the warlord Kymora Avedin. She was my late father's general. Since the division of our realm, she's been maintaining a large personal army—which she claimed was to keep other kingdoms from thinking us vulnerable.

"However, Kymora was only biding her time, gathering more soldiers to her cause. She intends to rule Ghadra herself. To beat every territory into submission under her rule. She has already accomplished this in my territory, and she is headed here now to do the very same with Marossa."

More murmurs, louder this time, arise from the mercenaries. Some start pacing in place, fidgeting noticeably. There's a lot of restless energy among these fighters. I worry some of them might bolt, but they stay in place for now.

Skiro continues, "I've come with my men and joined forces with Marossa. The other royal siblings have sent aid."

Very little aid at that, but the prince doesn't elaborate.

"But we hope to add you to our ranks," Skiro says. "That is why you have been called here today. Now, who will join our cause for country and liberty?"

Dead silence meets the prince's request.

He quickly adds, "You will of course be paid for your services."

More silence.

Then, someone shouts, "Is the tournament still happening?"

The prince, baffled by the question, says, "No, the warlord will be here by then."

"So I traveled all this way for nothing?" another asks. "Is someone going to reimburse my travel fees?"

"You could definitely take it out of the sum you will receive for aiding your countrymen," Skiro says diplomatically, but I can tell he's starting to grow impatient with the sellswords before him.

"How much are you paying us?" someone asks.

"It's a modest sum, but—"

"Isn't this warlord rich?" another asks. "I feel like she would give us a better wage if the tournament is out."

At that, Skiro's face turns to horror. I'm sure mine must match it.

Kellyn releases my hand to step up next to the prince. "Fellow mercenaries," he says. "Ghadra will be forever changed if Kymora conquers it. Think of your families and friends. Think of those who pay your wages. Everything will be ruined if you join her—if you don't agree to fight for us. I understand your minds. I am one of you. The sword is also my trade. But Kymora is evil. There will be no freedom under her rule. Think of your futures."

A pause.

Someone says, "Still sounds to me like working for her wouldn't be such a bad option. What does it matter who rules? A tyrant is a tyrant is a tyrant."

More gradual assent gathers as the mercenaries catch on to that idea.

And I realize, *It's not going to work.* We can't convince them to join us. If the prince can't do it and Kellyn can't do it—who else are they going to listen to?

They might listen to you.

The voice is the barest whisper in the back of my head; it sends a jolt of fear through my entire body.

Stop that, I command my limbs, the blood pulsing under my skin. The horror spreading throughout my very being.

It doesn't listen.

I won't do it. There's no way I would stand up there next to Kellyn. To speak to these people. I'm a nobody. Literally no one of consequence in the world.

But you made their weapons. You know what they can do and how best to use them. They respect you.

It doesn't matter. I'm not a ruler. I'm not a mercenary like them. I'm seriously one of the worst people with words on the planet. I am no public speaker. I would only make things worse.

More questions are directed at the prince and Kellyn. Some mercenaries start walking off. Others are arguing among themselves over who the better fighter is.

Some seem to have already forgotten the threat of Kymora and are arguing over nothing relating to the upcoming fight at all.

How quickly their attentions stray. Fighters aren't always the best listeners.

But as I look at the retreating backs of those who intend to leave the city with their weapons, my feet step forward of their own accord.

CHAPTER
TWENTY-SEVEN

Wait!" I shout.

I feel my voice drift up from my throat, but I have no memory of giving it the command to speak. I feel alight with painful electric shocks. My hands are shaking, and all my limbs feel some confusing mixture of lightness and unbearable weightiness at the same time. Like I'm not actually present.

The retreating figures halt in place. They turn around or look over their shoulders.

Kellyn puts what he hopes is a comforting hand on my shoulder, but I shrug it off. I can't stand to be touched right now. I'm already feeling way too much, and I can barely think.

Start with your name, the little voice encourages. The brave me who is always hidden in the far reaches of my mind.

"I'm Ziva Tellion," I say, weakly at first. I repeat the words again with volume. "I made your weapons," I tack on foolishly.

Some of them were made years ago. They might have forgotten what you looked like. And some of them only interacted with Temra, so they wouldn't even know you on sight. It's okay to introduce yourself.

I still feel like an idiot. Every word out of my mouth burns. I try to mentally validate myself. Assure myself I'm okay.

"I gave each of you a little piece of magic to carry with you through your travels. To keep you safe. I've watched you at this tournament over the years. I've seen you in action. You are all impressive fighters. The best Ghadra has."

Good, Ziva. You appealed to their vanity. Now you need to find their consciences.

Consciences? Do half of them even have those? They fight for money.

Stop worrying and keep talking. You don't know how long their attention spans are.

Just tell them your story.

"Warlord Kymora commissioned a blade from me some three or four months ago." The time blurs, I can't actually be sure. But that's not important to the story. "I made a broadsword that steals secrets from those it cuts, and that's when I heard Kymora's thoughts. She'd cut herself on the weapon, you see, and I heard her intentions clearly.

"It won't be like it is now under the rule of the princes and princesses," I explain. "It won't even be like it was with King Arund—for those of you old enough to remember his rule. Kymora is the worst kind of tyrant. She likes her power and doesn't want anyone else to match it. She doesn't want anyone to have choices anymore. You think you'd be better off receiving your wages from her? How about when she asks you to slaughter children when their parents don't hand over food for her soldiers? What about when she demands you do menial grunt work, patrolling her grounds?"

I gain a little courage when I see those who had started leaving return to the mass of fighters.

I clasp my hands together to try to cease my own fidgeting. I can't look anyone in the eye. Instead, I look above their heads. I hope that gives the illusion that I'm eyeing them all.

"You will have no choices. Whatever she wants of you and your magical weapons, she will demand it. And any resistance will result in immediate execution. She's a general. She doesn't have time for insubordination."

I swallow. "You will be lackeys. Not fierce mercenaries free to take jobs where you will. She doesn't care about people. She cares about herself. She cares about the land but not the people in it. She wants your weapons for her own. She wanted me to make more for her army. While I was able to render the initial broadsword useless to her, she still wants to get her hands on me and force me to make her and her men unbeatable."

I'm rambling; I must be. I can't see an end in sight to this nightmare that is public speaking, but I have to keep going.

"You don't know me that well. You only know what I've done for you. What I can still do. I know the odds aren't great. Kymora's numbers outweigh our own."

More grunts and grumbles. I steal a glance at Skiro, and he blanches. Clearly he hadn't intended to share that information.

"But!" I hurry to add. "I can magic armor for all of you. You are already fearsome with your skill alone. With my weapons, you're nearly unbeatable. With armor, you will be *untouchable*. I'm not asking you to fight for me or for Ghadra. I'm asking you to fight so you can keep your way of life."

I suck down heaping gulps of air, as though I hadn't been breathing during my pathetic little speech. Though I must have.

Do I need to say more? What else do I say?

Did I already mention how dangerous Kymora is?

Did I tell them my name?

Twins, I've forgotten everything I just said.

The silence drags on again, and I want to rip off my own skin.

A voice from the crowd says, "And we'll be compensated for fighting against this warlord?"

"Yes, damn you all!" Skiro snaps. "How hard is it—"

I cut him off. "You will be paid. You will receive armor for you to keep. And I will fight at your sides."

Stupid, I think after I add that last bit. What do they care that I'll be there?

But then someone says from the front, "I'm in."

"Me too. I want the free armor."

"Think of the stories we'll get to tell. Fighting side by side with the magical smithy herself!"

"A payday is a payday."

"Maybe they'll reschedule the tournament for after. Might as well stick around."

One by one, we get their assent. Except for Asel, who simply takes a stance at his father's side.

I glance around to the newest additions to the army in disbelief.

I did that.

"Wonderful," Skiro says to the crowd. "Now let us prepare."

Marossa and our soldiers arrive three days later. Their numbers? Four hundred and ninety-eight. With all the mercenaries added (whose numbers have increased as more have arrived for the tournament), that puts us at five hundred and forty-one.

Against nearly two thousand.

The last battle saw far worse odds, but Lirasu isn't like Skiro's Capital. There's no castle, no walls to encase the people. No high turrets to defend.

The enemy will have a much easier time surrounding us and overwhelming our numbers.

Not to mention the fact they're now led by Kymora, who is the fiercest strategist.

At the first war council in Lirasu, with Marossa, Skiro, and their advisers, Petrik shares his thoughts.

"I've gone over diagrams of the city. Coupling that with all the reading I've been doing on warfare, I have some ideas on how we can make the fight as fair as possible. We want the high ground. I want us to use the mountain. Set up a vantage point for most of our forces and set traps for Kymora's men as they try to climb up to us. The warlord's forces will be weary from marching. We want to tire them out even more."

Temra narrows her eyes. "What's to stop Kymora from ignoring us entirely? Why would she take such a risk when she can traipse right on past us and hit up Marossa's Capital now that it's undefended?

The princess flinches at that.

Petrik grins. "We have something that she wants."

I gulp. "Me."

Petrik nods and lays out the plan.

The prince and princess send scouts ahead to check the enemy's progress. When they return with the news that Kymora's army will be here in two days, a blanket of fear settles over the city.

Much of it is deserted. Those who can afford to leave, who have family or friends elsewhere who will take them in, do so.

The rest make camp up in the mountains or barricade themselves in underground cellars and other safe places.

Safe unless Kymora wins the battle, that is.

I magic more armor. Anything found in the city. The governor scrounges up enough of it to cover his own men and the mercenaries. Kellyn trains with the mercenaries and other fighters, running them through the plan until they have every speck of it memorized. Temra practices with them, pushing herself to be better than ever.

That leaves Petrik to plan the traps with Reniver, the governor's husband.

A night, a day, and a night pass.

It's time.

We crouch in the forest, waiting for the first signs of Kymora's approaching army. My heart is lodged somewhere up in my throat. Fear and anxiety mix in an unbearable pain that pierces my very center with each breath I take.

I only have one comfort right now, and I try to cling to it. Temra's safe for now, up in the mountain with over half our forces.

But, oh, how she wanted to be on the ground.

"I can fight with the mercenaries and other foot soldiers," she'd insisted.

Before I could think of anything to say to deter her from this plan, Petrik said, "We need someone to lead our hidden force up on the mountain. You're the only one I trust to do that."

Temra looked between the two of us. "I didn't get to fight last time, either! I was put on portal duty. Please don't keep me from the action again. I'm begging you."

"There will be action aplenty on the mountain," Petrik assured her. "You're not being kept from anything. You're just being held in reserve for the second wave. We need you when the fighting grows more desperate."

That silenced any more protests from her.

I'm so, so grateful to Petrik for knowing just what to say to her, though the selfish part of me wishes I could have her by my side right now. The comfort of her presence. At least Kellyn is beside me.

But the wait in the woods just might kill me.

From my other side, Petrik says, "Ziva, if this goes badly, I need you to do something for me."

Expecting something along the lines of *protect Temra at all costs*, I say, "Of course."

"Get to the mine," he says.

I'm not sure I heard him correctly. "The mine?"

"Yes."

"What am I supposed to do there?"

"You'll know when you see it. Maybe. If it's possible."

"*What?*"

"Just trust me. I don't want to explain, because then you'll just get overwhelmed thinking about it."

"You maybe know me too well," I say.

"Just believe in yourself," he says. "I know you can do incredible things, and if the battle takes a turn that we won't come back from, I need you to try something. Even if it seems impossible. Okay?"

"The thing that you won't explain because I'll overthink it?"

"Exactly. Promise me you'll try."

Before I can respond, the signal floats through the trees. The high trill of a bird not found in this area. The quiet murmuring of the men instantly ceases. I hold my breath as we all wait for whoever is approaching.

We've covered ourselves in green and brown to blend in with the surroundings. Many of us have even tied fern fronds around our arms and legs. Others lie flat on the ground, peering through the foliage ahead. Camouflaged from view.

A lone figure walks silently through the forest. She's not wearing Kymora's colors, but she's far too comfortable alone and traveling without any supplies to be anything other than one of the warlord's soldiers.

The small woman strides with a grace that allows her to flit between the trees quickly. She's not on the road, but just to the side of it. If we hadn't been looking for her, no one would have spotted her.

A scout, Kellyn mouths from beside me.

What do we do? Let her go to the city and find it mostly empty? What if Kymora doesn't attack because she suspects something?

The sound of a loosed arrow fills the quiet. It pierces right through the scout's left eye, the shaft exiting out the back of her head.

Princess Marossa lowers herself from the tree she'd climbed, striding over to the body. I look away just in time, as I realize she's come to *retrieve her arrow*.

When I turn back around, she's wiping the blood and other matter on the dead scout's clothing. As Marossa looks up, she finds the lot of us staring at her.

She says, "If the warlord wants to know what's ahead, she'll need to come see for herself. No one gets through us or has a chance to turn around and report." Then she climbs her tree once more.

Another hour passes, and the signal comes again. Another scout, this time a lean man.

When he finds the body of his fallen comrade, he bends down to examine her.

Marossa finishes him just like she did with the first.

A third scout arrives and meets the same fate.

Only then do we hear the marching of hundreds of feet, which can't be masked no matter how quiet they try to be. The ground trembles ever so slightly. I can only feel it because I'm kneeling so low to the forest floor.

Unlike Ravis, Kymora marches at the head of her army. She's in full armor, riding atop a horse, while most of her men walk behind. They march in perfect formation, taking up just the width of the road. She's clearly taken the time to train them a bit better.

At some unseen command, the entire party halts.

There's no possible way Kymora sees us (we've hidden the bodies of the scouts), yet some instinct has her surveying the greenery around her.

"Here we are," Kymora says. She doesn't speak louder than a conversational tone. "You wanted me walking into your city blindly. I am ready for you to spring your ambush now."

Petrik swallows from right next to me. For all his reading and planning, his mother is simply *better*. We can't really prepare ourselves to match against her skills and experience.

Not a soul moves in response to the warlord's words.

How are we about to spring a trap when Kymora *tells us to*?

Kymora crosses her arms above her horse. "I'm waiting."

Still, no one can find their wits.

The warlord sighs. "It's too quiet. The wildlife has disappeared, and you missed a streak of blood on that fern. Really, it's sad how you all think you can play at being warriors."

Still nobody moves from their hiding places.

"Was this my son's idea? I expected better. Surely you're—"

Marossa lets an arrow fly. The distance is ambitious, even for a skilled archer like herself. Nevertheless, her aim is true. The arrow sails right for Kymora's face.

In a motion I can hardly register, Kymora swings her sword, the arrow bouncing off the steel harmlessly.

Her eyes land on Marossa in her tree.

"Princess," Kymora greets.

Wrong, wrong. This is all wrong.

I look to Petrik with a desperate *What do we do now?* gesture.

We were supposed to wait for Kymora to cross an invisible line, then spring up to fight. But she's farther away than agreed upon, and she's singled out Marossa.

Kymora smiles. "My men know better than to show their hand." She says to someone over her shoulder, "Cut down that tree."

Men with axes spring forward. We're out of time to think. Marossa lets loose another arrow, fells one man, but others spring forward with shields to cover their fellow men while they chop.

I nudge Petrik.

With a loud exhale, he stands. The rest of us follow suit. There are about two hundred of us in total, including the mercenary company. With weapons drawn, we face Kymora and her men at the road.

"There you are," Kymora says. "I could hear the fearful heartbeats." And then she adds, still conversationally, "Loose, please."

Loose? Did she mean *lose*? Was she asking us to surrender?

But then a volley of arrows come at us from the sides, thundering down like a hailstorm.

It is my armor that saves us. The arrows glance off harmlessly, the magic protecting every soul in our company. Little *plink*s like thick raindrops staccato through the space.

"Ah, Ziva. You've been busy," Kymora says. Then, "Another volley."

There's no capable commander among our numbers. No one to take charge. Petrik was supposed to give the order to attack once Kymora and her soldiers were in place, but that never happened. Petrik eyes his mother, his knees suddenly locking in place, forgetting himself.

I can't even blame him; their relationship is the most complicated one I know of.

I stare down the woman who murdered my parents. Who tried to kill my sister. The woman intent on capturing me and destroying everything.

Someone needs to step up.

Feeling like an idiot all the while, I shout, "Advance!"

And I start running.

CHAPTER
TWENTY-EIGHT

The ferns whip against my legs. Brambles catch on my ankles, but they're ripped free by the force of my sprint. Impossibly, I hear more feet around me—the mercenaries, my friends, Skiro's and Marossa's soldiers—joining me.

Kymora scoffs. I can't hear the sound, but I see the way her head moves. "Go meet them," she says.

Her soldiers engulf her, racing to engage us.

I thought the fight in Skiro's Capital was utter chaos.

But it is nothing compared to the bedlam of fighting face-to-face on even ground. The clash as bodies strike against bodies. Shields and steel screaming. Grunts and cries piercing the air. My surroundings completely overwhelmed by red. First by the tunics of Kymora's soldiers. And then, of course, the blood.

My shield catches the man running straight at me. All the air leaves his body as he flies backward. I bring my hammer down, see his eyes widen just before Agony makes contact with his brow. I taste bile in my throat as I run for the next falcon-decorated soldier.

Out of the corner of my eye, men go flying as a magicked greatsword sends them pelting backward.

Magicked throwing axes fly not in a straight line, but in wide arcs, taking out many enemies with each throw before returning to the castor's hands. I hear laughter behind me and turn just in time to see a large mercenary with magicked knuckles on his left hand and a sword on his right knock enemies unconscious with every swing.

Our enemy's blows bounce off the magicked armor.

I don't relax, exactly, but some trembling part within me stills. I see the few magicked weapons I made for Ravis throughout the battlefield. They hold strong under blows, return to their masters' hands after they're disarmed.

But they are no match when pitted against all the weapons I've made throughout the years for the mercenaries.

Maybe I don't have to give up making magicked weaponry. As I see all the good it does right here, in this moment, I realize that maybe I can get back to doing what I love if I'm careful in who I allow to commission from me.

All these thoughts surge through my mind in the time it takes for my neck to turn.

Flashes of red come at us from the sides. Kymora's archers have advanced with spears.

Marossa and her archers take them down with careful shots out of the trees. Still, a few get through, and our men at the sides are forced to fight more than one opponent at a time.

"Go for the gaps in the armor!" Kymora shouts over the chaos. "Beneath the arms. Behind the knees."

And soldiers from our side start to die.

My arms swing in wide arcs, catching an enemy in the nose, cracking a knee out from under a soldier, caving in a collarbone.

Men fall beneath Echo, and other fighters on my side slit our enemy's throats before I have to make the killing blows myself. A short-lived respite.

There's always more killing to be done.

A commotion up ahead prompts me to look up from my latest kill. One of the biggest men I've ever seen races through the crowds, swinging a giant war hammer as he goes.

I can feel the magic from here. It calls to me because it is a piece of me, born of my surprise when Ravis interrupted me during a magicking session. Ravis called him by name to test out the weapon. I scramble through my memory to find it.

Izan.

I remember just as he sends the massive weapon down against one of our men, who explodes into a million minuscule pieces of bone and blood, sinew and flesh. Nearby fighters get doused in the remains of the fallen soldier.

One of our mercenaries approaches Izan, thinking to catch his next blow on his magicked sword, but that, too, explodes on impact, shards slicing into the owner of the sword before Izan finishes him off in another swing.

Another burst of innards flies outward.

But this time, instead of shame, something new takes root within me.

Fury.

That's my weapon. He's misusing it.

I'm not okay with that.

I'm going to stop him.

Rage dowses the fear. My anxieties are nonexistent.

After all, I have no intention of talking to the man.

I'd never thought about it before, but when in the thick of a fight, you're not watching the eyes of your enemy. Your eyes are on their weapons—their movements—the whole time. For a moment, you can disassociate the being before you from a living, breathing human. Instead, it's a moving mass intent on your destruction, and you have to destroy it before you die. You pick out your next opponent by the colors they're wearing. There's not much thought to the action. As long as you're acting, moving, the battle rages on.

But this fighter? I picked him. I look him squarely in the eye as I advance toward him, my own hammers pathetically small compared to the sheer weight and size of his war hammer.

A smile glazes his lips, glee burns brightly through his eyes. He's a man who loves his job. Who takes pleasure in killing.

And he's excited to end me.

Not if I end him first.

I would have thought he'd be burdened by the sheer weight of the war hammer, but he runs at me, sprints full tilt.

I ought to be petrified. Sensible warriors are running away from this fighter, not toward him.

But I can't fear a weapon I made, a weapon that is a part of me.

When Izan and I reach each other, the brute raises his hammer in a practiced swing and brings it down.

I hide behind my shield just in time.

As I skid back in the dirt from the force of the blow, Izan goes *flying*.

The force of his own swing sends him soaring through the air over the heads of other fighting warriors. He knocks another pair over. Agony absorbs the blow, powering her next swing.

Echo is as strong as ever, unaffected by the magic in our opponent's hammer, because it didn't actually come into contact with her, just the invisible shield she projects.

It's beyond satisfying to watch Izan struggle to regain his footing, but eventually, he picks himself back up, shoves another fighter out of the way, grabs his war hammer, and zeroes in on me once again.

His first strike appears to have only enraged him. He charges again.

I extend my left hammer, hiding behind it, waiting for the next bone-crunching blow. Might as well let the brute tire himself out before I advance with swings of my own.

Instead, Izan flips the handle forward, testing it against my invisible shield. He taps the shaft against it lightly, moving outward.

Trying to find the edge.

I shove forward, pushing the handle aside with Echo. I swing my own hammer at the opening presented to me.

But Izan spins away with more agility than I would have thought possible of a man his size. I'm so stunned, in fact, that he gets the best of me. The shaft of his hammer finds the edge of my shield, and he flings it out of my hands, sending Echo skittering out of the way. Before I can react, he shoves a shoulder into me, sprawls me flat on my back on the dirt.

And then he raises his hammer high, preparing to crush me into the earth.

"Ziva!" A horrified scream comes from somewhere out of sight. I think, distantly, that the voice belongs to Kellyn, but I have no time to respond to it.

I roll as fast as I can, out of the reach of that hammer. It sinks deep into the earth where my head was just a second ago. I feel the *thump* of it, somehow still painful on the back of my head. The reaction of the earth to the blow. Clods of dirt fly upward, rain down on me, pelting my face with exploded bits.

Undaunted by his miss, Izan raises his hammer again, a maniacal grin on his face. He swings again.

I keep rolling, slightly slowed by the unfamiliar armor I wear, trying to stay out of reach of that hammer. Agony feels insignificant in comparison. I pull my own hammer tight to my body as I move, keeping a fierce grip. I don't have time to raise it, to send up a strike of my own.

All I can do is move and move. I'm getting dizzy.

Izan grunts something low that sounds like "Hold still."

As if.

I keep rolling, realizing how foolish I was, thinking to take him on. So what if I made the weapon he carries? It's capable of killing me just as much as anyone else. I'm not invincible. I'm not even that talented of a fighter. I just got so angry. But that fury seems to have fled as I now fight for my life.

I roll once more, my body smashing into a hard surface.

A boulder—impeding me from moving any farther.

I look up in horror at the next swing. He knows he has me now. He raises his hammer higher; it disappears from view behind his head.

I don't have time to think. I act.

My boot swings up, catching him in the crotch.

He chokes, drops his hammer behind him, his hands going to the wounded area.

With a scream, I rise up onto my knees and send my hammer smashing into whatever part of him I can reach.

I hear a thundering crack. A sound I cannot describe comes out of the brute, and he staggers to the side.

I think I hit his pelvis.

But I don't stop to examine. I swing again.

And again.

This time higher and higher. Smashing ribs. Breaking his sternum.

And then a final crunch at his nose.

I'm screaming. I'm growling. I'm something completely unrecognizable to myself. But reason fled long ago.

"Ziva," the voice calls again. Arms come around me, hauling me up to my feet. I don't attack on instinct, because I recognize that voice.

"Kellyn?" I try to remember there is more in the world than just me and the dead brute. There's an entire battle. More foes to fell. More blood to spill.

My breathing is coming fast, the starting of a potential panic attack, but I don't have time for that now.

My body doesn't care.

The feeling of impending doom settles deep in my head, reclines lazily, like it has all the time in the world. I grip Kellyn tightly, my hands slicking against the blood on his armor.

He holds me to him with his left arm, and I try to slow my breathing. Meanwhile, I think he must be holding Lady Killer in his right hand, *one handed*, and he begins defending me while I disappear into hysterics.

Sacred Sisters, now is *really* not the time.

I try to focus on the smell of Kellyn, but it's mixed in with blood and dirt and other foul things. He spins me this way and that with his one arm, trying to keep me safe while he battles foes I cannot see. My head is still pressed between his neck and shoulder. I'm quivering. I'm falling. I surely must be dying. How can this be anything else?

And then all at once, I can breathe again. My hand clenches around my hammer, feeling the weight of it. The texture of the handle. The comforting sturdiness of it. I spin out of Kellyn's arm and help him fight off the man trying to take advantage of his distraction.

Kellyn's blade slices into his neck, stopping against the bone, taking the head halfway off.

I scramble to find my fallen shield hammer.

"I thought he had you," Kellyn says in a panicked voice.

"Me too."

"Next time, go for the crotch sooner and save me the near-death experience, please."

I think my hammer flew this way. I stumble around fallen bodies, duck away from fighters. Kellyn is right at my back.

"I'll do my best," I say. *Come on. Where are you?*

It's pandemonium all around us. I can't tell if we're winning or losing. Fighters have extended beyond the length of the road. Marossa and her archers pick off the lone enemies, but they can't risk hitting their own men in the thick of it.

I finally catch sight of my hammer.

But there's a boot right next to it. I look up, prepared to take on the enemy with Kellyn.

And then I see that it's Kymora.

Only, it's not *just* Kymora. There in a row, in a neat line, are *five* Kymoras. They wear identical tunics, hair pulled up into a neat bun, buckled boots with the same amount of shine. Beside the last one is a girl I recognized instantly.

The cotton spinner, Elany, looking pleased at all the carnage around her.

What has she done?

The Kymora in the middle bends over, retrieves my hammer, holds it delicately in her left hand. "The first of many such weapons I plan to hold," she says.

She cocks her head to the side, waiting to see what I will do.

Kymora has Echo.

I'm not getting it back.

Four others are wearing her face to confuse and scare our fighters out of their wits.

I feel Kellyn's hand clamp down hard at my shoulder.

"Retreat!" he shouts, giving the order Petrik was meant to give as soon as the time was right. But that time is most definitely now.

We were meant to let the enemy's numbers overwhelm us. Let Kymora get a good look at me. Then make a run for it up the mountains.

But Kymora has a magic weapon now, and who knows where Izan's hammer landed?

The time to run has come. It is no farce. Kymora already has the advantage in skill alone, and now she has my shield hammer.

We break through fighting pairs, turning tail and sprinting. We cut through the city, traveling on deserted streets until we reach the other side, to the steep incline of the mountain.

I hear Kymora's voice shout over the sound of running feet, but I can't make out what she's saying. I'm too focused on fleeing. Getting away from the dangerous woman who now has *my* hammer.

This is exactly what I feared. Magic getting into the hands of those who would misuse it. Imagine if it had been Kellyn's sword.

I shudder involuntarily.

We take a careful path up the mountain, avoiding the snares we've set. The path is rigorous, a steep incline that makes my lungs and legs hurt from the effort. But death waits below. We need to let them think they're winning. We need to convince Kymora to follow.

And they are winning; their numbers are still far superior to ours. But I try not to think about that. Temra is at the top of this rise. Marossa's calvary is waiting for us. We just need to climb.

Kellyn's breathing is just as labored as mine. I take his hand, haul him up with me. Or maybe he's dragging me after him? Impossible to tell.

When I finally reach a certain point on the mountain's side, I look down. Most of the mercenaries are still with us. I'm relieved to see their numbers. The princess is with them, but I don't see many of the other archers. They must not have made it down the trees and away from the enemy in time. They weren't wearing the magicked armor like the rest of us. How could they and still climb the trees?

A horrible sinking sensation takes root in my stomach. I feel like I'm falling, plummeting to some horrible death.

I knew there would be losses. There were losses in the last battle, too.

It's still shocking. Painful. Horrible.

"Well?" Skiro asks when we reach him.

I spot Petrik next to the prince, Temra at his side. The scholar says, "They're coming. She's taken some losses. The mercenaries have really wheedled down her numbers, but we've accrued losses of our own."

"Then let's hit her even harder with the next wave."

Kymora and her men have regrouped. Reformed their marching ranks. They cut through the trees now that the archers have been dealt with, wend through the city, and approach the mountain's edge.

The Kymoras form a line at the front of the battle, but I can tell which one is the real threat. She holds my hammer. She's the one scanning the surrounding area, looking up at the mountain questioningly. Her eyes fall on me. She's hundreds of feet away, yet I feel her gaze like a jolt of cold water to the senses.

I read her lips as she says simply to her men, "Climb."

We watch as her soldiers and the four other Kymoras start the trek up the mountain. It's a slow process—her men are even more tired than we are, having marched for most of the day before the battle. Their chests heave with exertion, their brows dripping with sweat.

Marossa looses the few arrows she has left upon the advancing men. Others cut loose boulders and tree trunks we'd carefully positioned. They roll down the hill, taking out the red-breasted soldiers as gravity pulls them down to the base. Kymora's fighters are crushed, bruised, broken as we send parts of the mountain sailing toward them.

But there are always more soldiers to replace the fallen.

And Kymora is no fool.

"Climb the sides!" she orders. "Don't attack straight on."

Her fighters obey orders without question, taking positions to the right or left of our huddled masses. Out of range of the traps we've set.

I take my sister's hand when the warlord's forces are halfway to us.

Temra puts a horn to her lips.

From even higher up than we are, hidden behind the trees and natural crevices of the mountain, Marossa's calvary descends.

The horses charge into the enemy, knocking them down, sending them tumbling head over heels. Swords swing down, taking off heads. Spears are thrown. Axes cleave through armor.

By now, half of Kymora's forces are gone, compared to only a third of ours—by my guess.

But it's not enough to convince me we'll win this fight. Not yet.

After the initial surprise, Kymora's men start fighting back.

Her archers let their arrows fly, sinking into horse flesh. Some of the poor beasts go down, taking their riders with them, both tumbling end over end down the mountain. Kymora still waits at the base, watching her men fight, shouting out orders, telling them exactly what to do to achieve victory.

We just don't have the experience or the knowledge to counter her instincts.

But we do have men and women willing to fight for what's theirs.

Let it be enough.

The fight commences in full force once again when Kymora's soldiers reach us. Fighting on uneven ground is supremely more difficult. Still, the more tired party is the one likely to make a mistake first.

I stay close to my sister, my back to hers, as we fend off attackers. She swings Midnight with a furious determination. Though Petrik does his best to throw his staff at anyone who tries to approach her, some still get through.

She fights like a lion, with quick slashes and quicker feet. It's terrifying to see soldiers flinging steel at her, but I have my own foes to focus on.

Though I've no shield hammer, I dodge and swing for all I'm worth, protecting Temra's back with a ferocity that could likely bring down this mountain.

Our magically assisted mercenaries do a remarkable job killing Kymora's men by the dozens. But when even more red-clad fighters reach the mountain's top, our fighters are surrounded. And they begin to fall in earnest.

When the imposter Kymoras enter the fray, resolve weakens. Men flee at the sight of her. Some hesitate in fear, which is just enough time for the enemy to get the upper hand on them. Just the nearby presence of the fierce woman in enough to cause more pandemonium in a fight that we're already losing.

Horses scream. Men scream. Metal screams.

Pain and chaos.

Death. So much death.

More and more of the enemy reach the top of the mountain. Arrows pick off anyone who tries to separate from the thick of the fight. More red tunics surround me and my friends than ever. Skiro and Tazar stay close. Marossa and Algarow. We all fight with everything we have.

An arrow flies right for Algarow. Takes him down before he can finish his exhale.

Without the princess's head guard to defend her, a sword sails right into Marossa's unarmored gut.

She looks up, outrage on her face. "Rude!" she screams before slumping against the ground.

Skiro is thunderstruck. He and Tazar sail forward, fighting off her attacker.

Petrik freezes, looking at the scene as though it can't possibly be real. His staff drops from his hand, but as soon as it makes contact with the ground, the magic sends it back toward his fingers.

Finally, his eyes reach mine. "Ziva, it's time," he says.

"No," I argue. "I can still fight. We can still fight. It's not over."

But just because I say so doesn't make it true.

We're finally overwhelmed by their numbers. There's too much red. The princess will die if we don't get her to Serutha. We have to end this.

Petrik's eyes flit to the mountain's base, where the real Kymora once stood.

I follow his gaze.

The warlord is gone.

Likely joined the fray.

When she reaches the top, there will be no stopping her victory. No one can beat her in swordplay.

"The mine," Petrik reminds me. "Take Temra and go. We'll cover your backs."

I hesitate.

"Now!" Petrik orders as he flings his staff to take out another enemy.

My eyes reach Kellyn's for the briefest moment.

I grab Temra's hand, and together we run.

I've never approached the mine from this way. In fact, I've never approached the mine at all. I've seen it before, at least—the gaping hole in the mountain is visible from the southern edge of the city.

"Do you know what we're doing?" I ask as we run and skid and slide our way across the mountain, veering for the base in a slanting arc.

"Yes, Petrik told me the plan."

"And?"

"We're not to the mine yet."

I let out a growl of frustration. "How am I supposed to do something if I don't know what it is? I swear, if this is some trick he's concocted just to get you and me clear of the fight—"

"Then we'll turn right back around and die with our friends."

"Twins, Temra. Do you have to be so callous about death? Couldn't you have said *fight* with our friends?"

"If this doesn't work, the fighting will be brief."

With that cheerful thought, we travel west along the mountain's base, looking for the dark opening. I know it's here somewhere.

There!

I pick up the pace, trying not to think about Kymora entering the fight, slaying the people I care about right and left.

There's a torch on the ground just outside the mouth of the mine, next to flint and steel. I light the torch, then hoist it high before entering the darkened opening, Temra just behind me.

An empty track on the ground meant for mine carts weaves farther into the dark tunnel. Temra and I step on either side of it, following it deeper and deeper.

The place smells of earth, coal, dampness. And something else that I can't place.

"How far into the mine are we going?" I ask.

"I'm not sure. We'll know it when we see it."

The walls are barren, all the iron ore having been mined closer to the surface. We follow the track even deeper.

I feel like a screw wound too tight. Like metal just before it reaches its boiling point.

"Temra, I don't know how much more of this I can take." We're too far from the fight to hear anything, but that only gives my imagination free rein to go wild. Imagine all the different ways people could be dying right now.

"Just a little farther," she says. "It must be."

And then I see it.

A cart locked on the track. It's empty, though caked in a black residue.

But behind it, pressed against each wall of the mine—a line of coal. I bend down to examine the line on the right, and that other smell grows stronger. A shiny residue atop the coal.

Oil.

Accelerant?

I remember that word written in Petrik's notebook.

Temra and I stare at the two lines of coal. They're thin, extending deeper into the mountain, as far as I can see by the meager torchlight.

"Do we keep going?" I ask.

"No, here's fine."

"*Now* do I get to know the plan?"

"Yes. First, you need to light it. Both sides."

I press the torch against the first line of coal. The oil catches quickly, and the fire snakes down into the tunnel lightning fast, lighting up the path. I do the same with the other side.

I hold my breath, waiting for something to happen. Waiting for Petrik's plan to become obvious to me.

At least it's no longer freezing down here. Or so dark.

"Hello, girls."

CHAPTER
TWENTY-NINE

Kymora has my shield hammer in her left hand, her broadsword in her right. She blocks the only exit out of the mine.

"Ziva, run," Temra says. "I'll hold her off. You carry out the plan."

I still don't know the plan! And she should know better than to think I would ever let her do that. "I'm not leaving you."

"She wants you. You need to go."

Kymora makes a face I can't quite interpret. "Aren't we past all this? Trying to flee. Trying to fight. Surely you know by now exactly how that will end."

I do. Temra dead. Me caught.

"I'm not making weapons for you," I say. "Just leave me alone!"

"You *will* make weapons if you wish me to spare the lives of all the prisoners my men have taken. The battle is over. I have won."

I look to Temra.

"Your sister's life is already forfeit," Kymora says. "There's no escaping that. It's punishment for what you did to my sword. For all the actions you've taken since fleeing your city."

I swallow. "Please—"

"No. You don't get to ask for anything. My mind is decided. Come now, and your remaining friends need not die."

"Petrik—" Temra starts.

"Is alive for now. Can't say the same for that mercenary fellow, though. What was his name?"

"Kellyn." I choke on my next breath. My limbs go limp. My mind blank.

But my heart—my heart breaks into a throbbing heap. Each beat sends an aching pain so exquisite through my body, I nearly collapse.

"That's it," Kymora says. "You have no one but me now, Ziva. Let me take care of you. Let me put your skills to use. Let's build something great together."

Live for yourself.

You give me hope.

Ziva, I love you.

I close my eyes, let Kellyn's face fill the blackness behind them, let the memory of his voice fill my head.

I love you, I tell that image. And I will regret forever never saying it to his face.

I want to break down. To curl in on myself and weep for everything I've lost. But there is no time. Not when I still have a sister to protect. Not when the whole of Ghadra still depends on me. I still have things to fight for. I can't quit yet.

The heat from the coal warms me from the outside in, and my eyelids fly open. On the wall, I can see a vein of iron winking in the firelight.

And all at once I realize what Petrik wants me to do.

He's delusional! I want to scream. We are going to have *words* when I see him next.

I can't magic an entire mountain!

My knuckles turn white. The left on the torch, the right on my hammer.

"Back up, Temra," I say, keeping my eyes on the warlord as I take a step away, putting more space between me and the danger.

"You're going to run again?" Kymora asks, advancing a step. "How many people are you going to let die for you? First your parents. Then your sister. Your friends. Now everyone who fought for your cause. Is there nothing you hold dear? Nothing you're unwilling to sacrifice?"

I continue to retreat, Temra keeping behind me, unwilling to blink and risk missing a movement from Kymora.

"Does this mine even have an exit?" the warlord asks. "You can run, but I will catch you. You're exhausted from the fight. I haven't even raised my sword yet. I'm fresh. I will overwhelm you."

"Ziva," Temra says, a note of fear entering her voice.

Kymora keeps pace with us, stepping around the mine cart, stepping between the two lines of burning coal.

"I have sacrificed nothing," I say, answering Kymora's earlier taunt. "I have fought for what I believe in. I have loved. I have lost. I have *lived*. But you? You missed out. Your son is one of the best men I know. You should have stayed close to him, loved him, learned from him. Perhaps you would have turned out better. You should have cared for the people under your protection, instead of seeking to overthrow them. You should have been content with the power you had. You should have lived for the people around you, instead of intent on conquering them."

"Why?" Kymora says with a laugh. "I'm about to have everything I've ever wanted."

"No," I tell her. "You're about to die. You're about to die for *nothing*."

Kymora sighs. "I'm weary of this. Let's be done with it, Ziva."

Yes. Let's be done.

I stand completely still, yet inside, I'm a raging inferno of emotions. Grief, rage, desperation, anxiety—always anxiety. They pound against my skin as though trying to burst free. They beat against my skull, trying to force me to examine them, to become completely overwhelmed by them.

I look to the walls, where the coals have heated the base of the iron deposits.

"*Move*," I say, channeling all that emotional energy into the metal surrounding the warlord.

The iron vibrates, sending fissures up along the walls. A few thick clumps break free, the heat from the coals the only thing allowing me to manipulate them.

"Ziva," Kymora says, a hint of warning in her voice.

With my will alone, I send pieces of iron sailing toward her. Kymora raises Echo to fend them off. Rock crumbles against the shield hammer, rains uselessly to the ground. I break off more of the mountain, send it toward her with even more force.

Kymora tries to bat a particularly large piece back toward me, but I change its course midair, send it right back toward its intended target.

"Ziva!" the warlord shouts, her irritation showing. She bends at the knees to make herself smaller and charges with my hammer extended.

I send rocks at her feet, tripping her as Temra and I now

continue into the mine. Kymora rolls once before jumping up onto her feet, as though she doesn't feel an ounce of pain.

The air is sweltering. So much heat and very few places for it to go. It warms everything and anything caught in the path between the two lines of coal.

I feel for the magicked hammer in Kymora's hand, tug at it gently with my magic.

"Oh, no, you don't," Kymora says, gripping it more tightly.

I need to draw more from myself.

The hazy image of my parents' faces flashes into my mind. Kellyn's smile. Temra laughing. Petrik determinedly reading a book for answers. These are the people I love most, the ones Kymora has threatened or already taken away from me.

I let my love for them burn through me as I fix my magic on the hammer once more.

Instead of pulling Echo toward me, I push it away, and Kymora jerks backward with it, her left arm at an odd angle, as she's tugged by the hammer back toward the mine's entrance.

I seize my chance, charging forward, Agony prepared to swing. Kymora releases her hold on the other hammer so she can grip my shoulder with her left hand, catch my hammer swing on her sword.

But what she hadn't realized was that Agony had been absorbing every blow she'd taken on Echo. Every piece of iron pelting toward her. Building and building.

The force of it sends Kymora's own sword swinging backward from it.

Right toward her neck.

Metal slices into flesh. Eyes widen in surprise.

Kymora tries to speak, but gasping air is all that makes its way through her throat.

"You had a chance," I say. "Mercy is not extended a second time. This is for my parents."

I step back, focus all my magic on the sword partly imbedded into her throat.

And I *push*.

Two separate bits of flesh hit the ground with sickening *thud*s.

I turn around and pull my sister into my arms before I weep.

I can't make any sense of time as Temra tries to console me. She murmurs into my hair, strokes my back as I weep for Kellyn. Weep for my parents all over again. Weep for the soldiers lost in the fight.

"Ziva," Temra says gently. "There is still work to do. Kymora's men still hold everyone captive. You know what you have to do next."

It doesn't matter if Petrik is delusional, if he places too much faith in me. I have to try.

"All right."

I sink to my knees, spread my hands along the nearest heated wall of rock. Tears and snot still drip down my face, my knees ache against the rough ground. But I ignore all of that.

I close my eyes, feel the metal that beats at the heart of this mountain, that slides just under its skin. Beneath the city. Around all of Lirasu.

It's not difficult to imagine what I want the metal to do. It's what I've always wanted. What I've strived for my entire life.

Safety.

I've always wanted to feel safe. To be rid of the fear I feel every time I step outdoors. Whenever I'm surrounded by people. It's an internal struggle that no amount of magic could ever cure.

But the physical and very overwhelming threats in the city *can* be dealt with.

So I pour that deepest and truest desire of mine into the iron, mix it with all the pain I'm already feeling. I put everything I am into the magic.

I feel a pulse of heat so strong that it sends me flailing onto my back, my eyes temporarily blinded by the white light.

When I can see again, I feel curiously empty inside.

No fear. No panic. No pain.

But also no joy. No triumph. No relief.

The magic took everything from me and put it into the iron.

The smoke in the mine becomes too thick for Temra and I to withstand much longer. Temra doesn't speak, though she sheaths her shortsword and takes my hand. After retrieving Echo from Kymora, I slip both hammers back into my belt.

We bolt for the exit, coughing and clinging to each other the whole way. Temra is weakened from the fighting and the running and the smoke inhalation. I feel like I could run for days and never stop, despite the smoke affecting my lungs.

With every step, I can feel the pulsing flow of magic around me. The same way I'm aware of all the weapons I've made. But this last magic was cast on no singular weapon. I cast it on the veins of ore in the mine, which connect to the whole of the mountain. To the deposits beneath the city.

After all, when I heat the tip of a blade, am I not still capable of magicking the whole sword?

I've magicked all of Lirasu.

We find the warlord's men gathered at the base of the mountain, near the city's edge, just beneath where the second wave of fighting took place. Our soldiers are there with them, bound on the ground, kneeling, weapons removed.

Prince Skiro sits cross-legged next to the princess. Serutha is there, too. To the average onlooker, she appears to be applying pressure to Marossa's wound. I know better. She's magicking it where none can tell. She hid in the city for the fight, but I'm sure the wounds of the dying called to her, encouraged her to make an appearance even though we've lost.

It's not long before Temra and I are spotted by Kymora's soldiers. They eye us carefully; some even put their hands on their sword hilts.

I see a pile of weapons near the warlord's horse. She likely wanted them all gathered so she could sift through for the magical ones.

While I process everything around us, Temra says to the group before us, "The warlord is dead. You'll find her body in the mine."

"Thank the Twins," Skiro says. He stands.

"Back on your knees, Prince," a woman out of sight says. Skiro glares at her before kneeling on the ground again. She steps forward.

It's Elany. "If Kymora is truly dead, then we, her loyal followers, will take things from here. Starting with the executions of the prince and princess."

A few soldiers detach from the rest and approach the royal siblings, but as they bend down to grip them with their hands, they pause.

One of the guards squints, adjusts position slightly, tries to reach for the prince again.

"What are you doing?" Elany asks of them. "Grab them."

"They can't," I say, my mind still devoid of all emotion. Talking to Elany now has no effect on me. My anxiety is absent. "You cannot wrong another human in the boundaries of Lirasu. This is a safe haven. Magically protected."

Elany scoffs, draws a bastard sword, and strides for me. Temra tenses at my side, but I hold her in place with a raised hand. Elany raises her sword to strike.

And it meets invisible resistance in the air.

She tries again. Again. Again.

I wish I could feel pride at what I'm seeing, but still there is nothing within me but clarity. I poured a lifetime of anxiety—which was brought to unbearable levels by all Kymora put me through—into that iron.

That magic will hold forever.

I say to all of Kymora's listening soldiers, "I am Ziva Tellion, known for my magical blades. But that is not the extent of my powers. I can bend heated iron to my will, and I've magicked the ore beneath your feet, the ore in the mountains. Lirasu is a place of refuge and safety to all who come here. And you cannot conquer it."

Elany's face scrunches into fury. "Then we'll leave and take the rest of Ghadra. I will have my vengeance!" She encourages Kymora's soldiers to retrieve the pile of weapons. Asks that the wagons be loaded.

But as Kymora's soldiers try to reach for the stolen weapons, they find themselves unable to touch a single one, as though they'd all been placed in an invisible box.

"Those aren't yours," I say. "Ghadra is not yours. These soldiers don't have to follow you. You need to let this go, Elany. Find another way to achieve justice, because I will stop you if you try to hurt another innocent soul in Ghadra."

"We'll all stop you," Skiro proclaims, standing again.

"We've already beaten your forces once. You surrendered," Elany says with satisfaction.

"And you took great losses," Skiro responds. "You don't have the numbers to take on Ghadra anymore. My brother Verak didn't send aid, but he has hundreds under his command. With his numbers beating you from the north and ours coming at you from the south, it would be a quick fight."

I look around at what remains of Kymora's soldiers. "These fighters aren't loyal to you like they were to Kymora. How many do you think are interested in following you into a lost cause?"

For the first time, Elany loses some of her confidence. She does a sweep of the area with her eyes, taking note of the fidgety fighters.

And then Governor Erinar appears from seemingly nowhere. "I'm also curious how you intend to pay these soldiers? You won't reap any spoils from the land as you go. You won't make it that far. I have vast resources here. And now this land is protected. Maybe some of them would be interested in full-time honest work here? Also I'd wager the prince and princess could use more hands now. Why would they have reason to fight a lost cause when they can take safer work now that Prince Ravis and Warlord Kymora are dead?"

"Someone needs to rule Ravis's Territory now," Elany says. "We'll march there, return—"

"You will not," Skiro says. "My siblings and I will discuss what is to be done with Ravis's land. You have no claim to it. The people do."

"I have all the claim I need! I am a magician. A fighter. Now, we march!"

Not a single red-breasted soldier moves.

"The war is over," I say. "Stop now before you forfeit your life, too."

Elany looks about her for a single fellow devotee. Finding none, she climbs atop the warlord's horse, gives the entire scenery a nasty glare, and gallops away from the city.

Finally, it's over.

And everything comes rushing back in at once.

I stagger to the ground as my grief, anxiety, pain, exhaustion—everything slams into me, the effects of the magic finally receding.

Tears stream from my eyes at the pressure of all of it finally allowed to come to the surface.

We may have won, but I still lost far too much.

Temra's arms cradle my shoulders, pull me against her side. Though there's movement all around me, I can't bother to focus on any of it. They're probably gathering the dead, tending to the wounded, doing whatever else needs to be done after a battle. We weren't exactly able to stick around after the last one.

And I know I should help. I should get up and move, but I'm not ready.

"He's gone," I say through my sobs.

"I know," Temra says.

"I never told him, Temra. I never told him I love him back. Why didn't I tell him? It was so stupid and petty, and now he'll never hear it."

Footsteps approach, and I feel a twinge of embarrassment, but it's nothing when compared to my grief.

"What's wrong?" Petrik wants to know. "Is she hurt? Are either of you hurt?"

I feel Temra's head shake, and then she stiffens. Her arms fall from my sides. "Ziva," she says.

"Can you hold me just a little longer?" I ask. "I'm not ready."

"Ziva, open your eyes right now."

On my next sniffle, I obey.

And I think I must be hallucinating, because Kellyn is standing there. Impossibly tall from where I'm slumped to the ground, his hair a burning beacon with the sun lighting it from behind.

"Sweetheart, what's wrong?"

I'm too scared to blink, afraid what I'm seeing will all go away. I've done impossible magic; who knows what toll that's taken on my body?

"Kymora told her you were dead," Temra explains. "She's weeping for you."

"Dead? With Ziva's sword to protect me? Not a chance. Oh, honey, come here."

He bends down and holds his arms out to me. I'm afraid to touch them. What if my hands pass right through?

Kellyn's face turns to uncertainty. His hands drop. "What is it?"

"You're not real."

"Yes, I am."

"Prove it."

He reaches for me so quickly that I don't have a chance to react. Very solid hands grasp me, yank me off the ground, and crush me to an even more solid chest.

"Kymora was a manipulative bitch," Kellyn says. "Are you going to believe her or the very real person standing right before you?"

I start crying again.

CHAPTER
THIRTY

Petrik waits until I've calmed down before gloating.

"Everyone thinks it's the big tough fighters who win wars, but it's the little guys, the smart guys, that change everything."

The royals try to organize everyone into cleaning up the city now that the fighting is over, but our little group of four huddles together outside of it all.

"I think you mean it's the talented *women* who get things done," Temra tells him.

"Ziva did the work, but it was my idea. Give me some credit."

Temra raises one brow at him. "Your idea?"

"Okay, so she made the idea better! That doesn't mean—"

"Wait," I say. "You didn't intend for me to magic the whole city?"

"Not exactly," Petrik says sheepishly, "I thought you might magic part of the mountain, so we would be safe up here. Or render weapons useless or something trivial. Whatever you could manage. I didn't realize the whole city was built upon the iron deposits."

Kellyn flexes the arm he has wrapped around me. "Of course she went above and beyond."

"But it was a good idea," Temra tells Petrik, kissing him on the cheek. "Thank you for making all the preparations."

He blushes at her praise.

"However, I'm more impressed by all the speeches Ziva's been giving of late," Temra says. "You convinced the mercenaries to fight for us. You talked down the cotton spinner, turned Kymora's men to our side. I've never seen you speak with such confidence."

"I cheated on that last speech." I explain how the magic took my fear away temporarily.

Temra shakes her head. "You could have done it regardless."

Maybe so, but I'm glad I didn't have to.

I'd already given so much.

The next few days are exhausting. Serutha heals the wounded. The rest of us bury the dead. Messengers are sent to take the news to all that the warlord is gone.

Princess Marossa is up and helping in no time. ("Where is my bow?" she asked upon first waking.) The governor and his husband go door to door, seeking out the families who barricaded themselves within, letting them know all is now well.

The dead warlord's men are interviewed individually, given tasks and assignments based on their skills.

And the mercenaries who survived the fight come to collect.

It is a long time before the bank is up and running again, but the sellswords are more than happy to wait.

I feel nothing more than a wistful sadness to hand over every ockle I've ever earned, because I still have everything I need.

My sister. My Kellyn. My friends.

Money is nothing when compared to all that.

It takes a month for the city to get back to what is mostly normal. *Mostly* because crime has vanished. The governor doesn't need a personal guard anymore—no one can attack him in the city. Theft and murder cannot be committed. Violence is not a possibility in Lirasu.

It's safer than any place in the whole world.

And yet, it can't protect me from my sister leaving.

She and Petrik stand with loaded packs on their backs, ready for the trek back to Skiro's Capital. The prince has long since left, but Temra wanted to stay a little while—for me, I suspect. And I was too selfish to insist she go any sooner. But she informed me yesterday that now was the time.

Silent tears fall down my cheeks as I eye the two of them. "Do you really have to go?" I try one more time.

"It's time," my sister says. "Skiro needs me, and I know the library is missing Petrik something fierce."

"It's true," Petrik says. "I've been neglecting my duties there. And I have another book that needs writing."

"The one on magic users?" I ask. The entire reason we met in the first place.

"Well, that one, too, but I meant the one about our battles against Kymora. The sequel to our first journey. The world should know what we did. Half of it had no idea that Ravis and Kymora made a play for all of Ghadra. They don't know that they were ever in any danger."

"I bet most will assume it's fiction," Kellyn says.

"Ha, even I'm not that creative."

The two men shake hands.

"You're all right, scholar," Kellyn says. "Safe travels. Try not to trip on your dress."

"Try not to be so obnoxious that someone kills you the moment you step outside the city."

"No promises."

They share a smile, and Petrik steps up to me next.

We stare each other down. "Should we—do we hug?" he asks me.

I shrug before wrapping my arms around the silly man. It's not entirely unpleasant.

"I meant what I said before," I whisper to him. "The bluntest tool in my forge."

"Got it," he says as he steps back.

"You keep my sister safe."

Temra laughs. "More likely I'll be the one keeping him safe."

"Very true," Petrik says.

Temra and Kellyn embrace. Kellyn says something to her about stretching out her arm, and she flexes her left bicep for him. He laughs at what must be an inside joke for them.

Then my sister stands before me, and I feel myself starting to cry again.

"Hey, none of that," she says, pulling me to her.

"I'm going to miss you so much."

"But not for long. We'll see each other all the time! I'm not stuck in Skiro. You're not stuck here. Besides, you'll be in Amanor all the time, won't you?"

I slide an uncomfortable look Kellyn's way, but he and Petrik are busy saying something to each other.

"We haven't talked yet. I don't know . . ."

"Ziva." Temra flattens me with her stare. "You defeated the most powerful person in the world. You used magic beyond the parameters that have ever been achieved. Now go talk to the man you love and make a *plan*. Write me so I'm not left in suspense. I love you."

"I love you."

"Oh, and when you do decide where to settle, I happen to know a painter who might want to help us find ways to see each other more *conveniently*." She winks.

With that, Temra and Petrik walk hand in hand away from our childhood home. I watch them until they disappear around the bend in the road.

Oh, but Twins it hurts. Kellyn ushers me inside, holds me as I cry. I let myself have one minute of this, and then I abruptly stop. I wipe my eyes, school my features, and refuse to think about what I'm losing.

"It's okay to be sad," Kellyn says. "I bawled my eyes out the first time I left home."

"You did not."

"Okay, maybe not quite so hard. But I shed a tear."

We seat ourselves on the small sofa in the living room. I try not to think about how empty the house feels without my sister's beautiful personality.

It's the way of life, I tell myself. Children grow, and they leave their homes. I know Temra isn't my child, but she might as well have been, since I raised her.

When I've got myself under control, I finally allow myself to look at the beautiful man before me. I reach out and take his hand.

"What's next?" I ask.

"Are you hungry? Should we grab some lunch?"

"I mean for us, Kellyn." I take a very deep breath.

"I don't understand. Why do you look like the end of the world is coming for us again?"

In a sudden movement, I stand, putting distance between us. I pace the space in front of him, because I need to *move*.

"You brought up marriage. We talked about how we felt about each other. But we never talked about how we would make it work." I risk a glance at him. "I'm terrified of this conversation because I don't want to lose you. But we want different things. I want to be safe. I don't want to go adventuring all over the world. I'm a homebody. I like staying indoors.

"But you want to travel. You want to swing that sword and meet new people. And I just don't see how we can be together when we want different things."

"Oh," Kellyn says. He stands with me, paces his own little line. "I hadn't thought of that."

And I feel myself about to dissolve into tears again. *Get it together, Ziva.*

I hoped so badly that he would have an answer. That I would just lay out the problem, and he would laugh and say he'd already thought of that!

But he doesn't. And now he's pacing, and that's making me fidget with my fingers.

Kellyn halts. "Well, first things first, where do you want to live? Here in Lirasu?"

I'm a little stunned by the question, but I answer. "No, I think I'm done with this city."

"Really? Even though it's the safest place in the world thanks to you?"

"Actually, I always felt safest when I was in Amanor."

I look at the ground.

"You want to live in Amanor?" Kellyn clarifies, his tone one of disbelief. "Where my massive family lives?"

"Yes. It's close to Temra, and I love your family."

"Just my family?"

I expel a breath of air before looking up. "I love you, too, you stupid brute."

Kellyn bites his lip, fighting a laugh. "Was that so hard to say?"

"Yes! Now it'll hurt more when we go our separate ways. When—"

He cuts me off with a lingering kiss. "Could you do me a favor and say it again without the 'stupid brute' bit?"

I'm dazed by the kiss, but I bite out, "I love you, you arrogant ass."

"Hmm."

He kisses me again, and I forget all about my sister and my nightmares of war when it's just him and me like this.

He pulls back, and my words come out in a whisper. "I need to know the plan."

"We'll live in Amanor," he says simply. "There, one thing solved."

I splay my hands on his chest and push back slightly, so I can look at him. "But you won't *be* there. You'll be traveling the world. And I'll only see you once every couple of years!"

Kellyn looks into my eyes, and my breathing picks up at the serious consideration he gives me. "What if I only take four jobs a year? That's once every three months that I'll be gone?" But then he smiles. "And what if you come with me for two of them? That's only twice a year that we'll be apart."

"What?" I ask.

"We'll build a house in Amanor. I happen to know it's in need of a good smithy. You can forge. I'll work the fields. The land will provide everything we need. I'll take four jobs a year so we'll make extra money. And if you're up for it, maybe you'd want to join me for half of them? We can see a little bit of the world together. In small, perfectly safe doses."

I don't know what to say. "Four jobs a year? Is that enough for you? What if you grow miserable? What if you resent me? What if—"

He silences me with yet another kiss. It makes my rising fear all but disappear.

"I would never resent you," he says. "I'm choosing this. It's what I want. I want to travel, but I want to spend most of my time with you. Could you consent to two trips a year with me? Am I asking too much?"

His face looks worried, and his mind is turning, already trying to think of a new solution if I say no to his suggestion.

So I just kiss him. I bury my hands in his hair, breathe him in, feel the hope of a new future together.

"Really?" I ask. "That's it? That's all it took for us to come to a compromise? Of course I'll travel with you twice a year."

He grins. "Why do you sound so surprised?"

"I've been stressing about this for *weeks*. I was too scared to bring it up because what if it ended things prematurely?"

"Ziva, I told you; you are my forever. You thought that could be undone so easily? That we couldn't come up with something to make things work?"

I'm doing something between a laugh and a cry, and when will I finally get my emotions under control?

Our foreheads come together, and I relax for the first time in as long as I can remember.

"I love you," I say.

"I love you," he says.

I don't feel worthy of this happiness. But I accept it. Because what else can I do? There will be other things to figure out as they come up, but we can do it. Together. I have that faith in us.

For right now, I'm not afraid.

I'm excited.

"When can we start?" I ask.

"The rest of our lives?" Kellyn asks. "I'll go pack."

ACKNOWLEDGMENTS

It's unreal to have this second series completed! The Bladesmith duology was so very different from the Daughter of the Pirate King duology, but I love these series, and I hope you do, too. For those longtime readers of mine, I promised you in the acknowledgments of *The Shadows Between Us* more kissing scenes just for you. While it wasn't possible to work them into *Blade of Secrets* with the emotional journey Ziva needed to take, I hope you feel I've delivered with *Master of Iron*.

While there were different people who worked on these two series, there are several people who remain constants on all my books: Rachel Brooks, my incredible agent; Holly West, my fantastic editor; Brittany Pearlman, my talented publicist; and many more behind-the-scenes folks at Feiwel and Friends. Thank you to all of you for your hard work!

I wouldn't be able to do what I do without all the support of my amazing friends and family. You know who you are. Thanks for listening to me complain when things got tough and brainstorming with me when I needed it. Being an author can be such a lonely profession. I don't think any of us could do it if we didn't know there were people rooting for us.

I need to give a special shout-out to all those TikTokers out there who are recommending my books on their accounts. Thank you also to all the Bookstagrammers and BookTubers and other social media folks for showcasing my books on your feeds. I'm so grateful for all that you do for the book community. Thank you to the librarians and booksellers who recommend my books to patrons. Thank you to everyone who has ever left a glowing review for one of my books on GoodReads or other platforms. That truly does help!

Lastly, thank you to my readers who stuck with me for this series. I know Ziva is a bit different from my typical Slytherin protagonists, but I felt this story was one I was uniquely qualified to tell, and I just had to get it out. I hope you're all looking forward to my upcoming releases. I'm excited to be returning to two different worlds as well as my first ever trilogy! I have many more stories to tell, and I'm so grateful for those of you who read them so I can keep doing what I do.

THANK YOU FOR READING THIS
FEIWEL & FRIENDS BOOK.

✦

THE FRIENDS WHO MADE

MASTER of IRON

POSSIBLE ARE:

JEAN FEIWEL, Publisher

LIZ SZABLA, Associate Publisher

RICH DEAS, Senior Creative Director

HOLLY WEST, Senior Editor

ANNA ROBERTO, Senior Editor

KAT BRZOZOWSKI, Senior Editor

DAWN RYAN, Executive Managing Editor

RAYMOND ERNESTO COLÓN, Director of Production

ERIN SIU, Associate Editor

EMILY SETTLE, Associate Editor

RACHEL DIEBEL, Assistant Editor

FOYINSI ADEGBONMIRE, Associate Editor

LIZ DRESNER, Associate Art Director

ANGELA JUN, Designer

VERONICA MANG, Associate Designer

KAT KOPIT, Associate Director, Production Editorial

MANDY VELOSO, Senior Production Editor

✦

FOLLOW US ON FACEBOOK OR VISIT US ONLINE AT FIERCEREADS.COM.
OUR BOOKS ARE FRIENDS FOR LIFE.